Love
Me Not

by
Jacqueline Falcomer

Reviews

"Vivid and breath-taking observations sing from the pages capturing the soul of by-gone Tuscany. Aside of food descriptions that will cause you to weep with longing, Jacqueline's scintillating turns of phrases and progression of memorable characters will strike you deep in your heart. Another late night page-turner."
— Klaus Weixelbaumer Cape Town, South Africa

"Warning: Eat before you read. Have you ever read a story where *food* is a character? Ms Falcomer pulls this off with aplomb, and turned me into a willing slave to the Tuscan table."
— Molly Zucknick, Texas, USA

"Jacqueline Falcomer's *Love Me Not* is an insightful and magical story of a woman who is a survivor. With the help of a magnificent and imaginative cast of characters, Hortensia brings her little spot of Tuscany into the modern world. Falcomer's writing is lyrical, her story completely entertaining, and the meals memorable."
— Toni Morgan, Idaho, USA, author of
Patrimony, and, *Two-Hearted Crossing*

"*Love Me Not* is a wild ride around the Tuscan countryside, complete with villains, some you'll love to hate; family members whose affections turn on a dime, and then back again; marvelous descriptions of local Italian meals; and Hortensia, a plucky heroine who fails, succeeds, fails again, and finally emerges victorious— whew! I rarely read magical realism, but this story caught my attention, and I'm glad I succumbed. The magic is subtle and unobtrusive, but it plays its role magnificently. Written by an author who lives where she writes, with great authority. Jump on board and enjoy the ride!"
— Madge Walls, Oregon, USA, author of
Paying the Price and *Buyers Are Liars*

"Hang onto your hat. Jacqueline Falcomer's *Love Me Not* is magical mystery tour of Italian characters, the Tuscan countryside, fabulous food, and unexpected storylines. Follow the amazing story of Hortensia as she overcomes enormous odds to find her happy ending."
— Kathryn Munn, California, USA

About *Love Me Not*

Abandoned at the age of three, Hortensia is raised by three peasants to serve the greater good of others. As Hortensia matures, shedding her naivety and innocence, she realises her role in the game plan and fears for her unborn son.

Her well-intentioned plans to provide her son with a secure future, fail. She breaks the one promise she has made to herself – she gives him up. In return, she gains a girl whom she raises as her own.

When life starts to go as planned, her son's biological father, a past lover, and a man desperate to make her his lover, threatens all she has strived for.

To save her children, herself and the valley's livelihood, Hortensia must make the biggest sacrifice of all.

Dedication

In the light before dawn you appeared
Guided by your words
I embraced freedom

Personal Thanks

To my family and friends, beta readers and critters, for joining me on this journey, your encouragement and support – my deepest thanks.

Tuscany, July 2018

Foreword

Be prepared for a sprightly and salivating read. Jacqueline Falcomer's sensuous *Love Me Not* whisks you away to the Tuscany that exists in our dreams: a sunbaked valley filled with ripe vineyards, colorful characters, and the ever-present aromas of fine Italian cooking. The cooking roots the book in reality, but the heroine, Hortensia d'Ambrosia, carries the reader to where the magical is just a four-course meal away.

In Jacqueline's prose, post-war Italy is transformed to the world of classical legend. Nymphs and demons in pencil dresses and pearls battle for the souls of men, and the dragon to be conquered is the town mayor, with lust in his heart and pasta sauce on his mind.

Hortensia is up to the challenge. An orphan who believes herself born of a woman who transformed into a butterfly, she is raised by Maria the benevolent witch, Anna the master chef, and the wise Rubino, to lead their valley out of the ravages of war and neglect, to the glittering prospects of 1960's Italy. Her link to these three vibrant characters transcends the grave, but like the rest of the book abounds in humor and humanity.

You may never visit Tuscany, but you can feel it in these pages. When you do visit Tuscany, inspired by this novel, you will see Hortensia around every corner, driving the cart behind her intrepid donkey Long Ears, or speeding off in Pietro's Piaggio three-wheeled van to do battle with the mayor.

With storytelling ingredients like erotic nights in a vault under a church, magical dead men's teeth, and instructions on how best to tenderize an octopus for dinner, *Love Me Not* is the recipe for an unforgettable read.

— George Collazo, Seattle, USA, author of
The Pirate, Ghandi

LOOK BEFORE YOU LEAP,
FOR SNAKES AMONG
SWEET FLOWERS DO CREEP

— Tuscan Proverb

While picnicking in a clearing surrounded by ancient Tuscan chestnut trees my mother metamorphosed into a butterfly.

At first I cooed. Then, when I could no longer identify her from the others, I wailed. On a warming current, clouds of iridescent, emerald-green and sapphire-blue chitonous wings dipped, looped and rose above the treetops and drifted away.

My wails turned into hiccupping sobs. Terrified, I succumbed to sleep, trusting, that upon waking, my butterfly mother would be restored and returned to me.

With her black cloak billowing about her, Maria Fortunato, our valley's prescient midwife, found me huddled between the exposed, iron-hard roots of one of those giant chestnuts. Already aware there was no point searching for my mother, Maria rescued and raised me with the same love she lavished upon her adored pygmy goats.

I was three years old. I never saw my mother again.

———————— ◆ ————————

As I woke, the dream-memory of that event faded only to be replaced by an orchestra of chirping crickets leaping in anticipation in my belly.

It was 5 May 1946, my fourteenth birthday, the day on which Maria had said my life would change.

It was time to say my goodbyes. I stared up at the smoke-darkened beams supporting the roof of the shepherd's hut, my home for eleven years. Instead of winter raindrops, glinting arrows of sunlight sneaked through the cracked terracotta tiles and dotted the hard-packed earth.

I turned my head and focused on the rickety table and two chairs in front of the hearth in which fragments of coals, nestled in ash, winked red. Maria's bed at the far end was empty. She'd left before dawn to move her flock of goats to a distant meadow.

What the room lacked in furniture was remedied by Maria's stock-in-trade. Hanging from the airing rack suspended in the middle of the room were clusters of still-drying, leafy stalks and tubers as well as roots of dandelion, borage, calendula, nettles, bay laurel, fennel and mint. Scents ranging from earth musk to cucumber crisp suffused the air.

Dried herbs – left whole, crushed, pounded into powder, suspended in oil, or made into salve using snow-white lard rendered from pigs' kidneys mixed with ash and perfumed with lemon – filled numerous bottles stored on shelves. More bottles contained the carcasses of small mammals and reptiles, toadstools and other fungi. Sticky, wagon-wheel-shaped spiderwebs layered between dry leaves rested on the deep window-sills.

Maria's black cloaks, all stitched with various sized pockets, and in different weights for varying kinds of weather, hung from nails serving as clothes hooks. A few nails stood free as my clothes were already bundled into a ball tied with twine.

The peal of the church bell sounded from the valley floor, beating the cock to his first crow. It was time to leave. I rose and reached for the bundle. As the door crack widened, it revealed the splendid distant view I never tired of – the opalescent Tyrrhenian Sea. Effervescent salt air, gathering the fragrance of wild sage and honeysuckle as it rose from the coast to the hills, filled my lungs.

I turned to face the grey mountain with its jagged ridge resembling the spine of a crested lizard. Accompanied by a trilling chorus of early morning songbirds, I made my way uphill.

To my right, on the opposite valley ridge stood our neighbour's, Claudio Trianni, sprawling villa with a splendid turret rising high above the extended olive groves. I sighed. For reasons still unexplained, the property was forbidden to me. One day, I had promised myself a hundred times or more, I'd gather my courage and visit the crumbling villa, especially the turret.

I shifted my gaze ahead. In a few minutes, with the rising sun warming my back, the perfectly proportioned, three-storey, apricot-walled and green-shuttered Villa Angeli – where I was to live and serve as a personal maidservant – came into view.

Leaving the wild Tuscan countryside, I stepped through the arched, pine-scented cypress door set in the stone wall and entered the enclosed, cultivated vegetable garden. Alternating bushes of rosemary and lavender awash with bees lined both sides of the path. Beyond the bushes, patches of Cook's plants and herbs flourished.

'Good morning, Hortensia. Happy Birthday.' Anna, Villa Angeli's cook and housekeeper, almost as wide as she was tall, embraced me. Anticipating her next move, I scrunched my face. But nothing happened. Disbelieving my good fortune, I sneaked a peak through my lashes.

Sparkling lights danced in Anna's raisin-black eyes. 'From today no more cheek-pinching for you.' She still reached out, but all I felt was the feathery caress of air, between her fingertips and my face. It was a feeling I loved. Then she spoiled the moment, with her next words. 'You are now, after all, a young woman.'

My face flushed. Even though I had known her all my life, and loved her as if she were my grandmother, I cringed at the slightest mention of my first, recently experienced, menses.

'Here,' Anna said, 'let me help you.'

I released the bundle into her hands, which she casually tossed into the kitchen fire.

'My...my cloth...'

The flames surged and engulfed the bundle, which fragmented, and in a shower of bright spitting sparks, dissolved. Cross breezes carried away the stench of burnt cotton.

'I've had new dresses and aprons made for you. They're on my bed.' Anna's apple-cheeks dimpled. 'Go. Bathe before the water gets cold. And, Hortensia, with all your clothes off.'

My face flushed hotter.

Anna waggled an index finger in the air. 'Yes. You heard right. *With all your clothes off.* Wash your hair. Don't forget behind your ears. And scrub your nails and hands. Once you're dry, get dressed and return here.' She indicated a spot on the floor.

I entered Anna's small bathroom off the kitchen and eyed the copper bath warily. Curling wisps of vapour rose from the still surface. Until that moment, I had bathed infrequently, standing in a large bucket of tepid water, wearing a cotton shift. The fragrance of rose-scented geranium filled the room and eased my trepidation. I did all Anna instructed and in record time.

The ankle-length linen dresses, each a patchwork of different colours, thrilled me. The full skirts swished around my legs, and when secured, the white cotton apron ties revealed the narrowness of my waist, of which until then I had not been aware. The triangle-shaped headscarves sat upon my head, and with little effort turned into what I imagined could be a small crown, like the one the Virgin Mary wore.

Holding my shoulders back and belly in, I returned to the kitchen and stood exactly where Anna had indicated.

She circled me. 'My, oh, my. The maids did a good job with the dress and apron.'

I felt a twinge of sorrow. I had hoped to hear a compliment. But the truth was, I was hardly anything to look at, even if my new clothes made me feel all grown-up.

Anna unwrapped several pairs of boots. 'See which pair fits best.'

Judging by their good, albeit used condition, the peddler had likely traded hard. Even after the war, leather goods were difficult to find, and expensive. I dreaded imagining how many bottles of Anna's renowned pickled vegetables and marmalade filled the peddler's cart.

The best fitting pair was tight.

'Loosen the laces,' Anna said. 'That'll make a difference.'

But it made no difference at all. Within half an hour, blisters bulged on my heels. My squashed toes begged for release, and when the pins and needles feeling disappeared, I believed my toes had died. Later, when Maria arrived for lunch and Anna was out of earshot, I lowered my voice and lamented my sore feet.

More often than not, the silver bangles on Maria's right wrist saved her the effort of communicating by releasing a pre-emptive sound. Today was no different. They jangled once prior to Maria's snort of disapproval.

'Bah. Be grateful for the fact your job gives you a roof, a bed, food, clothes and a pair of boots. A small price to pay given your orphaned state.'

While my heart ached from Maria's reminder, my feet and boots went to war. I could not help but wonder which would surrender first. It would take weeks before the skin on my feet hardened and the leather eased.

I knew my way around the Villa Angeli kitchen, having taken my meals there for as long as I could remember. But now, under Anna's instruction, I learned how to be a personal maid. Later, on my own, I learned to listen hard when Maria and Anna or the housemaids lowered their voices.

That afternoon, for the first time, I followed Anna up the staircase. Arriving on the wide landing, Anna indicated to double doors on the right.

'Here is the library. The door opposite is a guest bedroom.'

We continued down the corridor.

She lowered her voice. 'And here is Master Giovanni Angeli's bed-chamber.'

I suppressed a shudder. The housemaids had clutched their throats and stuck out their tongues when they told me about our master, who lay slowly drowning in the liquid that gathered in his chest, sometimes even bubbling out of his mouth.

'Where am I to sleep?' I whispered. The night before, as Maria told me my life was about to change, I had been filled with hesitation. But learning I would have a bedroom of my own, all resistance disappeared.

Anna pushed a door open and stood aside.

My belly contracted with excitement, and then released with disappointment, when I stepped into a small room. It was furnished with a single bed and a set of drawers and there was only one window. In my head, I heard Maria's bangles rattle their reprimand, reminding me of my former humble home. I pressed the heel of one boot down hard and relished the solidness of the two-hundred-year-old floor underfoot. In the shepherd's hut, I feared the hard-packed earth would open and swallow me whole. As small as my new bedroom was, there were three doors.

Anna noticed my confusion. 'That connects to Mistress Letizia's bedchamber, the other to the guestroom. Come, it's time for you to meet her.'

We returned to the corridor and stopped in front of the last door at the far end.

'Hortensia, remember what I said.' Anna spoke in her lowest voice. 'Under no circumstances react when you see the size of her.'

I felt confident. Aside from Anna's warning, the housemaids' gestures had told me all I needed. When Anna wasn't looking, they blew out their cheeks and extended their arms to indicate Mistress Letizia's size. But their exaggerations did her no justice.

Though it was mid-afternoon, Mistress Letizia still lay abed. She was not dissimilar to a giant snowman: round, squashy, about to melt into a blob. With metres of yellow silk swaddling her form, she appeared even larger. Her hair, thick as a tied bundle of wheat and shiny like the treasured bobbin of gold thread in Anna's sewing box, appeared to have no end. From either side of her face it hung like curtains and pooled in her lap.

The moment I got a full view of her, my immediate reaction was to step back. But Anna gripped the knot of my apron's bow and held me firm. I took in the rest of the room.

Six shepherd huts could easily fill her chamber. Furniture, the likes of which I had never seen, included two Cararra-white, marble-topped bedside tables, a dressing table with a fixed centre mirror flanked by two smaller adjustable ones, a wardrobe whose doors were carved with the Angeli coat of arms – an angel in the centre of a shield, atop of which rested a knight's helmet and below the motto *pax et fides* – and a chaise longue. Plush rugs with intricate designs lay on the floor. Better than all this, through the gauzy curtains covering the windows, I glimpsed that view I never tired of.

The sound of Mistress Letizia's voice, sharp and reedy, was at odds with the rest of her. 'How old are you, Hortensia?'

I steeled myself and returned her gaze. 'Fourteen, today.'

Her cornflower-blue eyes, almost hidden by the fatty folds of her eyelids, opened wide. 'Younger than me by three years.'

Anna steadied me again by tightening her grip.

Mistress Letizia focused on Anna. 'You did remember to bake chocolate cake, didn't you?'

Her acerbic tone hurt my ears.

'Of course, mistress.' Anna bobbed her head.

I was shocked. I had never seen Anna display subservience to anyone. But now I saw Anna for who she was: a servant. Given Maria and Anna had schooled me to respect my elders, I felt a rare surge of fury against Mistress Letizia.

Anna's grip increased.

'What about dogs? Do you like small dogs, Hortensia?'

Our valley's hunting dogs were thin but their long legs made them seem big. They were excellent trackers with howls that could wake the dead. But a small dog? I'd never seen a small dog.

Mistress Letizia snapped her fingers. 'Foxy. Here, boy. Come.'

It was then I noticed the size of her hands, and instinctively knew that her unexposed feet were delicate and small, too.

From beneath the coverlet, a shiny black nose, pointed muzzle, black dots for eyes, perky ears, and fluffed white body emerged. 'Ah, there you are.' She caressed the dog. 'Foxy will decide if you will be a good maidservant to me.'

I froze to the floor aghast. *A dog! Making decisions? This is madness. No. Heresy. What would Don Antonio, the priest, say?* I watched with curiosity as the formally known *volpino italiano,* looking exactly like the small, white arctic fox, first trotted, then skipped, towards me. He stopped at my feet. His diminutive standing height reached the middle of my calves. He lowered his head, sniffed my boots with keen interest and licked the leather with his tiny, bright pink tongue. His tail, a smaller ball of fluff, wagged. He pranced a step backwards and then, pressing his nose to his tail, began to spin and executed several faultless pirouettes.

'Ah, good,' Mistress Letizia said. 'He thinks you'll do.'

By late afternoon I had traipsed up and down the staircase several times, and each time my toes begged for mercy. First with a tray carrying a pitcher of mint-infused lemonade, followed by a pot of tisane, and then the chocolate cake Anna had baked. The cake almost did not reach its final destination. As I bent to pick up the tray, pain raced from my feet up my legs causing me to lose my balance. My hands fumbled. The tray lurched, sending the cake sliding from one end to the other.

'Hortensia,' Anna hissed, 'be careful. Get that cake to Mistress Letizia in one piece.'

I ignored my sore feet. 'All of it?'

Anna nodded. 'Don't worry. I have another for us to share after dinner when we celebrate your birthday.'

I was relieved to hear it. I had only recently been introduced to chocolate, it being impossible to source during the war. From the moment I had taken my first bite, I loved chocolate above all.

After setting the trays for Mistress Letizia's afternoon tea within easy reach for her, she called, 'Foxy, fetch the ball.'

The dog shot out from under the bed and, using his nose, nudged a small ball towards me.

'Take Foxy. Play with him. I'll ring when I've finished.'

I tucked Foxy under one arm – he was as light as one of Anna's meringues – and headed out to the meadow beyond the kitchen garden where I hastily removed my too-tight boots, spread my toes and massaged each foot in turn. My feet offered grateful thanks for the cool, soft grass. Thus barefoot, I extended the game of catch with Foxy until his tongue lolled sideways out of his mouth and, happily exhausted, he collapsed with the ball firmly wedged between his front paws.

I sat beside the dog and turned my thoughts to Mistress Letizia, her father, and Villa Angeli.

From Maria, I learned that Mistress Letizia's mother had died a few hours after childbirth. Grief consumed Giovanni Angeli, and he sent his days-old daughter to live with his wife's family in the north of Italy. Fearing for her safety when the war started, they placed eleven-year-old Mistress Letizia in a nunnery across the border in a country called Switzerland.

When the men in our valley were called to arms, Giovanni Angeli put Anna in charge of the villa. After she shrouded the furniture in dustsheets and secured the windows and shutters, he locked each room's door leaving only Anna's en-suite bedroom, cantina, kitchen, and vegetable garden open for her use. He placed the keys in a tin box and under cover of darkness he buried it. Then he left. Some claimed he joined the Italian army. Others whispered he had been seen in the valley's woods. No one knew for certain.

From the time Maria rescued me, I spent my days with Anna. She taught me how to garden, and I watched her prepare food. I ate my meals with her in the Villa Angeli's kitchen, and at night Maria and I returned to our shepherd's hut. When Anna's attention was elsewhere, I roamed the land beyond the kitchen walls and often visited the forest clearing where I'd last seen my mother. Thus, while the interior of Villa Angeli, with the exception of those few rooms, was unknown to me, the Angeli Estate's land was as familiar to me as my own hands.

One early morning, a week after the war had ended, Giovanni Angeli, stooped, and so thin and filthy he was barely recognisable, returned home. He placed the dug-up tin box on the kitchen table and instructed Anna to call back the maids and reopen the villa. After three successive hot baths, nail clippings, haircut, and removal of his unkempt beard and moustache, he changed into fresh clothes. Had there been a competition, he would have won first prize for best scarecrow. Taking up the reins and following what his father and his father's father would have done, he returned to the vineyards.

Valley men also returned, looking not much different to Master Angeli when he had returned home. Within days, they joined him in the vineyards even though there was no mention of payment, immediate or future. After the war, nobody had anything, and it was accepted that proceeds from the next harvest would go towards restoring and improving the vineyards. Should there be any left, and only at Master Angeli's discretion, would it be divided among the workers.

As Master Angeli's wife's family had all perished in the war, it took him a year to discover the whereabouts of his daughter and arrange for her to come home. Thus, Mistress Letizia had arrived a month ago. The housemaids had said she refused to get out of the wagon until darkness fell.

Only then did she enter the villa, and to this day, she hadn't left her bedchamber.

———————— ◆ ————————

Anna's voice sounded in the distance. I squeezed my protesting feet into the boots, and with tears pricking my eyelids returned to the kitchen.

'Where have you been?' She looked cross.

'As instructed, playing with Foxy.'

Though Anna's face softened, she was still upset. I did not venture to ask because I knew I'd learn why. The answer came sooner than expected.

'Your mistress has already eaten dinner.'

I glanced at the cake tray on the table. All that remained were crumbs. 'She ate it all?' I could not hide my sheer disbelief.

'What's more, she had seconds for dinner and the chocolate cake I'd baked for you. So, I am very sorry, Hortensia, but your birthday dinner is in your mistress's stomach. We will all be eating bread and cheese. Tomorrow we'll celebrate your birthday. I promise.'

I swallowed my disappointment and gave Anna a quick hug.

'Here, take this to your mistress, settle her for the evening and come back downstairs.'

I sighed. 'More chocolate?'

Anna's mouth pressed into a thin line. 'Yes. And, Hortensia, make sure you deliver the box to her intact. Not one chocolate is to go missing. Do you understand?'

I nodded. I'd heard that despite her vehement protestations, this was the reason for the last maidservant's dismissal. She'd opened the box, eaten one and then tried to rearrange the rest of the chocolates. But Mistress Letizia knew exactly how many chocolates there should have been.

I knocked and entered.

She reclined on the chaise longue with her long hair spilling over the backrest like a golden waterfall. I handed her the box and then waited as she counted the chocolates.

Mistress Letizia waved her hand in the air. 'Don't just stand there. Bring the brush. It's on the dresser.'

I moved swiftly. I had no desire to subject my ears to her vexed voice which could shatter glass. On the dressing table stood several crystal perfume bottles, an ivory comb, a brush and a handheld mirror. I picked up the brush and, remembering Anna's instructions, sectioned my mistress's hair before brushing with long, even strokes.

Her hair ran through my fingers like silk ribbons. Before long, at the end of each downward stroke, strands lifted in an arc, seemingly intent on following the upward movement of the brush returning to begin the next stroke. In the gathering dusk, pinpricks of blue light snapped and intensified until the room filled with crackling sparks. The heat in my palms and arms burned, yet I could not stop. I felt an overwhelming desire to abandon myself to the warming trance taking hold of me. Much how frogs felt, I supposed, when Maria slowly brought them to a simmer.

The jarring sound of Maria's silver bangles in my head broke the spell. I opened my eyes and saw Mistress Letizia sleeping peacefully but with one delicate hand clutching the box of chocolates, already half-empty.

I slipped out of the room, shaking my burning hands in the hope of restoring them back to normal, and headed to the kitchen. Knowing we only had bread and cheese for dinner, and from the garden likely a platter of raw, crunchy vegetables drizzled *with* olive oil and sprinkled with salt, I looked forward to it. I loved raw vegetables and cheese, especially Maria's goat cheese. I was, I realised, very hungry.

I did not see Maria until she materialised in front of me outside Master Giovanni Angeli's bedchamber.

'Hortensia.' She spoke in her no-nonsense voice. 'Go and fetch your mistress. She is to come to her father's bedchamber. He is dying.'

Upon hearing Maria's words, my toes and belly, for different reasons, insisted I shout *No!* But I knew better than that. Ignoring them both, I retraced my steps.

Waking Mistress Letizia was one thing. Getting her up and off her bed was another. Finally, she stood, and leaning heavily on me, we shuffled one step at a time to the master bedchamber.

'Thank you, Hortensia,' Maria said. 'I'll take care of Mistress Letizia from here. But when you get downstairs, tell Anna to send for Dr Baldi.'

I fled to do her bidding.

Blessed with a sixth sense, Maria entered valley homes already prepared to administer her potions easing discomforts of all sorts. Unlike Dr Baldi, Maria was always present before a birth and a death.

So, it was no different that evening when Master Angeli took a turn for the worse. Maria and Mistress Letizia sat by his bedside for two days and nights during which time Dr Baldi visited twice. When Mistress Letizia, reeling with exhaustion, and noticeably less gargantuan, succumbed to her bed, only Maria was at our master's side when he breathed his last breath.

With few exceptions, everyone from our valley attended Giovanni Angeli's funeral. As soon as the bronze doors of the Angeli mausoleum shut, questions, deemed unseemly to voice while he lay dying, ripped through the crowd like an end-of-summer wildfire. With no male heir to continue the Angeli ascendancy, what would happen to the estate? Would it be sold? And if so to whom?

Trianni, our neighbour, had abandoned his olive estate decades ago. Now with their last wage-earning option in jeopardy, the workers returned to their homes likely feeling the nooses around their necks pull tighter.

In the afternoon, on the same day Master Giovanni Angeli was buried, *avvocato* Fini arrived to read the will.

'Hortensia, I will wear the black dress,' Mistress Letizia said as I stood before her wardrobe.

I helped her find the armholes in the swaths of cloth and then pulled and tugged the dress down over her torso, stomach and legs. I could not decide if her golden hair was enhanced by the black silk or if the black silk was enhanced by her hair. Either way, it reminded me of my mousy-brown, wispy hair that was far from Mistress Letizia's crowning glory. She leaned on me again until she found her balance, but to my pleasant surprise she negotiated her way down the corridor to the library unaided. Foxy pranced daintily ahead.

Propriety demanded that Mistress Letizia, not yet eighteen, be accompanied. Also, in the absence of living relatives, and as I was her maidservant, the task fell to me.

In the library, though my chaperone chair was some distance away, I had an unobstructed view of her. The nearsighted lawyer, thin, pale, also dressed in black, sat with his back to me, but I saw his reflection in the gilded wall mirror. His hushed voice was no match for my young, well-trained ears; I could hear a pin drop.

While *avvocato* Fini shuffled papers, I took a good look at the rectangle-shaped library. The short, north wall behind me held floor-to-ceiing book-lined shelves as did the long east wall. The south wall showed off the gilded wall mirror. Cream-coloured drapes framed the sea-facing windows on the west wall. Light flooded the room. Mistress Letizia's portrait, flanked on either side by a portrait of each of her parents, hung between the windows.

A crystal chandelier said to have come from Venice hung from the centre of the wood-beamed ceiling. While Anna complained that keeping the five thousand books dust-free was a thankless task, she also bragged that it was a library second to none, containing books on subjects about which I knew nothing: mathematics, mythology, science, poetry and art.

The only subject I was beginning to think would be of interest were those books called novels that were mainly about love. At least, that was the conclusion I'd come to after eavesdropping on the housemaids, who all had an intense interest in the subject. Love caused them to alternately giggle and cry with equal intensity and, most surprising of all, caused them to change their minds as fast as fickle cross breezes switch directions.

A table big enough for spread-open maps furnished the light and airy room, as well as chairs, smaller side tables, a sea chest, a ceramic floor-standing vase stuck with hand-painted flowers and birds, and a sofa that easily accommodated Mistress Letizia.

The lawyer found the document, held it up to the light and read aloud. 'Your father's will states that to inherit, the last surviving member of the Angeli family, in other words you, must be married, and have borne a son by the first anniversary of his death.'

'You are mistaken.' Mistress Letiza spoke in her tinny voice. 'How can I possibly meet a man, fall in love, marry and have a son, all in the space of twelve months! My father must have been out of his mind when he wrote this.'

Avvocato Fini began to sweat. He dragged a handkerchief across his brow. 'I can assure you, he was of sound–'

'On whose say?' Mistress Letizia's tone sharpened.

The lawyer indicated the three, blue-inked signatures. 'The witnesses, of course: Dr Baldi, Don Antonio and myself.'

While Mistress Letizia paused, I glimpsed dust motes moving within a bright ray of sunlight that cut through one of the tall, sea-facing windows. Then I saw it before the lawyer did, even though he was sitting directly opposite her.

One after another, hairline cracks appeared in Mistress Letizia's porcelain-glazed face. After cracking, her face, the maids had told me, would inevitably crumple, and tears would gush much like the waterfalls that poured down our valley's steep sides in the full flush of winter rain. What I saw next surprised me. Mistress Letizia employed the mightiest effort and managed to keep her tears in check.

'It's an impossible order.' Her tone hit a note that caused both the lawyer and me to wince. Despite the fact that there was no breeze, the chandelier's crystal drops shimmied.

Avvocato Fini recovered. 'Have hope. God has his eye on you, and you may be blessed yet.'

'What nonsense you speak. I wonder if it is you who is not of sound mind. Perhaps you should be relieved of your duties…'

'Mistress Letizia, I am executor of this will. You are in no position to exercise that power.'

'Enough. Tell me what fate I must await in a year's time, when I am without husband or son.'

My ears strained. I concentrated, knowing I would be expected to report back word for word.

The lawyer took up the will again. He held it close to his face while he read. 'In the absence of a marriage and grandson, the Angeli Estate shall in its entirety be gifted to his Holiness, Eugenio Maria Giuseppe Giovanni Pacelli, Pope Pius XII. My daughter, Letizia Angeli, shall enter a convent of his Holiness's choice, where she shall remain until God calls upon her to join him in heaven.'

While the lawyer spoke I realised the dust motes had stopped moving, and the shock of a knife-blade slicing through my heart turned my body cold. I could not fathom how Mistress Letizia must have felt. Then she surprised me again.

'If that is all, you may leave.' Her voice was low and cold.

I jumped up and held the door open for him to pass. Only then did the first waterfalls of tears slide down Mistress Letizia's cracked face. I was surprised again; I felt sorry for her.

She cried so hard upon returning to her bedchamber that she left a trail of tears in her wake, causing me to notice the hem of her dress dragging on the floor. *She is losing weight!*

By the time we entered her bedchamber, Mistress Letizia had begun to chant. Her voice, like a seesaw tipping back and forth, rose, 'What am I to do?' and then fell, 'Dear God, tell me, what am I to do?' She barely paused, repeating the refrain over and over. She seemed oblivious to my presence. I felt torn between sorrow and growing irritation. My mistress's chanting was enough to conquer Job's patience.

I could not stand it a second longer and so I left. The moment I closed the chamber door, I rolled my shoulders and inhaled deeply. From the kitchen came the tantalising aroma of sautéing *porcini* coated with garlic, parsley, salt and a squeeze of lemon juice cutting through crisp and fatty cubes of bacon.

Thoughts of Mistress Letizia and her insurmountable woes cast aside, I hastened along the corridor, down the staircase and across the entrance hall, and dashed through the dining room to enter the kitchen.

'Ah, Hortensia, here you are, at last.' Maria tilted back her head so that her turned-in eyes, pointing towards the tip of her hooked nose, skewered me like a pin would an insect. 'Sit. Tell us about the reading of our master's will.'

Villa Angeli's estate manager, Rubino, whom I loved but did not realise how much until it was too late, folded the month-old copy of *il Tirreno* and set it aside. Maria and Anna, who had definite, but often differing opinions on everything, caused Rubino to take the path of least resistance. But when it came to decision time, he made the final call.

Anna placed the black iron pan of *porcini* on the table and sat. As I took my place, my thoughts raced back to the moment Mistress Letizia and *avvocato* Fini settled themselves at the library table. I took a deep breath and related, word for word, what I had witnessed.

The kitchen fell silent. Rubino investigated the bottom of his glass for any remaining wine. Maria stared into the distance. Anna shut her eyes and tapped her temple with a finger.

Unusually so, Rubino spoke first. 'This could be the opportunity we've been waiting for to assume control of the estate and secure the valley's livelihood for decades. But how?'

Anna stopped tapping her temple. 'Give me ten days.'

From the corner of my eye, I caught Maria and Anna exchange glances. Whatever it was, they clearly did not wish me to know. But taking my cue from Rubino, I said nothing. Time would reveal all.

'Anna, you've got ten days from tomorrow. In the meantime, no one is to repeat a word of the will's conditions,' Maria said. 'Understood?'

The bangles on Maria's bony wrist jangled. I glanced up to see three pairs of eyes staring at me. We stood, made the sign of the cross together. Then I received warm hugs from the most important people in my life. All of whom I trusted implicitly.

My belly grumbled. I could wait no longer. 'Can we eat, please?'

The following morning, I entered Mistress Letizia's bedchamber. She was still asleep. Fearful she would start chanting and crying once awake, I left her. Foxy appeared to be of the same opinion. He did not bark but sneaked out from under the bed with a ball in his mouth. I scooped him up and left.

By mid-afternoon, the situation was no different from the day before. Upon waking, the waterfalls of tears flowed, and Mistress Letizia began her incantations.

I discharged my duties as fast as I could and when evening fell, I left the chamber and expelled a huge sigh of relief.

My nostrils went on instant alert. Although the light fragrance hinted asparagus, I was almost certain our meal would include *carciofi ala giudia*. The new season's baby artichokes, left whole, looked much like closed rosebuds when deep-fried to a crackling-crisp. Served lightly salted with a squeeze of lemon, the ancient recipe with Jewish origins made a delightful appetiser while Anna would prepare the next course.

I raced to the kitchen.

Though I was decades younger, Maria, Rubino, and Anna always waited for me before starting our meals.

'How does your mistress fare this evening?' Maria asked.

I took my place at the table. 'She still suffers.' I said this with certainty. Like me, Mistress Letizia was now parentless. But unlike her, I had no idea who my father was and had, for reasons still unknown, been abandoned by my mother. This grief I bore each day; the pain never lessened.

Maria waved her bony hand, setting her bangles jangling with disdain. 'Oh, never mind.' She glanced at Anna. 'Soon, Mistress Letizia will have reason to get over it.'

I should not have been shocked by Maria's words. She was not only a midwife but with her highly developed sixth sense, she was an augur, too. She always knew what was to come, and it was said, though very quietly, that she could change what had already been written in heaven. There were few people in our valley whose future had not been shaped by

Maria's interpretation of omens when she held a newborn in her arms and slipped from skilled midwife to gifted augur.

At my mother's birth, the pair of dissolving fragile wings – iridescent green on top with bright purple spots below – attached to her minuscule shoulder blades had caused Maria to say, 'This child will leave our valley', immediately upon which tears cascaded down my grandmother's face. But for Maria's quickness wresting the newborn from her arms, my mother was sure to have drowned.

Anna, whose rotund form was the polar opposite of stick-thin Maria, always sat to my right. Throughout my childhood, whenever I raised the mystery of my mother's transformation and disappearance, Anna would enfold me in her plump arms and say, 'Your mother got lost in the swirl of butterflies. She never ever meant to leave you.'

Despite her fervent assurances, supported with home-baked biscuits and cups of warm, honey-sweetened milk, I did not believe her. Secretly, I vowed I'd never abandon a child of mine. Not for anything.

Anna's raisin-dark eyes opened wide. 'You and I will help Mistress Letizia get over the loss of her father, won't we?'

I wanted to shout out loud: *Mistress Letizia was not grieving the loss of her father, a man she hardly knew, nor her mother, whom she knew not at all. Rather, she was wholly grieving her bleak future.*

But I took a lesson from Rubino who always advised that, in order to get attention, one should lower their voice. And so I did. 'No. I believe my mistress would be best served if we helped her prepare for the certain fate awaiting her.'

I caught Anna and Maria exchange glances again while Rubino placed his huge hand over my much smaller hand.

Through years of toil, his fingers had swollen like sausages about to split their skins. Solid and steady, he represented the centuries-old giant chestnut standing as strong above ground as it was rooted below. And like the tree's wrinkled bark, so too were the years etched upon his face. Rubino gave my hand a gentle squeeze. 'How right you are.'

My anxiety was eased by the warmth of his words.

'And,' he added, 'what a lot you've already experienced working alongside us.'

Anna placed the dish of piping hot and crunchy rosebud artichokes on the table. Her face beamed with pride and joy. '*Buon appetito.*'

———— ◆ ————

Each evening Anna led the prayer before we ate, or, more accurately, feasted.

'Mmm…delicious.' I licked the last crumbs of golden polenta mixed with a generous quantity of grated *Parmigiano-Reggiano* from my fingers.

Rubino refilled our glasses with the Angeli's sought-after *Sangiovese* wine, plum red, with a surprising savoury pinch to the back of the tongue. 'To Anna. The best cook in Tuscany.'

We raised our glasses.

Anna's cheeks dimpled. She loved it when people enjoyed her cooking, and she wasn't shy of appreciating her own food either. She placed an ancient nutcracker and a wicker basket filled with walnuts in front of Rubino and, before each of us, tiny bowls of damp coarse salt.

Rubino cracked the shells and passed them to us. With metal skewers shaped like toothpicks but with hooked ends, we teased the kernels from their wrinkled shells, dipped them into the salt and popped them into our mouths.

Anna filled glasses with ice-cold *limoncello*, the unctuous liqueur made from alcohol and the fruit of lemon trees found on the island of Capri. A teaspoon of the bright liquid drizzled over vanilla ice cream on a hot summer day was as refreshing as taking a forbidden dip in the river that ran through Trianni Estate's abandoned olive groves. Or, like this evening, rolling the liquid around the inside of my mouth then letting it slide down, igniting a fire in the pit of my belly.

The meal over, Maria turned her attention to me. Before she even opened her mouth, I knew what her question was going to be. I shook my head. 'She has not improved.'

Maria turned her attention to Anna.

Anna responded to Maria's unvoiced question, 'Any day now.'

———— ◆ ————

I lay in bed in the small room alongside my mistress's and counted out on my fingers the number of times Maria had asked me how my mistress fared. Tonight had been the tenth. And just like that, I knew time was up. I could not begin to imagine what the next day would bring.

Before the church bells pealed, I entered my mistress's bedchamber to wake her. But, on that morning, two weeks into the year-long mourning period, she was already awake. Her round face was flushed and celestial blue eyes uncommonly bright. 'Mistress Letizia, whatever is the matter?'

'I've not slept. The smell of warm chocolate has driven me to distraction. Is Anna baking?'

'You gave her orders not to.'

'I know I did. But someone is trying to sabotage my best efforts to reduce my weight.'

'Sabo–'

'There! There's that smell again. Quick, Hortensia, open the window and shutters.'

The moment I flung them open, I inhaled and caught the alluring hint of chocolate carried by the fresh Tyrrhenian breeze.

'Now do you believe me? Where is it coming from?'

I leaned over the sill and only saw the steep slopes upon which the regimented Angeli vines stretched. On the opposite valley slope, the Trianni's centuries-old grove of gnarled, evergreen olive trees spread up to the sprawling stone villa, which was overshadowed by the olive oil mill. Attached to the mill rose a splendid turreted tower. *Il fiume Frigido,* the

Frigid River, snaked along the valley floor that since the last earthquake now flowed only through the Trianni lands.

The garden bell rang.

'Goodness! On a Sunday.' The space between Mistress Letizia's crescent-shaped eyebrows, furrowed. '*Who* can it be?'

I rose to the tips of my toes. Twisting sideways, I caught sight of a boy – or was it a man? – standing at the wrought-iron gate set between two stone pillars. I looked harder. It was a man dressed in a suit. At his feet rested a brown case, looking much like the kind travelling salesmen use.

'A salesman, I think.'

'Ask him who he is.'

'*Lei, chi é?*' I called out.

'*Al vostro servizio,* Gennaro Di Napoli.'

My spine tingled. I had never heard a voice vibrate with so much energy and self-confidence.

Upon hearing his surname, Mistress Letizia inhaled sharply. He was a *napoletano*, against whom she, and others like her, had been warned. In the presence of a Neapolitan one had to be on the alert. Especially virtuous women with no male protector.

'Ask what he's selling.'

It was unnecessary; I already knew. He had flicked open the lid and, holding his case above his head, waved it about. The breeze, now heavily laden with the intoxicating scent of chocolate, rose and entered the chamber. Desire filled my head until I thought it would burst. Behind me, Mistress Letizia released a soft moan. But I asked anyway. '*Lei cosa vende?*'

'I bring gifts fit for gods.'

Mistress Letizia's stomach rumbled. 'Let him in through the front door and show him into the parlour.'

A jumble of confused feelings coursed through me. Tradesmen and peddlers were directed to the kitchen entrance. Never did they see the inside of the parlour. But then this salesman dressed and held himself differently than others. His voice…

'And offer him refreshments,' Mistress Letizia said, interrupting my thoughts. 'Then come back. I want to change into a fresh gown. The blue one.'

———— ◆ ————

I t took all my strength to slide back the iron latches, turn the heavy key and push open one half of the double front door. I hastened down the broad stone-flagged path to the gate, unlocked and pulled it open.

'Good morning.' The salesman's voice caused taut strings in my chest to vibrate.

He was short and swarthy like most Neapolitans. His slicked-back hair was well pomaded, exuding the smell of beeswax.

In concert with the vibrating musical notes resonating from deep within me, his gaze travelled from my feet, up my legs, lingered upon my chest, my throat, to the top of my head.

He was blessed with obscenely long eyelashes, much longer than mine. Most striking of all, he had large, dark pools for eyes. Though I was still learning to swim, I saw myself, mermaid-like, gliding effortlessly, hardly rippling the glossy surface, blissfully biding time until he joined me, which, every tingling fibre in my body told me he would.

'And you are...?'

To my astonishment he leaned towards me and I found my hands clasped between his. Close up, the skin on his face was like that of a youth. Was the rest of his body as smooth? Or was his head of shocking rich and thick hair replicated elsewhere on his body? While those indecent thoughts exploded in my head, Di Napoli kissed the backs of my work-roughened hands. 'Hortensia.' I barely heard the sound of my voice.

'Because of you,' he said, 'the world is finer.'

Fearful of the rising heat sure to colour my face, and the shock of first-time flutters in other parts of my body that left me light-headed, I said in a rush, 'Please, follow me,' turned and led Gennaro Di Napoli into the parlour. 'My mistress will see you soon.' I escaped to the kitchen. To my surprise, Anna was already there.

'He's arrived?' Her voice was low.

'Who? Oh, you mean the travelling chocolate salesman?'

Anna looked at me very carefully, as though she was seeing me for the first time. 'Yes. Gennaro. My nephew from Naples.'

Then I remembered. The ten-day deadline was up and here was the person who was going to help solve Mistress Letizia's inheritance problem.

———— ◆ ————

'Hurry, Hortensia,' Mistress Letizia said, as my fingers fastened the buttons on her gown which matched the colour of her eyes. She stood, feet apart, balancing her weight while I tugged and straightened her dress. She reached into her bosom, lifted and settled one enormous breast into the triple-stitched bodice, swapped hands and did the same with the other. A cleavage formed so deep, things hidden there might never be found.

'Use the blue bow,' she said, 'for Foxy.'

Hearing his name, the fluffy white dog stuck his head out from under the feather-filled bedcover.

I snapped my fingers. 'Come, Foxy.'

He bounded with legs locked stiff to where I stood. Under the pretence of a caress, I clipped the bow to the top of his head.

Our mistress lumbered towards the door. Foxy scooted under the bed and then emerged with a ball in his mouth.

'Not now,' she said.

Foxy dropped it and trotted behind as our mistress, much quicker than her usual pace, made her way down the corridor towards the library. Size and speed combined created a current of air that caused her dress to billow and ruffle my hair. Entering the library, she took up her position on the long sofa, the only seating in the villa other than her bed that accommodated her without restriction. She flounced and spread the fabric of her skirt to hide her fleshy folds, then patted the sofa. Foxy settled himself next to her.

'Bring me the Neapolitan,' she said.

———— ◆ ————

D i Napoli stood statue-still in the parlour.

'This way,' I said and turned quickly, so as not to be trapped in those dark eyes again. As I climbed the stairs, I sensed him appraising me from behind. Reaching the landing, my spine, of its own volition, straightened, and my hips moved with an unaccustomed swing. About to grasp the handle of the library door, I prayed. Please God, don't let his face register shock upon seeing her. I entered. Mistress Letizia looked much like a giant, overblown rose. I stood back and let the salesman pass.

Though Di Napoli did not come close to touching me, my body flared like a struck match. I clutched the door handle for support.

'Mistress Angeli, I am humbled.' The timbre of his voice resonated against the book-lined walls. Copying his mistress, Foxy cocked his head and stared unblinkingly at the chocolate salesman.

With courtly manners reminiscent of a bygone age, Di Napoli bowed deeply, not raising his head until bid. Then he smiled, and Foxy growled. Both displayed their teeth.

'Gennaro Di Napoli, you are welcome.' Mistress Letizia hooked a finger around Foxy's collar. 'Tell me, what delights do you bring?'

I twitched with surprise. The tone of her voice had changed. Foxy detected it, too, and changed the direction of his cocked head.

From the erratic movement of her eyes, I watched Mistress Letizia struggle to tear her gaze from Di Napoli and lower it to the suitcase at his feet. The next second, as though drawn by the pull of a magnet, her gaze slid back up and locked on his. Then the colour of the robin's breast stained her cheeks.

I released my grip on the handle and closed the door. Slipping into my chair, I once again swapped my maid's role for that of chaperone.

'Delicacies,' Di Napoli said, 'I am now loath to display.'

Mistress Letizia fluttered her fan with vigour. Beads of sweat covered her expansive chest. They would soon turn into trickles, then rivulets and soak the front of her gown.

'Do not toy with me. You are here for a purpose, are you not?'

'Yes.'

'To sell me something?'

'I came with that intention,' he said. 'But, now that I am in your resplendent presence, I cannot.'

With breakfast still not served and the air rich and heady with chocolate fragrance, Mistress Letizia stifled an irritated sigh.

He lowered his head. 'My wares are not worthy of you.'

The tone in her voice sharpened. 'I shall make that decision for myself. Show me.'

The tick-tock of the grandfather clock filled my ears.

With the heel of one pointy-toed shoe, he nudged the suitcase to rest behind him, causing it to release another cloud of aromatised chocolate. 'Alas, no.'

Only the increased fluttering of her fan kept my mistress from swooning. 'Gennaro Di Napoli, are you playing me for a fool?'

'I swear I am not.'

'Then show me your wares.'

Foxy saved the conversation from going any further. He flew off the sofa, raced over and demonstrated what he thought of Di Napoli and his suitcase of wares by lifting his leg.

'Foxy!' Mistress Letizia shrieked. 'Bad dog.'

Di Napoli stepped aside, but too late. The damage was done. He stared at his fouled, black, pointy-toed shoes. 'You see. Your dog has concurred.'

'Gennaro Di Napoli, remove your shoes. Hortensia, have them cleaned. Take Foxy with you. Lock him in the garden.'

'Mistress, I cannot leave barefoot.'

Like a trapped bee, the timbre of his voice hummed in my ear.

'Leave?' Unable to bend because of her barrel stomach, Mistress Letizia slipped off her morning slippers. Her feet, like her hands, were delicate and slender while the rest of her was swollen like a water-filled balloon. 'See? We shall both remain here shoeless until you have shown me your wares.'

To his credit, the chocolate salesman did not flinch, but bowed with exaggeration. 'As it pleases you.'

'Hortensia, serve my breakfast. Gennaro Di Napoli will join me.' Though she spoke to me, her eyes were fixed on his. 'Hide his shoes until I instruct you to return them.'

Gripping a squirming Foxy under one arm and carrying the fouled footwear in my other hand, I headed for the kitchen.

As if Anna had overheard our mistress's instruction, two trays were already prepared. 'Hortensia, don't mix them. The pink one is for Mistress Letizia. The blue for Gennaro.'

Before re-entering the library with the trays, I stopped, amazed by the musical sound of my mistress's laughter. In the three weeks as her personal maid, it was the first time I heard her laugh. My heart warmed.

But no sooner had I entered than I froze, as though I'd been dunked under the swift current of the *Frigido*.

Di Napoli sat alongside my mistress in Foxy's place. Compared to her he looked diminutive. He'd slung his jacket over my chaperone chair, upon the seat of which his scrunched socks rested. His tie was missing and the buttons of his shirt, down to his navel, were undone. His soft-brimmed hat, with its white silk band rested upon my mistress's head.

From where I stood holding the trays, I could clearly see my mistress's toes flexing and contracting, like the kitchen cat kneading a pillow. Di Napoli's perfectly chiselled feet and toes rested dangerously close to hers.

My mistress and Di Napoli barely turned towards me.

Her moon face was radiant, blue eyes aglow, mouth smiling without end. Then realization dawned. *This is what Maria meant when she had said Mistress Letizia would soon have a reason to get over the shock of her father's death.*

Gennaro Di Napoli's eyes deepened as I drew closer. I bent to place my mistress's tray directly in front of her and his before him. He jumped up to help, closing his hands over mine. Our foreheads almost touched. Not even when I'd suffered a three-day fever had I been so hot. The trays almost upended, but with a panther's grace, Di Napoli set them to rights. I reclaimed my hands from under his.

'Be careful!' My mistress's voice shrilled. Startled, I glanced at her while she gave Di Napoli her full attention. And he gave me his.

The bodice of her dress no longer stretched tight. She had indeed benefitted from her diet.

'Hortensia, take a walk in the garden and play with Foxy. I'll ring should I need you.'

I could not identify the feeling that caused me to hesitate. It was more than the confusion I felt over her sudden weight loss. I stood immobile.

'Hortensia…?' My mistress's voice penetrated my ears as though relayed over a long distance.

My intuition dredged hard, something was rising from the dark, coming into light. Alarm bells began to ring.

'Hortensia?'

That's it. It's dangerous to leave Mistress Letizia alone in the library with Gennaro Di Napoli. 'Yes?'

'Go.'

I turned to leave. Again, I sensed his gaze upon my body. My spine straightened. This time I prayed for my hips not to sway.

After playing ball with Foxy in the walled garden until he was happily exhausted, I re-entered the kitchen.

Anna's face glowed. 'Our mistress bids you make up the guest room. Gennaro is invited to stay.'

'Guest room?'

'Yes. The one alongside yours.'

My heart missed a beat. That room and mine shared an interconnecting door. Did not my mistress or Anna remember that? 'But…' I stopped, thinking it better than to verbalise my retort.

'Is there a problem?' Anna asked.

'No. I'm just wondering where I will find the bed linen.'

Anna's dark eyes flashed. 'Where all linen has been kept for the last two hundred years.'

I aired the room and made up the bed. It did not escape me it was the perfect size for two.

Later that afternoon, I delivered another tray to the library. This one was laden with a plate of Mistress Letizia's favourite cakes and a pot of tisane, concocted by Maria, who knew more than anyone about the effects of flowers and herbs.

Foxy, dizzy with delight at having been released from his garden banishment, streaked ahead and stopped short of the sofa.

Mistress Letizia lay recumbent, her eyes closed. Di Napoli perched at the other end bare-chested. With his sculpted pectorals and washboard abdominals exposed, he read to her from the book written by Salvatore Di Giacomo, another Neapolitan native.

To the rhythm of Di Napoli's voice, rising and falling, and water swirling around and over the smooth, half-exposed pebbles in the *Frigido*, Mistress Letizia's breasts rose and fell, accompanied by little gasps escaping her soft lips.

That he spoke in the Neapolitan dialect that Tuscans regarded foreign mattered not. From the rhythm and intonation, the meaning of the song's words was as clear as if he had been speaking our own pure Italian.

Quando la luna esce in Marechiaro,
anche il pesce fa l'amore
When the moon comes out in Marechiaro,
even the fish are making love

And then, if that was not enough, Di Napoli picked up the mandolin that had lain hidden at the bottom of a sea chest buried by rolls of ancient hand-drawn maps. He strummed and sang the lyrics.

Foxy sat with his head cocked, staring at the crooner.

Reluctant to disturb, and still holding the tray, I sat on the chaperone's chair. But the truth was I did not want to interrupt my dream wherein I was Caroline at the tower window overlooking the sea, serenaded by an admirer playing his mandolin from his small fishing boat.

Before the song came to an end, Foxy lay down and rested his head upon his outstretched paws. Only his furry eyebrows moved to the sweet notes of the mandolin.

Mistress Letizia's eyes snapped open. 'Gennaro, that was wonderful.' And with a quickness I had never seen, she swung her legs off the sofa, stood, clapped her hands and called out, '*Bravo.*'

Earlier that day, her blue dress had stretched to the point of popping. Now it hung loose and relaxed about her frame. I looked harder. She had lost even more weight since I had served lunch. *How is this possible?*

'Ah, Hortensia, you've brought afternoon tea. Good girl. I'm famished.'

I rose, walked to the table and placed the tray upon it. Di Napoli did not jump to my assistance this time. He remained at the end of the sofa with the mandolin held against his naked chest.

'Thank you, Hortensia,' he said.

I was confused. Things had changed since I had last entered the library. Mistress Letizia referred to our Neapolitan guest by his first name, and now he had the audacity to thank me for my service. *Who do you think you've become?*

And then, the veil of naivety that shrouded – or perhaps protected me – lifted. No sooner had I glimpsed the contents revealed of what I supposed was an augury, I wished I hadn't. So, promptly forgot.

———— ◆ ————

From the aromas flowing from kitchen, I knew Anna had surpassed herself.

Crostini, titbits of toasted bread, rubbed with a zig-zag flourish of garlic were topped with tiny cherry tomatoes, sliced in half and sprinkled with salt, causing them to sweat their juices.

Rubino had started the fire some hours before. When the coals glowed an even red, he cast a T-bone steak three fingers high upon it. When the thick layer of fat sizzled and spat, Rubino turned the steak over, added a sprinkle of rough salt and a generous quantity of olive oil to the upside. Four minutes later he removed the steak, and sliced and placed it on a hot serving platter. Accompanying the *bistecca alla fiorentina*, Anna had prepared yellow potatoes, roasted in the wood-burning oven, covered with sprigs of rosemary, salt, whole garlic cloves still in their skins and more olive oil.

She had poured a bottle of the Angeli Estate's finest vintage *Sangiovese* into a hand-blown glass decanter, allowing the wine to breathe. For dessert, she had blended cream cheese, sugar, hazelnut liqueur and roughly chopped chocolate pieces, and a handful of bruised raspberries. She poured this mixture into a terrine and left it to set in the marble cooler.

Everyone who passed through the kitchen during the preparation of the dessert had a taste of their favourite ingredient. Mine was the dark chocolate, Maria and Rubino the rich cream cheese and Anna the hazelnut-based liqueur.

Once the meal had been laid out on the table in the library, my mistress instructed everyone to leave. 'And Hortensia,' she said, 'take Foxy with you.'

As I picked up the dog, whose tail dipped at his mistress's words, I glimpsed another augury, but this one refused to be forgotten. Warnings or attempts to stop Mistress Letizia would serve no purpose. She was doomed, already helplessly trapped.

I fell on my bed and tucked Foxy beside me. A silver moon peaked through the window, bathing the room in light. To the memory of Di Napoli's singing voice, I fell asleep.

For the first time, I dreamed of my mother. She appeared as a butterfly and flitted here and there in the company of others.

'Come,' she whispered. 'Come with me, before it's too late.'

My eyelids opened to the sound of fading words. I shook my head; just a dream. It was morning. I dressed and tiptoed to my mistress's room. Her bed had not been slept in. I cracked open the door adjoining the guest bedroom. Its bed was as pristine as I had left it the day before.

'Foxy. Let's go to the kitchen.' But I knew I would take a peek through the library's keyhole to see what there was to see.

My head jerked back from the keyhole. *Am I seeing correctly? What on earth has happened?* I held my breath, eased the door open and entered the library.

Dawn's filtering light coloured the room pink.

Empty *Sangiovese* bottles, too many to count, lay abandoned between upended chairs and tables. Empty shelves stared forlorn, their books piled into towers on the floor. A chill ran up my spine. My former master, Giovanni Angeli, would have turned in his grave to see these books, his pride and joy, treated with such disrespect.

Oh no! The curtains! The maids would have a hard time repairing the heavy drapes torn from their rails, which dotted the floor like giant scoops of vanilla ice cream.

But the most sacrilegious of all: Mistress Letizia's portrait, painted when she was fourteen – wearing a novice's black habit and white whimple – rested on the floor facing the right way, festooned with branches of the pink rambling rose that grew over the metal-framed arbour in the garden. Her parents' portraits had been turned to face the wall. The waist-high, free-standing *capodimonte* porcelain vase, depicting painted mythical scenes and encrusted with clusters of flowers and birds lay in shards.

Torn from their stems, flower heads reduced to petals filled the room as if a snowstorm had blown through the room.

The gilded mirror, through whose reflection I had matched the lawyer's words during the reading of the will two weeks earlier, was nowhere to be seen. *Where is the suitcase? Where is my mistress and the salesman?*

Mistress Letizia's blue gown lay under the table, her fan on top of it. Ribbons, which she always wore threaded through her golden hair, dangled over the back of my chaperone chair, the only one remaining upright.

I closed the door and tiptoed further into the room. From behind a pile of books stacked on the floor, creating a low wall, I heard a sound. A whisper. Or was it a sigh? Then the lightest groan tinged with pain floated up, swirled over the wall of books, slithered towards me and closed around my ankles like a noose. My feet were stuck to the floor. My heart missed a beat.

The light groan was joined by another, deeper one. It too wrapped around my ankles. Licks of warmth rose from my feet, passed my ensnared ankles and caressed my calves. My knees would have buckled but for the fact my body had stiffened with alarm. The tepid warmth grew warmer as the sounds from behind the wall of books grew louder. Reaching down I gripped my burning inner thighs in an attempt to stave off the tide of searing heat racing towards the cleft between my legs. The air had disappeared. Unable to breathe I panicked. At the same moment, I noticed movement coming from the outer edge of the wall of books.

The creamy soles of my mistress's delicate feet pressed hard against Di Napoli's dark calves, moving in rhythm to the floor which had begun to rise and fall. The books teetered, and the library walls undulated as if I were standing on the deck of a boat on a stormy sea, moments from being swamped by the final wave that would drown us all.

Crossing my arms, I braced myself, anticipating the wave's force. My temples throbbed and a series of stinging shocks rippled through my body. The wall collapsed. My mistress and Di Napoli were revealed. Naked. They lay upon the mirror that doubled the image of their thrusting bodies.

Her transformation awed me, a vision of voluptuous beauty. Her long golden hair fanned out in a half-moon dotted with rose petals and her skin radiated with phosphorescence. But I was unable to tear my eyes away from Di Napoli's sculptured chest, his taut, indented buttocks.

With open mouths, and in unison, my mistress, with her eyes closed, and I, with my eyes wide open, gasped and panted.

Di Napoli's turned his head and focused on me. In his dark eyes I saw myself, a beguiling mermaid, one second rolling in frothy white waves, the next, a shy minnow, flicking my tail to whip away into the deepest crevice. And there, with only my hurt and shame for company, hide forever.

He raised himself from her and turned to rest on his side. I was transfixed by the sight of his glistening, rigid shaft protruding from, as I had correctly imagined, a dense patch of dark pubic hair. I raised my eyes to meet his. He mouthed, *Non amarmi*, love me not.

The spell broken, the noose released my ankles and in loose coils lay at my feet.

Snapping my panting mouth shut and feeling my face brighter than the rising sun, I fled from the library and crashed into Anna. She righted herself and glanced at the keyhole.

You've been peeking! What had she seen?

'Go. Straighten your clothes and then attend to your mistress. Afterward, come to the kitchen.' Though her raisin-dark eyes flashed me a warning, her apple-cheeks dimpled and a smile played around the edges of her mouth.

An ominous cloud of confusion followed me to my bedroom. I closed and locked my door and then did the same with the interconnecting door, which, the night before I had left closed but unlocked. *How foolish I am*. I had imagined I was Caroline of the song, *Marechiaro*, about to receive an admirer's midnight visit. I cringed with embarrassment. I could make no sense of what had happened to me standing in the library. Yet I trembled with desire for it to happen again.

No sooner had I set my dress and apron to rights did I hear sounds coming from the guest bedroom to my left. I held my breath, half

expecting the door handle to turn. Relief, swiftly followed by disappointment, flooded me when it did not.

From my mistress's room, to the right of mine, came the sound of
her voice. She was humming. I entered. She sat at her dressing table with
her long tresses partially covering her nakedness. It had not been my
imagination after all. Her former gargantuan body had slimmed down to
sleek curves.

Her blue eyes sparkled like sunlit jewels. 'Ah. Hortensia.' Her
voice, piercing and strident at times, had transformed into a soothing,
honeyed tone. 'A most wonderful thing has happened!'

'Mistress?'

She clapped her hands in delight. 'I am in *love*. With Gennaro Di
Napoli.'

The dog who was lying in the middle of the bed suddenly yelped.

My mistress twisted in her chair. 'Foxy! No need for jealousy. I will
always love you.'

Foxy hid beneath the bed.

'You silly dog. Come here.' She soon gave up trying to coax him
out. 'Hortensia, go and see if the maids have finished stitching my dress.'

I felt taut with the unfamiliar sight of my mistress lovelier than I
could ever have imagined. The memory of her pale body entwined with Di
Napoli's dark body, and his never-ending slicked member easing out from
between her legs, refused to leave my mind. My skin began to burn, and
before the breast of the red robin could leave its calling card upon my
cheeks, I turned on my heel and left.

Foxy scooted out from under the bed and attached himself to my
shadow.

———— ◆ ————

Anna set about preparing dishes I later learned promoted virility. She
sent Rubino with a basket in hand to the patch of land where wild
asparagus plants send up their spears. 'Pick as many as you can,' she said to
his retreating back and turned to me. 'Hortensia, don't return until this

basket is full.' She nudged me out of the kitchen and handed me a stained apron to wear over my white one.

My heart sank. The sun already burned ash-white and the path to the cherry trees was difficult and distant. While I loved eating cherries, I hated picking them. Once the birds who'd taken up residence in the trees perceived my intent, they would take turns dive-bombing me.

I made it without incident to the first tree, shimmied up the trunk, and wedged myself safely in a fork. To the cacophony of tweets and whistles, wing-whirrs and feather-flutters, bobbing heads and beady-eyed looks, I filled the basket.

On my way home, I first heard the steady hum of Pietro the Fisherman's Piaggio Ape's engine, and then a buzz like a bee – which is what *Ape* means – as he shifted gear and ascended the slope. Then I spied him in his small, light-blue, three-wheeled van bouncing along the potholed track.

'Hortensia,' he shouted as he slowed to a stop. 'Hop in, I'll give you a lift.'

For as long as I could remember, Pietro had delivered Anna's fish order on Fridays. He always had a kind word to say to me, and when I was younger brought me gifts of seashells. More than the lovely shells, it was the snaggle-tooth poking between his lips that left me gasping in wonder. As I grew older, I became aware of his bad breath and began to keep my distance. Whenever he sat repairing his nets, felines gave him a wide berth as did desperate women in search of a husband even though men, after the war, were in short supply. Nevertheless, today, I accepted his offer.

'So,' he said, as I squished next to him in the van's cab designed for one. 'The Angeli household has guests?'

At first, I thought the temperature in the cab was due to its size. But then it dawned on me that the heat came from Pietro's body. It was not the dangerous burning kind like Di Napoli's, ready to explode at any minute, but rather inviting, warm, and comforting. The van hit a pothole, causing the top layer of cherries to leap into the air before landing back into the basket. This forced us closer so not even a mouse could have squeezed through.

Pietro straightened the scooter-style handlebars. 'Whoa. Sorry about that.' He turned his head and gave me a quizzical look.

Remembering my oath, I furrowed my forehead. 'No guests.' It was not a lie, there being a difference between a guest and guests.

'Nonsense,' he said. 'With the amount of oysters I've got packed on ice, the Angeli household must be hosting an important dinner for more than several guests.'

Time to change to the subject dear to your heart. 'So, when will the dentist pull your last tooth?'

One hand flew to his throat to touch the gold horn suspended on a chain around his neck, which warded off the *malocchio*, the evil eye. Pietro's other hand scrabbled to align the handlebars then, let go for a second to make the sign of the Holy Cross. 'Please, I beg you, don't speak of it. It's the last tooth I have. Twice a day I pray to God that the tooth will outlast me.'

Just how old are you? Through a quick, furtive glance, I concluded he was nowhere near Rubino's and Maria's great ages. *Older than Di Napoli but a little younger than Anna, perhaps?* If God were kind, he'd have years left to fish. But, despite these racing thoughts, I concluded he belonged in the early stages of a most horrifying category – old.

The van's clatter had alerted Anna, for she stood waiting for us. She threw me a sharp look. I passed her and made the sign of holding a key to my lips and turning it to the locked position. Relieved, she turned her attention to Pietro.

He carried the dripping basket that contained the oysters packed in seaweed. Anna directed him to the marble sink. 'Place it there.'

He did as ordered, turned and surveyed the kitchen.

A bunch of wild garlic stalks topped with tiny white onion-shaped heads lay alongside asparagus spears piled high at one end of the broad-planed kitchen table. A new wheel of aged *Parmigiano-Reggiano* had been split – no mean feat given its tough rind – its glorious creamy-yellow nubbly interior exposed.

In anticipation of rolling the tiny rough grains smoothed out by a drizzle of translucent chestnut honey from the jar standing beside the wheel, my tongue slid against the roof of my mouth.

While I had been picking cherries, Anna had prepared the pasta. Hand-cut ribbons of *linguine* draped over cord lines stretching from one end of the kitchen to the other. I knew by the ribbons' pale hint of yellow, our Leghorn flock had been scratching through the fallow field, smothered in clover and dandelion. Clover and dandelion flowers turned the yolks to dark yellow. But once incorporated with the flour and salt, the colour faded, lightly darkening the dough.

In another pile, *datterini*, mini oval-shaped tomatoes from Sicily, still attached to their thin and brittle, pungent-smelling vines, lay clumped together.

Anna would finely dice the garlic, chop asparagus spears, halve the tomatoes and in a little hot olive oil toss these ingredients together until almost cooked through. After a splash of white wine, she'd mix the cooked *linguine* into the heady, fragrant sauce and serve it with generous quantities of grated *Parmigiano-Reggiano*.

My belly contracted, reminding me there were hours to go before dinner.

'Hortensia, don't remove your dirtied apron,' Anna said. 'You are to shuck the oysters.'

I stared at the heap of rough, whitish-grey shells. I'd never shucked or eaten an oyster before.

Pietro eyed the crates of chilled bottles, pursed his lips and whistled. 'Hey. You *must* have guests coming. What's so hush-hush that you won't share the news?' Though his eyes twinkled, his voice sounded serious. 'Are *you* getting married, Hortensia?'

'Don't be daft,' Anna said. 'And anyway, as you've been told before, she's still too young.'

Pietro stood with his feet planted solidly on the floor. 'Mistress Letizia. Is she getting married?'

Anna sighed, leaned towards him, lowered her voice and told an untruth so easily it was magical. 'It's a birthday surprise for Mistress

Letizia. But given her father's recent death, we are keeping the celebration quiet, just for her and us.'

'Oh.' Pietro matched his voice to hers. 'I knew something was up. Tell her I wish her *Buon compleanno.*'

But something told me Pietro was more relieved that no-one was getting married.

'Don't stand there. Make yourself useful. Show Hortensia how to shuck oysters. Hortensia, search through that drawer and find the shucking knives. They're short and stubby.'

After finding them, I tested the handle of one; it fit neatly into the palm of my hand.

Pietro busied himself unpacking the first layer of seaweed from the oysters. He took up the second shucking knife. 'Like this. Place the flat shell side on the cloth. Fold this flap of cloth over the top, curved shell. Keep your hand covered in case the knife slips. You don't want to cut yourself. Lodge the tip of the knife into the nose point. Right here, see?'

Despite his odorous smell, I leaned in closer and saw exactly where.

'Slide the tip of the blade in as far as it can go. Lever the knife and there...'

The oyster popped open with a sharp crack. It sounded like a bone snapping in two. I shuddered.

'Be gentle now. Run the knife along the top shell until it is separated from the bottom and pulls away. Then scoop the knife's curved tip under the meat. You will feel a little resistance. Saw through the muscle that connects the oyster to the shell so that the whole oyster is free and can slide around the bottom shell. Don't spill the liquid. Understand?'

'Yes.' I followed Pietro's methodical instructions and opened my first oyster.

'You're a natural.'

A candle's warmth glowed in my heart.

'Ever eaten one?'

I shook my head.

'Watch and copy.' He picked up the oyster he'd shucked. 'A drop of lemon and…' He tilted back his head, raised the shell and, eyes closed, tipped the oyster into his mouth. His lips smacked with pleasure. 'Go on, try.'

The shock of the cold silky texture sliding down my throat was followed by a burst of fresh, salty seawater. After chocolate, that oyster was the best thing I'd ever tasted.

Anna gripped Pietro by the elbow. 'Okay. That's enough.' She steered him towards the kitchen door.

But he was not going to be hustled past the crate of bottled *vermentino*, a hundred percent pure white bubbly wine that came from our Ligurian neighbours and was the perfect accompaniment to seafood dishes.

Anna slipped a bottle under his arm and escorted him out of her kitchen.

Pietro smacked his forehead with his hand. '*Dio mio!* I almost forgot. Your nephew has been seen in these parts. All women are locked up. So, Hortensia, be careful.' His voice bristled with concern. 'Don't let Gennaro Di Napoli come near you.'

Knife blades nicked their way up my spine. *Your warning's too late.*

Pietro headed down the rutted track and on towards the Tyrrhenian Sea, whose opalescence shimmered under the sun's dancing rays.

Anna returned to the kitchen, slapping her hands together as though trying to rid a nuisance from them. Then her dimples imploded and her mouth split into a lascivious grin. 'You loved the taste of the oyster, didn't you?'

I nodded.

'Well, I'm too old, and you're still too young to partake of this aphrodisiac men and gods worship above all else.'

I turned from Anna so she'd not see my red-hot cheeks caused by the infinite double image of naked, thrusting and heaving bodies that flooded my vision.

I raced down the stairs and into the kitchen. 'Anna, Mistress Letizia wants to see you now.'

Anna dusted her hands free of flour. 'What for?'

I shrugged. She straightened her apron as we made our way up the stairs. Given Anna's seniority, I held the door open and let her enter first.

Mistress Letizia sat facing the dressing-table mirror, brushing her long golden hair. 'Ah. There you are, Anna.' She waved the brush through the air like a conductor's baton. 'It's time to prepare for my wedding night.'

In the month Di Napoli had been with us, Mistress Letizia had not slept in her bed, nor he in his. The sofa in the library was adequate for two. Especially given my mistress was now half her former size.

Anna frowned. 'You mean the master bedchamber?'

'Exactly.'

That afternoon, after lunch, four housemaids, Anna and I assembled in the oversized room. The maids came prepared, carrying cloths, buckets, brooms and a carpet beater.

'First,' Anna said, 'we are going to flip the mattress.'

Shortly after the death of Giovanni Angeli, the family lawyer removed letters and bills from the writing desk and checked under the lumpy, kapok-filled mattress for hoarded paper money. That did not stop the maids from scanning every inch of the bed frame as they heaved and turned the mattress.

I replaced the bedside books on the library shelves, while Anna boxed Giovanni Angeli's personal items including his collection of walking sticks. The maids ferried armloads of his clothes and stored them in the attic, alongside those of his dead wife, his parents and grandparents.

'Here.' Anna thrust a basket of freshly cut spiky twigs into my hands. 'Slip one or two between the layers of clothes. And tuck more into lapels and pockets.'

I frowned.

'It's to ward off silver moths who love to eat fabric.'

In a short while, the musty attic air smelled of sun-warmed rosemary.

The maids turned their attention to the master bedchamber's three windows with an unobstructed view of the cobalt sea. They eased the windows wide open and removed the gauze curtains for laundering. They cleaned the panes with soft cloths dipped in white wine vinegar, and then polished them with newspaper until blue sky rather than glass filled the frames.

Taking turns, the maids beat years' worth of dust from the dense-woven carpets draped over the balcony rails. They washed and dried the floor to reveal the inlaid herringbone wood pattern. On their hands and knees, they rubbed beeswax into the parquet until it gleamed.

'Now, the most difficult task of all.' Anna waggled a finger. 'Pay attention.'

Atop four wobbling ladders, maids pulled and tugged trying to remove the canopy stuck with decades of ingrained dirt to each post.

'Hold on to it!' Anna yelled at the first maid to free the canopy from her corner. 'Or the fabric will tear!'

When the last corner was prized free Anna raised her voice again. 'On the count of three, let your end go. One, two, three...'

The fabric dropped to the mattress, releasing a cloud of dust. In seconds, we all began to cough and sneeze. Rolling the fabric into a long sausage was, I imagined, like wrestling a slippery eel intent on escape. Finally contained, the four maids carried it down the staircase and into the laundry room where it was washed and rinsed until the water ran clear.

Bent under the wet weight, thyme shrubs released their fragrance into the canopy as it dried under the sun. It took two maids a whole day to smooth the creases using hot flat irons.

A day later, once again wobbling atop a ladder, each maid held on-to her corner, and, following Anna's instructions, tugged back and forth until the canopy stretched taut between the four pillars. Bow-tied ribbons secured the canopy's side drapes, which when released fell about the bed. I reined in my thoughts from imagining what would go on in that bed enveloped in total privacy.

'Hortensia,' Anna said, 'now is the fun part. Go into the garden and cut enough flowers to fill these vases.'

Once I had completed the floral arrangements, Anna called the maids into the kitchen. 'Pick up the vases. Don't drop them. Follow Hortensia.'

I directed the maids to place the vases filled with Mistress Letizia's favourite fragrant pink roses where I thought they looked best.

Anna sent up a bowl filled with apricots, nectarines and pears, along with a carafe of wine and two silver-rimmed goblets. These I placed on a long, narrow table pushed against a wall. A curlicued-framed mirror, as long as the table and double in height, hung suspended from the wall. The composition looked similar to a painting by Caravaggio, famous for his dramatic *chiaroscuro*, still-life works of flowers, fruit bowls and wine carafes.

Anna entered and surveyed the chamber. Her gaze lingered on the table and its light and dark reflection in the mirror. She clapped her hands for attention and pointed to the door, dismissing the maids. 'Hortensia, you stay.'

When the last maid left, Anna turned to me. 'Good work with the table.'

I felt my face open into a smile.

She rolled up her sleeves. 'Now we are ready for the task only you and I will do.'

From the bottom of the cedar-lined chest at the foot of the cano-pied bed, we removed densely embroidered ivory-coloured sheets and pillowcases. In tiny stitches, generations of previous bridal couples' names and wedding dates appeared in the centre of the vine-embellished heart on the top sheet.

I looked closely and traced my fingers over a spot of uneven fabric. 'What happened here?'

Anna did not reply. I glanced up.

She stared at me with an unwavering gaze. 'Hortensia, can you keep a secret?'

A wave of tingles washed over me. My mouth turned dry. I nodded.

'You are not to tell anyone I told you this. Promise?'

'I promise.' My voice rasped.

Anna paused again. 'I,' her voice was low, 'unpicked a bride's name.'

I copied her lowered voice. 'Which bride?'

Anna changed her focus and squinted at the eye of the needle she held in one hand. 'Giovanni Angeli's first bride.'

'Why?'

Glints of stabbing, silver-bladed knives appeared in her raisin-dark pupils. 'The bride, a young maid from this villa, ran away on the very morning of her wedding.' Anna aimed the almost invisible thread poking from between her thumb and index finger at the needle's eye.

The question slipped from my mouth. 'Did she have a lover?'

Anna's forehead crinkled. 'How do you know about her lover?'

'Just guessing. Did they marry?'

As she pulled the thread through the needle she sighed, and the glint of those stabbing, silver-bladed knives faded. 'No. The rotten bastard. Though he promised, he had no intention of marrying. Ever. Yet, at the same time, he did not want her to marry. Thus, he destroyed her chance to marry Giovanni Angeli and enter a new station in life, which comes only once in a blue moon.'

'A blue moon?'

Anna slipped the needle into the fabric. 'Not really blue. Just an extra full moon in a month.'

'And the child?'

The crinkles in Anna's forehead deepened. 'Another lucky guess?'

'Yes. What happened?'

Anna began to stitch. 'When she fell pregnant, her lover–'

I interrupted and finished her sentence. 'Ah. Disappeared.'

A rush of vehemence escaped Anna's mouth. 'Yes.'

I wanted to ask who the bride was, but the words froze in my mouth. Instead, I asked, 'What happened to her?'

'Don't know.' Anna sighed. 'No one ever saw her again.'

A painful niggle sprung up in my heart for the runaway maid. 'And Giovanni Angeli?'

'His broken heart mended when he met and married Mistress Letizia's mother. But when she died in childbirth, it cracked.'

I had picked up enough snippets of maids' conversations to understand that Giovanni Angeli suffered greatly after the death of his wife.

'And then,' Anna continued, 'it broke in two again be–'

Clarity, as clear as a glass of fresh water, descended upon me. 'Because, the child born – Mistress Letizia – was a girl and not a boy.'

'Yes. That is correct. But, regarding this marriage today, I'm willing to bet my life that the bride and groom will turn up.' Anna said this with the same certainty as the sun takes its place in the sky each day. She tugged the needle, pulling the silk thread through the linen sheet for the last time. She snipped the thread and returned the scissors and needle to the sewing box. 'There.' She showed me her needlework. 'What do you think?'

The names Gennaro Di Napoli and Letizia Angeli were beautifully stitched in gold thread.

'Lovely.'

Anna's cheeks dimpled. 'Hortensia, it's time to make up the bed.'

Standing opposite each other, we lowered the weighty and elaborate top sheet. Lavishly ruffled with *Valenciennes* lace, the sheet skimmed the floor. After a final smoothing, and placing the plumped pillows side by side, we left, closing the door behind us.

Anna preceded me down the stairs. Halfway down, she stopped and turned to me. 'Remember your promise.'

I nodded and as we descended, these questions began to spin around in my head: Who was the runaway bride? To whom and where did she run? What happened to the child?

———————— ◆ ————————

The next day, the myopic lawyer, *avvocato* Fini, returned. Mistress Letizia received him in the rose-covered arbour. She appeared much like Botticelli's Venus – her hair was loose, her body barely concealed by a diaphanous shift.

When his weak eyesight made her out, his Adam's apple bobbed and jammed against his starched collar. He released his shirt's top button and flapped his hat to fan his face.

'Mistress Letizia, you have called me here because…?'

'I am to marry.'

'This is good news!' You see, I told you God had his eye on you. Who is the lucky groom?'

'Gennaro Di Napoli.'

The lawyer flapped his hat harder. 'Gennaro Di Napoli? *The* Gennaro Di Napoli?'

'Yes.'

'From Naples?'

'The very same.'

'This is terrible news. Mistress Letizia, do you not know–'

'I know everything about him.'

'But–'

'I will not be swayed. My father instructed me to marry. He did not specify to whom. And besides,' Mistress Letizia said with a beatific smile, 'I am in *love*.'

'When is the wedding to take place?'

'Now.'

He gasped. 'The wedding banns?'

'Announced three days ago.'

The lawyer dropped his hat and broke into a coughing fit.

'Rubino,' Mistress Letizia called, 'fetch Don Antonio and tell Anna to bring water. Hortensia, find Gennaro and Foxy and bring them here.'

My heart bobbed to the surface like the float on a cast fishing line. I had a legitimate reason to go in search of him. I was sure to find him alone.

Rubino and I set off in opposite directions. Passing Maria in the kitchen, I asked, 'Do you know where Di Napoli is?'

'No.'

'Foxy?'

'Under the table.'

'Take him with you and join Mistress Letizia in the arbour, please.'

Maria's knees protested as she bent down. With her forehead almost touching the floor, she reached out one arm to grab Foxy.

With a spring in my step, I made my way upstairs to the sounds of Maria's voice first coaxing and then damning the dog for its stubbornness.

Di Napoli was not in the library, the room subjected to nightly bacchanalian mayhem. It had become the playground after the garden, orchard and vineyards got too cold for Mistress Letizia's and Di Napoli's unshod feet.

I turned down the corridor and headed towards the bridal chamber. It was empty, but that did not stop my imagination visualising two pulsing bodies beneath the canopy.

Forcing myself from the chamber, I stopped outside the guest room that had become Di Napoli's room. Though I heard no sound, I tapped lightly and entered. It too was empty, but the interconnecting door to my room stood ajar. My heart thudded in time to each tiptoed step I took across the room. I peeked through the crack.

Bea, Villa Angeli's youngest household maid, sat on the window ledge. A bucket of soapy water stood on the floor. Her arms were raised, bracing her body centre to the window frame. In the background, the pearlescent sea shimmered. Her head tipped back, her eyes closed, and her mouth open. The buttons on her bodice were undone down to her navel, exposing her small breasts Di Napoli was biting. Despite it looking painful, my nipples tingled.

The floor beneath my feet began to shift in time to the thrust of Di Napoli's dark, taut buttocks. To support myself, before the wave I'd experienced before caused me to lose my balance, I gripped the door frame with one hand. Eager, and with intent, I sought to touch the cleft between my legs through the fabric of my dress with my free hand. My knees buckled, I lost my grip and fell against the door, causing it to swing open. Di Napoli stopped mid-thrust and turned. I slid to the floor. Freed, his slicked manhood bounced and waved, as a wizard draws his magic wand through the air.

Coitus interrupted, Bea's eyes flew open. Even though it was only me, she hurriedly shielded her bosom and lowered her skirts. Di Napoli hoisted his wedding trousers. Just as I had, Bea lost her balance. Only, she tipped backwards – out of the window.

'Bea!' Though I lay sprawled upon the floor, my arms reached for her, but my hands clutched air. Her scream was short and swift, followed by a dull thump as she landed in the garden two floors below.

Di Napoli's eyes clouded with what I believed, was regret. '*Merda!*' His deep voice vibrated around the room. He spun back round to the window, leaned over the sill and looked down.

The former wave of pure, infinite pleasure reversed in an instant and engulfed me in unspeakable horror.

Di Napoli turned to face me, grabbed my wrist and hauled me up from the floor. 'Sweet Hortensia, now do you understand my warning? No good comes to anyone who loves me.' His voice carried the same mournful note of a lone wolf howling at the moon. He held me close. The words he'd uttered turned into ice daggers slicing through to my core. My eternal hopeful and romantic heart overrode all common sense. Not only did Di Napoli and I stand at the same height, but we fit like two parts of a puzzle. *We belong together.*

He stepped under the arch of the connecting doors separating his guest bedroom from mine. 'Listen.' He lowered his baritone voice. 'Close and lock your door from the inside. I'll lock mine. I was never here. Do you understand?' Then he kissed me hard.

What I lacked in experience, I made up for with fervour. Thus he discovered this was my first kiss as clearly as if I had proclaimed it aloud.

He released me and murmured, 'Sweet, sweet Hortensia.' For the second time, his eyes clouded with regret as he stepped past me. 'Lock it.' He shut the door in my face.

The sound of anxious voices filtered up through the open window, now showcasing only the sea. Shaking and fumbling, I managed to do as ordered.

'Oh dear God! Bea.' Pressing a closed fist into my mouth to stifle my screams, I raced down the corridor, past the library, down the stairs, through the kitchen, out the door and into the garden. With each footfall, Di Napoli's unfathomable hold over me tightened. My hopeful heart's voice was overridden by a masculine voice, one I could not pinpoint. It asked, *How to tell a lie and get away with it?* The voice answered its own question, *Always keep the lie as close to the truth as possible.*

Bea lay sprawled upon the earth like a rag doll. My mistress, the lawyer and Don Antonio stood on one side of her. Rubino, Anna and Maria stood on the other.

Curiosity overcoming wariness, Foxy inched towards the body.

The three people I trusted and owed my life to focused on me. 'What happened?' they chorused.

'Is she…is she…?' I could not utter the last word.

'Yes,' Don Antonio said. 'Broken neck.'

The walls of my world collapsed, burying me alive.

As Maria bent down and re-buttoned Bea's bodice, she lowered her voice and repeated, 'Hortensia, what happened?'

I fought my way out of forever-limbo. 'She was sitting on the sill, cleaning the pane, and when I entered she got a fright and fell. I am so sorry. If only I hadn't…'

The lie slipped smoothly from my lips. Thus Di Napoli and I coalesced, becoming just as I believed us to be, but for the wrong reasons: one and the same.

'Where is Gennaro?' Mistress Letizia asked.

I shrugged and began to sob. Anna wrapped her plump arms around me and held me tight.

'Rubino, can you hook up your cart and provide a makeshift coffin?' Don Antonio asked. 'I need to get Bea to the church and inform her family as soon as possible.'

'What about my wedding?'

Heads, including mine, jerked against my mistress's lack of respect for the dead.

Don Antonio's lips quivered. 'Where is the groom?'

Anna's apple face paled. The wager she'd blithely offered – her life in exchange for neither groom nor bride turning up – hung in the balance. Then we all heard Di Napoli's arrival before we saw him. Anna's apple face flushed.

'*Eccomi qui, pronto.* Here I am, ready.' Shirtless, he strutted around the corner displaying his sculpted chest, stomach and arms, no different to how the yard cockerel shows off his fine plumage. He halted. '*O Dio mio.* What's going on?' His voice deepened. He moved to Mistress Letizia's side and took her hand.

'An accident.' The lawyer's eyes had grown round and large, taking on the shape of his glasses.

Di Napoli looked deeply into Mistress Letizia's eyes. 'Are you all right?'

She nodded abruptly.

'We'll postpone the wedding, of course,' Di Napoli said.

'We'll do no such thing. Rubino, fetch the coffin and return.'

Rubino and Don Antonio left, walking as though they each bore the weight of a crucifixion cross.

'No!' Mistress Letizia shrieked. 'Bad dog.'

Holding their hands over their ears, everyone turned to look at Foxy. He had his nose buried in the region of Bea's crotch and was sniffing through the fabric of her dress. Used to only sweet coos when being addressed, he jumped back.

'Come here!' Mistress Letizia yelled.

Foxy headed towards her, stopped, lifted his leg and urinated against Di Napoli's black, pirate-styled trousers.

I stopped crying.

The lawyer looked down. His face screwed up in surprise when he realised neither Mistress Letizia nor Di Napoli were wearing shoes.

'Letizia, my love, are you sure you want to marry me?' Di Napoli's voice took on a sorrowful tone. 'Once again, your dog has expressed his disapproval of me.'

Mistress Letizia's chin jutted out. 'Don't be silly.'

The lawyer adjusted his glasses. 'The dog may have a point.'

'Careful.' Mistress Letizia's cornflower-blue eyes narrowed. 'Or there may be two coffins heading for burial.'

The lawyer tore his shocked gaze from the naked feet and peered up at Mistress Letizia. His weak eyesight may have missed her daggers-can-kill look, but his ears clearly heard her hissed words.

Rubino and Don Antonio returned with a burial box. They lifted and placed Bea into it. But for her lolling head, she looked as though she were taking a nap.

'Here. Take this.' Mistress Letizia pulled a pink rose from her wedding bouquet and handed it to Don Antonio.

He sandwiched the stem between Bea's hands, placed one over the other. Rubino fastened the lid.

'Everyone to the arbour,' Mistress Letizia ordered.

'The arb-?' Don Antonio's mouth snapped shut. Unlike the lawyer, he had no difficulty seeing the look on Mistress Letizia's face.

The ceremony was short and the signing of the marriage contract shorter. The lawyer witnessed the signatures and, for good measure, told Maria, to add hers.

'I must attend to a sack-load of work,' the lawyer announced. He placed his unfinished glass of *Prosecco* on the arbour's table and left.

Rubino and Don Antonio drove the cart to the church. Anna returned to the kitchen to put the finishing touches to the celebratory meal she had been preparing for days. At a distance, Maria and I followed the wedded couple to the villa's large and imposing front door.

Instead of sweeping Mistress Letizia into his arms to carry her over the threshold, Di Napoli fell on all fours. She straddled his back and rode him as he crawled through the front door, into the entrance hall and up the staircase.

Maria placed the tip of her bony finger to my chin and pressed my gaping mouth closed. 'Come, Hortensia, let's take a walk in the orchard.' She showed not a jot of surprise at what we had just witnessed.

I whistled. Foxy appeared with a ball in his mouth. We walked through the garden, down the slope and entered the orchard that the first generation of Angeli's had cultivated one terraced level below the villa. In this way, the trees were protected from the too cold descending night air, and, facing the sea, received the maximum amount of sun all year round.

Planted among standard fruit trees were some notable exceptions: Zagara orange trees, whose blossom scent was the strongest but sweetest of all, a date palm, an avocado, vanilla bean and passion fruit climbers. These exotics had been brought home and planted by an Angeli son three generations ago, for whom the wine-producing Tuscan estate had been an anathema to his roving soul.

I threw the ball for Foxy, who repeatedly fetched and dropped it at my feet. I took comfort in this ordinary practice given the extraordinary events in the last few hours. 'Game over.'

This Foxy understood and, having had an exhausting play session, lay panting happily at my feet.

Maria sat, and I stretched out on the grass bursting with creeping buttercup and white clover. Close by stood the chasteberry tree. Its aromatic, delicate-textured leaves, soft and silky, looked just like the wings of the butterflies it attracted. The only other tree of its kind grew close to the *canonica*, the house attached to the church in the valley where Don Antonio lived. Like sunflowers, our heads tilted, tracking the summer sun's progress across the cloudless sky.

Maria took her time before questioning me, as I knew she would. But I was prepared.

'Did you know Di Napoli was in your bedroom when you went looking for him?'

'Of course not. I only entered my bedroom to collect the bag of confetti to throw over my mistress for good luck.' I had stamped out tiny circles from white paper using the two-hole paper punch I'd rescued from a clean-up session in the library. It had taken many hours to amass several handfuls. 'Now it is too late to use.' Overcome by that morning's events, I began to sob; for the recurring memory of Di Napoli's neat buttocks indenting with each thrust and Bea, tilting backwards out of the window, and for the futility of trying to make sense of the terrifying and glorious feelings that spiked and danced between my legs each time I saw or thought about Di Napoli.

Maria drew me into her bony arms and cradled me like she had done upon finding me abandoned. I sobbed harder.

The sun's arc increased, warming everything and causing the orchard's trees and plants to release their heavenly scents.

My sobs subsided to hiccups. Drifting off to sleep, I heard Maria ask God the same question I recalled at my birth when she turned from being midwife to augur.

'For what purpose have you made her such an innocent?'

Try as hard as I might, I could not remember His answer then, nor did I hear His response now.

The thought struck me. Perhaps he'd chosen not to. *Why?*

From the moment Letizia Angeli said, 'I do', Gennaro Di Napoli became the head of the Angeli Estate until they produced a child.

On my fingers I counted out the number of months left in which to fulfil the requirements of Master Giovanni Angeli's will. If everything went as planned, they'd make the deadline. But would the child be a son? For that, they would need a whole lot more than just God's blessing.

The following morning, in the early but still dark hours, Anna entered my bedroom. 'Hortensia. Are you awake?'

I rubbed the sleep from my eyes. 'Now I am.'

'Get dressed. Go and wake Rubino. He's to fetch Dr Baldi.'

'Mistress Letizia? Is she unwell?'

'Yes. And so is my nephew.'

My heart thumped. I struggled into my blue patchwork dress with a detachable lace collar cut to the curve of my neck that ended in two rounded corners. 'What's the matter with her?'

'You know. Womanly troubles.'

I understood, having experienced my first menses three months earlier.

'Don't bother with the apron. But put on a cloak. It's cool outside.'

'And him?' I asked.

'Hotter than a midsummer's day. Be quick. Help Rubino set off and come back here. Oh, and Hortensia, *only* Rubino is to go. Tell him to stop on the way back and inform Maria.'

I nodded, immediately envisioning the shepherd's hut in which I'd been raised. Since I'd left, Maria's beloved pygmy goats had taken to sleeping in her bed. Whenever asked, she would say, 'They keep my old bones warm.'

Rubino took a while to wake and even longer to pull on his boots and get onto the donkey a yard boy had saddled.

After seeing him set off, I returned to the master bedchamber. Dread had grown heavier with each footstep.

Di Napoli lay shaking and sweating under a pile of blankets on his side of the bed. Anna held a wet cloth infused with white wine vinegar to his forehead.

I bit my lip. His once swarthy skin was now alabaster pale. It had to be something he had eaten. But then, Anna, Rubino, Maria and I had eaten every last crumb of the leftover wedding celebratory meal. None of us had fallen ill.

'See to your mistress.' Anna jerked her head in the direction of the bathroom from whence came the sounds of retching.

———— ◆ ————

After Dr Baldi had been with both patients for some time, he clumped down the stairs and entered the kitchen. 'Good news, good news and bad news,' he said, ticking off three fingers. 'The first good news is that Maria will have the pleasure of delivering Mistress Letizia's child. Besides early pregnancy nausea, she is well. Light toast for her for the rest of today. The second good news is Di Napoli's fever has broken. The bad news is I don't know what caused it. A blood infection, perhaps? But he is present-ing the same symptoms as I have seen in men of the cloth when they've taken too much chasteberry.' Dr Baldi cleared his throat. 'Though I hasten to add, he is clearly not a priest.'

Chasteberry?

The bangles released three slow, muffled beats.

The sun had risen, and its light glinted off the copper pots and pans hanging on the walls, highlighting Maria's and Rubino's solemn faces as they gazed at Dr Baldi.

'Make him drink copious quantities of fresh lemon juice diluted in a little water. It will fight the infection. I'll be back this afternoon.'

To my surprise, neither Maria nor Rubino said anything after the doctor left. My bones told me none of what the doctor had said was news, especially to Maria. She always knew far more than the doctor and of events yet to happen. But the official news that Mistress Letizia was pregnant was a relief. Now all the valley workers' energies could be directed at lighting candles and praying for a boy.

The day passed calmly enough with either Anna or I traipsing up and down the stairs, taking the two patients light meals, all of which Di Napoli rejected. Recovered from her bout of nausea, Mistress Letizia ate with gusto. Much like she'd eaten before Di Napoli's arrival.

———— ◆ ————

'Either Mistress Letizia is getting fat again or her baby is growing very fast,' I blurted out after dinner one evening several weeks later.

'That happens to some women during their pregnancy,' Maria said.

Anna held up two fingers. 'Some eat for two.'

'And some,' Rubino said, 'no matter how much they eat, don't put on any weight.'

I went to bed with Foxy tucked beside me. From the day of Bea's fall to her death, and the wedding, he refused to be in the same space as Di Napoli. As he and Mistress Letizia remained in each other's company, dog and mistress hardly saw each other. Of this, neither appeared too fussed.

Mistress Letizia spent her days supporting her ever-growing stomach. She lay in bed or on the sofa in the library taking the occasional stroll with Di Napoli in the garden or orchard. Meanwhile, Foxy became my second shadow.

I worried about Di Napoli. He was losing weight as fast as Mistress Letizia was putting it on. His former swarthy skin had turned yellow.

Sometimes, when he was free from fever, I caught him watching me, his sunken eyes clouded with remorse and regret. Perversely, my maid's heart fluttered with joy.

From the master bedchamber's nightly silence, it was clear the bride and groom had lost interest in coupling. It may have been because she was pregnant, or because Di Napoli still broke out into a fever every other day, leaving him drained.

I fell asleep accompanied by these swirling thoughts, but dreams of butterflies, wizards and magic wands replaced them.

——————— ◆ ———————

Over the next few months, the library returned to its former state. Mistress Letizia's parents portraits were turned to face the right way and rehung. After much haggling, but still at great expense, Di Napoli had a new *capodimonte* vase shipped from the ceramic factory close to his hometown.

The maids rehung the curtains while I replaced the books in alphabetical order on the shelves. The mandolin, which Di Napoli had strummed while singing songs and reading poems to Mistress Letizia, was replaced at the bottom of the sea chest, buried under rolls of ancient hand-drawn maps. And the gilded mirror was bolted to its former position on the wall. While the library looked as before, it gave off the sense of violation and thus tainted. And that was just how I felt.

——————— ◆ ———————

About to enter the kitchen one morning, I spied Anna and Maria talking quietly, their heads close together. I sidled behind the door, held my breath and listened.

'How much more can he stand?' Anna asked.

'Not much. I'll start reducing the chasteberry dosage tonight. The child is due any day now. Please God, the potions worked, and it is a boy, then Di Napoli can go home and never return.'

My hand flew to cover my mouth. *Chasteberry? Potions? Never return?* I stepped through the door and entered. The women separated.

'Ah, Hortensia. We were just speaking about you. Come here.'

The first lie. Dutifully, I stepped closer.

'Do you remember our oath less than a year ago?'

I nodded.

'Now, more than ever, you must keep it. Changes are going to happen in this household. Changes that are going to affect us all.'

Maria and Anna exchanged glances.

'What changes?'

'Well, Mistress Letizia is soon to give birth,' Anna said. 'Don't you think that's a big change?'

I nodded.

'Di Napoli has made himself ill, pining so much for his own home.' Maria said. 'As soon as the baby is born, he'll go home to celebrate the birth of the child.'

'Will he return?'

The women's gazes fastened on my face.

'Why wouldn't he?' Anna asked.

The second lie. A thought struck me like a clap of thunder out of the blue. *What other lies have I been told?* Accompanying my shaken belief, the wood shutters rattled on their hinges.

Maria sniffed the air that had turned hot and dry. 'Ah. The *scirocco* is about to pay us a call.'

Anna's ruddy face paled. 'Hortensia, go to the second floor. Close every window and fasten every shutter. Be sure to turn the locks. 'I'll see to the ground and first floors.'

'And I'll remind Rubino to put the chickens in the coop and stall the donkeys,' Maria said. 'Then I'm going home to gather my goats and wait out the storm. Who knows how long this one will last.'

Just then a forceful wind blew, setting the villa's shutters and windows to banging.

'Tell Rubino to lock down the well's cover,' Anna said to Maria's departing back.

I doubted Maria heard Anna with the ensuing noise. I turned on my heel and rushed up the stairs. Apprehension knotted my belly.

Anytime a wind blew harder than usual, valley workers downed their tools and headed home. I got to hear this story one evening when we were at the end of our meal nibbling bits of cheese and grapes.

———————— ◆ ————————

'Maria, Anna,' Rubino suddenly said, 'do you remember the last great *scirocco?*'

'How could we forget?' they chorused. They downed the last of their wine and thumped the empty glasses on the table, challenging the memory to escape.

Rubino turned to me. 'It had been the perfect autumn morning, calm and clear, on which to start the *vendemmia*, grape harvest.'

Anna frowned. 'Isn't she too young to hear this story?'

'No,' Rubino said. 'It's better she knows than get caught by surprise one day.'

The bangles sounded their agreement by tinkling.

I wanted to inch my chair towards Anna. It was from her I would seek comfort if the story got rough. Then, I thought better of it, and with my insides frozen, sat still.

Rubino continued. 'Every able-bodied man, woman and child from the entire valley stood along the rows that stretched down the slopes to the valley floor.'

Anna piped in. 'It promised to be the best harvest for years. Vines groaned under the weight of plump, purple grapes.'

'I remember a sudden flurry of breezes causing the vine leaves to shimmy,' Maria said. 'Do you remember how the shadows elongated? How the sun turned to a pale orb of hazy light?'

'Yes, and how the increasing wind dislodged our headscarves and caps,' Anna said. 'Then, with the next, stronger, red grit-filled gusts, they lifted and like flying coffee saucers spun off into the air.'

I unfroze enough to pour more wine.

'Thank you, Hortensia,' Rubino said. 'And the donkeys. Oh God. Weren't they something!'

The three clinked their glasses, drank another mouthful of wine and fell into the silence of remembering.

I had seen the donkeys harnessed to the carts that stood between the vine rows, which had been planted wide enough for the carts to pass through. The donkeys pulled their carts along in time with the valley workers who emptied their baskets full of gathered grapes into the cart. When the cart was full, the donkeys, of their own volition, trundled into the barn which housed the stone presses. Here the next process of turning grapes into wine would commence.

Their memories were taking too long. I squeezed Rubino's hand. 'The donkeys?'

'Donkeys,' Rubino said. 'I swear on all that's holy they are more intelligent than we give them credit. Aware that those were no ordinary breezes, they stamped their feet. When our headwear went flying off into the air, they began to walk and then run, pulling the carts towards their stables. Without a single bunch of grapes loaded, the carts were empty and light, and the donkeys flew. I lie not. Their feet did not touch the earth.'

Rubino saw my furrowed brow. 'So, they arrived at the stable entrance at the same time, smashed the carts trying to get through and damaged the stable doors.'

'What did you do?'

'Workers' safety always comes first. Remember that, Hortensia.'

'But then?'

Rubino cupped his hands and pretended to shout. 'Take your baskets. Go home.' He lowered his hands. 'When I was younger, I could shout really well. But my voice was lost in the strengthening wind, and besides, I was forced to hold my hand over my mouth for fear of swallowing grit.'

'Yes. But everyone understood and dispersed,' Maria said. 'A few made it back home without injury. But most suffered cuts and bruises from flying debris.'

I used my encouraging voice. 'And?'

'We barricaded our windows and doors,' Anna said. 'The wind grew stronger, and we could hear unsecured terracotta flowerpots, furniture, and tools caught up by the *scirocco* ricocheting off roofs, walls and trees. Oh, the banging and the crashing.' At the memory of it, Anna held her hands over her ears.

'Mmm. But that wasn't the worst,' Maria said. 'Young or old, everyone endured broken sleep for the four days and nights the *scirocco* blew. Its relentless energy made us all fidgety, anxious and disoriented.'

Rubino swallowed another mouthful of wine. 'But do you remember how the wind filled wells with red sand carried from its origin? In the fields, huddled animals suffocated, their nostrils and windpipes clogged.'

One hand flew to cover my mouth.

'Birds and waterfowl tried to escape, but, enveloped by the abrasive and stinging cloud, died mid-air. Their wind-plucked feathers mingled with the aerial grit and swirled upward.'

I spoke from behind my cupped hand. 'Did you see all this?'

'Sadly, yes, while I was freeing the donkeys from the damaged carts. They were terrified and even when freed and re-secured in their stalls, they kicked the walls, bucked and reared, and brayed nonstop.'

'But the donkeys,' I said, 'were safe, weren't they?'

'Not exactly. I had to shoot two who broke their legs trying to kick their way out of their stalls.'

In response to clapping both hands over my mouth, Rubino steered the conversation away from life and death. 'Anything made of wood or metal was left sandpapered or pit-marked, reducing paint to a mere hint of its original colour.'

I'd heard that the wind madness, anemomania, struck several valley dwellers. To block the wind's shrill they talked. And talked and talked.

A wife, no longer able to bear her husband's voice fluctuating to the wind, beat him to death. Given the act was committed during the time the *scirocco* had been blowing, she received a pardon. Every time the wind blew, her second husband locked her up and released her only once the wind had died.

Another member of our community hanged himself from the rafters. He had bound his head with cloth to hold in place the cotton wool he'd stuffed into his ears.

Friends and loved ones confined to their small houses, quarrelled. Memories of broken promises, forgotten disappointments and old disputes resurfaced.

When homes' internal water supplies diminished, with no chance of replenishment from the external wells, love turned into hate. What criteria determined who was more entitled to a mouthful of water than another?

That time, the *scirocco* faded before midnight on the fourth night. Blessed silence rang loudly, and exhausted people abandoned speech. The valley's population fell asleep wherever they were and regardless of what they were doing.

'No. I think the worst of it was the following day,' Anna said. 'Heavy dew had settled upon the thick layer of dust. When the sun rose, it baked the wet dust, entombing everything. People were obliged to break their way out of their homes by cracking the hardened crust first.'

'Oh yes. I forgot that,' Maria said. 'Then possibly in an attempt at reparation for the havoc wrought, the heavens opened and poured rain for twenty-four hours. Blood-coloured mud slid down the slopes, dislodging vines, shrubs, trees, animal shelters and water troughs. The mass flooded the valley floor, flowed down to the sea and for a long while, turned the blue Tyrrhenian red.'

Rubino covered his face with his hands. 'Oh, the losses we suffered.' He peered through his spread fingers. 'It affected all those who depended upon the Angeli harvest for their livelihood.'

'But, wits soon recovered,' Maria said. 'Valley workers cleared the water wells, mended roofs and walls, replaced livestock and repaired tools.'

Rubino expelled a deep breath. 'We propagated the Angeli's *Sangiovese* vines and two seasons later planted the new cuttings. God. How hard we worked to restore the vineyard.' He wiped his brow at the memory of his labour. 'Fortunately, it survived. In contrast to the devastation to the vineyards, the Trianni's olive grove benefitted from the sand-dumping wind.'

'Nature is amazing,' Maria said. 'The *scirocco's* force naturally pared trees down to trunks and their four primary branches. Relieved of its excess load, each tree, despite being in its fourth century, underwent a growth spurt.'

'What,' I said, 'does that mean?'

'It means,' Anna said, 'that in the following years, while the Angeli vineyards still struggled in the aftermath of the *scirocco*, the Trianni olive grove thrived, yielded wonderful harvests. But best of all, the valley workers had work.'

At the mention of the Trianni Estate which was forbidden to me, I was all ears. 'Because the wind pared down the trees, it produced a good harvest?'

The trio stared at me with interest.

'Yes.' Rubino said. 'Remember this for the future, Hortensia: olive trees produce great quality if they are cut back after each harvest. And, the red Sahara sand harboured chemicals, which, once absorbed, improved the quality of the oil.'

'But then why isn't the Trianni Estate producing any more?'

The bangles rattled.

Rubino held his gaze steady.

'That,' Maria said, 'is a story for another time.'

I had touched on a very sensitive subject. Exactly what, I could not fathom. Then I caught Anna's guilty flush. *Does this have to do with our secret about the runaway bride?*

To the sound of the bangles' diminishing rattles, I made a decision. I'd ask Anna to tell me more about the runaway bride.

———————— ◆ ————————

By the time I returned to the kitchen, the villa, now completely shuttered, was dark and stifling. Anna had lit an oil lamp and placed in the centre of the table along with two trays.

'Hortensia,' she said, 'take the trays upstairs. And don't forget, the pink is Mistress Letizia's and the blue Di Napoli's. I've lit a few candles on the staircase to guide you.'

I nodded my understanding and thanks, but the candlelight was unnecessary. My feet had gone up and down those stairs so often they could find their own way.

A single candle lit the bedchamber. Despite having secured all windows and shutters, the wind sneaked through the tiniest cracks, causing the wick to flutter, and create grotesque, moving shadows on the walls.

Mistress Letizia lay like a whale marooned upon the beach. 'Is that my lunch?'

'Yes.'

'Good. I'm starving.'

Di Napoli groaned. 'The smell. I can't bear it. Take it away.'

'But, my love, I must eat, if only for our child. Why don't you go to the guest room and...'

Before she'd finished speaking, Di Napoli swung his legs over the edge of the bed. 'Hortensia. Help me.'

He leaned on me as I led him from the faltering light into my dark bedroom, and stopped at the interconnecting door, which had remained locked since Bea's death. Deftly, I turned the key and led him directly to the guest bed, upon which he clambered. We were in the pitch dark.

'Thank God, the air is cleaner here.' He'd lowered his deep voice.

The *scirocco's* speed increased, bumping the stone villa from all sides and rattling the shutters harder.

Di Napoli groped my hand and to my surprise, dragged me on top of him. Like a starveling, he held my head in his hands and covered my face with kisses. And then he slid his tongue into my mouth.

I melted into him like an ice cream dropped onto a cobblestone street on a midsummer's day. If I died at that moment, I would be the happiest I'd ever been.

He released my head. Even before he slid his fingers between the buttons of my bodice, my nipples sprang up as though called to arms. His hot touch made me shiver. Through the fabric of my skirt, the palm of his other hand followed the contours of my thighs and came to rest on the curve of my buttocks. As his fingers pressed through the fabric, digging into my flesh, he thrust his hips upward.

The *scirocco* whistled and whined harder around the villa, tightening its grip, squeezing what little air there was away. Sweat formed on my brow, and soon I felt as wet as if I'd just taken a bath. He stopped kissing me.

'O *Dio mio,*' his voice boomed in my ear.

Gripping me harder, he pulled me down in time to meet his upward thrust again and again. Not even the cloth of my skirts could cushion the painful jarring to my mons pubis. He did not have to say anything. Through his frantic actions, I understood there was something terribly amiss.

The *scirocco* pitched itself into full battle to which the shutters responded, protesting against being ripped from their hinges.

I did not need to feel Di Napoli's forehead. Under me, his body radiated enough heat to melt a thousand ice creams. In one ear, I heard Mistress Letizia's faint voice crying out, 'Help me.' In the other, Di Napoli yelped, 'Go. Get away from me. You are only adding to my malaise.'

After one more fruitless thrust, Di Napoli pushed me from him. I rolled onto the floor and landed with a bump.

With my honour still intact, and thankful for the darkness hiding my ashamed bafflement, I crawled on all fours to the interconnecting door. Using the door frame to haul myself up, the memory of Di Napoli pulling up his wedding trousers and Bea falling backwards out of the window flashed, lighting the room.

Enlightenment dawned. I experienced a rush of relief. I knew what Di Napoli's problem was. His cock could no longer bounce and wave like the wizard's magic wand. Indeed, all the while he had thrust his hips at mine, there had been no hint of turgidity – it had remained the size of a *pisellino*, a miserable little pea pod.

'Someone! Anyone! Help!' The screech of my mistress's voice shattered the vision.

Darkness returned. With arms stretched ahead feeling my way, I entered her bedchamber. The candle had blown out.

'Mistress?'

'Bring Maria. The baby. It's coming.'

Oh God no! Please, not now. Blind fear set my body to tremble like a leaf in the wind.

Mistress Letizia's frantic voice announcing her baby's imminent arrival rang in my ears. I turned, and with arms stretched ahead, made my way out of her bedchamber and down the corridor. The *scirocco*, which entered the villa through every crevice, had blown out the candles on the stairs.

Holding onto the balustrade and tapping the ball of one foot ensuring its firm placement on each step, I descended. Nineteen steps later, I reached the entrance hall's stone floor and continued towards the kitchen.

'Anna?' I bumped into the table. 'Where are you? Mistress Letizia says the baby is coming. She needs help. Anna!' My shriek rivalled the *scirocco's*.

I patted my hands over the table and found the oil lamp and the box of matches next to it. A torrent of sweet relief surged through me. I struck a match. It flared then died before I could remove the glass cover and light the mantel.

On the third attempt it caught, and I turned up the lamp's glow. Anna and Foxy were nowhere to be seen, but I noticed the kitchen door latch. It was up instead of down. Had she gone out? *Why?* Then I remembered. *The well.* She'd likely gone to ensure it had been covered and, curious as always, Foxy must have followed.

I was as alone as on the day my mother abandoned me. Loneliness clawed its way up from my belly and swallowed me. Then it registered. Mistress Letizia had stopped screaming. Or perhaps the *scirocco* had increased and blocked out all other noise. *Di Napoli.* There was nothing I could do for him. He'd have to sweat it out alone as long as the fever lasted. And, just when I needed – or to be precise, just when Mistress Letizia needed Maria – she had returned to her shepherd's hut.

Pressing my hands against the heavy kitchen door, I turned the handle. The door blasted inward, smashing against me with such force I lost my balance. Gritty, choking dust swirled into the kitchen, stinging my eyes. Throwing my body against it I cried out, 'Please God, help me.'

The *scirocco* stopped, inhaled and sucked back all the air it had blown into the kitchen. The door sprang from my hands and shut with a terrifying bang. Tears of relief cascaded down my face as I turned the key. *Dear God, make the lock hold.*

I rubbed my eyes, which made them burn all the more. Again, I could see nothing. The force of the wind had blown out the oil lamp. Panic from the centre of my belly raced forward, threatening to spill from my mouth.

The *scirocco* started up again and rattled the kitchen door, sounding like the monster that had haunted my childhood. 'Let me in, let me in, little girl,' it shrieked and drummed.

A memory flashed through my head. When I was a child and lost in our Tuscan hills, often chasing butterflies like my mother once had, I only had to shut my eyes and, in my head, call out to Maria. Her voice would lead me home.

Though I'd not communicated with her like this in years, I prayed she would hear my call. I squeezed my eyes shut, blocked out all sound and said, 'Maria, help me.'

Maria's voice entered my head. *Calm yourself. Breathe.*

I took in a mouthful of hot, gritty air and slow-released it.

Good girl. You've heard enough over the years to know birthing is a natural process. Listen carefully and do as I say.

'Where is Anna? Foxy?' I asked aloud.

Never mind them. Now's the time to focus on Mistress Letizia. She needs you. Walk back towards the table. Find the lamp and matches. Relight it, then…

I followed Maria's instructions and found myself standing outside the master bedchamber. In one hand I carried the lamp. In the other a bottle of water, a small sharp knife, a bobbin of silk thread, a needle and a pair of scissors.

Hortensia. There will be blood, and your mistress will be unresponsive.

I entered. Like Maria had warned, Mistress Letizia lay still, atop the blood-soaked sheets. The smell, combined with the stifling heat and the noise of the *scirocco*, was enough to make me turn and run. But to where?

If Maria heard me, she ignored it. Her voice filled my head again. *Focus. Place the lamp on the side table. Keep the knife, scissors, needle and thread close.*

I peered at Mistress Letizia's face. Her full lips quivered with the release of her last breath.

Tears welled and my throat constricted.

Hortensia! There is no time to lose. Take the scissors. Cut Mistress Letizia's skirts away.

Swallowing hard, I did as instructed and in a moment I stared at Mistress Letizia's taut, naked stomach that looked like our valley's church dome.

Take up the knife in one hand. Place your other hand above her navel. Plunge the knife tip to just beyond the blade's curve.

'What! No, I cannot!'

You must. Or Di Napoli's child will die too.

Perhaps it was the sound of his name that shocked me back into the task at hand. Gritting my teeth, I followed Maria's instructions.

Good. Now slice downward in a straight line. Go through her navel and stop when you hit the bone of her mons pubis.

The domed stomach split open like a ripe pomegranate, revealing its ruby seeds. I threw down the knife. Without being told, I reached in and pulled out the slithery form.

It should be a boy.

It is.

Quick. Turn him upside down and spank his bum. He must take his first breath and cry. Or die.

I spanked the newborn and after a second, he squalled.

In unison, Maria and I exhaled and I heard the hushed sigh of the bangles echo our relief.

Use the scissors. Snip the cord. Wrap the child in his mother's skirts. Place the child upon its mother's chest.

So I did.

Thread the needle. In the way Anna has taught you, sew up Mistress Letizia's stomach.

The sound of pulling thread through flesh was like no other sound I'd ever heard.

The child lay in a quiescent state. Unlike other newborns, his eyes, large deep pools like his father's, stared unblinkingly at me while I sewed.

Good. Now you need to put Mistress Letizia into another dress. Make sure her stomach is well covered. No one must see the stitches.

I moved the child and nestled him on a pillow.

Even though Mistress Letizia's was the first dead body I'd touched, there could never have been one heavier. I sweated out the last of my body's water. A crust of salt tightened my skin. Tugging and pulling, I managed to get an old and large dress over her head. Shoving her uncooperative arms through the armholes took longer. Finally, I was able to draw the dress down her torso, past her abdomen and thighs to reach her ankles. Her stitched stomach was well concealed. No sooner had I finished, Di Napoli staggered into the bedchamber like the risen dead.

The *scirocco* had increased its strength, determined to rip the villa apart. I saw Di Napoli's mouth move but did not hear a word. I believe he called my mistress's name. He clasped her round, porcelain face and with tenderness, kissed her. Receiving no response, he pulled back and looked closely. His face registered shock swiftly changing to grief.

I saw it clearly. Despite the countless women he'd pursued, Di Napoli had loved his wife. I swallowed the sharp blades of pain.

He turned his attention to the bundle nestled on the pillow. Euphoric awe spread across his face as he picked up and cradled the newborn. Father and son stared intently at each other. Trembling, the new father lay on the bed with the child between him and his dead wife. He shut his eyes.

Not once did he acknowledge me.

Take everything away with you.

Driven by Maria's voice in my head, I gathered the sewing articles, entered my bedroom and hid them under my mattress. I lay down. To block out the screaming wind, intense darkness and my dawning comprehension of what had taken place, I shut my eyes and held a pillow over my ears.

I had no idea how long I slept. But all too soon Maria spoke again.

With her instructions circling the inside of my head, I rose feeling drier than one of Foxy's old bones and barely able to breathe. The *scirocco* still raced around the villa, alternately pummelling and caressing the walls. I entered the bedchamber.

Mistress Letizia sat propped up, her arms clasped around her son. His mouth latched onto one breast and was nursing. I heard Maria's sharp intake of breath.

Looking closer, I saw Mistress Letizia's wrists, one crossed above the other, lassoed with a curtain cord anchored around her neck. Her eyes were closed.

'There was no other way to stop his crying,' Di Napoli's voice rasped.

He looked bad. His skin was parchment-thin, and his once-generous lips had shrunk into a thin gash barely covering his teeth.

'I...I need water.'

My gaze strayed to the bottle I had brought up earlier. It was empty. My body twitched, desperate for water, too. 'I'll be back.' I returned to the kitchen and drank until my skin oozed a new film of sweat. I filled several bottles from the kitchen's supply contained in the earthen pot and noted how much water was left. Grabbing a wedge of cheese, a piece of bread and a bowl of cherries from the marble cooler, I headed back upstairs and gave thanks my feet knew their way so well. With each step, the oppressive heat and smell grew worse.

The child was asleep. He lay secure, nestled in his dead mother's tied arms that formed a sling. Di Napoli lay alongside his wife, with one arm resting over her legs. After shaking him, I held a bottle to his lips. At first, he could barely swallow. Then, as if waking from a fabled, hundred-year-long sleep, he drank greedily, finished the first bottle and the next. Before my eyes, I saw his skin expand and the colour change.

'Did you bring something to eat?'

I held out the wedge of cheese and hunk of bread. Before one could say 'alakazam', Di Napoli wolfed both down. Then he started on the bowl of cherries. With each mouthful, energy, at first like a trickle of water in a parched riverbed, grew into a thin rivulet, then a stream, then a current until he was overflowing like a river spilling its banks. The Di Napoli of old emerged.

A thought struck me. If Maria had interpreted the augury at the birth of Di Napoli's son, I did not hear it. Or, she had deliberately not shared it.

———— ◆ ————

The *scirocco* took its leave just as quickly as it had arrived. The moment I threw open the bedchamber's wooden shutters, a scene I would never have imagined faced me. The landscape down to the sea was bathed in red. From the position of the hazy sun it was early morning, but not a single bird chirped.

Turning from the window, I saw the internal havoc the last forty-eight hours had wrought.

Mistress Letizia's body had stiffened in its upright position, her wrists still tied. Her son now lay in the crook of his sleeping father's arms. The child's large, dark pupils followed my every move. Everything was dirty. I glanced down at my clothes and saw I too was rust-tinged. Raising my hands, I patted my puffed-out hair, dense with gravel dust.

Through the open window, I heard the bangles' distinct bell-like tinkle announcing Maria's imminent arrival. I leaned over the sill like I'd done on the morning of Di Napoli's arrival a year ago. I raised my arm and waved. Walking behind Maria was the valley's wet nurse.

'Don't lean too far,' Di Napoli's deep voice warned me from behind.

I turned. He looked unimaginably well. His skin had returned to its dark and sleek elasticity. His lips had regained their fullness. His torso and arms had reclaimed their original sculpted lines. His eyes were darker than before. I wrenched my thoughts from appreciating his handsomeness and turned to pressing matters at hand.

'Take your child. Unlock the kitchen door. The wet nurse has arrived.'

The sound of my firm command surprised me. He noticed it too, said nothing, but with a quizzical look on his face, eased himself off the bed and left, carrying his son in his arms.

A minute later, Maria entered the bedchamber. The tip of her hooked nose wrinkled.

The bangles jangled with alarm.

Only then, did I realise the full impact of the foetid odour. We both looked at Mistress Letizia, from whence came the worst smell.

'Hortensia, you did exceedingly well delivering Di Napoli's child.'

'I could never have done it without you.'

Maria looked at me curiously. 'What ever do you mean?'

'You. Your voice…telling me what to do.'

'What did I tell you to do?'

Pinching my nose, I raised Mistress Letizia's skirts, displayed her stomach and the neat row of gold-thread stitches. For the first time in my life, I saw Maria's jaw fall open in surprise. The bangles fell silent.

Maria jerked the dress back down. She coughed, snapped her mouth shut, opened it to say something and thought better of it. 'For your sake,' she hissed, 'promise me, that of this, you will say nothing. Not ever. Not to anyone. It must remain secret.'

'I promise.'

'Good. But, know this. I am proud of you. Go. Bathe and change. The maids will return within the hour to start getting this villa back into order. I will deal with Mistress Letizia.'

'But…' Before I could finish the question, a shout went up.

I rushed to the window, leaned over the sill and craned my neck in the direction of the kitchen garden.

Rubino came around the corner of the villa and stood in the same spot where Bea had landed. With his cap in his hand, he looked up.

'They are found,' he said.

'Who?' I asked.

'Anna and Foxy.'

'Where?'

'In the well.'

My heart contracted with grief. Then contracted again when I realised I would never get the rest of the runaway bride story from Anna.

———————— ◆ ————————

Before Rubino could begin to hammer the lid closed, Di Napoli rushed around the bedchamber. 'Wait.' He pulled open drawers, extracted several items and tucked them around the dead body in what little space was left.

Items included were Mistress Letizia's gold wedding band, photographs, Salvatore Di Giacomo's book of songs, and the last boxes of *gianduiotti* chocolates – whose shapes were of upturned boats covered in gold or silver foil.

During the past year, boxes of chocolates arrived in a never-ending stream from the chocolate producer in Turin, for whom Di Napoli worked as a travelling salesman. Mistress Letizia loved all *gianduiotti* but her favourite was the dark variety, mixed with roasted ground hazelnut and almond praline paste.

Rubino frowned. 'What's all this?'

'I'm sending her off with the things she loved best. Then she has no reason to return to haunt me. You know, to pay me back for the times I was…er…disloyal to her.'

Rubino rolled his eyeballs heavenward. He picked up the hammer and a nail.

'Wait.' Di Napoli raced out of the bedchamber and returned a few minutes later, his sculpted chest heaving. 'One more thing.' Di Napoli held up a wet hessian sack.

From the shape, I had no doubt the sack contained Foxy, Mistress Letizia's first love, and likely Di Napoli's first-ever canine competitor.

Without hesitation, Rubino challenged the rank of master that Di Napoli had achieved through marriage to Mistress Letizia. 'Absolutely not.'

Such was the firmness of Rubino's voice, Di Napoli dropped the sack to the floor. Rubino raised the hammer and banged the first nail into the lid of Mistress Letizia's coffin while I, to the sound of my wailing heart, retrieved the soggy sack.

Di Napoli and two yard boys loaded Mistress Letizia's coffin onto the cart. Anna's was already on board and sealed. Rubino drove the cart while Di Napoli, Maria and I walked to the cemetery. Other families began arriving with their dead. Determined to have the dead buried without further delay, Don Antonio kept his blessing of each coffin down to a few words.

With speed, Mistress Letizia's coffin covered with several boughs of pink climbing roses Di Napoli had salvaged, was taken into the Angeli family mausoleum and placed on the next free ledge.

Unlike at his wedding, Di Napoli was fully dressed and wore the suit in which he'd arrived. Including his pointy-toed shoes. Seeing him dressed so, I knew Di Napoli would return to Naples as soon as possible. My maid's heart shrivelled.

After a hasty prayer and benediction, Don Antonio locked the mausoleum's bronze doors and pocketed the key.

Rubino drove the cart to the unmarked grave section where Anna's coffin was interred. Once again, Don Antonio spoke the briefest words, made the sign of the cross and indicated to the gravediggers to fill in the hole.

I neither saw nor heard anything while riding home on the back of the cart. I believe I grieved with even more intensity than I recalled when my mother abandoned me; my heart overflowed with tears for Anna, Foxy, and Mistress Letizia.

Upon our return home, we joined *avvocato* Fini who waited in the library. During our absence, the maids had done an admirable job ridding the room of the worst of the dust.

Di Napoli conferred with Maria, Don Antonio and the lawyer. By their nods, it appeared none of them objected to what he had proposed.

He took his child from the wet nurse's arms, and to my surprise placed him in mine. In my mind, Di Napoli, the child and I represented the eternal triangle. As we stood side by side in front of the *capodimonte* vase I was painfully reminded of just how well I thought we fit height-wise. Yet I let go of the flimsy dream-thread, wherein I had believed, that somehow, one day, we would be together.

Don Antonio used the *capodimonte* vase, filled with water, as the baptism font. It did not escape me that the water was red, courtesy of the Sahara's sand colour. As he dribbled the stained water over the child's crown, Di Napoli named me, Hortensia d'Ambrosia, the child's godmother forever after. It was cold comfort.

Maria was requested to witness Don Antonio's, Di Napoli's and my signature on the baptism certificate. The ink had barely dried when Don Antonio left, hurrying back to the cemetery.

Just as I thought everyone present was amazed that the seemingly impossible instructions of Giovanni Angeli's will had been fulfilled, *avvocato* Fini spoke. 'The conditions of Giovanni Angeli's will have been fulfilled. The management of the estate will pass directly to Mistress Letizia's firstborn son, Massimiliano Di Napoli upon the occasion of his eighteenth birthday. In the meantime, Rubino Sapienti shall continue the management of the Estate for as long as he is able, failing which he shall nominate someone else, and failing him, I will nominate another.'

My intuition picked up both Maria's and Rubino's responses, which they thought in unison: 'Over our dead bodies...'

'Er...there is of course,' Di Napoli said, 'the matter of my remuneration.'

Avvocato Fini was unable to hide the flash of dislike he had for Di Napoli. 'Don't worry.' He peered myopically in Di Napoli's direction. 'You shall receive your remuneration for being Mistress Letizia's husband and the father to the heir of the Angeli Estate as was negotiated.'

This was news to me. I had no recollection of such a negotiation ever having taken place. I glanced at Rubino and Maria. By their inscrutable faces, I realised not only did they know, but they had likely arranged it all.

———————— ◆ ————————

As expected, Di Napoli, Massimiliano – shortened to Max – being far too much of a mouthful for a baby, and the wet nurse, left. Di Napoli carried his suitcase long ago emptied of its chocolate samples. Every fibre in my being urged him to look back. I would take it as a sign, rekindling my hope we would one day be together. He did not. When I could no longer see him, resurrected hope died. The door to my foolish maid's heart with Di Napoli's name written upon it slid closed.

Maria left to attend to other matters in the valley and Rubino returned to the vineyards.

I entered the stable and from that section of the massive wall adorned with tools, I selected a spade.

'Can I help?' a new yard boy asked.

I nodded, handed over the spade, picked up the hessian sack and headed out to the orchard.

The yard boy dug a hole where I indicated. I removed Foxy from the sack. Red mud clogged his white fur. I stroked him and whispered, 'You were such an annoying but charming little pest with your love of chasing the ball. I shall miss you. Farewell.'

I lowered Foxy into the hole, reached into my apron pockets, pulled out his favourite ball and placed it between his paws.

From the first clod of earth the yard boy shovelled over Foxy's defenceless body, my heart turned inside out, and I began to grieve all over again. For Foxy, Anna, Mistress Letizia, my mother whom I hardly remembered, and father I had never known. And I cried for myself and Di Napoli.

'Hortensia.' The yard boy shook my shoulder. Exhausted, I'd fallen asleep. I woke in the dark. He helped me to my feet.

'Thank you. Oh dear, I don't know your name.'

'Iacopo.'

He walked me back to the villa. Halfway there, he removed his jacket and placed it over my shoulders. I realised then he was older than the usual age group of yard boys, almost a man. I was grateful for his consideration and the warmth of jacket. It smelled lightly of sweat and another smell I knew but could not place. I got distracted from those thoughts, for upon a steady stream of night air funnelling down the mountainside, fireflies floated, blinking their lights as they passed us by.

When I stood upon the kitchen step, I returned his jacket. 'Thank you, Iacopo. Goodnight.'

I entered the kitchen. The maids had done another miraculous job. It was dust-free and everything in its place, just like Anna had always insisted. Rubino fussed over a pan resting on the woodstove. By the aromatic cloud of aniseed, I knew he was preparing bell-shaped mush-rooms.

'I was beginning to fear I'd have to eat dinner on my own.'

Rubino believed eating alone was not good for one's digestion.

'Is Maria not joining us?'

'No. She's still down in the village. So, it's just you and me. Hungry?'

'Famished.' I washed my hands at the sink and took my place at the table. Anna's seat screamed its vacancy. I found my feet searching for Foxy, who, had he been alive, would have sat under the table, ready to gobble all spilled human food.

Rubino ladled out portions into bowls while I poured him a glass of *Sangiovese*. And then, for the first time, I poured myself a glass. If Rubino noticed, he said nothing.

I tore apart a slice of bread Rubino had flame-toasted and zig-zagged with garlic. It left a sticky residue glistening like a snail's filigree track glinting silver. I dipped the piece of warm bread into the sauce and popped it into my mouth.

At the end of the meal, eaten in companionable silence, a question which had been playing at the back of my head thrust itself forward.

'Rubino?'

'*Sì.*'

'Why do priests take potions of chasteberry?'

After the *scirocco's* departure and laying the dead to rest, outdoor activities resumed. But indoors, life underwent notable changes.

I replaced Anna as cook and ensured the maids kept house, as if expecting the imminent arrival of its owner. But that was unlikely, given Massimiliano Di Napoli, my godson, was one month old.

Travellers stopped by, bringing news. Hearing Max was thriving, my soul warmed. Variable accounts of his father's health caused my heart to contract with concern, and then pain, for I never received word from him. As more evidence of Di Napoli's past and present single-minded dedication to the pursuit of women came to light, my smitten, broken heart began to heal.

I no longer slept in my little room between Mistress Letizia's bed-chamber and the guest room, which I considered Di Napoli's. The memory of what took place in those rooms in the last year of Mistress Letizia's life remained acute. Thus, I took over Anna's former accommodation, just off the kitchen, as my own.

The maids cleaned and dust-sheeted the furniture in the rooms on the upper floor and closed the doors. Their duty reduced from full-time to once a week, the maids returned to their homes.

Maria, Rubino and I gathered most nights for dinner in the kitch-en. Since Anna's death, her family no longer sent delicacies from Naples. This forced me go in search of alternative ingredients. With a torrent of advice from the valley housewives, I tried my hand at a variety of Tuscan recipes. Maria and Rubino suffered many less-than-good meals in silence. Little by little, I began to serve more than passable versions of Anna's recipes.

Ribollita was such a dish, perfect for a cold winter night. A twice-cooked soup made of beans and kale, which has the colour and consistency of seaweed and is served piping hot with a generous splash of olive oil. *Acquacotta*, another soup, made with chopped vegetables and served with poached eggs floating on top.

And my favourite, *Pappa al pomodoro*, a tomato soup, refreshing on a hot summer evening, made with crumbled stale bread soaked in the juice of the reddest, softest squished tomatoes, mixed with finely chopped red sweet onion, and a handful of basil and olive oil. The trick: let the mixture stand overnight so all flavours meld, and then serve cold.

Rubino oversaw my first attempt at cooking a light sauce of white *tartufo*, truffles, served over *tagliatelle*, and Maria, a dark sauce of *lepre*, hare, served over *pappardelle*, both of which I adored. Later, when I realised the hare pasta had been Di Napoli's favourite and the white truffles, Iacopo's, I found myself unable to stomach either dish and never ate them again.

When Anna had been alive, our meals ended with any number of her desserts. We all still hankered after something sweet. So, in this too, I persevered and managed to turn out two desserts. *Castagnaccio*, a chestnut flour cake eaten hot or cold and, *cantuccini*, semi-hard biscuits with almonds.

———————— ◆ ————————

One Sunday evening after that season's harvest, we sat down to eat. More than a year had passed since the *scirroco's* last and most notable visit.

Rubino pulled the cork from a bottle of the previous year's vintage. 'Praise be to God. Di Napoli has stuck to his side of the bargain and in exchange for his monthly *stipendo*, salary he has given us no interference.' He held the cork to his nose and sniffed. The look on his face changed from curious to thoughtful. He poured three glasses, held his up to the light, turned it to an angle rolling the stem between his fingers. The liquid swirled against the bowl's translucent wall in a never-ending undulating wave. He plunged his nose into the bowl and inhaled deeply. He repeated the action three times.

'This wine is as capricious as a woman who doesn't know what she wants. Its aroma goes through several changes before settling.' He proffered a glass each to Maria and me. 'Here, what do you smell?'

We copied his actions. After a few moments, Maria responded. 'Plum.'

'Grass,' I said.

'Both are correct.' Rubino took a mouthful, gargled and swallowed. 'Now you try. Tell me what you taste.'

Maria quaffed back the wine in her glass. 'Berry jam.'

I followed suit. The taste of Di Napoli's mouth filled mine. *Damn you*. I held the liquid for as long as possible, then swallowed.

Rubino looked at me keenly. 'Well?'

It was crazy, but I said it. 'Chocolate.'

'*Brava*. We'll make a wine taster out of you yet. Now try this.' Rubino poured from another bottle. In silence, we repeated the smelling procedure as before. I took a good mouthful, anticipating Di Napoli's mouth.

'Ugh.' I spat out the turned-to-vinegar wine.

Rubino and Maria guffawed, and the bangles burbled with mirth. I grabbed the edge of my apron, stuck out my tongue and gave it a thorough rub.

Still laughing, Rubino handed me a glass of water to rinse out the liquid's acridness.

'Oh dear,' Maria cackled. The look on your face is priceless.'

'So? What do you think it's good for?' The wrinkles around Rubino's eyes deepened.

'Unblocking the sink?'

They laughed harder. My face broke out into a smile at the joke played on me.

'This,' Rubino touched the bottle of the chocolate-tasting wine and his voice changed to serious, 'is going to put the Angeli Estate on the map. It should sell at a good price.'

'And, everyone will get a share of the profits. From the oldest to the youngest who worked in the vineyards.' Maria looked carefully at me. 'Including you.'

I kept my mouth closed and my face immobile. What Maria had said was akin to heresy. Other estates' profits, no matter what they produced, went directly into the pockets of the owner, with the workers subsisting on a low salary paid after each season. And depending on the harvest, their meagre earnings dropped greatly or increased marginally. The *scirocco's* last visit destroyed the grape harvest and everyone in the valley had suffered.

'An American buyer is expected in a few weeks,' Rubino said. 'I have already inferred we have other interested parties. That way I'll hold the price firm.'

Plans, masterminded by Maria, Rubino, and Anna while she had been alive, and more complex than a labyrinth of mole tunnels, began to make sense. But what was my role? In time to my next heartbeat, the question was answered.

Maria sucked her teeth clean. 'Hortensia, all your improved cooking skills will be put to the test for the welcoming dinner.'

I gulped.

'Because,' Rubino said, 'a different vintage will accompany each plate you prepare. This method of tasting will be crucial to securing the sale.'

I nodded while at the same time I wished harder than ever that Anna was still alive.

Like a fickle breeze, Rubino and Maria changed direction.

'Do you remember the yard boy, Iacopo Lenzi?' Rubino asked.

His face flashed before me and I felt the warmth of his body, while my nose filled with the alluring fragrance I could not place. As casually as possible I deflected stabs of excitement plunging through my belly like sharp knives, and said, 'I think so.'

'Yes,' Maria said.

'He's completed his civilian army service,' Rubino's eyebrows crept upward. 'And he's in need of work.'

'What do you have in mind for him?' Maria asked.

'He could give me a hand overseeing the next harvest.'

The bangles clinked their curiosity as Maria waved a bony hand in the air. 'Is he to live down in the valley, or here?'

I looked from one to the other as their questions and answers flew back and forth. Then I realised, their conversation had been rehearsed, for my benefit. *Why?*

'In the stable,' Rubino said. 'Like before.'

'Am I to include him for meals?' I asked.

'A packed lunch to eat in the fields,' Rubino said. 'But dinner is to be taken here with us.'

'Fine with me,' Maria said.

My thoughts returned to Iacopo's skin's subtle fragrance that I could still not pinpoint.

The snap of Maria's fingers in front of my face brought me back to the present. 'Fine with me, too.'

I locked the kitchen door after Maria and Rubino left. Entering my bedroom, I caught sight of the window. Of all the ground-floor windows, it was, I realised, for the first time, the only one without wrought-iron bars.

I checked the windows and night shutters were not only closed but locked. Succumbing to past fears, I prayed the monster who stole children away in the night through forgotten-to-be-locked windows was not lurking under my bed. With a quick hop and skip, I dove into bed, blew out the candle and stared hard at the darkness.

Other than Christ crucified on the cross attached to the wall above my head, I was alone. As prescribed in the Holy Sacrifice of the Mass, I repeated Iacopo's name for each of the three times I struck my breast. Shivers raced through my body. I had offered myself to Iacopo even before he had arrived.

That night, I dreamed of Di Napoli, wizards, wands, a runaway bride and a mermaid swimming in the pupil of an eye. I woke with Iacopo's alluring smell fading, and still I could not identify it.

Maddening.

The next day shortly before the sun hit its high point, I heard a light rap on the kitchen door.

Iacopo Lenzi stood framed by the doorway. He had filled out. He had well-defined lips, a small dent in his chin and pupils made bluer by the surrounding unblemished white. He removed his four-point knotted kerchief from his head and held out his free hand to shake mine. Though his grip was firm, my hand got lost in his. His nails were square-cut and clean.

'Iacopo. Welcome.'

His face flushed. 'Thank you.'

Muscles in my lower abdomen contracted and released. 'It's been a while.'

'One year and two months,' he said.

You've been counting. I almost skipped for joy. I handed him a lidded bowl and a fork wrapped in a kitchen cloth and prayed he did not notice my trembling hand. 'I'm sorry. It's nothing like what Anna used to make.'

He smiled his thanks, took the dish and left. Later, I found the bowl and fork, washed clean, placed on the marble draining board. *The boy has manners.*

In the early summer months, we sat down to eat dinner at eight thirty. Later, when it got really hot, we would eat only once the earth had cooled, often close to midnight.

The wall clock's hands had just passed eight-thirty. Iacopo was the last to enter. He had changed into a fresh shirt. As he took his place and sat down, I caught a whisper of that tantalising smell again. But it was lost when I placed a black iron pot in the centre of the table and lifted the lid. A cloud of steam rose, obliterating any other smells.

I had boiled various pieces of meat, notorious for their toughness, together with a bay leaf, parsley, garlic, peppercorns, carrots, celery and onions. In the last hour, I discarded the boiled-almost-to-nothing vegetables and replaced them, including whole potatoes.

By the aroma alone, I knew this dish, *bollito misto*, was one of my better attempts. The meat was butter-soft and the vegetables cooked to the right crunch. The crowning glory: a bowl of glossy green sauce made from parsley, green peppers, capers, fresh chilli, salted anchovies, a few tarragon leaves, salt, pepper and olive oil, all blended and left to stand for several hours.

While I served the boiled meat in the traditional manner – piping hot – I served the piquant green sauce cold rather than at room temperature. The contrast of the rich hot meat and cold and oily green sauce is one of the most delicious shocks a tongue can ever receive.

Dessert of baked *cantuccini* served with a bowl of *mascarpone* followed. The ritual is to dip and soak the finger-sized biscuit in the *vin santo*, then run it through the cream before biting off the soaked and cream-blanketed biscuit tip. The secret is not to over-soak the biscuit, so the slivers of almonds still give a satisfying snap.

At the end of the meal, Iacopo politely wished us all a good night and left. Rubino rubbed his stomach in slow circles, and Maria held her bony hands cupped to her mouth while poking the cracks between her teeth with a toothpick.

Rubino eased his chair away from the table. 'Can I place my order now for one more *bollito misto* before the summer sets in?'

'I'll second that,' Maria said.

My face blushed with pride. I had finally produced a faultless meal. 'Of course.'

———————— ◆ ————————

The next day, after Iacopo left carrying his lunch, I followed him. He headed to the orchard to eat and took a seat on the ground near Foxy's grave.

Taking advantage of the cover the trees provided, I took my time and looked him over. He was the complete opposite to Di Napoli's swarthiness.

Iacopo's fair hair fell to his shoulders in heavy locks, highlighting his nose's prominent bridge and lending him an air of nobility and courage.

Most noticeable of all were his long and lean limbs. He moved with agile grace whereas Di Napoli had represented a ball of dangerous energy, ready to explode at any second. *Why am I thinking about you again?*

Having finished eating, Iacopo stretched out on a patch of grass, interlaced his fingers and rested his head in the palms of his hands. He looked peaceful, sandwiched between the green earth below and blue sky above.

Until they moved, it was impossible to tell the butterflies apart from the leaves of the chasteberry tree. Forming a giant cloud, they drifted down to alight upon the clover's tiny yellow flowers peeking through meadow grass and obscured Iacopo.

I headed back and with each step remembered the evening when Iacopo accompanied me home, our path lit by the fireflies and his jacket comfortingly warm over my shoulders.

That evening, Iacopo was the first to arrive for dinner. I greeted him first. 'Hello. Where's Rubino?'

'He said to tell you he's been invited for dinner in the valley.'

'*Che noioso*, how annoying. Maria won't be here either. She sent word earlier to say she's helping at a birthing.'

Iacopo remained standing in the doorway, looking unsure. 'Er...I could...'

'Don't be silly. Come in, sit down. We'll have dinner like always.' Turning on my heel, I headed downstairs into the cellar, wondering if I had seen a look of relief flash across his face. I pulled a dust-covered bottle of the chocolate wine from the racks. Pausing halfway back up the worn stone steps, I pinched my cheeks, rubbed my lips and popped open the next two buttons on the bodice of my dress.

'Here, open this.' I thrust the bottle at him with one hand and the corkscrew with the other. The action forced my breasts to press together. 'It'll go well with the dish I've prepared.'

He had more than noticed my cleavage through the widened peephole space. Before my face flushed, I spun around, pulled open the iron door to the wood-burning stove and reached in.

From behind me, the cork burst from the bottle's neck just as the cloth slipped and I closed my unprotected hand on the scorching pan. The kitchen filled with my yowl of surprise and pain. I held my burnt hand in the air and jumped from foot to foot.

In a second, Iacopo stood beside me. 'Here.' He took my hand and plunged it into the water jug standing on the table.

The relief was instant. Yet I was more aware of his palm resting over the back of my burnt hand.

'Keep it submerged for as long as possible.' He slid his hand out from the mouth of the jug. 'It's the best antidote for the pain and to halt the burn from further damaging the skin. Untreated, some burns can continue to blister for hours after the initial burn.'

'Where'd you learn all that?'

'The civilian army. I trained in first aid.'

'Oh.'

'Let's take a look. No, don't remove your hand from the water.'

We studied my hand, magnified, through the glass. A red welt rose across my palm.

'That's going to be painful for a while.'

He was right. Despite the water's cooling effect, my hand throbbed.

Iacopo pulled out a chair, cupped my elbow until I sat. 'Have a drink of this.' He poured a glass of wine and held it to my lips.

The wine slid down my throat, warming yet calming.

'Where's the honey?'

I tipped my head in the direction of the pantry. 'Top shelf to the right.'

Iacopo placed the honey jar on the table.

'What's that for?'

'To be used as a salve on the burn. It'll aid healing.'

I sat back, allowing Iacopo to do what he needed. He dried my hand with a clean cloth. Then he took another and, using his teeth, tore the cloth strips. He had even, white teeth.

'Rest your hand on the table palm facing up.'

I did as requested. He twisted off the jar's lid and there it was: the smell I associated him with. Honey? Not quite. But then again, maybe.

Iacopo smeared a thin coating of honey over the angry red welt. Taking up the clean strips, he flat-knotted each to the other and wrapped it around my hand. He twisted and tucked the end under the homemade bandage. It fit snug.

'Oh my goodness.' I twisted around in my chair. 'The rabbit.'

'I'll get it.' Using a cloth, he hauled the roasting pan out of the oven.

The slices of lard wrapped around the rabbit pieces had melted into a transparent film. The black and green de-stoned olives rolled around in the sauce, the air was heady with the fragrance of garlic, rosemary and oregano.

Iacopo looked into the pan. Hunger clouded his eyes. At that moment I wished I was the rabbit. I wanted to be devoured. By him.

'There's one more ingredient to add.' I removed a crocheted cover from a porcelain bowl.

Iacopo looked at the bowl and then me. 'Lemons?'

'Not just lemons; salted lemons. Empty the bowl into the sauce and give it a good stir.'

Iacopo did as I said. 'May I serve?'

'Yes. Please.'

While Iacopo plated the rabbit, I downed the rest of my glass. The liquid added another layer of warmth and calm to my insides.

I was not hungry, but sensed the need to keep up the façade of being all right, so I took a mouthful of rabbit. The sharp sour lemon cut through the bitter taste of the plump olives. Smoothed by the rich lard covering, the silky, moist meat was delicious.

I added wine to my glass and swallowed another mouthful, sat back and watched the expression change on Iacopo's face. It was clear his mouth was in the throes of undergoing a taste explosion.

He sighed, and pushed his empty plate aside. 'I am without words. May I...?'

I enjoyed watching him while he helped himself to another portion and ate with slow deliberation.

At some point, I remembered thinking how much I would like to lie down. The wine had gone to my head and my palm throbbed so, it was as if my heart had relocated and taken up residence there. Then the light faded.

———— ◆ ————

Before I opened my eyes the next morning, I knew by the bangles' short, sharp, plinks Maria hovered over me. *Had anything happened?* I remembered Iacopo carrying me to bed. I tried to feel what clothing condition I was in, starting with my feet. I had no need to go any further. I was still wearing my boots.

Maria shook me by my shoulder. 'Hortensia. Wake up.' I could no longer pretend. But I took another second preparing to face Maria's turned-in eyes, pointing towards the tip of her hooked nose, before opening mine.

'How are you feeling? That's a nasty burn on your hand.'

The bandage had come undone sometime during the night and my hand was free. 'All right, I think.' I gazed at the blistered flesh and the events of the previous night returned to me. 'Oh dear. The kitchen must be in a mess.'

'Not at all. Iacopo cleared up after you fell asleep. The kitchen's spotless. And he can't stop talking about the meal you prepared last night. He said he ate the lot after he put you to bed.'

I tried to flex my hand and winced with the pain. Then I remembered the American buyer and the dinner I was to prepare. I winced again.

'There is news from the Trianni Estate.'

Whether it was good or bad, news from our rival neighbour was always interesting. Immediately, my pain and the dinner were replaced by dancing shadows, and the runaway bride.

The valley buzzed with the news that our long-absent neighbour, Claudio Trianni, had unexpectedly returned and brought with him a surprise.

The bangles shrilled.

'Of all people,' Maria said, 'he should know better.'

'Know better?' My head got caught under the clean dress Maria shoved me into, muffling my voice. 'About what?'

'He should have married her here, rather than in Liguria. After all, weddings are meant to be celebrated with everyone participating in the event. And more so,' Maria continued while tugging the dress to rights, 'given he made us wait until he was seventy-five years old before bringing home a wife.'

'But the last wedding in our valley wasn't celebrated like that.'

The shrills changed to hissing which Maria's voice matched. 'Mistress Letizia had no family, and Di Napoli family members never leave their hometown. Not for anything.'

Knowing I had been lied to, and paying attention to the hisses, I knew better than to press the point.

'It's bad enough she is a *ligure*, rather than a *toscana*. But worse, she arrived with her personal maid.'

The bangles snapped once and silenced.

But Maria still had more to say. 'At least, as a sign of goodwill, she could have employed one of our own.'

By the jittery movement of Maria's eyes, I experienced a spark of sorrow for the maid. Her life would not be easy. She'd likely go home soon.

In addition to being thirty years younger than him, the twice-widowed, middle-aged, Angelica Barberi was rumoured to be the most beautiful woman anyone had ever seen. *Bellezza* was the visible aesthetic assessment standard against which valley workers judged all things. So, despite Trianni's multitudinous sins, the biggest being the vast amount of money he owed valley workers for years of unpaid labour, they would, because of his wife's unique beauty, begrudgingly offer him a sliver of respect. Of her beauty's depth, they cared not.

What the workers thought of his wife, or the amount of money he owed them did not hinder Claudio Trianni in the necessary task of impregnating his wife. He got down to business on the first night. The sound of his rutting squawks – he'd long lost the ability to bellow – that reached the valley attested to this. Lucky for her, Angelica Barberi did not have to suffer the indignity of having her soiled wedding-night linen flung over the balcony rails the following morning.

———————— ◆ ————————

The furore created by our neighbour's sudden return with his new wife and her two, equally beautiful daughters, similar in age to me, did not distract us from focusing on the American's arrival.

Rubino tacked a torn-off calendar for the month of June onto the kitchen wall. The calendar's pin-up girl for that month, no doubt, was still stuck on the upstairs stable walls where Rubino, Iacopo and a new yard boy, Arturo, had their quarters.

Rubino carefully circled and tapped his finger on Thursday 29, the American dinner date. 'Five days before they arrive. Lucky, it will be full moon. The weather should behave.'

'Never trust the weather. Plan to set two tables,' Maria said. 'One in the dining room and the other out on the terrace. And, Hortensia, the Americans will be sleeping here. Have the maids prepare two bedrooms.'

Had she forgotten? The maids now only came weekly. I sighed. My life had been much easier as a personal maid to Mistress Letizia. How helpful it would be to have another pair of hands like mine.

'Have you written out a menu?' Rubino asked.

I crossed my fingers behind my back. 'It's not complete.' I'd been going around in circles wondering how to present a meal that would show off six vintage wines and highlight the one with strong chocolate notes. More than ever I wished for Anna's presence.

'Later, I'll want to take a look.' He left.

Maria's cloak billowed as she followed Rubino out of the kitchen.

I sat at the table and pulled a sheet of paper towards me. I sensed Foxy's furry warmth on my feet. *Anna! Where are you?*

After weeks of agonising over the menu, the spinning in my head calmed as the kitchen walls excluded all other sounds and cocooned me in silence. I picked up my pen and to the sound of Anna's voice wrote out the menu on one side and the accompanying vintage wines opposite. I read it through once more, and satisfied, set it aside. I turned my attention to preparing our evening meal.

Two hours later, the clock's hands showed close to nine o'clock. *Where was everybody?*

Iacopo entered. Seeing him alone, my eyebrows rose.

'Rubino and Maria send their apologies. They've gone down to the valley.'

My belly flipped. It was the third time in ten days they had not arrived for the evening meal. Each time only Iacopo and I were present, I lost my appetite, and my mouth remained dry, no matter how much wine I drank.

'Shall I get the wine?' he asked, likely because he saw none on the table.

'Yes.'

'What are we eating?'

'Grilled quail with gorgonzola, pear and walnut salad.'

He disappeared down the cellar's steps. A few minutes later, he returned with not one, but two bottles. I held back from showing my surprise.

Iacopo took his time eating. He savoured each mouthful until his plate was wiped clean.

'Seconds?' I asked.

'Yes, please.' He helped himself and chewed slowly through the second helping.

I relaxed and enjoyed his quiet appreciation.

Iacopo wiped his mouth. 'You can add this dish to your menu. It was great.'

'I already have, but thank you.'

Iacopo scrabbled around the inside pockets of his jacket, hanging over the back of the chair. 'I have something for you.'

A gift? I had not received a gift since I was a child. He pulled out a small brown box tied with a gold ribbon.

'*Gianduiotti!*' Like greeting a dear friend, I clasped the box with both hands. Since Mistress Letizia's death and Di Napoli's departure, there had not been a single chocolate in the villa.

The look on Iacopo's face matched my delight. Carefully I opened the box. Nestled together were four upturned boats covered in foil: two in gold and two in silver.

I remembered my manners and offered the box to him first. He took one and much faster than me, peeled off its foil.

'Hortensia.'

I raised my gaze from the chocolate I held between my fingers, its foil still intact.

He brought his chocolate close to my mouth. 'Here.'

I bit it in two and then slipped the other half into his waiting mouth.

Our faces were close. While we savoured our half chocolates, I got a light whiff of the other smell I had tried to identify. Finally, I had it. Beeswax. Iacopo used a softer-scented pomade than Di Napoli had.

With light beeswax fragrance in my nose and strong creamy hazelnut chocolate in my mouth, I was firmly deposited in front of the gates of heaven. Iacopo leaned forward and pressed his lips to mine. As his tongue slipped into my mouth, slicked with chocolate, the gates opened.

◆

Iacopo climbed out of my bedroom window at dawn. I lay under the covers for a little longer, and contemplated the nocturnal event. Ours was poles apart from the abortive coupling I'd experienced with Di Napoli.

When I rose, I saw to my dismay blood soiled the bottom sheet. I'd have to secretly wash it before the maids did the weekly linen changeover in two days' time. A soaking in cold water with a good handful of salt should do the trick. But, how to dry the sheet without hanging it outside, which everyone would see? There was no time. I stripped the bed, replaced the bottom sheet and hid the soiled one under my mattress. I'd deal with it later.

Equally important, I needed to stay alert and make sure Maria, especially, did not get wind of last night. Yet, a little shiver of excitement ran up my spine. I looked forward to seeing Iacopo again. He was sweet and as the valley workers would say, *un bel ragazzo,* a beautiful boy. I did not want to think anymore about its evil twin, *brutto ragazzo,* which was how the valley workers referred to Di Napoli.

◆

On the appointed day, the American buyer and his learning-the-business son arrived. That they were related was unmistakable, right down to their florid faces and soft paunches. When the father spoke, the sound of his voice was like an assault upon my ears. The son's subdued parroting – an offset echo – of all that his father said was hypnotic.

'Welcome. Welcome to the Angeli Estate,' Iacopo said in English.

Aha! So, besides first aid, you also learned English in the army. Thus, his role in ensuring a successful sale was revealed.

The weather behaved. The Americans, our first foreign buyers, Rubino, Maria and Iacopo ate out on the lantern-lit terrace. The dinner, judging by loosened belts and red faces, was a success.

For the occasion of the contract signing, rambling pink roses filled and tumbled out of the *capodimonte* vase in the library. With exaggerated flourishes, father and son and then Rubino and Iacopo signed the wine sale contract. Maria signed as witness. Every last drop of wine, still fermenting in the wood barrels kept in the barn alongside the villa, had been purchased.

'Once it arrives,' the American buyer said, 'we'll use this wine as the base for blending other varietals and create a new wine. Do you have olive oil for sale?'

Iacopo translated.

'*Quando ne avrò la farò sapere,*' Maria responded.

Iacopo translated again. 'When we do, we'll let you know.'

The next morning, before leaving, the American father said, 'Don't forget the olive oil.'

'We won't,' Iacopo said.

After more broad grins, likely leaving face muscles strained, and a lot of handshaking which turned into vigourous hand-pumping, father and son left.

Olive oil? The closest olive oil estate was Claudio Trianni's across the valley from us. How did Maria plan to sell his olive oil to the Americans, especially when the two estate households had not spoken to each other in years? And, equally important, now Claudio Trianni had returned and was permanently ensconced there with his wife?

———————— ◆ ————————

A few weeks later, on a Friday, we heard the whine of Pietro the fishmonger's blue van approaching the villa.

'Rubino. A letter from *HA MER E KA!*' His voice carried up the hill and was loud enough to penetrate the villa's thick stone walls.

'What an imbecile,' Maria bleated, sounding like her goats. 'By now the entire valley will know. And why is he delivering the letter rather than the postman?'

'Perhaps, because the next post delivery is in two weeks' time,' I said. 'Likely he asked Pietro to deliver it with the fish order, saving us the wait.'

Maria stood and tugged at her shawl. 'Hortensia, bring three bottles of wine from the cellar for Pietro's trouble.'

Rubino rose. 'Not the good stuff.' He stepped out to meet the deliverer of the letter.

I walked out of the kitchen cradling the bottles wrapped in brown hessian.

Iacopo came to my side and relieved me of them. Though we had spent every night together, I marvelled at how my body thrilled at the brush of his fingers against mine. But with Maria, and less so Rubino, close by, I kept a straight face, turned and fixed my gaze upon Pietro. I could not help but notice he was missing his snaggle-tooth. His lips pressed together, sucked back into his mouth.

'Dentist got it?' I asked.

Pietro looked at me and quickly raised his hand to cover his mouth and nodded. Though he was toothless, I had underestimated him; there was nothing wrong with his sight or counting ability. He raised a finger for each bottle Iacopo and I placed in the back of his van. With the bottles settled, Pietro handed the letter to Rubino.

'I've also got oysters.'

Everyone turned to me. For a moment, I forgot I was the cook. 'Yes. I'll take them. Both baskets.'

'Only one. The other is for the beautiful Angelica Barberi.' He forgot to cover his mouth and exposed an all-gum grin.

Likely, Rubino, Maria and Iacopo ran their tongues gratefully over their teeth, just as I did, when confronted with Pietro's toothless mouth.

Hearing the deference paid to Angelica Barberi, whose Ligurian maid was proving to be more resilient than anticipated, Maria stiffened.

I carried the fish which had been swimming in the Tyrrhenian not four hours before into the kitchen. Iacopo followed, carrying an oyster basket trailing seawater. I indicated. 'Here, place it in the sink.'

Through the kitchen's opened door, Iacopo and I heard Pietro argue with Rubino.

'What are you waiting for?' Pietro demanded. 'Read it out loud.'

I selected the shucking knife from the drawer. My hearing increased to its keenest ability.

'This,' Rubino said, 'is Massimiliano Di Napoli's business.'

Lifting an oyster out of its seaweed packing, I placed it flat side down nestled on a kitchen cloth.

'But, the child is not yet a year old. Nor is he even here. I tell you, everyone knows it has to do with the *HA MER E KA NEE*. Is the Angeli Estate sold? The valley workers want to know.'

I flipped the end of the cloth over the oyster's curved back, held it firm while I slipped the tip of the knife under its nose.

Rubino lowered his voice. 'You have my word. If anything in this letter has to do with you or anyone else, I'll be the first to spread the news. On our mothers' graves, I promise.'

I levered the knife until the oyster popped open with a sharp crack as the van's door banged shut and the engine started.

Pietro bounced his way downhill to the valley floor, and then up the opposite slope to Trianni Villa, grinding the van's gears all the way.

I continued shucking until the oysters were laid out on a platter with lemon wedges.

Rubino and Maria entered. They sat down, one at each end of the table.

Rubino passed the letter to Iacopo sitting between them. 'Read. Translate.'

10

After Iacopo translated the American's first letter, Rubino called a meeting. On the appointed day, every worker in the valley laid down their tools and headed to the barn.

A representative from Rome sat at a makeshift table with a pile of application forms in front of him. Tacked to the wall behind him was a poster encouraging workers to join the recently formed labour union.

'But when do we get paid the money owing to us?' a voice from within the crowd yelled.

'Yeah,' shouted another. 'We want our money now.'

Rubino spoke without raising his voice. 'The Angeli Estate claims it has no money.'

Years of simmering discontent now boiled over. Indignant voices howled their protest, faces turned red and feet stomped the earth until the barn walls reverberated.

Rubino let the crowd rant, then raised one hand calling for calm. 'But, sign on as a member of the labour union and the Angeli Estate will be forced to pay wages, and on time. No more waiting.' Rubino paused, placed his right fist over his heart. 'On this, I give you my word.'

Another voice rose from the crowd. 'What about the back monies the Trianni Estate owes us and our fathers, and our fathers' fathers for seasons of olive harvests? Now that Claudio Trianni has returned, he must pay us.'

'Hear, hear.' Again, the barn's walls vibrated.

Rubino raised one hand. 'The Trianni Estate is a separate matter which will also be dealt with when the time comes.'

The air exploded with curses.

Rubino called for silence again. 'But, you have my word, it will be addressed. Let us deal with the Angeli Estate first.'

Having no other option, the valley workers joined the labour union and separately signed on as seasonal workers with the Angeli Estate. Each member was issued with a labour union membership number and a booklet that outlined the monthly subscription payment and benefits. When they realised the base wage was higher – many times greater than what their ancestors dreamed – and included fixed paid holidays and disability compensation, their rumbling discord dwindled until the barn was filled with silence.

'A new era is upon us. Praise God,' a voice whispered.

A chorus rose. 'Thanks be to God.'

The crowd trooped out of the barn each holding their booklet with as much reverence as they held their rosaries at church on Sundays.

The next day, the vats of wine were siphoned into barrels and sealed. With sleeves pushed up displaying an array of sun-bronzed muscular arms, workers rolled the barrels onto the back of horse and donkey-drawn carts. These were driven down to the valley floor and then to the harbour. Once there, the barrels were rolled up a gangplank, down another, stored side by side and lashed together in the bowels of the boat.

The carts of varying weights had churned up the bumpy track that had led to Villa Angeli for as long as even Maria could remember.

'Well, that's the first good thing we've had out of this wine shipment,' she said. 'A broad and flat road.'

The bangles tinkled their agreement.

Rubino's facial creases deepened with every hour. He barely ate. Each time another empty cart arrived, he asked, 'Do you have a letter for me?'

When the first letter had arrived, delivered by Pietro and translated by Iacopo, it stated a copy of the bank draft for the amount agreed would arrive with the next mail. It also expressed heartfelt thanks for our hospitality and asked that extra thanks for the 'stupendous' six-course meal be passed to me. Overwhelmed with their praise, and blinking back my tears, I handed over half of the Americans' gratitude to Anna.

The driver of the last cart, who had just loaded the final barrel, approached Rubino. 'Boss. Sorry, I forgot to give you this.'

Relief softened Rubino's crevices. He took the proffered letter that he had, with growing anxiety, been waiting for.

'Iacopo!' Rubino shouted in the loudest voice I'd ever heard him use. 'Kitchen.'

Rubino, Maria, Iacopo and I took our places around the table.

Iacopo opened the heavy envelope with care, withdrew several sheets and quickly scanned the first page. 'Attached,' he read, 'is a copy of the bank draft made out to the Angeli Di Napoli Estate.' He paused, 'But, only for half of the original sum agreed.'

The kitchen wall clock seemed to stop ticking. The bangles fell into ominous silence. Maria's eyes closed and Rubino held his breath.

'There's more,' Iacopo said. 'The balance will be paid when the wine shipment arrives in good order, and,' he lifted his head, his eyes sparkled, 'I am to accompany it.'

Maria, and Anna, who had put in an appearance, breathed in unison. The bangles renounced their silence and tinkled joyously.

Rubino whistled. 'Well, my boy, imagine how all the mothers will be clamouring for your attention to show you their daughters upon your return from *HA MER E KA.*'

I bit my lip and thought about chocolate in case Maria saw into my head and discovered my relationship with Iacopo. I found myself biting harder, to suppress a rising feeling of disquiet, threatening to drown me.

Maria had other things on her mind. She tapped a bony finger against the copy of the bank transfer. 'So far, we only have half the payment. Iacopo, be sure the Americans pay the balance. I repeat, be sure.'

Iacopo swallowed hard. Maria looked like a witch.

That night we ate a simple meal of bread, cheese, home-cured wild-boar salami, olives and a plate of fresh celery sticks, fennel and carrots.

'Pack and get a good night's sleep,' Rubino said. 'I'll hitch the donkey and take you to the harbour myself at daybreak. The boat will leave midmorning at high tide.'

The three of them left, and I locked the kitchen door. Stunned by the swift turnaround in events, my mind went blank while I cleared the dinner table. Tidy at last, I headed to bed and undressed. I didn't bother putting on my nightdress, slipped between the covers and fell asleep. I woke when Iacopo cleaved his naked body to mine.

Because of the narrowness of my bed, and, in order for neither of us to fall off it, we lay wrapped in each other's legs and arms.

Iacopo nuzzled my neck. 'I'll be gone for six months, at least.' His member hardened against my thigh. 'I shall miss you.'

I stared into the darkness not knowing what to think. Each night for the past fortnight I had joyfully accepted the union of our bodies but found something to be missing. What it was, I had no idea. Having both been first-time lovers put us on the same level. That was a good thing, I supposed. Except each time we engaged intimately, his groans of pleasure wholly exceeded mine to the point where I felt excluded. But, he was sweet, truly a handsome young man and he smelled good.

'Hortensia?'

'Yes. I'll miss you too.' *Why am I whispering?* Except for Christ eternally suffering on the cross above our heads, there was no one to hear us.

'Will you wait for my return? You won't…er…go with anyone else, will you?'

I hugged him closer. 'I'll wait for you. And no, I won't go with anyone else.'

With his manhood hard and strong, he climbed upon me again.

———————— ◆ ————————

Iacopo and Rubino left before sunrise. Throughout the rest of the day sadness, mixed with a hint of foreboding, hovered like a cloud of pesky gnats above my head.

The next afternoon, while I was preparing vegetables for dinner, Rubino and Maria entered the kitchen.

'Hortensia,' Maria said. 'Sit.'

They've found out about Iacopo! I sat and promptly Foxy's warm furry body rested upon my feet.

Rubino pushed the American's sale contract offering to purchase all the wine, towards me. 'Tomorrow, you are leaving for Naples. X marks the spot where Di Napoli, as the current head of the Angeli Estate must place his full signature.'

I glanced down and then stared hard. The original sale amount had been halved.

'Yes,' Maria said. 'We have taken half to cover what was promised to workers years ago for housing repairs and upgrades. And from this half,' she tapped a bony figure on the document, 'will come Di Napoli's share and payment to the workers for bringing in the harvest. And yours.'

Before I could get my head around all that Maria had said, my belly flip-flopped. Suddenly I was nauseous. 'But…' I wanted to gag. 'I've never travelled before. Not even out of the valley.' My voice sounded weak and feeble to my ears.

'Consider it an adventure,' Maria said. 'And, you'll get to see Naples.'

'Pietro is collecting you tomorrow morning,' Rubino said. 'He'll accompany you.'

'You mean travel by boat?'

'Yes,' Maria said. 'You'll be there by nightfall. Why? Is there a problem?'

'I'm afraid of the sea.'

The bangles clunked and stalled.

'What nonsense,' Maria said. 'The sea is lovely. You'll feel like you've known it all your life the moment you step on board.'

'Where will I stay?'

'With the nuns at The Cloister of the Poor Clares,' Rubino said.
'What's that?'

'A nunnery,' Maria said. 'It has a garden of ceramics. You will be enthralled.'

'But who will cook and keep an eye on the maids?'

Maria pointed to the American's document. 'My child, this is far more important than cooking or maids.'

'How long will I be gone?'

'As long as it takes you to get Di Napoli to sign it.' As she had with Iacopo, Maria turned into a witch. 'And, Hortensia, don't come back without it signed.'

The bangles released a warning rattle.

Despite my concerns, my nose filled with the heady smell of beeswax and my mouth filled with the taste of chocolate. *Di Napoli. God help me.*

————— ◆ —————

The journey to Naples was far less terrifying than I had imagined. The steady breeze kept the sails full and taut while the fishing boat tacked along at a good knot, hugging the shore.

Still wary, I remained sitting in the centre of the deck, nestled between fishing baskets and ropes. From my vantage point, I could see the shoreline on the left and an expanse of limpid sea, the perfect shade of cerulean blue, on my right. I focused on the land as we sailed southward.

Every so often, Pietro yelled out the name of a beach, an inlet or an island. Two hours into the journey, with an even louder voice, he shouted, 'Look to your right. In the far distance you can see the southern tip of Corsica. Right here we pass from the Tyrrhenian into the Mediterranean Sea!'

I could not tell one sea from the other. It dawned on me then how cocooned I had been living in our valley, never venturing out and terrified of getting lost. Clearly, my mother had been braver. She ventured forth and had gotten lost. Was breaking out of the cocoon the reason why she fled under the pretence of chasing butterflies? Would I ever find where she had gone? And why, oh why, did I have a bell ringing in the back of my head hinting a man was involved? My father? Had she gone to join him? Why did she not take me with her?

I promised myself that during the journey I would close my thoughts to Di Napoli and not think of him. After all, I would be seeing him soon. But, as each hour passed, my belly tightened in anticipation. Despite my best intentions, I found myself comparing him to Iacopo.

Never were two men so different. I recalled how within hours of first seeing Di Napoli, his stature was forgotten. Now that I had Iacopo to compare him to, Di Napoli's diminutive size was overwhelmingly apparent. But, despite the differences in height, Di Napoli's manhood, from what I'd seen when he had been coupling with Mistress Letizia and Bea, far exceeded Iacopo's. A thrilling shiver ran up my spine.

Several hours later I awoke to the sun, cut in half by the horizon. Water lapped the sides of the boat moored in the Port of Naples.

'Hortensia,' Pietro shouted. '*Andiamo*. Let's go.'

I dragged myself up, straightened my clothes and followed Pietro down the gangplank.

'Jump on,' he said.

My belly knotted as I eyed the hired Vespa.

'There's no time to lose,' Pietro yelled. 'Saint Clare's Convent closes its doors at nine o'clock. We don't want to find ourselves on the streets. Not in that area.'

Realising I'd worried about the sea voyage unnecessarily, I shoved my fear of riding the Vespa aside and perched stiffly on the passenger seat sitting side-saddle.

'If you don't want to fall off,' Pietro shouted, 'I suggest you hold onto me.'

My grip around his waist tightened as the scooter pulled away. I was surprised at the hidden firmness and strength of his body, in stark contrast to his wrinkled, sunburnt face and coarse hands. Perhaps he wasn't as old as I'd thought.

All accounts had been true. Naples was a fiercely dirty and chaotic city. We zipped through narrow cobbled streets, past tiny doorways and under buildings whose balconies almost touched, and lines of washing fluttered above our heads. In the distance, strings of home lights decorated the calm and benevolent volcano's lower slopes. At every turn, there were more fearless pedestrians and riotous traffic. Clouds of mostly foreign noises and jumbled odours battered me anew.

However, it was what the women were wearing that grabbed my attention most of all. Flouncy, layered skirts, plain and polka-dotted in colours that rivalled the rainbow. Broad and buckled belts, cinched at the waist, buttoned cardigans over which lay single-stranded pearls, lacy, see-through gloves, and heeled shoes. For the first time in my life, I experienced a new feeling: shame. What must I look like in my ankle boots, long straight dress and shawl?

By the time Pietro pulled up outside the convent's wrought-iron gates, the upper half of the sun had disappeared. He tugged a long chain and, in the distance a bell rang.

A nun, whose habit blended with the descending dark, hurried down the colonnaded path.

'Welcome,' she said. The gate opened. Reaching out, she pulled me into the confines of the convent walls. The gate shut. After a swift turn of a key as long as her forearm, she took me by the elbow and steered me along the path. I turned around, I couldn't see anything, but heard Pietro pull away into the darkness.

'He's staying at the monastery on the other side of the church. I'm Sister Peta. There's a meal for you in your cell. Eat. Go to sleep. You'll be up at four thirty for morning prayer.'

Not even for my weekly bake, did I get up that early.

Our footsteps echoed down a passage. I counted the doors. Sister Peta stopped midway, at door number twelve, opened it and stood aside for me to enter. She lit a match and held it to the wick of a candle stub. It revealed the inside of a windowless cell. A single bed, narrower than mine at home, stood in a corner, two hooks on the wall, one empty, the other upon which draped what I thought was a blanket. Another eternal suffering Christ on a wooden cross hung above the bed. A chamber pot sat in the corner. On a small table stood a jar of water, a bowl of soup and a slice of bread.

'Get up at the first bell. Put on the habit.' She gestured to the hooks on the wall. 'On the second, exit your cell and fall into line.'

She shut the door and was gone. The candle flame spluttered. I hurriedly ate the meagre meal before the cell plunged into darkness.

———————— ◆ ————————

The next morning, I woke at the first clanging toll, which caused the brick walls to thrum. As ordered, and in pitch darkness, I pulled on the habit. At the second toll, I stepped out into the passage in haste. Not so much to be on time, but to prevent my eardrums from splitting.

Matins took forever. Certainly, there had never been so much standing and kneeling at the Mass held on Sundays in our valley church. Not even at Easter or Christmas Mass.

Walking in pairs we entered the dining room, my belly growling. Laid out with precision, a bowl of polenta, milk, honey and a pear sat, ready for each nun. Ignoring my belly's desire for croissants filled with ricotta and blueberry jam and a large mug of hot milky coffee, I ate and gave thanks I had only to suffer one more of these breakfasts.

Without any visible or audible sign, we stood as one and still in silence, exited the dining room. I saw a clock and as I drew closer made out the hands. It was only six a.m. We entered another room whose glass doors overlooked the garden. As the day brightened, the doors were unlocked and swung open.

The nuns dispersed, randomly to walk, sit or stand – but all remained in silent contemplation, with their rosaries entwined around their fingers. As the sun crept higher and the shadows retreated, the cloistered garden along whose pillared walkway I traversed the night before became clear.

The dome of Santa Chiara rose higher than the walls of the convent. But these buildings, and the monastery, equal in size to the convent on the opposite side of the church, reflected a citadel, built, I later found out, in a style called Gothic.

Only the blind could have missed the glorious hand-painted tiles covering knee-high walls, benches, chairs and the columns. Each section of individual tiles told a story from the Bible. Maria had been right. I was enchanted with the garden within a garden, detailed in intricate, polished colour.

I found an unoccupied seat and sat upon its smooth, tiled surface. My thoughts slowed to where I could hold each one, turn and inspect them from all sides. Former memories traipsed across the inside of my forehead. I moved the pain-filled ones aside and spent more time on the pleasurable ones. The event that eclipsed all memories, and was neither pleasurable nor happy, was meeting Di Napoli.

As clear and peaceful as the garden was, I believed my soul was most assuredly affixed to his. *Is this love? Love for a man? Is that why I cannot get him out of my thoughts?*

In the form of a ray of sunshine that at first lightly crept upon my skin, and, as it heated, penetrated to my core, came the answer. It had the sweetest voice I'd ever heard, made, I was sure, by the collective Voices of God's angels.

'What you feel is not love, but…' The ray's warmth intensified. 'Morbid infatuation.'

I sensed it may be even worse than that. Around Di Napoli, I lost all reason and logic. I was fatally and helplessly attracted to him. 'I feel I am his puppet to do with as he pleases.'

'Correct,' the Voices said.

'What am I to do?'

'Resist him.'

'I want to but I can't.'

'Then there is nothing to do but be his puppet until you resist him.'

I swallowed hard. 'What about love?'

'Have no fear. When it comes, you will know.'

As the midday bell rang, the sun's ray vanished, knocking me back into reality. Just as fast, I forgot the conversation with the collective voices. The nuns reassembled, I fell into line and we headed indoors.

Lunch was a simple plate of pasta with spicy tomato *ragù,* fragrant with basil. Dessert reminded me acutely of my mother – a Bavarian cream custard thickened with cornstarch and sugar I'd last eaten on the day she abandoned me. My former memory and current taste coalesced. They were precisely the same.

Sister Peta appeared from nowhere. She bent and whispered in my ear. 'You have an appointment at three thirty this afternoon. Be ready.'

For a moment, my lunch threatened to escape from my mouth. Entering my cell, I found my clothes had disappeared. *Am I to meet Di Napoli wearing a nun's garb?*

A light tap at the door before it opened.

'Ready?'

I nodded and with the American's wine sale document needing Di Napoli's signature tucked into a conveniently large and hidden pocket under the habit, I followed Sister Peta.

After more twists and turns than my brain could keep up with, we came to a door set into the garden's wall. We entered, and Sister Peta closed the door behind us. We stood squashed together with only a tiny patch of blue sky high above our heads.

'This leads directly into the vestment chamber off one of the chapels within Santa Chiara. I will return in an hour.' Using both hands, Sister Peta twisted the dinner-plate-sized iron ring. She wedged her shoulder against the door and gave it a hefty push. The hinges squeaked.

I stepped through the door from light into darkness. Immediately, my nose caught the smell of pomade. My body turned into hazelnut chocolate, ready to be devoured.

Maria held my head as I retched into the basin. 'Tell me the child is Iacopo's, not Di Napoli's.'

   In my head, images of both men's faces, side by side, instantly sprang up. 'I cannot … I don't know.'

  The bangles whirred once and stopped.

  'No matter. We'll present Iacopo as the father. Do you hear me, Hortensia?'

  I threw up again.

  'Horten–'

  'Yes.' My voice squeaked like a mouse caught in a trap.

  'Write and let him know.' She released my head. 'It will give him another reason to conclude business and return.'

  I rinsed my mouth and spat into the basin.

  'Oh, you will give birth to a fine, strong son.'

  A boy. Dear God, did you hear that? I'm going to have a baby boy. Peace, so sweet, so exquisite filled my heart and caused tears of joy to bathe my eyes. Immediately, rage, which rivaled the fiercest tempest swept through me. *If you can tell me the sex of my unborn child, why won't you tell me where my mother is and who is my father? Or, at least, tell me who my son's father is?*

As those unguarded thoughts erupted, Maria's turned-in eyes jittered in time to the bangles' furious tinny chain-rattles. Her gaze pinned me fast without so much as a bat of her eyelids.

'This may surprise you,' she said. 'But even I have limits. Regarding your parents: things reveal themselves in their own good time. But right now, our valley's future is hanging in the balance. Do not wreck all the work Rubino, Anna and I have put into this. Never mention the fact that Di Napoli could be the father of your child. From here on, banish all thought of him forever. Understand?'

Feeling wretched, lonely and as forlorn as the futtocks of a wrecked ship scattered wide and far, I nodded.

'Hopefully, the augury at your son's birth will not scupper our plans either.' Maria's gaze released me, and she turned to leave.

To my surprise, she faced me again, her voice softened. 'My dear, remember, you are not ill, just pregnant. Tomorrow take up your duties. I guarantee you will feel better. And anyhow, be grateful. Violent morning sickness is a sign of a healthy pregnancy.'

She left. The bedroom door closed with a click.

Sliding down into my bed, I caught sight of the eternal suffering Christ nailed to his wooden cross, looking upon me from his position on the wall.

'No thanks to you.' I pulled the cover over my head and fell asleep. Like almost always when I dreamed, Di Napoli took centre stage. This time I dreamed of our first encounter in Santa Chiara, the church in Naples.

◆

'Hortensia, I need time.' Di Napoli's rich, hypnotic voice washed over me. 'It's unreasonable to expect me to sign a document concocted by a mere farmer who knows nothing about money matters. Let alone that witch who almost killed me.'

Despite the too-cool, dank air of the silent vestment chamber lit by a tallow candle, my body heat increased as blood pounded through my temples. I could not refute his statement about Maria. He was correct. She and his aunt, Anna, the cook, had almost killed him. But his words regarding Rubino caused me to bristle. *You mean the income for life, procured through marriage, arranged by him!*

I struggled to prevent a single word pass my lips, whether to defend Rubino or for fear of letting slip the true value of the wine sale to the Americans. Rubino's words echoed in my head. 'If Di Napoli knows, he'll demand a greater share, or worse, reject the sale outright.'

'What guarantee is there after signing this document I shall receive any money at all?' Di Napoli said. 'No. Rubino must demonstrate his goodwill by paying my share first. Hortensia, write and tell him.'

Where my response came from I had no idea, but it was as clear as if *avvocato* Fini had spoken the words directly into my ear. I lowered my voice. 'The Angeli Estate has no money. Only once you have signed, can the payment for the wine sale be transferred into the estate's bank account. Then, and only then, can you receive your share.'

We stared long and hard at each other. Neither of us moved. In my head I heard the bangles chime, and counted in time. Upon the thirtieth, I reached out to pocket the document. 'Very well then. I'll be on my way.'

Di Napoli beat me to it. He caught my hand and triumphant held it up in the air. Maria's ominous warning accompanied by the bangles pinging repeated in my head: 'Don't come back without it signed.'

I held out the pen with my free hand.

Di Napoli ignored the offered pen. Instead he chuckled, deep and low and drew me to him. 'Not so fast…'

In that moment the bubble, the fantasy world I had created, shattered. Naivety evaporated. Understanding dawned. I had been sent, not as the messenger, but thrown like the sacrificial lamb between lions, intent on achieving their own opposing goals.

Di Napoli enfolded me in a crushing hold. The sudden lack of breath caused my limbs to turn to jelly. At the same time, a pinprick of awareness lit up in the back of my head. *No matter what, this lamb will survive.*

Di Napoli stuck his tongue in my mouth. Or was it a piece of chocolate?

Then, in order to survive, the lamb surrendered.

L ike a hunting dog shaking its body free of river water, I shook myself awake, chasing away the memory of my first encounter in the vestment chamber with Di Napoli.

To my relief, the sun was up.

As Maria predicted, I felt better and miraculously, I was hungry. Encouraged, I bounced out of bed and headed into the kitchen. The coffee pot soon bubbled, the hot milk frothed, and my belly groaned with eagerness. I drank two large cups of milky coffee into which I dipped and savoured several hazelnut biscuits. Breakfast over, I reclaimed my position as housekeeper and cook at the Angeli Estate.

But first I had to familiarise myself with the new electric stove that had been installed during my six-week absence, along with learning to flick wall switches, which turned electric bulbs dangling from the ceiling, on and off. While the rest of Italy had benefitted from electricity for years, our valley had only just become a recipient of such a wonder.

I assembled the ingredients to prepare pasta for lunch and kneaded enough dough for bread and three persimmon tarts. Also, following the lingering memory of the Bavarian dessert at the Poor Clare's Convent, I made custard infused with the flavourful seeds scraped from the inside of a leathery brown vanilla bean.

With an added spurt of energy, I chopped vegetables and set them simmering, to which I would later add green fava beans and salted pork trotters, parsley, garlic, sage and oil. Soon, cross breezes laden with cooking and baking fragrances swept over the heads of valley workers, who were paring last season's vines.

A chorus of protests rose from the terraces. 'Aw, you're killing us, Hortensia.'

I giggled for the first time since Iacopo left for America. The realisation that I had never giggled or laughed around Di Napoli left me dazed like a bird flown into a windowpane.

When the ribbons of pasta started to harden, and the meat *ragù* in the cast-iron pot turned thick, rich and sweet, I heard the changing gears of Pietro's van coming our way.

My heart moved, like a butterfly testing its wings in slow motion before taking its first flight. *Is it too soon to expect a letter from Iacopo?*

'Hortensia.' Pietro stamped his feet upon the kitchen step, leaving sea sand boot prints.

He held a basket of fish. I had forgotten it was Friday, the day we always ate fish.

'I bring you–' He faltered and looked at me carefully. 'You look well.'

'Why shouldn't I be?' *Even if I am pregnant.*

'What I mean is you look exceptionally well.'

Encased in crinkled, sunburnt pouches, his cobalt blue eyes – I had learned from our voyage, they changed, reflecting the colour of the sea – appraised my body from the feet up, reminding me of how Di Napoli had looked at me the first time.

Maria materialized from nowhere. 'What did you bring Hortensia?'

'Er... the beautiful, exquisite Angelica Barberi...' Pietro faltered again. 'Has...has requested... Hortensia's help since her Ligurian maid and cook have returned to their homes...'

The bangles kept time and Maria's boots beat out a victory jig. *'Finalmente!'*

'...and if Hortensia would supply her and the ailing groom, the slightly redeemed *brutto,* ugly Claudio Trianni, with a few dishes each week.'

The tintinnabulation changed tone and sounded like Maria's pygmy goats' bells all ringing at once: this was important news. The request represented the first break in the silence that had held both households in a state of non-communication for years, the reason for which, no one had yet told me.

Pietro cleared his throat. 'Angelica Barberi has learned no one produces dishes the way Hortensia can. She is desperate to get Claudio Trianni to eat and keep up his strength. At least until after she has given birth to their child.'

'We'll consider it.' Maria left the kitchen in a billow of black cloth.

I had no doubt she would add this information to her stewing pot.

Pietro glanced over his shoulder to make sure Maria was no longer in earshot. And to make doubly sure, he lowered his voice. 'There's something else.'

I reached for the corked bottle of chilled wine standing on the table in preparation for lunch. By way of silent thanks, his mouth split into a grin that displayed his gums. He took the bottle with one hand, and with the other held out a letter. I slipped it into my apron's pocket without looking at it.

Pietro held up one hand to his mouth, simulated locking his lips and throwing away the key. Without another word he left, clutching the bottle.

'Hortensia,' Maria said at the end of lunch. 'I'll take care of the dishes. You have a rest and later, write to Iacopo.'

In the privacy of my room, I retrieved the letter from my apron pocket and turned it over. My heart broke into a gallop. The letter wasn't from Iacopo.

◆

That evening, streaks of orange and purple lit the autumnal sunset sky. Rubino entered the kitchen. He too had received a letter. He held up one hand and said, 'HA MER E KA'.

The bangles rallied and sparked with anticipation as Maria slit open the envelope addressed to our six-month-old master, Massimiliano Di Napoli, my godson and heir to the Angeli Estate.

Maria pulled out a sheath of papers searching for the flimsy American bank transfer. 'It looks in order, but for less money than it should be.' Maria handed the copy to me. 'What do you think?'

None of us read nor spoke English, so we could only go by the numerals on the transfer. That alone was interesting. The document had been printed by a typewriter: a machine we'd heard of, but not yet seen, despite it having been invented a century before by a Torinese some two-hundred kilometres away.

'Here's a note from Iacopo,' Rubino said. 'Your eyesight is better than ours, read it.'

I held the single sheet up to the light and read his spidery scrawl.

'*Greetings. As you will see by the bank transfer, the American has still not made payment in full. He is withholding one-third of the last payment of the wine purchase, and I quote, "…only upon delivery of top quality oil, full and final payment for the wine shipment will be made".*

'*Until then, he intends keeping me here, too. I cannot complain of this arrangement as there is a lot for me to learn. Specifically, blending.*

'*Write me your price and the quantity of oil that can be supplied, and I will negotiate the best possible terms for us all. Cordially, Iacopo.*'

A dreadful silence followed. I glanced up.

The angle of Maria's turned-in eyes increased.

Rubino sat still. More than ever he resembled the solid trunk of a giant chestnut. Three minutes passed before he broke the silence. 'Negotiate the best possible terms? We don't have the oil.'

The bangles called for attention by giving a strident ping.

'We will,' Maria said. 'Soon.'

I was sure my face reflected Rubino's surprise.

Maria turned her attention to me. 'Tomorrow, take a plate of pastries, a pot of rich broth and one other dish to Trianni and his wife. Include a couple of vintage bottles. Tell her it will be your pleasure to do as she asks. Get Arturo to drive you. Deliver it to her personally.'

While listening to Maria's instructions, I wondered how long it would be before Iacopo's return.

There was an almost imperceptible bangle ting.

'Have you written to him?'

Maria had clearly read my thoughts. 'Yes. But the letter's not yet posted.'

'Don't post it until I say.'

12

The following morning, wrapped against the cold autumn wind, and with all Maria had instructed me to take, I clambered aboard the cart.

'Ready?' Arturo flashed me a dazzling smile.

I nodded. My heart lurched in time with the cart. It was my first visit to the Trianni Estate; forbidden territory until now.

We arrived on the valley floor and passed through hamlets of clustered houses, built just so for safety, and with no visible division separating one crumbling stone façade from another. However, all roofs sported new terracotta tiles, and the repainting of doors and shutters was underway. Repairs were possible thanks to the sale of wine contract Rubino, Maria and, posthumously, Anna had secured.

Instead of continuing along the Etruscan track, straight as a ruler-drawn line leading to the opaline sea, Arturo turned the donkey left. The cart rumbled as its wheels traversed the *Frigido's* pebble-lined bed with barely a splash. Soon, winter rain would deluge the valley, and the swollen river would roar its challenge, daring all to cross it.

The riverbank gave way to dense woods swamped in autumn's mantle of reds and browns, after which the slope rapidly inclined and the woods thinned. The donkey's flanks expanded and heaved with exertion and the cart creaked in protest.

We encountered the first line of the ancient olive trees, standing like armoured knights guarding the perimeter of the Trianni Estate. Thereafter, we passed rows upon rows of twisted and gnarled trunks barely able to support the weight of cascades of pearly-black fruit begging to be picked before they withered.

I shuddered and pulled my shawl tighter. Though it was ludicrous, I compared the olive grove to my child. A profound emotion from the bed of the deepest ocean rose and all but swept me away. I embraced Nature's maternal need to protect the child I carried. Then I recalled my vow. I would care for and raise him to a healthy and happy being, at any cost. And never abandon him. Not for anything.

The Trianni's crenulated tower came into focus. The romantic dream I once had of myself as Caroline, the damsel in the song *Marechiaro,* being serenaded by an admirer playing his mandolin bloomed. *I'm pregnant. What am I thinking?* The dream evaporated.

With the bitter taste of regret in my mouth, I turned my attention to the crumbling arches and balconies. Despite its impressive size, the villa was dwarfed by the oil mill.

I glanced through the double-storey-high arched doorway leading into the cavernous mill and saw it contained not one, but two sets of stone wheel presses. The smaller press would be turned by a blindfolded donkey. The larger press would be turned by an ox, who, for some reason never got sick walking in a circle.

The presses stood dormant, with no hint of donkey or ox. The debris of broken farming implements littered the vast earth-hardened floor. Layers of dust covered the stacked oil barrels that were, I was sure, empty.

The cart came to a stop at the kitchen door. A few hens scratched in what ought to have been a vegetable garden, brimming with orange pumpkins, black kale, red-stemmed chard, purple broccoli and bushels of deep-green Brussel sprouts.

The door stood open and with Anna, vaporous and spectral beside me, I walked into the Trianni kitchen. We gasped in dismay at the kitchen's disgraceful disarray. *No wonder Claudio Trianni has given up eating.*

And then the rumour was confirmed. A heavenly creature sat at the table, immobile.

'Hortensia?'

I placed the heavy basket on the edge of the kitchen table. 'Yes.'

As Bernardino Luini's "Portrait of a Woman", a copy of which I had seen in an art book in the Angeli library, came to life, I was reminded, and ashamed, of how plain I was.

Both Luini's painted subject and Angelica Barberi had light copper hair that fell around their shoulders in long ringlets. In the former twice-widowed Angelica Barberi's case, her forehead was high – our valley attributed that to intelligence – and her skin was creamy unblemished, rosy on the cheekbones. Both shared similarly large almond-shaped eyes, the colour of green opals with iridescent gold flecks. The line of Angelica Barberi's naturally arched eyebrows tapered down the ridge of her nose and ended in a perfect tip. Her top lip looked much like Cupid's bow and the bottom lip plump, inviting and gracefully curved.

She wore an intricate embroidered robe I thought too light for the season. But then, perhaps such beings had no need for earthly comforts. The heavenly creature rose and with hands outstretched, glided towards me.

'Help me,' she said.

--------- ◆ ---------

My housekeeper's instincts kicked in, and by mid-morning I had cleaned those parts of the Trianni kitchen needed for preparation and cooking. It would take an army of maids to achieve the same order that reigned throughout Villa Angeli.

At the last stroke of twelve, Angelica Barberi entered the kitchen with her third husband, the infamous Claudio Trianni, leaning upon her arm. They took their places at the far end of the table, which I had laid with etched glasses, heavy silver cutlery, a linen cloth and napkins.

I served the bone broth first, deep-yellow and dotted with parsley. With a good sprinkle of grated *Parmigiano-Reggiano* over the soup, the alchemy was instant, enhancing the aroma so, my belly groaned.

I retired to stand at the other end of the table and found myself mesmerised, not by the lovely Angelica, but by Claudio Trianni. He bent his head, bald but for a few straggly hairs, over the bowl and inhaled. He stayed in that position for a while, and I fleetingly imagined he was lost in the memory when just such a bowl of soup had been set before him.

With the spoon trembling in his frail hand, he struggled to bring the liquid to his mouth. After the first taste, colour flushed his face, and his hand grew steady.

By the end of the course, Claudio Trianni had gained enough strength to take note of his surroundings. His face registered subtle surprise as he found himself in the kitchen and his eyes widened when they came to rest upon me.

'Fa...Fagio...?' Claudio Trianni stuttered.

I bit my lip. 'I'm sorry. I did not think to prepare beans.'

He shook his head slowly. Perhaps I had jumped to the wrong conclusion. Had he meant the fact they were eating in the kitchen? 'I'm sorry. I was unable to prepare the dining room in time for lunch.' I placed the dish on the table that had brought me the recognition of being a good cook – a casserole of tender rabbit pieces and olives with a dollop of stirred-in, finely chopped and macerated-in-salt lemon pieces. I lifted the lid, releasing another rich yet altogether different aroma to the soup.

'I'd...be the happiest man...' the scarecrow thin Claudio Trianni rasped, 'if my beautiful wife gives me a son and I could eat this food at this table until the day I die.'

'Hortensia,' the ethereal Angelica said, 'what will it take for you to come and work here?'

I needed no help. The ready-formed phrase was waiting on the tip of my tongue. 'I'll come if permission is granted to reopen the olive grove for harvesting.'

Claudio Trianni began to cough and choke – on the rabbit or at the mention of olives, I did not know which.

Fearful I would be the cause of his death, my throat seized until Claudio Trianni stopped coughing. Like an incoming tide surging its way up the beach, relief flooded me as he nodded his head, signifying his acceptance of my terms.

Another source of income had been secured for the valley workers in exchange for which I had simply swapped my servitude from Villa Angeli to Villa Trianni.

———————— ◆ ————————

I clambered aboard the donkey cart.

'Ready?' Arturo asked.

'Yes.'

He flicked the reins over the donkey's back and flashed me a quick, bright smile. He had an enviable set of evenly matched teeth.

But not even the flash of those lovely teeth could prevent the grey cloud that settled upon my head during the return journey to Villa Angeli. When I entered the kitchen I found Maria had already gathered my belongings. Clearly, there was no going back.

'Are you packed?' she asked as Rubino entered the kitchen.

'Almost.' Rubino took his place at the dinner table.

Before I could ask Maria if she intended to move to the Trianni Estate too, the sound of Pietro's van could be heard in the distance. Its clattering engine strained, which meant he was carrying a passenger.

'Lay another two places,' Maria said, 'and then sit down.'

I sat. Rubino placed one large weather-beaten hand over one of mine. This was serious. My ears begin to hurt with the strain of waiting to hear what Maria had to say.

'Hortensia, I'll get straight to it. Given yesterday's letter, there is no way Iacopo will return from America in time to marry you before your pregnancy shows. Don't repeat your mother's mistake. For your child's sake, you must marry.'

I wanted to pursue this line of conversation, but the pain – at the very mention of my mother – that rose in my heart was too much. 'My letter to Iacopo?'

'Destroyed.'

The van's engine cut. The voices of Don Antonio and Pietro carried through the window.

The cloud turned from grey to charcoal. No need to ask who my husband was to be. The memory of his firm waist under my clasped arms while sitting on the back of the scooter in Naples flashed into my head.

'Does he know I'm…?'

'Yes.'

'Am I…am I to share my bed with him?'

'It's the least you can do. After all, he is offering you and your child a lifeline.'

'And he's prepared to marry spoiled goods and be responsible for a child that is not his. Why?'

'He likes and knows you. Besides, he's never been married and now is as good a time as any.'

The cloud turned black. *How will I get around his having no teeth, and dead fish-stinking breath?*

In the seconds it took for my head and heart to process this information, silence reigned.

Maria pointed a bony finger in the air. 'He makes only one request of you.'

I held Maria's gaze by focusing on the bump in her hooked nose.

'From this moment forward, you never betray him with another man.'

Sexual relations. Argh! That was the very last thing on my mind. I nodded.

'One more thing, Hortensia. Remember, no matter what happens, now only the three of us are party to past and current events. Let it remain so.'

———————— ◆ ————————

After rudimentary greetings, we entered the library where Maria had lit the fire and the wall sconces, rendering the room in a soft glow. I studiously ignored the four-seater couch where Di Napoli had once wooed Mistress Letizia, strumming the mandolin and singing the words to Salvatore Di Giacomo's song, *Marechiaro*.

Pietro and I stood close to the waist-high, free-standing *capodimonte* porcelain vase which was filled with orange chrysanthemums, sprigs of lilac heather and lengths of yellowed vines trailing to the floor. In addition to having served as a baptismal font it now served as a marriage altar.

From the start of the ceremony, my feet warmed. I did not panic. It was not the burning heat I'd experienced when I had first seen Di Napoli and Mistress Letizia coupling upon the gilded wall mirror laid on the floor, but the warmth from Foxy's furry body sitting upon my feet. Or, was it the steady comfort I had always associated with Pietro?

'The ring?' Don Antonio asked, bringing me back to the present.

Pietro unclipped the gold horn suspended on a chain from around his neck, and placed it around mine.

Don Antonio did not skip a beat. He had married couples with far less, and sometimes with nothing to exchange at all.

I was strangely affected by this gesture. I knew Pietro, like other fishermen, wore the horn called a *cornetto* to ward off the *malocchio*, the evil eye, to protect him. Especially when he was out at sea.

After the shortest marriage ceremony ever, Rubino and Maria signed the marriage certificate as witnesses and we returned to the kitchen. Rubino uncorked a bottle of *Prosecco*, filled our glasses and toasted, saying, 'To the bride and groom – may you both be blessed with health and joy.'

'And wealth and freedom,' Maria added.

It was a simple meal and soon over.

Arturo and the donkey were roused from their slumbers to drive Don Antonio home. Rubino retired to his quarters above the stable. Maria walked along the moonlit contour path home. Though it was a windless night, I knew her cloak would billow out behind her and she'd call to the goats, 'I'm coming. Mamma's coming home,' warning them of her arrival.

Pietro and I retired to my room, where Pietro did what grooms do to brides upon their wedding night. All the while I tried not to inhale his stinking breath.

That said, he was vigorous, gentle and patient, making sure he satisfied me before taking care of himself. It was the complete opposite to my experiences with Iacopo, a boisterous pup with no end to his energy. And a whole other world to Di Napoli, whose desires plumbed the depths of terrifying devil-darkness.

Is this all my life will ever amount to? I sighed, squaring my shoulders with more bravado than I felt. *I'll make the best of it.*

———————— ◆ ————————

In the morning before leaving for the Trianni Estate, Pietro tied two ends of the sheet to the back of his van so all who we passed could bear witness to the proof of my former chastity. Only, it was the bed sheet upon which I had lain with Iacopo and hidden under my mattress.

As we drove through the hamlets, Pietro slowed, honking the van's trumpet horn. Residents poured out from their houses, abandoned their fields and gardens, and walked or half ran to keep up with us.

'We didn't think you had it in you, fishmonger,' one of the men yelled. The rest of them grinned, and some slapped the three-wheeler's metal roof.

Women trilled their congratulations, *'Auguri!'* Some older women looked at me with tired, knowing eyes. My past rushed towards me, and images in chronologic order paraded by.

My mother, for reasons still to be discovered, had abandoned me. I'd witnessed the death of a maid and cut a child free from its dead mother's stomach. Freely given myself to one man, was taken by another, one of whom was the father of my unborn child, then sold myself into servitude for an olive oil sale to benefit our community, and entered an arranged marriage with a third man – in order to protect my child.

No wonder I felt as tired as those women whose knowledgeable and pitiful stares sought mine, even though I was only sixteen years old.

13

On the first day of my marriage I took charge of the Trianni household, and valley workers under the direction of Rubino flooded the olive grove. It was also the start of the first *la raccolta delle olive* in decades.

But before the harvest could commence, workers cleared thorn-studded brambles as thick as a man's wrist. Rubino's forehead furrows deepened. *'Dio mio.* This thick bush is fit only for wild pigs.'

'Palmo a palmo,' responded the men, in Tuscan dialect. They cut paths that measured a hand-palm distance apart, one at a time, clearing the area surrounding and under the trees. As children and mothers nimbly picked fallen olives, the air filled with yells and expletives. Without exception, everyone suffered painful pricks from those vicious thorns. By noon several donkey carts were filled to the brim with the onyx-black fruit. Later, when the sun began its descent, the mounds of brush were lit sending pencil-straight smoke columns into the air.

While the land around the olive trees were cleared, another gang swarmed the dusty mill. They scrubbed the crushers' stones clean, swept the vast floor and broke apart cracked barrels for firewood.

Rubino appeared to be in all places at once, including repairing the non-functioning stone crushers' mechanisms. He had a spring in his step that hid his age. But come evening his old joints would protest so, it would take his breath away. I made a mental note to ask Maria for advice on how to relieve his ailments. No sooner was the thought completed, the bangles tinkled and Maria appeared.

She placed a sack on the kitchen table. 'He will need to soak in a bath of warm water and salt.' She looked around. Her eyelashes batted, revealing her alarm. 'I had no inkling of the state this villa has fallen into. You're going to need help.'

'I can't. Angelica won't have anyone else in the villa.'

'Ah. Yes, because of her daughters. Have you met them?'

'No. But I glimpsed the elder one staring out the window, standing statue-still.'

Both Maria and the bangles harrumphed. 'The younger one?'

'She sleeps during the day.'

'So, it's true.'

I wanted to ask what was true, but Maria returned her attention to the sack on the table.

'Hortensia, don't get this salt mixed with the table variety.'

I knew Maria poured a solution of this mineral salt on her goats' hooves should they begin to rot. But I had no idea it would also reduce joint swelling. 'How much am I to use?'

'Half, if you fill the copper bath that has come out of the mill.'

I glanced over her shoulder, out the kitchen door and into the courtyard. Two workers were wrestling the oval-shaped bath into the stables.

'Now, let's write a note to Iacopo.'

Since my marriage, my heart barely moved when I heard his name. I dusted my floured hands, sat down and took the pen and paper from her.

'Write: Rubino estimates one hundred and fifty thousand litres filling three thousand fifty-litre barrels. Shipment arranged for month's end. Advise your best price.' Maria signed the note and folded it while I wrote out the American address on the envelope.

'Give this to Pietro tonight to take to the post office on the way to harbour tomorrow morning.'

'Tonight?'

'Yes, my dear.'

My throat tightened. Like the spark of a match, the question flew out of my mouth. 'What remedy for Pietro's breath?'

From under the folds of her cloak, Maria withdrew another, smaller sack and handed it to me. I recognised the light seed as fennel for his breath. 'The dark seed?'

'Milk thistle for his liver. Make sure he swallows a tablespoon after each meal. Get him to stop drinking then the problem of his rotting organs will subside resolving his bad breath. If he doesn't, his bad breath will get worse, his organs will fail, and he'll die. Sooner than you think.' She turned on her heel and was gone.

I froze. *Has Maria just given me the knowledge to end my husband's life?* I reached for and touched the gold horn around my neck.

Considering the implications of Maria's advice caused me to sweat more than cleaning the disgraceful kitchen. I prepared lunch for Claudio Trianni and Angelica Barberi. Indeed, I was grateful that for once my carousel-turning thoughts of Di Napoli had been interrupted. The macabre idea of Pietro's death at my hands was in stark contrast to the excited hoots and hollers generated by the cleaners in the mill next door, and the valley workers chatter, floating up hill from the grove below.

At the first stroke of noon from the bell in the church tower, Claudio Trianni, leaning on his wife's arm, entered the kitchen. They sat at the far end of the table.

I served the first course: *tagliatelle* tossed in a light cream sauce with raw-grated black truffles and a twist of cracked pepper.

With his eyes closed, Claudio Trianni inhaled the earthy and nutty aroma with studied concentration. He dabbed his tearing eyes and without a word picked up and twirled the fork at the outer edges of the pasta. With his hand trembling less than yesterday, he raised the fork to his mouth.

I was sure that, in addition to its smell, the taste of the undisputed king of pasta dishes was nudging to the surface more of his forgotten memories. Perhaps happy times.

The workers had also stopped for lunch. I knew they would be eating traditional field-hands lunch consisting of slices of wild-boar salami, semi-soft pecorino cheese made from full-fat ewe's milk, pickled pearl onions and hard-crust bread washed down with a tumbler or two of *Sangiovese.* If the mill's stone wheels could be made to function, we would all dribble thick, bright green olive oil over bread and raw vegetables at the next meal. I swallowed in anticipation, knowing how the aromatic, rich and smooth oil would nip the back of my throat as it passed.

That evening, Claudio Trianni and the exquisite Angelica retired with a bowl of hot *minestrone* in their bellies to anchor them to their bed – an old wives' remedy to prevent sleep-walking – to which I had added green beans, diced and cooked until butter-soft.

Disappointment, because Claudio Trianni had not noticed the beans, added to my exhaustion, and I did not hear the clatter of the van's engine announcing Pietro's arrival.

He looked tired as he entered the kitchen. 'Where are we to sleep?'

I waved my hand towards a door at the back of the kitchen. It led into three rooms which would serve as our accommodation. The first room had a small wood stove and two broken chairs. The second, smaller room had a wrought-iron bed that occupied most of the space. On the bare mattress lay a pile of dusty linen and several blankets. A narrow door led into the bathroom.

After the final cleaning of the kitchen, I entered the bedroom. To my surprise, Pietro prepared the bed. He took my hand and he led me to it. He eased my feet from my lace-up boots, untied my apron and guided me onto the bed. As if I were a child, he drew the covers up to my chin and kissed me upon the forehead. I fell asleep in the time it takes to snuff a candle.

Later, I woke to the sound of the donkey's steady plod walking the tight circle, and the rumble of the two stone wheels grinding against each other. The smaller stone crusher was working. I rose, pulled on my boots, threw a shawl over my shoulders and passed through the sitting room. The repaired broken chairs stood in front of the grate in which embers glowed.

In the kitchen, I shifted the pots I'd filled with water the night before to stand over the stove's direct heat, added wood and then opened the kitchen door.

Lamplight blazed, and the unmistakable, pungent fragrance of pressed olive oil wafted out from the double-storey-high arched doorway.

Hobbling with tiredness and likely pain, Rubino led a blindfolded donkey. Walking behind the donkey, Pietro poured a continuous flow of black fruit through a funnel to fall upon the bottom stone. I got dizzy just watching.

'How much longer?' I called from my position under the arched doorway.

The two men looked up. It occurred to me then that Rubino and Pietro were related. Uncle and nephew, perhaps? I'd ask later.

'Half an hour,' Rubino said.

Concern flooded Pietro's face. 'Hortensia, you're still tired. Go back to sleep.'

Wholly surprised at his response, I pretended I didn't hear and returned to the kitchen. My heart was aflame with appreciation and my eyelids pricked with tears of gratitude. Never before had anyone considered my well-being. The thought that he would make a fine husband after all flashed into and out of my head.

One by one, I carried the pots across the courtyard into the stable and poured the hot water into the dulled copper bath. I added half the sack of salt and with the handle of a broomstick gave it a good stir, set the thin metal cover over the bath to retain the heat and left.

The grinding rumble stopped. The first stage in the transformation from solid to liquid was over. Again, I stood under the mill's archway. Rubino was unshackling the donkey, and Pietro had just finished pouring the last of the liquid into holding barrels where the water would sink and the oil would rise. 'Rubino, your bath is ready. Pietro, attend to the donkey.'

Neither man protested. Rubino leaned heavily upon Pietro, as he led the donkey to the stable next door.

'Pietro.' Men and donkey halted. 'After Rubino, you bathe.' After all, if they were related, what difference did it make? Men did not suffer the squeamishness women did about bathing in another's bath water. The trio exited the mill.

Ordering Pietro to bathe in the restorative salt water was the only way I could thank him for his kindness and acknowledgement of my tiredness. I felt a prickle of confused emotion. Did this feeling mean I might grow fond of him?

A noise from above came from the hayloft. It was too loud to be a rat. I stepped back and looked up. I recognised Camellia, Angelica Barberi's youngest daughter, who, it was said, roamed the countryside at night. She was a younger version of her beautiful mother, and naked.

Camellia vanished before I could raise my hand to greet her.

———— ◆ ————

In the hour before dawn, Pietro slipped into the bed beside me. He smelled clean, making me realise I was in urgent need of a bath for cleanliness rather than restorative powers, though salts would smooth and soften my work-roughened skin.

When dawn's light filtered through the window and turned the foot of the wrought-iron bedstead into an outline, I rose. I placed the bag of mixed seed on my pillow in direct line of Pietro's sight.

In the voice I had used to coax Foxy, I whispered in his ear, 'Pietro?' Like Foxy's, his eyebrows twitched. 'I ask for both of our sakes, stop drinking. And swallow a palm-full of seed twice a day with water.'

A few seconds passed. 'Okay,' he mumbled.

'Pietro?'

'Yes.'

'Here is the letter to be posted to Iacopo. Make sure it gets to the post office today.'

'Will do.'

'Oh, and Pietro.'

'Yes.'

'Thank you.'

His eyes snapped open – they were sea-grey that morning – and he reached out to grab me. Dawn's light was now bright enough for me not only to see the outline of his smiling mouth but its empty interior. I skipped away, evading his clutching hands. *Could the issue of his toothless mouth be resolved?*

An hour later, in concert to a meagre winter rising sun, valley workers hiked up the slopes. In addition to their lunch pails, they carried baskets, ladders, rakes and brooms.

Men strapped the baskets around their waists and climbed harvesting ladders whose pointed tops wedged between branches. Women picked olives from the lower branches and children gathered those that fell to the ground.

La raccolta delle olive of the Trianni's ten-thousand-olive-tree grove started in earnest, and no one would rest until the last fruit had been picked, washed, pressed, and the filtered oil transferred into new barrels.

While busy in the ordered and pristine kitchen – very different from the first time I'd seen it – a commotion erupted.

I pushed open the door and entered the Trianni dining room, next in line for a thorough cleaning. I dreaded thinking about the rest of the villa I had yet to see. I passed through the dining room and stepped into the grand entrance hall that boasted black-and-white marble floor tiles laid in a harlequin pattern.

Claudio Trianni and Angelica Barberi were wrestling a contraption down the stairs. I rushed to help.

'What is it?'

Relieved of its weight, Claudio Trianni gripped the balustrade with both hands, steadying himself. 'A gramophone.'

I had no idea what he was speaking about. Nevertheless, I bore most of its weight with the exquisite Angelica, whose feet I was sure did not touch the stairs. A giant petunia-shaped brass bell swung dangerously close to my head.

'Listening to music lessens exhaustion.' Angelica's breath carried the faint smell of celery.

Where have you found some to eat? I knew there was none in the abandoned vegetable garden. I put these thoughts aside as we reached the bottom step. 'Where's it to go?'

Claudio Trianni pointed a crooked finger towards the terrace.

'Wait.' I raced back through to the kitchen, out into the courtyard, looking for anyone to help. I spied Arturo. 'Come here.'

Pietro stuck his head out of the mill.

'You too,' I said.

Pietro pinched my bottom as he followed me. 'Giving those orders, you sound just like a *commandina*.'

Arturo choked back a laugh, at witnessing my bottom being pinched or called a commander, I knew not which, but likely a little bit of both. He grinned, showing off his perfect teeth, all the more evident, given Pietro's smiling-wide, stretchy mouth, displaying its gummy hole.

Under Claudio Trianni's directions, the men set up the gramophone on the terrace and turned the brass speaker towards the olive grove. He looked at me and then Angelica. 'Where are the records?'

'Here,' said a strange, new voice.

As one, we turned to see Angelica Barberi's oldest daughter, Delphina. The records she held clutched to her chest were partially obscured by the curtain of waist-long, pitch-black hair that dangled ramrod straight, releasing a distinct rattling, like the sound of the porcupine's clattering quills.

The men fell silent.

'Come.' Angelica held out one hand towards her daughter. No one could miss the shadow of anxiety that clouded Angelica's face.

The men stiffened. Even Claudio Trianni stood a little straighter. Each man protectively cupped his genitals.

By way of explanation, Maria's voice entered my head. *Delphina's hair has been known to impale and pin a man to the floor.*

My shudder was interrupted by Maria's imaginary bony finger prodding me towards Delphina. The rattling increased to an impossible decibel, a warning to keep my distance. I halted. She stepped towards me, but at the last second turned sideways and thrust the records at Arturo. He was forced to relinquish his protective genital hold in order to clasp the records.

Like the lighthouse's rotating beam, the pinpricks of light in Delphina's pupils opened to a wide angle, and brighter than the sun, blazed, blinding the men. Reversing the order, the angle diminished, and as the pin pricks of light snapped shut, she vanished.

I relieved Arturo of the records before they slipped to the ground. He and the other men rubbed their eyes. Assured their sight was restored and genitalia intact, they exhaled long and loud. Angelica cast me a pitiful look, begging understanding.

Claudio Trianni thumbed through the stack. 'This one first.' Though he handed the record to Angelica, it was me he looked at with, I thought, unnecessary intensity.

Angelica unsheathed the record and handed me the cover. The name Enrico Caruso singing 'Santa Lucia', stared at me.

With trembling hands and surprising reverence, Claudio Trianni placed the disc on the turntable, turned a handle and lowered an arm over the record. The stylus, no different to the stinger of the furry-orange bumblebee sank into the vinyl's first groove.

Released from the brass horn, rich and melodic, Enrico Caruso's voice rose up and with a feather-light caress, flowed through my ears.

I stood still better to hear the words about a calm night sea, silver stars and a boat.

A chorus rose from the olive grove, and in perfect pitch and tune, joined Caruso in the repeating refrain singing the words: *Saint Lucy! Saint Lucy! Come board my lively little boat, Saint Lucy, Saint Lucy!*

Though I had never heard this song, it felt familiar, and I hummed along with ease. For the rest of the day, I could not get the tune out of my head.

Enchanting. Maddening.

———— ◆ ————

Midafternoon, Rubino stuck his head around the kitchen door. 'Hortensia, for once, forget cleaning. Make soup to feed one hundred people. Throw in these smoked trotters.'

I followed Anna's voiced instructions that were as clear as if she were working alongside me.

The first day's work ended after sunset, and the exhausted valley workers, numbed with cold, dragged themselves into the mill. A fearsome fire burned in the hearth fed with pruned olive branches.

Women spread blankets over straw bales. Once the children had downed a bowl of soup, they fell asleep despite the cacophony of rumbling wheels, Rubino and Pietro's tinkering with the large stone grinder and raised adult voices.

Men took turns in leading a blindfolded donkey and pouring olives onto the exposed bottom stone of the smaller grinder.

Around midnight a victory shout went up. The ox, harnessed and prodded into walking in a circle, set the repaired, large grinder into motion.

And so passed each day and night for a week, until every last olive had been processed. Only then did the valley workers return to their homes.

Two weeks later, a flotilla of assorted carts and vans rattled up the valley come to collect barrels of Trianni's olive oil and deliver it to the ship harboured in our port that would leave for America on the next high tide. The valley's Etruscan track widened to road proportions with all the unaccustomed traffic. It was a fitting gift, highlighting the first olive harvest in decades and I prayed, with God's blessing, the first of many more to come.

———————— ◆ ————————

'Hortensia?'

I heard Pietro call before I saw him. Then he appeared at the door and, in his considerate way, stamped his feet, freeing his boots of dirt before stepping into the kitchen. 'I'm going fishing.'

'Why now?'

'Soon it'll be full moon.'

I frowned. 'Soon it'll be Christmas.'

'Fish don't know about Christmas.' His mouth began to stretch into a smile. 'But they do know about full moon and love.'

I ignored his comment about fish and moonlight. The night before he had dragged the bed under the window and opened the shutters. Moonbeams bathed us while he made the sweetest love to me all the while whispering the song *Marechiaro* in my ear. Lovemaking belonged in the dark, and now he was alluding to it in broad daylight and in my domain, the kitchen. More irritating than that, I could not bear to see his mouth stretching wider. I frowned harder.

Crestfallen dismay replaced Pietro's smile. With a quick return to seriousness, he said, 'Moonlight draws fish to the surface. The nets will be close to bursting.' He released a hurt-filled sigh.

Guilt and disappointment stabbed me in quick succession. Guilt, for the pain I had inflicted – he did not deserve it – he was a good man; disappointment, because Pietro would not be able to share the Christmas feast I had planned.

His lips brushed against my cheek. 'Take care of yourself.'

I did not turn my face. After several weeks, the seed and only one glass of wine at night had diminished his bad breath. But his toothless mouth remained a problem. It repulsed me.

For the umpteenth time, I caught myself thinking what a pity that was. Though he was double my age, he had a fine, strong body and coupled with his kind attention towards me, I found myself softening towards him. But whenever I saw the dark cavern of his mouth, those feelings turned into shooting arrows missing their target.

He placed the palm of his hand against my belly, and keeping his mouth as closed as possible murmured, 'Keep the child safe, too.'

Remorse rose and spilled like a pot of heating milk left unattended. I rubbed the gold horn around my neck, in the hope of keeping bad luck away from him. '*You* take care.'

Pietro sniffed the air like a hunting dog, his nostrils quivering. A wispy fragrance of candied orange and lemon peel, and currants and raisins had escaped the oven where two large Christmas *panettoni* were baking. 'Save me a slice or three?'

'I will.'

For the first time, I followed him and waved goodbye as the van bounced and rattled out of the courtyard. I pulled my shawl tighter and turned to re-enter the kitchen. From the corner of one eye, I saw Camellia, naked, flitting from the stable to the mill. *How can she stand the cold?*

Just then, Arturo appeared at the stable door, righting his trousers. Seeing me, his face flushed and then he grinned sheepishly, flashing his lovely teeth.

I entered the mill and called, 'Camellia.' There was no response. The ladder accessing the loft caught my attention. She had not pulled it up after her. I placed one foot on the bottom rung and wrapped my fingers around its rough, wood frame. I raised my voice. 'Camellia. It's me, Hortensia. I'm coming up.'

As I climbed to the top, I caught the scent of the flower after which she had been named. So, her mother, Angelica, had not been eating a secret supply of celery after all. Her natural body odour was of the wild celery variety, hence Angelica's name.

Upon reaching the top rung, I could not help but see the indentations in the hay bales; Camellia spent a lot of time in the loft. A thud, like that of a heavy door closing, resounded. Likely it was the door set at the far end. Curiosity drew me to it. I pushed it open. A ramp inclined towards a shaft of sunlight filtering through a grated aperture. Inhaling the scent of camellias, I walked along the ramp until I reached the end where I stood on tiptoe and pressed my face against the metal grate. The door led out to a former dream of mine – a turreted tower.

My heart thrummed with excitement as I stepped out onto the tower's stone floor. Though her scent lingered in the crisp air, I could not see Camellia. From a gap in the tower wall, I surveyed the vista. Immediately below, the ten-thousand strong, olive trees, expertly pruned, spread out in equal rows.

The chestnut and pine forest dropped down to the valley floor where the *Frigido* slithered its silvery current through Trianni's land down to the sea. My heart leaped at the unobstructed view of the Angeli vineyards, garden, orchard, apricot-walled and green-shuttered villa, barn and Maria's shepherd's hut.

From nowhere, a razor-sharp gust of wind sliced through me. I hurriedly retraced my steps to the hay-filled loft, down the ladder and into the warmth of the kitchen.

◆

I n addition to the Christmas cakes, I had already prepared a hazelnut and chocolate torte. During its preparation, I had a sip of the hazelnut liqueur Anna had so loved and stuffed my mouth with chocolate. Not the expensive kind Mistress Letizia and Foxy had often eaten for breakfast. Yet, I swore my son kicked his feet with pleasure at its taste.

Traditionally, fish was the focus of the Christmas feast. But with Pietro gone and no clear knowledge of his return, or access to fish without him, I had to rearrange my menu. I took up a pencil and stared at the blank sheet of paper. Foxy took up his position sitting against my feet.

Anna's voice entered my head. *Are you in need of help?*

Yes, please. In place of fish, what am I going to serve for Christmas lunch?

Always antipasto first. How about Rubino's favourite: a platter of prosciutto di Parma, sliced, translucent thin?

Good idea. And small discs of spicy salami studded with black peppercorns – the fragile, dry casing already removed – which Maria loves, even though she always coughs when the peppercorns burn her throat.

Anna chuckled. *That's just her excuse to have another glass of wine!*

I giggled. Anna was right. Maria never reached for a glass of water.

What about your favourite?

Mmm…yes. Large circles of silky, pale pink mortadella stuck with green pistachio.

Don't forget to accompany those meats with bowls of sour pickled onions, roasted red, green and yellow bell peppers and sweet pickled artichokes. They contrast with, yet enhance, the aroma and flavor of the sliced cured meats, each distinct from the other.

I scribbled down Anna's suggestions. *And what about the first course?*

Do you remember how to make tortelli? Those little pillows of pasta made with hand-milled flour, cold effervescent spring water, egg yokes, wet Atlantic salt and Trianni oil, stuffed with a teaspoon-sized mixture of fresh ricotta, toasted pinoli and chopped basil?

I do. And to be served with a sauce of browned butter with a hint of smashed garlic spooned over the soft yellow pillows.

Good girl, Hortensia. You remember well! What about the main dish?

Braised rabbit? No, wait. Veal?

You can decide later. As for the vegetables, I would suggest deep-green spinach sautéed in oil and lemon zest or oven-roasted yellow potatoes topped with sprigs of rosemary.

I'll make both. And, should anyone be hungry after that, and before dessert, I'll have to hand, a plate of semi-soft goat cheese, slices of crisp pears, walnuts and chestnut honey. What do you think, Anna?

She did not reply, and Foxy's warmth upon my feet subsided.

Pleased with the re-worked menu, I turned my attention to preparing lunch and food trays for Delphina and Camellia.

♦

After their lunch, Angelica settled Claudio Trianni for an afternoon snooze and returned to the kitchen to collect trays for her daughters. Though I saw her retreating up the stairs, I did not hear her footsteps.

In the beginning, the sisters' trays were returned with the food hardly touched. As the days passed, the trays had less and less food remaining. On that wintery day of Pietro's departure, there wasn't a single crumb. Thinking they had begun to enjoy my meals, my chest swelled with pride. Midway it stopped. In the month I had been at the Trianni Estate, I still had not had a conversation with them, cleaned their rooms or washed their clothes. I had not seen either of them for longer than a moment. Nor seen them together.

The truth was, having anything to do with them was scary. Their cold strangeness was beyond anything I'd encountered. I stuck to my decision. Keeping my distance was prudent.

By contrast, I saw Angelica several times a day. She rarely spoke, and when she did, it was a gentle request, which I obeyed without question. Not noticing her burgeoning stomach was impossible. Her pregnancy was at least two months ahead of mine.

After my fastidious cleaning of the Trianni kitchen, my obsession resurfaced, and I transformed the dining room. The parlour on the opposite side of the harlequin-patterned entrance hall remained unused. I managed to curb my compulsion and kept the parlour's double doors shut, hiding its disarray. In honour of approaching Christmas, I tackled the staircase that soared and curved graciously against two of the entrance hall's walls. It reminded me of the voluminous interior of Santa Chiara, the church in Naples. And in turn, Di Napoli.

The jolt I normally experienced when thinking about him had lessened. Perhaps it was due to my increasing belly and slow-growing relationship – or was it friendship – with Pietro? I rarely gave Iacopo a thought, but nevertheless, at that moment I put all three men right out of my head. I had more cleaning to do. Midway through cleaning the staircase, I heard a door above the stairs bang, its bolts rammed home.

'You will remain until I say.' Angelica Barberi's dulcet-toned voice had changed to iron. Its sound clanged down the staircase. An increasing, high-pitched rattling froze the marrow in my bones. I was in no doubt from which daughter this sound came. A second door banged, and more bolts rammed home. Angelica Barberi repeated her words. Camellia's unmistakable mournful keening – no different to how I cried when my mother abandoned me – wrenched my heart.

It took me far less time to clean the rest of the steps. My son, who had been rambunctiously knocking about in the squashed confines of my belly, stilled; much like prey gone underground, waiting for danger to pass.

14

In keeping with his atheism, Claudio Trianni paid no heed to the fact it was Christmas Eve. In his slippers, he shuffled into the kitchen wearing flannel pyjamas, over which he wore a velvet dressing gown.

Angelica Barberi dressed as though she were attending a prince's ball. She wore a mauve gown overlaid with silver lace looking like spider webs laden with early morning dew crystals, but no shoes.

With each course they ate, they fell deeper into silence that rang with contentment. I cleared away clean plates.

'To bed,' Claudio Trianni said after dessert. They struggled their way up the gleaming staircase with Claudio Trianni leaning upon Angelica. *I'll soon be serving his meals on a tray.* And, as one thought follows another, *possibly Angelica's, too.* In the last few days her stomach had again noticeably distended. Exhaustion for what was about to come flooded me – being a much larger house, the staircase in Villa Trianni had ten steps more than that of Villa Angeli.

When they reached the midway, Angelica's daughters released their distinctive sounds from behind their bedroom doors; Delphina's porcupine quills' high-pitched rattling, and Camellia's low, mournful keening. Their combined noise crescendoed, causing the locked doors to vibrate in their frames like earthquake tremors before splitting the earth. Or in this case, until the rattling door bolts sprang open.

Claudio's knees buckled.

Angelica turned. Despite the distance between us, and the roaring din, I heard her quiet, sweet voice clearly. 'Hortensia. Put Claudio to bed and stay with him until I return.' She disappeared down the corridor towards her daughters' bedrooms.

I raced up the stairs, jouncing awake my sleeping son in my pregnant belly. Placing my hands under Claudio's armpits, I lifted him to standing position – he was feather-light – wrapped an arm around his waist and positioned one of his arms around my neck. I struggled to remain upright against the force of the combined noises that threatened to tumble us backwards. Together we made slow progress towards the master bedchamber. I closed the door to block out the noise. Especially a new one of evenly spaced whistle-flicks and cracks that could only come from a whip. Blessed silence engulfed us.

'Thank you,' the old man rasped, as I drew the bedcovers to his chin. The skin covering his skull was parchment-thin. I could see bone, as smooth as the outgoing tide leaves sand.

How could Claudio Trianni have had the energy to impregnate his wife when he was almost at death's door? An image of the butterfly-leafed chasteberry tree rose before me. Could Angelica have given Claudio Trianni a dose? An illuminated vision arose – an augury perhaps? – *Yes! Like me, she was pregnant before she married.*

'Sit,' he said.

I pulled up a chair.

'Come closer.'

I did as he bid. His eyelids slid closed and I took the opportunity to look around. The bed was a canopy-less, four-poster, large enough for six. The walls of the room disappeared into dark shadows, making them seem endless. Heavy curtains trailed onto the floor. *What a waste. All that extra fabric getting dirty and needing cleaning!* My boots sank into the soft carpet.

His eyelids fluttered open. 'I'm dying.'

I caressed his cheek with the back of my hand. He sighed, sounding like me whenever I thought of my mother. The words slipped from my mouth. 'Shall I call Don Antonio?'

The muscles around his mouth twitched. I could not make out whether it was in a grimace or a smile.

'No. You shall hear my confession.'

'But I'm not allowed–'

'Hear me out. Only then will I be able to recount the best story of my life, the story of Little Bean. The unabridged telling of which will garner my place in heaven.'

But, you don't believe in God. You said so yourself.

Maria's voice entered my head. *A change of heart when nearing death is common.*

After a faltering start, Claudio Trianni's voice strengthened though it remained low. I had to incline my head to catch every word.

Nothing could have prepared me for the recitation of wrongs Trianni had done unto others. No wonder he did not wish a priest to hear his confession. And no wonder the valley workers despised him. Behind his back, they called him *mascalzone,* scoundrel.

By his account, he had broken all the Holy Commandments. Had God made more, he would have broken those too.

With the telling of each injurious action, the lines in Claudio Trianni's face relaxed and his pallid skin tinged pink. *Confessing one's sins is cathartic, after all.*

The never-ending litany was mesmerising and overwhelming. I lost all sense of time and to protect myself from the very worst horrors, I must have dozed because when he stopped, I raised my head from his chest and whispered, 'And Little Bean–'

The bedchamber door opened and Angelica, calm, fresh and lovelier than ever, entered.

'Thank you, Hortensia. You may leave.'

The corridor was silent and bathed in full moonlight. As I passed, the mixed scents of wild celery, delphiniums and camellias crept up my nostrils.

Do I have a scent of my own?

I recalled playing among the hortensia shrubs in the gardens of Villa Angeli when the round heads resembling giant pom-poms were in deep-blue flower. Their consistent shade was an indication the *Sangiovese* vines were in good health – the harvest likely to be abundant and quality excellent. If the colour of the flower heads, God forbid, changed to pink or white, the vines were not well.

The hortensia's vivid blue was easy to recall. Its scent was not. It had none. I had just answered my question. *Neither do I.*

Though Maria's clothes often smelled of her pygmy goats, like me, she too had no smell of her own.

And my mother's scent? She had the very best smell – vanilla to which her name, Lucia, bore little relation save for an -i and an -a. But on reaching the last step realisation dawned. My mother's nickname referred to a slender green bean which, except for the colour, resembled the vanilla pod.

What Claudio Trianni had said at the first meal I served him became clear. He had taken me for my mother and had called me by her nickname, *Fagiolina.*

For some unfathomable reason, my mind made a giant, cricket-like leap and landed upon Anna's story of the run-away bride. An image rose of a bride whose progress along the torturous ridge path connecting the two estates was being hampered by her white wedding gown, rose. Brilliantly illuminated, I easily recognised it: an augury revealing the past.

————— ◆ —————

Rubino, Maria and Arturo were already seated at the table.

'Sorry, Hortensia. We could not wait any longer.' Rubino stuffed a slice of *prosciutto*, followed by a piece of bread dipped in oil, into his mouth.

Had they not heard the sounds coming from the daughters' bed-rooms?

Maria's eyes jittered once and so fast that no one but me saw. And though she sat next to me, her voice entered my head. *I did. But not Rubino or Arturo.*

Claudio Trianni knew my mother.

Yes.

He is a terribly bad man.

Yes.

He is my father.

Yes.

I regretted having prepared so much food. The new-found knowledge that Giovanni Angeli's runaway bride was my mother, and Claudio Trianni, to whom she ran, was my father, made the inside of my head swirl. All I wanted was to crawl into bed. But, with the delighted oohs and aahs over each course, and several mouthfuls of *Sangiovese*, the swirling stopped. My exhausted spirit lifted, further buoyed as Arturo jumped up and served, saving me the bother.

'Hey, slow down boy,' Rubino cautioned as Arturo brought the platter of pears and honey to the table. 'What's the rush?'

Arturo flushed beet. 'No rush except I had planned to attend midnight Mass.'

None of us had been to midnight Mass in years.

His eyes grew large in child-like innocence. 'Would you like to join me?'

Rubino and Maria could barely contain their mirth.

Rubino's face contorted in an effort to stem his laughter. 'Er...no, thanks.'

'We'll go,' Maria said, 'tomorrow morning.'

But I knew they would never get out of bed early to attend Mass. Not even if it was Christmas morning.

I knew too, Arturo wasn't going to mass. He had an appointment of a different kind, but clearly had no idea the person he was to meet sat bolted in her room.

'I have to get going. Thanks a lot for the meal. But...er...' Arturo cast me a beseeching look. 'Please save me a slice of *panetto-*'

'Of course, I'll save you some Christmas cake.'

He flashed me a brilliant smile, showing off his lovely teeth. As he opened the kitchen door, moonlight streamed in framing him in the doorway. '*Buon Natale.*'

'*Buon Natale,*' we chorused as he shut the door behind him.

I cleared the table and Maria placed a glass filled to the brim with *limoncello* in front of each of us.

'Down to business,' Rubino said. 'Pietro is expected back two weeks from now. He's gone on to Naples…,'

Naples? Di Napoli! 'Why?'

'He will have delivered his fish catch to the market in Naples. It's much larger than ours and should bring him in quite a bit of money. 'But, more important than that,' Rubino paused to swallow a mouthful of *limoncello*, 'we are expecting a letter from Iacopo.'

'Remember,' Maria said, 'we are waiting to hear the price the Americans will pay for the oil.'

I knew all this but had forgotten about it. Perhaps it had to do with my being pregnant? A woman from the valley not only forgot how to cook during her pregnancy, but to her husband's consternation, did not recognise him!

Rubino placed one of his large hands over mine. 'Which brings us to the next hurdle. Hortensia, are you listening?'

I returned to the present to find both Rubino and Maria staring at me. 'The hurdle?'

'You are to get Claudio Trianni to sign this document, giving me, and in my absence, Maria the right to manage and–'

'Sell future oil production until his unborn heir reaches *maturità* at age eighteen,' I finished for him.

Grinning, Rubino's chestnut-bark wrinkled face deepened into crevasses. 'Precisely.'

Like a gypsy playing a pair of castanets, the bangles click-clacked their approval.

Rubino and Maria left. I bolted the kitchen door, entered the bedroom, and after checking that the window and shutters were locked, slipped beneath the covers and turned out the lamp.

Wishing Pietro was there to keep me warm and safe, I curled into a ball to protect my belly, but sleep cruelly evaded me. In my mind's eye, one after the other, the men in my life, Rubino, Di Napoli, Iacopo and Pietro, marched by. My father, Claudio Trianni brought up the rear. On the fingers of one hand, I counted out two *bello*, two brutto and one *mascalzone.*

15

I woke, sweating and clawing my way out of a nightmare. Colossal butterflies filled the sky, and human victims who dotted a rocky landscape bled rivers of blood. Like a pebble lodged in my throat, the knowledge that Claudio Trianni was my father had choked me dry.

I swung my feet to the floor and trod upon something, long and thin, similar to a strand of spaghetti. My housecleaning instincts screamed, 'How did that get there?' But my desire for water was stronger than my need to investigate. I padded barefoot into the kitchen. It was bathed in light from the dipping moon, suspended low in the sky and framed by the open kitchen door.

Mixed delphinium and camellia fragrances assailed my nostrils while the fleeting image of quill-straight hair and a naked body caused shivers to cascade down my spine. If the daughters were free…

I placed one hand upon my belly, and with the other I rubbed the gold horn around my neck, wishing for the sun and Pietro to arrive.

Should I shut and bolt the door again? Will it make any difference to the sisters should they return? I knew of no barrier that could stop them. To ensure night animals did not enter, I closed the door but did not bother bolting it.

Slaking my thirst with icy water from the jug, I returned to bed. The cylinder cracked underfoot as I trod upon it again. *It can't be spaghetti. Or is it?*

Afraid, I didn't care to find out and slipped into bed where, wide-eyed, I waited for the sun to arrive, which it did, and Pietro, who did not.

———————— ◆ ————————

In the morning Rubino entered the kitchen. 'Hortensia, have you seen Arturo?'

'No.'

'He did not return last night.'

My spine froze with dread followed by a melting rush of warm hope. 'Perhaps he stayed in the village after midnight Mass?'

'I'll check as I pass through. But if you see him, tell him to come to the Angeli Estate. I'm transporting wine from there to here. I need his help.'

I tucked several escaped wisps back into the bun at the nape of my neck. 'Is Maria going back with you?'

'She went home after dinner last night.'

In my mind's eye, I could see Maria, her cloak billowing behind her, stepping lightly along the treacherous ridge connecting the two estates, calling out her arrival to her goats.

It neared mid-morning, and no one had breakfasted. I picked up Claudio's tray and headed for the staircase with the Right to Manage and Sell document tucked into my apron pocket.

The door to Delphina's bedroom listed, torn from its hinges. Camellia's door stood open with its hinges and bolts intact. It was obvious that Delphina's fury surpassed Camellia's. I peered into rooms that were pristine. Had these rooms been occupied? A thought I'd had once before repeated. *Did the sisters exist?* and rejected it as soon as it materialised. *Of course they existed. Others had seen them. Hadn't they?*

I knocked on the master bedchamber's door and entered. Somehow I knew Angelica would not be there but Claudio Trianni would.

He sat propped up in bed. *Why did I feel strangely drawn to it?*

Time's phosphorescent-lit passage sprang up and raced back into the past to reveal another augury: my conception and birth had occurred in that bed.

The light in Claudio's eyes had dimmed and his skin was pale again. 'Fagiolina, at last you have come. I have been waiting and waiting.'

'I am not Fagiolina. I am Hortensia.'

A spark flashed in his eyes. 'Oh yes. The little cook. I've been waiting for you too.'

I wasted no time. 'Now I am here, you can tell me about my mother.'

'Who is your mother?'

Am I going mad, or, are you? I looked closely. The spark had died. How could he have confessed the sinful events of his horrible life with such clarity the day before and now not recall my mother? 'Lucia d'Ambrosia.'

'I don't know a Lucia d'Ambrosia.'

I paused. 'Okay. Then tell me what Little Bean was to–'

His voice wavered. 'Fagiolina is dead?'

An acute memory of the glorious taste of Bavarian custard I'd eaten at the Convent of the Poor Clare's in Naples, and which my mother had served me on the day she disappeared, filled my mouth. I had no way of knowing, but I said, 'She is alive.'

His chest contracted with relief and in his rheumy eyes a new spark turned into a small, steady light. 'Thank God.'

My chest contracted with relief, too. 'Tell me.'

'Give me something to eat first.'

Holding back my growing frustration, I offered him a bowl of yellow *polenta* mixed with warmed cream and sugar. His hands shook so, I retrieved the bowl and spoon.

Feeding him was slow. With each swallow, his Adam's apple bobbed under his neck's crepey skin. The trembling in his hands, which rested like gnarled corkscrews on the coverlet, began to subside.

In awe, I watched a great war play out before me – a body that wanted to die and a spirit that refused.

Right on cue, Maria's voice entered my head. *Remember, he's fighting to stay alive for the birth of his heir.*

I wanted to scream, 'What are you talking about? *I* am his heir.' But I did not, realising at the same moment it would be to no avail. I was illegitimate and female. Instead, my next thought, in time with raising the last spoonful to his mouth, was understanding it would not take much to bring about Claudio Trianni's death – stop all nourishment.

Not before he signs the sale document.

Hastily, I pushed both evil thought and Maria's reminder aside.

Claudio Trianni pointed to the cup of rich, milky coffee I'd prepared, no different to the way my mother had once prepared for him. His eyelids paused midway, indicating bliss at the first sip. And after a nibble of coconut cake, they closed.

For a moment I thought he'd died so still was he. I tapped one of his hands. 'Fagiolina's story.'

He took his time to respond. Likely he had been visiting a memory and was not ready to leave it. His rheumy eyes fastened on mine. 'It's long. Promise you will listen to the end?'

Nothing at that moment was more important to me. Yet something warned me to check my enthusiasm. Like a card player's bluff, I kept silent.

'Hortensia. Do you promise me?'

'Okay. I promise.'

He took a shallow breath. 'I was forty years old, chafing at the bit, praying for my father to die so I could leave.' Claudio Trianni waved a feeble hand in the air. 'How I hated this place.'

It would become a pattern: asking Claudio Trianni a question about another, and him responding with something about himself.

'And how I hated the olives. They came before anything or anyone else. My life was governed and ruined by them.'

'But,' I said, 'olives made your father rich and your life comfortable, didn't they?'

'What good are riches, if there is nothing to spend it on? Buried in a God-forsaken Tuscan valley whose sides soar,' he took another shallow breath, 'leaving only a patch of blue to behold, and which is served by a goat track for a road?'

Instinct told me his question did not require a response. Nor did I inform him the rutted path he spoke of had turned into a road.

'Immediately after my father's funeral, I left.'

Maria's voice entered my head. *And took all the money from under the mattress.*

'I was free. Able to do all I had ever wanted.'

Maria's raised voice echoed in my head. *And more.*

I blinked hard. *Maria. Enough!* I turned my attention to Claudio. 'But what does that have to do with the story of Fagiolina?'

'Everything.'

I was about to yell, 'Tell me!' when Angelica entered. *Che sfortuna!*

'My daughters have returned.' Her lovely face glowed with serenity. 'They have eaten and are resting in their rooms. Thank you. You may leave.'

Clearly, in her mind, all was well. Cursing my bad luck, I picked up the tray and, with the unsigned Right to Manage and Sell document crackling in my apron pocket, returned to the kitchen. With Delphina's door repaired, both daughters' doors stood closed, but not bolted. Right then I was more concerned with a million bee stings worth of frustration than those two crazy sisters.

Only Angelica appeared for dinner.

My heart doubled its beat.

'My husband is tired. I'll take him a tray once I've eaten.'

From the size of her stomach and the slowness of her movements, Angelica appeared tired, too. *How much longer before I reach that stage?* 'I'll help you.' My serving meals on trays began sooner than I expected.

16

The following morning Rubino was waiting for me in the kitchen. Though it seemed impossible, the bark-like crevasses in his face had deepened. Doom sprinted up my spine, erasing all hope. I could hardly articulate his name. 'Arturo?'

'He did not go to midnight Mass. No one in the village has seen him. I've called the hunters for help.' Rubino twisted one of Arturo's shirts in his hands. 'I'm hoping the dogs will pick up his scent.'

Before Rubino finished speaking, the distinct sound of barking dogs and their belled collars rose from the valley floor as they made their way to the Trianni Estate. Rubino went out into the courtyard to meet them.

I watched with rising indignation as the courtyard filled. *This is meant to be a search to find a missing man, not an excuse to hunt wild boar!* Each hunter carried his rifle. From their dishevelled hunting clothes, dirty beards and ragged caps, they looked like they lived permanently in the woods. Jacket pockets bulged with wine bottles. No doubt provided by Rubino in exchange for the search.

Through the kitchen window, I saw Rubino press Arturo's shirt against each scrawny hound's nose. One after another they sat upon their haunches and quieted. At a signal, each hunter bent down and untied the rope attached to his dog's collar. The dogs sprang up, lowered their heads and with their noses skimming the ground trotted here and there, some in tight circles. They picked up Arturo's scent, yipped and streaked away. The hunters followed in quick pursuit.

Rubino stood alone in the centre of the courtyard with Arturo's shirt. He caught my eye, rolled his eyes to heaven, and I shrugged. With a brief wave, he left the courtyard.

Half an hour later, the dogs' barking coalesced, coming from one direction, deep in the chestnut and pine forest. By their altered pitch, I knew they had found something. Then the sound of two shots echoed around the valley. Likely, they had flushed a boar, and just as likely, the hunt for Arturo would be abandoned.

An hour later, dogs and hunters re-entered the courtyard. Four men carried a thick branch resting upon their shoulders from which a boar, secured by his feet, hung. Like the dark patch around the boar's neck, from where it had bled out, dark patches of sweat marked the bearers' heavy winter jackets. They grimaced and grunted as they eased the branch off their shoulders and dumped the boar onto the ground.

A few hunters started a fire in the wide and long firepit at the far end of the yard directly on the earth. When the flames licked at an even height, they hauled up the boar and passed it back and forth over the pit.

More in frustration that Arturo had not been found than in anticipation of the acrid smell of singed coarse hair that would permeate the air, I slammed the windows and kitchen door shut.

Through one of the side-by-side kitchen windows, I saw Maria. She stopped to talk with a group of hunters who stood in a tight circle, a cloud of purple cigarette smoke suspended above their heads. One hunter squatted, resting his hand upon his dog's head. The dog trembled with the shock of its wound, a cut, sliced clean from shoulder to rump. Maria reached into the folds of her cloak for one of the many small tins of ointments she carried. I'd seen her treat injured hunting dogs many times, often with more care than she treated humans. In a second, the dog lay stretched on its side, induced into sleep by the small black stone Maria had pressed in the space between its brows. Despite her stiff fingers, she worked quickly, smearing ointment into the cut.

The dog's owner opened his tobacco pouch and crumbled tobacco fragments directly into the ointment-smeared wound. I knew without seeing Maria would pinch the two sides of the wound together and hook it closed with the thorns from the Angeli's rambling rose she had collected and dried.

The boar's coarse-haired coat had been singed clean. It took six men to heave the body up onto a table. They scraped the burnt skin with specially chiselled stones they carried in their pockets and then the boar was swiftly gutted and butchered. Each hunter went home with a bag of raw meat in one hand and a bag of blood-specked bones for his dog in the other.

Maria entered the kitchen and placed Rubino's bagged share on the table.

My eyebrows rose. 'Where is Rubino?'

'Searching for Arturo.'

'You don't have any idea where he is?'

'No. But I'm going to look for them both.' Maria left.

I did not believe her but banished the thought lest she discern it.

It was time for me to assemble the ingredients for fresh wide-ribbon pasta with wild-boar sauce stewed in tomatoes.

Spectral, Anna stood alongside me, and the sound of her voice entered my head. *The secret to a good sauce is a fresh bay leaf as opposed to a dry one, milk and three hours of simmering.*

Following her further instructions, I set the black pot on the stove when something caught my eye. I looked through one kitchen window and saw nothing. I was drawn to look through the other.

Naked, Camellia stood before the firepit. She raised her arms sideways to shoulder height and like a toppled tree, fell face forward into the glowing coals.

'*Dio mio!*' My shriek pierced my eardrums. As I opened the kitchen door something fast and airy-light streaked past me. The odour of burning flesh filled my nose.

I lifted my skirts and ran, following in Angelica's wake. Despite my desire to pull the burning girl from the fire, an invisible barrier with the might of two opposing magnets held me fast. Angelica and I stood beyond the reach of the fierce heat.

Delphina materialised, crouched at the edge of the pit. Her tawny-dark pupils glowed. Her stiff, pitch-black hair released the rattling sound of her enraged porcupine signature call.

Angelica stared hard at Delphina. 'Did you push her?' Her voice was colder than the *Frigido* and sharper than the jagged mountain peaks behind us.

'No.'

Angelica's tone turned to iron. 'Are you sure?'

'Yes,' I yelled. 'She's telling the truth. Camellia stepped into the fire on her own.'

'Delphina,' Angelica said. 'Help your sister.'

'KA ME LEE YA,' Delphina's sing-song voice echoed around the courtyard. 'Mamma says for you to come out.'

No sound came from Camellia's writhing body melting into the coals.

'Delphina! Get in there and help your sister.'

'No.'

But Angelica was wise to Delphina. 'What did you do to cause Camellia to do this?'

'Not me. Her.'

'What did Camellia do?'

'She wouldn't share.'

'Wouldn't share what?'

But I already knew. Camellia had not wanted to share Arturo with her older sister.

My voice rang in my head. *It's official. The sisters are crazier than their beautiful mother.*

The eerie calm found only in the eye of a storm enveloped me. As if that wasn't enough madness for one day, my mother's voice entered my head. *Hortensia.* I pinched myself. I was awake. *Leave. Leave before it's too late.* Hearing her voice, my body rippled in delight. But now was not the time to renew our acquaintance. I saved that for later and returned to the immediate situation at hand.

To survive the shock of witnessing the fire-burning, I erected an impenetrable barrier and cast that memory behind it. But not before accepting I had living proof that Angelica and her two daughters were none other than The Furies. Camellia, who, naked, flitted around the countryside in the dead of night, and Delphina, who took her revenge on those who thwarted her by wielding her hair spikes. I did not attempt to imagine everything Angelica had wrought, but the image of a spider ensnaring victims in deceivingly fragile, gossamer threads, sprang to mind.

With the barrier in place and thus protected, I returned to the kitchen and went about my day as if it were simply another ordinary day.

Evening came. The air filled with the fragrance of wild-boar sauce. Mounds of soft, butter-yellow *pappardelle* sat ready to be tipped into the pot of roiling, well-salted water.

Angelica entered. Though her mouth did not move, I clearly heard her words as if she'd spoken them. 'Hortensia, thank you for your understanding this morning.'

She looked at the two trays I had laid for her and Claudio and said aloud, 'Er…um…the girls are looking forward to their dinner, too.'

Oh no. A fountain of both rage and heartfelt sadness spurted up inside my chest. The sisters may have returned, but I knew Arturo never would.

17

New Year's Day dawned bright, setting the intricate and perfect feather-pattern of the frosted crystals on the windowpane aglitter. Pietro had been away for eleven days, the last seven of which Arturo had been missing.

A series of light raps told me it was Angelica knocking at my door. I scrambled out of bed and opened it. Delphina and Camellia stood behind her. For once, they were all warmly dressed, and the sisters each carried a prayer book and a rosary.

'Good morning Hortensia,' they chorused, their faces wreathed in seraphic smiles.

The chill of the stone floor beneath my feet told me I was not dreaming. Since the firepit event, the sisters had turned into earth-angels. At least, so it appeared.

Likely at the sight of my mouth turning down in bafflement, the corners of Angelica's curled up. 'We're on our way,' she said, 'to confession and Mass.'

With cleansed souls, New Year resolutions will get off to a good start.

'We'll be home in time for lunch. Please, serve Claudio his breakfast.'

'I will.' *Thank you, God. Uninterrupted time with the old man alone!*

As Angelica made to leave, the sisters fell in behind her, and as one, they all exited into the courtyard.

Visible through the kitchen doorway, Rubino sat hunched on the donkey cart bench. He too was dressed in more clothes than I had ever seen. His mouth pressed closed, and likely not only because of the unusually cold morning, but from the pain in his aching joints. My heart contracted in sympathy for him. He was in need of another warm, salt bath. When he caught sight of me, he rolled his eyes.

I pulled on my boots, struggled to fasten my skirt's buttons over my expanding waist, tied on an apron and slipped the still unsigned Right to Manage and Sell document into the deep pocket.

Pregnancy had done me no favours. Angelica, so much older than me had become even more beautiful with her pregnancy. I walked past the mirror without bothering to peek.

A few minutes later, carrying Claudio's breakfast tray, I headed upstairs. I'd have at least three hours with him.

'Fagiolina?' His voice quavered, and the light in his eyes was dim.

Oh no. I sighed with exasperation. *I'm going to have to start all over again.*

With each mouthful, Claudio's wan complexion improved. By the time he sipped the rich, milky coffee, the light in his eyes gleamed steadily.

'Hortensia,' he said. 'Are you ready?'

Good. He's back on track. I feigned innocence. 'Ready for what?'

His face flashed annoyance. 'To hear the story of Little Bean.'

I had tried to communicate with my mother in my quiet moments. To my crushing disappointment, she had not responded. I realised what further information I would glean would only come from him. Yet, I held back my excitement. 'Do I have to?'

'You promised, remember! If you don't, I…I won't go…' He began to cough.

'Won't go to heaven?'

His face turned blue.

I held my panic in check. 'Are you too afraid to say it?'

With herculean effort, Claudio Trianni struggled to pull himself further upright and waved away my offer of help. 'Me? Afraid? Never in my life.'

I had to give him credit. He was a tough old bird. 'Prove it. Say, "I am not afraid of going to hell."'

He fell silent. His face took on the light of understanding. 'Ah ha! Now who's the foxy one? What do you want in exchange for listening?'

I pulled out the document from my apron pocket. 'Sign this.'

'Women,' he sighed. 'You are all the same. Scavengers. Well, you're too late. I've nothing left. Only land, bricks and mortar.'

I bristled but ignored the insult. 'Keep your land, bricks and mortar. I only want the right to manage, harvest and sell the oil produce until your heir reaches maturity.'

He glanced heavenward and punched the air with a fist. 'Again with the damn olives. God, can't you wait? Do you have to punish me on my deathbed?'

'That behaviour won't get you anywhere with Him.' Even to my ears, my voice sounded clipped.

Claudio Trianni collapsed against the pillows.

I glided over a twinge of guilt as smoothly as a card shark's sleight of hand. 'You sign, I'll listen. Then you'll get a place in heaven.'

'You're sure?'

Behind my back, I crossed my fingers. 'Sure, I'm sure.'

'Hortensia?'

'Yes.'

'I've already given permission for the olive grove to be harvested and produce sold in exchange for you coming to work here.'

Argh! Scoundrel. You're smarter than I thought. This time I crossed my fingers until they hurt. 'Yes. But that's only for this season. What about the seasons to follow? And in any case, someone must take charge and restore this old pile of stones. Unless of course, you don't care if it falls around your wife's and heir's ears.'

Claudio Trianni shifted in his bed.

'Besides, restoration work will provide additional work for the valley.'

His rheumy eyes focused on me. 'Is the villa really in such bad shape?'

With truth ringing in my heart as clear as a bell, I nodded. 'And when the building inspectors make a surprise visit, I have it on good authority they will declare it unfit for habitation, turn your wife and heir out and block up all the doors and windows.' I tilted my head, placed the tips of my fingernails under my chin and flicked my hand outward; the classic hand gesture meaning, what do you care? 'You'll be safe in heaven.'

'Give it to me.'

While Claudio Trianni read, in my head I began to count. Thirty seconds passed.

'Why does your name replace Rubino's and Maria's?'

'Because of their age.'

Claudio paused. I counted another thirty seconds.

'*Va bene.* Give me a pen.'

I pocketed the signed document giving me the sole right to manage and sell the olive production until his heir turned eighteen.

'Are you ready now to listen to the story of Little Bean?'

Getting him to sign had been easy. But would listening to the story of Little Bean be easy? I bit my lip, pulled the chair close, sat with hands folded and waited. From the light, sweet fragrance of vanilla, I knew with certainty my mother's spirit entered the bedchamber and likely listened more intently to Claudio Trianni's recollection of their relationship than I.

At the start of the telling, I turned into a leaf floating calmly upon a gentle stream. As the events of my parents' troubled past unfolded, the stream became a torrent that churned white froth and then squeezed through a narrow gorge, hurtled down a vertical waterfall, slammed upon rocks and raced down into the sea. And still it was not over.

———— ♦ ————

Claudio Trianni wept. 'And, th…then…four years later, she arrived as I had instructed.'

'Why did you send for her only four years later?'

'You've not been listening! Despite enjoying myself, I hankered after my old life. More importantly, I desired to be in the presence of pure innocence rather than the depravity drowning me a little more each day.

'I had written, begging forgiveness, declaring my true love to her. Said that this time I would marry her. Madness gripped me while waiting for her reply. Determined to make good my promise to myself, I foreswore my past lifestyle, wanting to be as clean and innocent as she.'

Only a week's worth of cleansing for a lifetime's worth of depravity? *What nonsense!* But, I held my tongue.

'The morning the letter came, with a simple yes to everything I had written, I fell to my knees. God had smiled upon me. I'd been granted a reprieve. Hope was restored. My life spared. Having had no sleep, and fasting and abstaining for days, I was quite out of my mind.'

'Abstaining from what?'

Claudio Trianni never skipped a beat. 'On the morning I was to meet Fagiolina, an Oriental woman with the pipe that causes dragons to breathe fire in my brain arrived. She persuaded me Fagiolina would be disgusted by my body's relentless jerks and shudders, the result of my attempt to desist the opium. My resistance vaporized and I succumbed. My life's path spiralled down into another, much deeper hole.

'I heard much later Fagiolina waited for five days and then disappeared. When I entered normality, I searched for her.'

'And the child? Did you look for the child?' The pain from hearing my voice say those words aloud caused me to press my hands over my heart.

Time stopped. Claudio's lids closed. Not even his eyeballs moved under the thin skin.

Finally, his lids reopened. His eyes shone bright with wonder. 'There was a child?'

'Yes.'

'A boy?'

'A girl.'

Wonder evaporated in a snap. 'Bah.' His mouth curled in disgust. 'What use would a daughter be to me?'

I ought to have been elated – I'd succeeded in getting both signature and story – but the pain of his rejection cut deep.

An oyster shell, thick and calcareous, encapsulated my heart.

———— ◆ ————

New Year's Day passed in a mindless fog. Angelica and her daughters returned. I served lunch, but don't recall what. The first moment I could, I returned to my room to rest. My eye fell upon Delphina's cylindrical hair spike. I sat on the bed and held it while reviewing each piece of information in sequence as Claudio Trianni had recounted. The shell surrounding my heart dulled the pain of phrases such as 'cleaner and cook'. My mother's voice entered my head. *Show him. Show him what use a daughter has.*

Why did I feel strangled every time I heard the word 'use'? Why was I not accepted and loved simply for being me?

My mother didn't miss a beat. *Pietro accepts you.* She was right. He married me knowing I was pregnant, and more, he loved me.

I longed for his return. *Perhaps from the tower, I'll see his fishing boat in the distance?* With a lighter heart, I headed to the oil mill. I climbed the ladder, pushed past the bay hales and walked up the inclined ramp.

Sharp, late afternoon sun shafted through the grated aperture. A gentle push and the heavy door swung open, smooth and silent.

I froze not ten paces from Rubino and Maria, both of whom were crouched over Arturo's naked, rigor mortised body. Thickly scattered around them lay black spaghetti, too many to count. It was clear: Arturo hadn't stood a chance. He clenched a handful of spikes in one hand. Of those that were skewered deep into his flesh, some remained intact, and some had snapped off above entry point.

So intent were Rubino and Maria, they did not hear or see me.

Rubino's cheeks inflated as he blew out through his pursed lips. 'Who'd have believed extracting teeth would be so tough.'

Maria patted her cloak pockets. 'Here, try this. It's the smallest pair of pliers I have.'

'Ah. That might do it.' Under the fabric of his jacket, the muscles in Rubino's back bulged from the effort. His elbow moved sharply as he levered his large hand up and down, giving me a shuttered view of Arturo's face. His jaw, dislocated, wedged unnaturally wide open.

'It looks loose enough now,' Maria said. 'Try pulling down.'

With a tug, the tooth released with a sucking pop and Rubino tumbled backwards. Triumphant, he held the prize aloft, gripped between the pliers. 'Success!'

Maria helped him return to his crouched position. 'Only thirty-one more to go.'

'Won't Hortensia be surprised when she sees Pietro with teeth?' Rubino said. 'You know, of course, I wouldn't do this for anyone else.'

Maria held out one of her small metal tins. 'Nor me. I hope once they're fitted, her feelings for him will blossom.'

Rubino released the tooth. It landed in the proffered receptacle with a tinny plink. He wedged the pliers back into Arturo's gaping mouth. Rubino's elbow began to move sharply again as he levered the next tooth. 'The problem is, until we receive the final payment for the wine and first payment for the olive oil, there is no money to buy gold for the dental wires and plate.'

The opportunistic desecration of Arturo's mouth for my benefit flooded me with abject horror. One hand flew to the horn around my neck, the other clamped my mouth shut. I could not stand to hear or see anymore. I backed away until the view of Rubino, Maria and Arturo's dislocated jaw faded.

———— ◆ ————

Arturo's funeral was held two days later. It was said he had been found in the chestnut and pine forest, thanks to Rubino, who had not given up the search. Because of the body's state of decomposition, the casket lid was firmly nailed down. No one got to view his toothless mouth or hundreds of deep wounds made by Delphina's piercing hair spikes. Nor his manhood, shredded beyond recognition.

That evening, before Rubino and Maria rose from the dinner table, I unclasped the chain from around my neck. 'For Arturo's er…Pietro's teeth.' While I slid the chain and gold horn smoothly across the table, my insides churned. *Dear, poor Arturo.*

Rubino and Maria stiffened.

'You saw?' Rubino asked.

'Yes.'

Maria's bony hand covered mine. 'We did it for you and Pietro. For your happiness.'

'I know.'

Rubino and Maria relaxed. Rubino palmed and pocketed the chain and horn. 'Years ago a dentist made a wax model of Pietro's gums. I'll go to him.'

I wrestled with the vision of Arturo's mangled jaw and tried desperately to focus on something mundane. My forehead furrowed. 'Years ago?'

'Yes. But when the dentist told Pietro the cost, he cancelled. The dentist said he'd keep the wax model until Pietro could afford it. It'll take only a few days and hopefully be completed before Pietro's return.'

I nodded. The wall clock ticked.

'By the way,' Maria said, 'Are you any closer to getting Trianni to sign the Right to Manage and Sell document?'

I nodded. 'Yes. Any day now.'

The lie slipped out smoothly and easily. My spine prickled, but my heart gave a little kick of triumph. Maria had believed me.

In my head I heard my mother sigh and say, *good girl*. I had mastered the art of lying. I had held back handing over the document because I had been practicing forging Claudio Trianni's signature. I needed a little more time to perfect it for the Paternity document I had begun to compose that would need his signature before he died.

That night I fell asleep counting out the days. Two weeks were up, and still I waited for Pietro's return.

———————— ◆ ————————

In the town's community hall, Arturo's death on the certificate was listed as, 'Death by Misadventure'. In the minds of the villagers, however, Arturo's death was linked to the crazy sisters. Valley mothers forbade their sons to apply for the vacant position of yard boy at the Trianni Estate. So, in addition to cleaner and cook, I now added courtyard gardener to my duties.

The soil crying out for attention had driven me mad. I could bear it no longer. I grabbed a spade, fork and hoe and set to turning over the hard earth that had once supported a flourishing patch of vegetables.

While hacking at the hard soil, I wondered if this was what the village women referred to as 'nesting'. Except for the parlour, I'd cleaned Villa Trianni Villa from top to bottom so it was understandable that I now turned my attention to the yard.

The sisters emerged from the kitchen. 'Can we help?'

I hid my surprise and more so when they proved skilled at working the garden tools. In next to no time, upturned clods were broken down and re-forked into the loosened earth. Dry rasping turned to excited murmurs as the sisters watered the turned-over earth. The soil breathed and sighed, waiting in anticipation to nurture plants.

I straightened and stretched my back. My unborn son kicked his feet in displeasure from having been cramped. From my apron pocket I removed two cloth seed bags. 'Delphina, these are spinach seeds. Sow them this far apart and this deep.' I indicated using the span of my hand and the length of my middle finger. 'Camellia, you sow these Brussel sprouts seeds in alternate rows. This far apart and this deep.'

In my mind's eye, I could already see spinach and Brussel sprouts plants lush and verdant, growing side by side. 'After you've tamped the soil down, make sure to cover the rows with hay in a thick layer so the seeds don't freeze. Understand?'

'Yes.' Their voice mimicked each other's.

So far, the sisters' change of behaviour for the better continued. They had turned into polite, helpful and happy young women. Though different from each another, there was little doubt they were Angelica's daughters. Each day, they grew more beautiful, in contrast to my plainness.

Why they had been what they once were, and how and what they were now, I would never know. Yet, I was grateful for the current status quo and prayed it would continue. In the meantime, I would continue to err on the side of caution when dealing with them.

In the kitchen, I washed my hands and turned my thoughts to preparing lunch.

'Hortensia.'

I jumped. One hand flew to protect my belly, the other to touch the gold horn that no longer hung around my neck.

'I did not mean to startle you.' Maria stood still. Her turned-in eyes jittered madly. I knew she had news.

'The good first, please.'

'Pietro has docked. He'll be here tomorrow.'

My heart contracted with joy. 'The bad?'

'Iacopo has returned.'

My heart stopped beating, and my knees gave way.

Maria's clutched my elbow, preventing me from falling to the floor. 'There's more.'

I regained my balance. 'Let me guess.'

So terrible was the thought that sprang into my mind, I gave a strangled laugh. 'Di Napoli has returned, too.'

The bangles released a drum roll.

'Yes,' Maria said. 'He has.

18

'Iacopo coming back is bad enough, but Di Napoli!' Rubino winced as my voice hit a note reminiscent of Mistress Letizia's. I lifted the cheeseboard lid; two small goat rounds lay revealed. 'I tell you, it's too much,' I groaned as I pulled away the paper from one round, revealing the cheese's cracked black pepper crust. 'Especially, unannounced!' I peeled away the paper from the second round, revealing its slivered almond crust. 'Why? Can someone tell me what on earth have I done to deserve them both arriving at the same time?'

Rubino, Maria and the bangles remained silent.

Since lunchtime, when Maria had informed me of their arrival, I felt as though I had turned into a tornado racing around from one end of the kitchen to the other.

I rarely complained. But now, I whined and wept. I felt sick and dizzy, boiling hot and frozen stiff all at the same time.

'That's enough, Hortensia,' Rubino said. 'You're giving me indigestion.'

I took a breath, forcing myself to calm.

The pocket knife flashed as Rubino flicked it open. He selected a dark red apple and rotated it in one hand as the honed blade sliced through the outer red and inner yellow pared skin, falling away in a single long curl. He cut the apple into three, neatly removed the core, speared one piece with the tip of his knife, offered it to Maria, speared another and offered it to me.

Maria glanced at Rubino. 'Between us,' she said, 'we'll find out what they want.'

'Do you think they will come here?'

'Yes,' Maria said.

I stopped my belly muscles from contracting and disturbing my sleeping, unborn son.

'But, you are a married woman now, under your husband's protection and in his absence, under Maria's and mine.'

Rubino's words were comforting. I rested my palm over his large calloused hand. 'What am I to do and say?'

'Stay calm,' Maria said. 'Admit nothing.'

Rubino's brows crinkled. 'You never received or wrote a personal letter to Iacopo, did you?'

'Not even one.'

'And Di Napoli?' Maria's stare held me fast. 'Did you receive any more letters after his first?'

She knows. How silly I had been. Of course, Maria would know I'd received a letter from Di Napoli. She knew everything. Well, almost everything. Quickly I added up the lies I had told. Mine were far less than the lies I believed that Maria, and Anna, when she was still alive, had told me. 'No.' I placed my right hand over my heart. 'I received nothing after the first.'

'And you never replied to it?'

My thoughts flew back to how many times I had reread Di Napoli's letter. And how many times I had written a reply, burning each one immediately thereafter. 'No.'

Maria's stare released me. 'All's well, then. Remember, no matter who fathered your child, in the eyes of the law, your husband is legally your child's father.'

After she and Rubino left, I locked the kitchen door and hastened to bed. When I laid my head upon the pillow, the signed Right to Manage and Sell oil, and the Paternity documents crackled.

I fell asleep. Before long, the tornado returned and not only did I swirl in the grip of a spiraling vortex, but so, too, did butterflies, my father, Di Napoli, Iacopo, Arturo's teeth, Pietro, and The Furies turned to earth-angels.

The next morning, in the still and icy predawn, the clatter of Pietro's van announced his return. I wrapped a shawl around my shoulders and unlocked the kitchen door. The waning crescent was barely visible. Another sixteen days to go to full moon, which would confirm if the daughters' transformation to earth-angels was permanent.

Even before the engine cut, Pietro bounded out of the van's little cab. Excitement rippled from my feet up. In one hand he held letters and in the other a bunch of dried hortensia flower heads. Their faded colour exactly mirrored my plainness. But I pushed that thought away and focused on greeting my husband.

By his crisp, clean smell, I knew he had already bathed before changing into fresh clothes. His face cracked into a closed-mouth smile. *You've remembered your lesson well.*

He picked me up and carried me into the bedroom. 'I've missed you.' His voice was low and gruff. He kicked the door closed behind him.

'Wait. I've something for you. Close your eyes.'

Pietro obeyed. From the puzzled look on his face and upturned corners of his mouth, I knew he was bemused. I reached under my pillow and brought out the full set of dentures. I cupped both hands around them and held my arms out straight. 'Open your eyes.' I lifted my top hand and revealed two rows of teeth, bound with gold wire strands attached to a thin, flat, roof-of-the-mouth plate.

Pietro took the dentures and in the dawn's strengthening rays, looked upon them from every angle. Reverence and awe illuminated his face.

I held up a hand mirror and angled it towards him. 'Try them.'

Getting the dentures into his mouth proved awkward. They stuck, he gagged, his face turned red. I refused to panic. But once in, and after several jaw slides right and left, the dentures fit.

'Smile,' I said.

His mouth expanded, stretched sideways, lips parted, revealing the square tips of Arturo's lovely teeth. Then, like the sun, creeping above the horizon, Pietro's smile broadened. '*O Dio mio*. 'Look. I have teeth!' He opened his mouth wide and holding the mirror closer, he inspected and counted each tooth. 'Hortensia?'

'Yes.'

'What do you think I want to eat?'

I giggled. The days of sucking the flesh from fish-bones were over. 'Mmm…let me think.' I tapped a finger on my temple as though it were the most difficult question in the world to answer. 'A large and thick, chargrilled *bistecca alla fiorentina?*'

'Clever girl. And, only if you're good, and after these beauties have chomped their way through the meat,' he snapped his teeth together until they chattered, 'I'll allow you to gnaw the bone with me.'

'Why thank you, husband dear. You are very kind.'

We laughed. He, for the first time, with wide, open-mouthed freedom, that was a joy to behold. *Thank you, Arturo.*

Pietro took the mirror from my hand and placed it on the table. He swept me into his arms once more and whispered in my ear. 'A million thanks, a million times over.'

I closed the shutters against the sun's warming light and then abandoned myself to his lovemaking.

Later, as he enveloped me in his arms and was about to fall asleep, he asked, 'Where is the gold horn?'

'In your mouth,' I replied.

He gave an amused snort and fell asleep. I opened the shutters permitting the morning sunlight to flood the room. While he slept, I marvelled at how his face had filled out. He was a handsome, mature man. Close to how I had imagined the fisherman in the song *Marechiaro*, serenading a damsel in a tower.

The vision of Di Napoli, with his muscled stomach, playing the mandolin and singing to Mistress Letizia, flew like an arrow striking the centre of my forehead. *Damn you.* I swatted the image away. But it returned, again and again, each time stinging harder.

———— ◆ ————

The feeling of being watched crept over me. I looked carefully through the first kitchen window and saw nothing but the courtyard and the recently hoed and planted vegetable patch. The view from the second window also revealed nothing.

Shrugging off the feeling, I picked up the trays and headed upstairs to the master bedchamber. Angelica opened the door before I could knock. No matter how I prepared myself, her beauty always shocked me. Even now, heavily pregnant, she was divine, seeming to belong more to heaven than earth.

'Hortensia.' Regardless of who it was, or what the time was, Angelica always simply said the person's name.

Over her shoulder, I saw Claudio Trianni sitting slumped. My heart contracted. My thoughts flew to the Paternity document I had written, now hidden beneath my pillow and which I needed him to sign. 'How is he?'

'Weak. Send Rubino for the doctor.'

I nodded, passed her the trays and raced down the stairs. I entered the courtyard and headed to the stable. 'Rubino. *Rubino!*'

He poked his head around the stable door. 'Yes?'

'Fetch the doctor for Claudio Trianni.'

Without a word, he disappeared back into the stable. I knew he would harness the donkey and set off in a matter of minutes. Movement from the oil mill caught my eye. Dread caused me to shudder. *Have the sisters already reverted to their old, Furies style behaviour?*

I paused under the double-storey high arch and stared hard into the gloom. The vast floor space was clear. The two stone presses stood like statues, waiting for the next season when they would come alive, turn, and grind the olives until the bright grass-green oil flowed.

'Pssst. Over here.'

I turned. A row of oil barrels partially hid Iacopo. 'What are you doing?'

'Searching for you. Why are you not at the Angeli Estate?'

At the first sound of Iacopo's voice, my son kicked his feet in joyous greeting. Then I knew Iacopo was the father of my unborn son. 'Iacopo, I–'

'Hortensia.' Pietro's voice drifted from the kitchen's open door. In another second, he would appear in the doorway and see me standing under the mill's arch.

Trapped between my husband to my right and my first lover to my left, I stepped into the mill.

Iacopo grabbed my wrist and pulled me towards him. 'God. Hortensia, I have missed you so.' He began to cover my face with kisses, pressed me close, and then froze. 'What's this?' He held me away and looked down at my belly. 'You're pregnant.'

'With my husband's child.'

Iacopo's hands fell lifelessly to his sides. 'You're married?'

'Yes.'

'But you promised! You promised you'd wait for me.'

Though Iacopo had matured these last six months, he still sounded like the youthful boy who had left. In addition, now he sounded hurt and vexed. And I felt the first twinges of irritation.

'Hortensia.' Pietro's voice was louder and closer.

Recognition followed by a wave of disbelief caused Iacopo's mouth to fall open. 'That stinking, toothless old man? Your husband? You married Pietro *il Pescatore*, the fisherman?'

'Quick. Follow me. He mustn't see us together.' I scaled the ladder as if all the beasts in the world were snapping at my ankles. Iacopo followed. Together we pulled up the ladder.

Just as the last rung slid over the edge, Pietro stepped under the arch. 'Hortensia?' His voice skimmed over the floor and ricocheted off the stone presses.

I frowned, raised my finger and pressed it to Iacopo's lips. We lay on our sides, face-to-face, our noses touching and our hearts thumping. We breathed in each other's breaths while our son continued to kick against his father's stomach.

The sound of the donkey's hooves thudded against the courtyard's cobblestones.

'Good morning, Rubino. Have you seen Hortensia?'

The bale-filled loft muffled Rubino's response. 'Likely she's upstairs serving breakfast.'

'Right. Where are you going so early?'

'To fetch Dr Baldi for Claudio Trianni.'

'It's that bad?'

'Apparently so.'

'Get off that donkey. I'll drive you. It'll be faster. And then I can show you my new teeth.'

The van's engine coughed into life and then clattered. As Pietro drove Rubino down the rutted road, its sound diminished.

Our heartbeats and breathing returned to normal. But the welcoming foot drumming continued.

Iacopo rolled away from me. 'Hortensia, what have you done? What's going on? You promised me.'

I was lost for words. Then remembered. 'You said you'd write.'

'I did. Many times.'

I twirled a curl of hair around my finger. 'You did?'

'Yes. You never replied. That's why I am here. I have been awfully worried.'

Dear sweet boy. 'I never received them.'

'That's not possible. You received my letters regarding the wine and olive oil sales, right?'

'Those were addressed to Rubino. If there had been letters, Rubino would have passed them to me.'

'It's all that witch's doing.'

I knew exactly *who* he meant. But the truth struck home. Pietro always delivered our mail. It was *he* who never passed on Iacopo's letters.

Would Iacopo's letters have changed my current position?

'I've come to marry you.'

'You can't.'

'I must. I have already told everyone I am bringing my wife, Hortensia, to America.' Iacopo's voice sounded distinctly peeved and churlish.

In that second, I gave thanks Pietro had never passed on Iacopo's letters. And in that second too, my unborn son's feet halted their welcoming beat.

19

Despite the distance between the hayloft, where Iacopo and I were hiding, and the master bedchamber, I heard Angelica call my name. An icy wave washed over me in response to the urgency her voice conveyed.

Iacopo held the ladder steady while I scrambled down. 'I'll be back.'

Maria waited in the kitchen. I had long given up trying to understand how she knew to arrive where and when she was most needed.

'Hortensia!' Angelica's voice skittered down the staircase like a bag of spilled marbles. 'Has the doctor arrived?'

'No. But Maria has.'

'Send her up.'

Maria placed her cold, bony hand on my arm. 'It's all right. I know where to go.'

Of course, she did. She had assisted my mother giving birth to me in Claudio Trianni's bed, in which he now lay dying. When Maria reached the top of the staircase, I returned to the oil mill. The ladder had been pulled up. I cupped my hands. 'Iacopo?'

His head popped over the edge of the loft floor. Despite the gloom separating us, it was evident he'd been crying. I reined in the impatience building in my chest. 'You have to leave. Maria has arrived, Dr Baldi will be here soon, and Pietro must not find you. I have my hands full.'

'But what about me? I have a problem. A big one. I've already told everyone I am returning with my wife.'

He looked pathetic and sad. My heart softened. I had to do something. 'I am sure we can find you a good match with one of the many girls in the village. After all, they are much better-looking than plain old me.'

'That's true.'

My heart stopped softening. 'Take a stroll into the village. Let the barman know. Within an hour, you'll have multiple offers.'

'Good idea.'

My heart turned to flint.

'But, Hortensia?'

'Yes.'

'It's you I love. I'll take the child as my own. Just come with me.'

It was difficult to maintain a sympathetic tone through clenched teeth. 'Iacopo, I can't. Please try to understand. I need to stay, and you need to go.'

His young, handsome face cracked, like the *Frigido's* dry bed at summer's end. A wave of inspiration hit me. I placed my hands one over the other and rested them upon my heart. Using the tone I'd once whispered in his ears only, I said, 'You'll forever be my first.'

'Forever?'

'Forever.'

We looked at each other through the gloom.

I broke the silence. 'Iacopo?'

'Yes?'

'When you've found a wife, let me know who she is. Okay?'

'*Va Bene.*'

'Iacopo?'

'Yes.'

I softened my voice. '*Mi dispiace.*'

'I'm sorry, too. Hortensia?'

'Yes.'

'I love you.'

Despite myself, I tied Iacopo's words with ribbon and mentally filed them away. The clatter of Pietro's van announced his return. 'If you truly love me don't let Pietro catch you here.' I turned and left the oil mill.

As I reached the kitchen step, Pietro drove into the courtyard. He waved and flashed me a great big Arturo smile. I still hadn't decided if I would ask him about Iacopo's letters. It stood to reason that if Di Napoli had written again, Pietro would have kept his letters, too. Perhaps that old saying about letting sleeping dogs lie would be wise.

———— ◆ ————

I heard the tinkles of the bangles and then Maria's voice before I entered the kitchen.

'Hortensia, Claudio Trianni needs something to heat his blood.'

Have you gone mad? 'Chastebury?'

'No. *Zenzero.*'

I sighed with relief. 'Ginger.'

Maria fixed me with her stare. 'Go to the Angeli Estate. Dig up a couple of rhizomes and brush them free of soil. But, Hortensia, this is very important. Only when you are ready to serve, grate and stir a heaped tablespoon of the ginger into the broth. Otherwise, the medicinal benefits will be lost.'

'Chicken broth?'

'Yes. For good measure, throw in some crushed garlic.'

I placed a large pot of water on the stove. My brain was already sorting through the flock. The white cock's old bones would make good stock. Besides, it was time to make way for the younger male before he spurred the white cock to death.

At mid-morning, the flock was alert while foraging, the very worst time to kill a chicken, and above all, the old white cock. I'd have to be extra careful, especially given his wily tactics. Thankfully, the flock responded to the sound of my voice. I spread broken corncobs on the floor of their coop and called. The flock paused and, curiosity getting the better of them, began to move towards the stable where they roosted at night. No surprise, the white cock arrived first. I let him be, pecking at a piece of corncob until the entire flock arrived. I sat on a rickety three-legged stool and threw out a few more kernels.

It was peaceful, with the flock making soft peeping and trilling noises and the odd tuck-tuck when something of particular interest had been discovered. The cock strutted closer. Irked at the hens gathered at my feet, he wasted no time pushing his way through, delivering well-aimed pecks left and right. I reached down, grabbed him behind the neck with one hand, his feet with the other and laid him chest down across my thigh. I pulled his neck downwards and with a flick of my wrist twisted his head backwards. Though he was unconscious immediately, his legs jerked, and wings flapped. To minimise the sound, which would upset the other birds, I braced my hands around his body and stifled his movements.

I sat for a few minutes longer. If the flock understood what had happened to the white cock, they made no show of it.

At the far end of the kitchen, I hung up the bird by his scaly feet, slit the artery in his throat where I had dislocated his neck and left it to bleed out into a bucket.

The water was almost at a boil. Holding the feet, I dunked the cock headfirst into the pot, waggled it about and removed it. In a matter of minutes, I had de-feathered and gutted the bird, set the heart and liver to one side, and chopped off and discarded the head, feet and entrails.

Carrots, a sweet red onion, celery, parsley, a single garlic clove, a dried bay leaf, along with the bird, went into the stockpot. I filled it with water and set the heat on low. The stock would simmer for two hours. Time enough for me to go to the Angeli Estate, dig up some ginger and return.

It was a perfect early spring day. No wind, a warm sun and a powder-blue sky scattered with cotton tufts for clouds. Stepping carefully, I took the shortcut along the apex of a precipitous cliff.

Although only five months had passed since my arrival at the Trianni Estate, it seemed longer. No different to a butterfly, my thoughts, in no particular order, alighted upon those events that had been most shocking and revelatory: cutting and pulling my godson out of his dead mother, the deaths of Mistress Letizia, Bea, Foxy and Anna, Iacopo my first lover, spending six weeks with Di Napoli in Naples, discovering I was with child, marrying Pietro, gaining Arturo's teeth, realising who my father was and hearing my mother's tragic love story.

I turned past the row of cherry trees, and dropped down into the Angeli's terraced, sea-facing orchard. My eyes were immediately drawn to the place where I had buried Foxy, with Iacopo's help. I paused at the little dog's grave. 'Dear Foxy, I miss you still.' I wiped my tears and turned to search for the clump of ginger.

The thin, green stalks were half their normal height. Once opened, the buds would change colour from white to yellow. I removed the large kitchen spoon from my apron pocket, sank onto my knees and scraped the earth. Just below the surface was the first light brown plump and knobbly root. I removed two, placed them and the spoon in my apron pocket, and with my pregnant belly weighing me down, I struggled to stand. I caught a whiff of beeswax pomade.

'Here, let me.'

At the sound of Di Napoli's deep, rich voice, my mouth filled with the taste of chocolate, and my son began to drum his feet with urgency.

Di Napoli reached out and helped me to my feet.

The blow came from nowhere and without warning. Indeed, I believed it was a bolt of lightning until, sprawled upon the earth gasping in pain and surprise, Di Napoli fell upon me. His hands gripped my shoulders. 'Why did you not write?' With each word, he shook me, and like a rag doll my head bounced against the earth and flopped forward. 'Did you think you could make a fool out of me?'

I could have been thrown into Dante's Inferno. I could not breathe. One hand fluttered uselessly at my throat, the other cradled my belly. My vision blurred. The air filled with the shapes of the chasteberry's leaves. Like my mother, I too turned into a butterfly and lifted into the sky.

'*WHY? WHY? WHY* did you not respond to my letters?' He released a single sob. Not an ordinary sob. But one that exploded from the centre of his being with the force Virgil described Mount Etna's volcanic eruptions. Di Napoli gathered me in his arms, cradled the top half of my body, rocked me and howled.

I could barely make out his words, drowning in a waterfall of tears cascading from his face onto mine, and tried to breathe. The inside of me turned to ice.

Di Napoli began to kiss my face. 'God, I'm sorry. I beg you, forgive me. Tell me you forgive me.'

Even if I had wanted to, I could not respond. My attention turned wholly to my belly. From his drumming feet, which had been a warning, my son had not only gone dead still but compacted himself to the point of almost non-existence. And then, as if to reassure me he was well, he gave a single, quick kick.

There are no words to describe my relief. Di Napoli licked my tears, all the while murmuring his sorrow. To my horror, the chocolate taste returned. Finding no obstacle, it flooded my mouth.

With my belly almost flat, Di Napoli ravished me on the green grass, like a starveling at a banquet. In the warmth of the midday sun, my body rose, met his and in an act, hitherto always taken in the gloomy dark, we fulfilled our need of each other in broad daylight.

When all was done, Di Napoli clasped my face between his hands and kissed me. Truth be told, that kiss was more intimate than the savage act that had just taken place. He pulled up his trousers and without saying a word, he strolled up the terraces, heading back towards Villa Angeli, just as if nothing had happened.

Under the beating sun, the reminder of the vow I had made pierced me. Pietro had been betrayed – unwittingly, yes. But, should he know, he would consider it betrayal. A part of my heart curled up and hid with shame.

My return journey to the Trianni Estate was swift, during which my son took up his natural position. I entered the kitchen.

Pietro stood so quickly his chair tipped backwards and crashed. His face was drained of colour. 'Dear God, what happened?'

'I slipped and fell, but I'm fine. Shoo. Out of the way, I have stuff to do.'

'But–'

I lied like never before. 'No buts. I'm fine, truly.' I stood on tiptoe to kiss him on the cheek. 'Now out. Before the rest of the day runs away without me.'

———————— ◆ ————————

With the simmering stock strained, I added a clove of crushed garlic and a large tablespoon of grated ginger. Immediately a cloud of aromatic fragrance filled the kitchen, causing my nostrils to burn and my eyes to weep. I clamped a lid over the bowl, placed it on the tray and began the climb up the stairs. I entered the master bedchamber. 'Where is everyone?'

Claudio Trianni tried to sit up. 'At the village Spring Fair.'

I plumped the pillows behind his back. 'What did Dr Baldi say?'

Claudio Trianni snorted with derision. 'Bah. Promises I'll be back on my feet in days. What does that old fool know?'

'Perhaps he was being kind?'

'What's to be kind about?' Claudio Trianni grimaced. 'I am a dying man. Anyhow, what have you brought me to eat? I'm starving.'

Somewhere in my chest, hope glimmered. 'Those are not the words of a dying man.'

Claudio Trianni gave another, but this time, exaggerated, snort. I couldn't help but giggle.

When I removed the lid, Claudio Trianni wrinkled his nose and peered into the bowl. 'Witches' brew?'

'Specially made to pay you back for all the horrible things you did to Little Bean.'

'What! Do I have to be reminded? Wasn't confessing and giving you the authority to manage and sell the oil enough?'

'If you eat this, I won't remind you.'

'Dear God in heaven! What planet do you come from? The softest part of you is your teeth.'

I growled and curled back my lips. 'Open wide.' I spooned the broth into Claudio Trianni's mouth.

He grimaced and fussed, but curiosity stained his face. By the time the bowl was half-empty, his cheeks flushed pink. A sheen of sweat covered his brow. 'Are you trying to kill me? Open the windows. It's hotter than hell in here.'

'Consider this a practice run.'

'What do you mean?'

'You know how I had to listen to your story about Little Bean?'

The old man looked at me warily. 'Yes?'

'Well, I have something you must listen to.'

'And if I don't?'

'You'll go to hell and be the most miserable creature there.'

'And if I do?'

'You'll go to heaven and be the happiest man there.'

'Not much of a choice, huh? Be serious, Hortensia, you know what will make me the happiest man in the world.'

I knew all too well. 'A son.'

'*Precisamente.*'

'A grandson would be just as good and would solve your dilemma, wouldn't it?'

'Don't make jokes, Hortensia. Who in hell is going to give me a legitimate grandson?'

Suddenly, shyness overcame me. My voice lowered. 'I am.'

'But that means…?'

'Fagiolina is my mother, and you are my father.'

After what I seemed like an eternity, Claudio Trianni broke the silence. 'Prove it.'

'If I say her love name for you, that only you and she knew, would that be enough?'

Claudio Trianni turned statue-still, his rheumy eyes fixed on mine.

'You called her *Fagiolina*, Little Bean, and she called you, Jack, after the childhood story, *Jack and the Beanstalk.*'

The old man's stiffness crumpled, and he sank into his pillows. 'There might just be a God after all.' After a pause, his uncooperative, litigious attitude resurrected. 'Of course, I knew you were her daughter all the time. Plain and simple. You're her spitting image.'

That he'd said, 'her daughter' rather than 'my' or 'our daughter' resounded in my head to the thundering beats of kettledrums. He patted my hand, and like the livestock's branding iron, his words were indelibly stamped upon my heart.

He cocked me a wily, jackdaw eye. 'How do you know you're carrying a son?'

'Maria augured it. But for him to be your grandson, you have to recognise me first.'

More slippery than all of God's eels, Claudio Trianni changed direction. 'What of Angelica? She may be carrying my son, too. Then I won't be needing yours.'

I could strangle you. 'Ah. But you will.'

That got his attention. Claudio Trianni watched me like a rat in a trap.

I held up two fingers. 'First, she is carrying a daughter.' His body flinched. I ticked off one finger. 'And,' I paused for effect, 'the child is not yours.' His body flinched harder as I ticked off the second finger.

'How do you know this? No. Don't tell me. Maria…'

'Yes. And you know she's never wrong.'

His lips pressed into a straight line. 'Enough! What am I to sign?'

From my apron pocket I pulled out the Paternity document. 'Sign where I have marked X.'

'What's it say?'

I read aloud. 'I, Claudio Trianni, recognise Hortensia d'Ambrosia-Trianni as my daughter, and her firstborn, my grandson, to be my rightful heir.'

'What about Angelica and the child she is carrying who, through marriage, I am responsible for?'

I pointed and, bringing the document in line with his sight, read aloud again. 'My daughter, Hortensia d'Ambrosia-Trianni, and her son, my yet unborn grandson and heir, will care for my wife, Angelica, until she remarries or until her death, and will care for the child of my marriage to Angelica Barberi until *maturità.*'

'Hortensia, not even the Devil could dissuade me from accepting you are my daughter.'

I took it as a backhanded compliment, the only praise I would likely ever receive from this man.

'Give me that pen you have lurking in that apron pocket.'

Claudio Trianni held the pen poised above the document. 'Hortensia?'

Oh no. What now? 'Yes'.

'You know, there is nothing for nothing in this life.'

'What do you mean?'

'What do I get in return for signing this?'

I wanted to scream out loud, what more do you need in the little life you have left? But I did not. I clamped my teeth down onto my lower lip and shrugged.

'For me to sign, you have to give me something in return.'

I tasted blood in my mouth. 'What's that?'

Claudio Trianni lowered his voice. 'Come close.'

I moved forward.

'Closer,' he said. 'I need to whisper it in your ear.'

I moved closer and angled my head towards his mouth. Claudio Trianni's whispered words were so terrible, I gasped in horror and my head jerked away.

'I'm not finished. Come back.'

'I won't.'

'Ah. But you will.'

'I won't.'

'Then I shan't sign this.' He dangled the pen in the air.

My mind began to spin. *He has to sign. He must sign.*

'Come close again. We don't want the whole world to hear now, do we?'

Once again, I leaned in and angled my ear towards his mouth. My eyelids closed tight as the enormity of what he was asking began to sink in.

'So, you promise?

I remained mute.

'Say, "On my son's life, I promise."'

I'm so close yet so far. I can never make a promise like this on my unborn son's life. It would be aligning myself with the Devil. I shuddered.

My mother's voice entered my head. *Don't be ridiculous, Hortensia. Of course you can. Remember, promises are only made to be broken.*

But my son. What about my son?

He'll be fine. But now, just say you promise.

My eyelids flipped open to see Claudio Trianni's rheumy eyes locked on mine with surprising steadiness.

'I guarantee,' he said, 'it's no different to killing a chicken for the pot. Swift and easy.'

I digested this in silence.

'Well?' rasped my father's voice. 'Don't just stand there. Tell me. What's it to be?'

'I promise.'

'Good wench.' Claudio Trianni signed the document with a flourish.

I stared at his signature, not quite believing my eyes. Then the reins holding my heart in check released and gave an almighty sky-high bounce of pure elation and then dropped to the ground. *My son. Oh my God, what have I just done?*

'Hortensia?'

'*Si?*'

'And one more thing. Don't show this to Angelica until I'm buried.'

'*Va bene.*'

'Hortensia?'

'*Si?*'

'Is there any more of that hell-hot witches' brew?'

'Iacopo could not have singled out a prospective wife closer to home if he tried,' Rubino announced to Maria, Pietro and me at the dinner table that night.

Pain pierced my chest. *He did it. I've been replaced.* To hide my surprise at my disquiet, I stabbed the spiral-shaped pasta with my fork. From the corner of my eye, I could see Pietro looking for my reaction to Rubino's announcement.

Pietro dabbed his mouth with the napkin. 'What are you thinking?'

'I'm thinking I won't be preparing this delicate sauce again. In another week or two, when the summer heat sets in, cream will turn, and peas will be out of season. So, *buon appetito* everyone!'

Maria saved me from asking who she was.

Rubino picked up his glass. 'Angelica's daughter, Camellia.'

My overly full mouth prevented me from blurting out, 'Oh no!'

Rubino swallowed a mouthful of wine. 'That's not all. Di Napoli put in an appearance at the Spring Fair. That sent all the men scurrying to round up their wives and daughters. Despite the entire female population batting their eyelashes at him, Di Napoli only sought out…' Rubino looked at each of us in turn. 'Well, don't you want to know? Go on. Take a guess.'

Like most men, at the mere mention of Di Napoli, Pietro turned red-faced and balled his hands into fists.

'Delphina,' Maria said.

Like our valley's favourite fireworks, pinwheels, exploding against a night sky, so, too did my feelings.

I reached for my glass and gulped a mouthful of wine. The idea of Di Napoli doing to Delphina what he had done to me was more than I could bear. But it could never be compared to what she had done to Arturo. No different to how my father used slippery eel evasion tactics, I veered far away in order not to remember either incident.

To the sound of a rogue strike of lightning, that only I heard, I understood why Angelica asked me to prepare an early dinner for six people. It was to entertain two prospective husbands, which she and Claudio Trianni would host, if he lasted that long.

My father had made a remarkable recovery since eating the ginger-spiced broth. Even now, his voice could be heard all the way down the staircase and into the kitchen. But it was only Life's last rally.

I twirled the glass stem and watched the russet-hued liquid flow in a never-ending, undulating wave. 'Do they know Iacopo is to return to America?'

'Not yet,' Rubino said. 'But when Angelica finds out Iacopo is our wine and oil agent…'

I frowned. 'When did that happen?'

'While you went in search of ginger, I met with Iacopo and confirmed his position as our agent. He'll take his new wife with him to America.' Rubino paused. 'I'm sure Angelica will feel safer knowing her interests in the Trianni Estate will be better served having one of her daughters married to him.'

The Paternity document Claudio Trianni had signed the day before, was now, after my son, the most valuable thing in my life. I made a note to move it to a safer hiding place and then allowed myself a second to imagine Angelica and everyone's surprise when I would reveal it after my father's death. 'Speaking of Angelica, she has requested a dinner for six tomorrow. Maria, can you give me a hand?'

The bangles were silent, but that did not mean Maria hadn't read my thoughts.

'Certainly. What do you want?'

'Lamb. Can you barter for one and have it slaughtered?'

'Certainly,' Maria said. 'Oh, we need more wine. Pietro, please could you go down to the cellar?'

The moment Pietro disappeared down the cellar steps, Maria lowered her voice. 'Has Trianni signed the Right to Manage and Sell Oil document?'

I reached into my apron pocket and passed it to her.

Maria's gaze slid down to the bottom of the page, where Rubino's and her name had been crossed out and replaced with mine. She raised her head and stared unblinking at me as she passed the document to Rubino.

I gave a light shrug. 'He said that as you and Rubino are even older than him, the management of the grove and oil sales must go to someone younger. I did not want to let the opportunity to slip by debating who that person could be, so I said you and Rubino have been guiding me in the management of harvests for as long as I can remember.'

'That was good thinking on his and your part,' Rubino said. 'For, it is the truth. I've taught you well.' He folded the document, raised his glass and waited for Maria to do the same.

Setting her glass on the table, Maria said, 'You secured our valley's olive harvest livelihood for another eighteen years.'

Together and quietly they said, 'Hortensia, *brava.*'

While they drained the wine in their glasses, in my heart I apologised to them for having lied. If either of them intuited my lie, they showed no inkling of it.

Pietro returned from the cellar with another two bottles. Eager to play a part in the upcoming pre-wedding dinner, Pietro asked, 'What can I do to help?'

'It's not warm enough to have dinner on the terrace,' I said. 'Can you bring wood for the fireplace in the dining room and start the fire around four o'clock? That way Claudio Trianni won't get cold.'

'What has that old scoundrel done for you to deserve your solicitous care?' Under the guise of flashing Arturo's lovely teeth, Pietro watched me carefully.

You'll know soon enough. 'He's frail and not long for this world.' I glanced at Maria, Rubino and Pietro in turn. 'Do you mind? I'm exhausted. Tomorrow will be another busy day, and my bed is calling.'

I left them to finish the meal, knowing Pietro would clear up.

Aside from being tired, I needed time alone. I wanted to make sense of what had happened to me with Di Napoli under the chasteberry tree in Villa Angeli's orchard.

———————— ◆ ————————

Tired from the previous day, I remained in bed a little longer than usual. When I finally rose, I could hear the daughters' footsteps through the kitchen ceiling as they moved between their bedrooms. Their incessant twitterings flowed uninterrupted down the staircase as they tried on each other's dresses, arranged their hair and selected shoes.

I carried the breakfast trays upstairs, knocked and entered the master bedchamber. Angelica rested alongside Claudio Trianni, who snorted and grumbled in response to the girls' high-pitched squeals. Even I desired to clap my hands over my ears.

'Have those girls any brains?' Claudio asked. Angelica murmured soothing words. As the sisters' giddy excitement increased, their bodies released the heady scent of their floral fragrances. Soon the air was thick and barely breathable.

'*Basta,*' Claudio Trianni groaned. 'Let me die in peace, will you?'

Later, when I entered the chamber carrying the lunch trays, he said. 'Hortensia, I beg you, poison those daft girls.'

Ooooh. Don't be misled. They're more crazy than daft. The next moon would be a full moon. Then I'd know if the daughters would revert to their old behaviour. Or not.

At five o'clock, I cast my gaze over the table laid for six. The matching silver candelabra gleamed as did the Trianni family's crested cutlery and hand-etched Venetian glassware. The blazing fire in the hearth warmed the cavernous room.

In the kitchen, the sweet fragrance of lamb roasted with rosemary wafted from the oven. Accompanying the lamb was a dish of boiled *cardi gobbi,* hunchback cardoon, served with a bowl of *bagna càuda, a* sauce made with a head of peeled garlic simmered in milk until soft, mashed with salted anchovies, olive oil and lemon juice. A sauce for those who planned to share kisses.

Uncorked bottles of the Angeli's vintage *Sangiovese* released hints of chocolate.

Torta di riso a cake rich with sugar, eggs, rice, lemon peel and milk, cooled. Its golden-yellow top glistened, oozing the scent of anise, the liqueur made from soaking crushed fennel seeds in alcohol.

Goat yoghurt, a light sour contrast to the rich cake, chilled in a marble bowl.

I'd already snipped off the smallest mint leaves, separated the petals from a single head of bright orange calendula and picked lilac violas with which to decorate each serving of rice cake.

Pietro carefully stamped his feet freeing his boots of dirt and at the same time inhaled. '*Mamma Mia. Che profumi fantastici!* I can't believe I'm going to miss this feast like I did at Christmas.'

'Are you going somewhere?'

He placed his arms around me, and lightly nipped my neck with Arturo's teeth. 'You remember what fish do under full moonlight, don't you?'

After the encounter with Di Napoli, I'd sworn off intimacy. The night before, I'd turned away from Pietro for the first time.

'Are you not feeling well?'

'Just exhausted. Sorry.'

Pietro had pulled me close and folded his arms around me. 'No problem.'

The image of Di Napoli, whose body had perfectly fit, violently and then sinuously coupled with mine less than twelve hours before, was replaced by that of Di Napoli and Delphina. I had spent most of the night beating that image until it disintegrated.

Now, I gave Pietro a playful punch, but he caught my fist. He stared hard at me. 'You'll be okay serving?'

'Of course. And Rubino and Maria will be here to clear up.'

Though I alluded to Rubino's and Maria's help, I sensed his question was a cover for what *he* likely meant: me being in close proximity to Di Napoli. But my husband's concern was too late. He'd already been betrayed, and I prayed to God he would never know it. I threw myself into his arms and rested my cheek upon his broad, strong chest. 'When will you return?'

'As soon as I can.'

I tilted my head and kissed him. 'Take care and come back soon.'

'I will.'

To my surprise, Pietro opened his mouth and with some difficulty, removed Arturo's teeth. Immediately, his face collapsed back into the old, toothless Pietro.

Thank God for the dentures. He looked truly awful without them. 'Why?' The pitch of my voice rivalled the daughters' squeals.

In the old way, he lifted his hand to cover his mouth and said, 'I don't want to risk losing them on the boat. And, as you're not there to see me you can't be offended.'

A deep pang of remorse for how carelessly I had hidden my distaste of him and his toothlessness in the past lodged like a boulder in my heart.

'Keep them safe, will you?'

I slipped the dentures into my apron pocket. 'I will.'

'One more thing.' Pietro pressed a black iron key into my hand. 'Hold on to this. It's the spare key to the safety box I keep on the boat.'

The van's engine coughed to life and clattered out of the courtyard. Without looking back, Pietro stuck his arm out the window and waved goodbye.

I was shocked at his swift departure. But relieved, too. I surveyed the kitchen and mentally ticked off my to-do list. I could take a quick break before Iacopo and Di Napoli arrived for dinner.

I registered that Pietro's van had stopped. He would have reached the river crossing. *Has the engine stalled?* I listened hard. After what seemed too long a while, the van started up again and continued on its way to the harbour. I found myself releasing a breath of relief. But the unknown reason for his stop, like a burrowing worm, niggled.

Camellia, who had been dressed and ready for most of the afternoon, entertained Iacopo, who arrived unfashionably early. Later, Delphina joined them. Questions and answers about his life in America flew back and forth. I shut my ears. I did not wish to hear about the life I could have had in America.

Di Napoli arrived fashionably late. Angelica showed him into the dining room where the daughters and Iacopo were already seated.

In Di Napoli's presence, the daughters' carefree giddiness changed. Camellia to subdued anxiety, and Delphina to overt excitement. Either way, both girls had never looked more beautiful demonstrating, once again, how plain I was.

I entered the kitchen with the dirtied *antipasti* plates in my hand. 'You're quiet tonight, Rubino. Anything the matter?'

Rubino rubbed his wrinkled brow. 'I would never have believed it possible that people like us could sit at Claudio Trianni's table as equals. Much less celebrate the permission granted to Di Napoli and Iacopo to marry the daughters.'

I was quick to set the record straight. 'Remember, they are only his stepdaughters. And, from the moment Di Napoli married Mistress Letizia, he entered a higher social class. And, Iacopo, too joined a higher class simply by going to HA MER E KA. You said so yourself, remember?'

Rubino nodded.

I continued. 'It just goes to show how changes are coming, even to these backwaters, and how life, as we knew it, is chang–'

Angelica entered the kitchen. 'Hortensia, help Claudio to the dining room. Maria, please serve the first course.'

The tintinnablating bangles were shocked into indignant silence. I held back a laugh. Even Rubino struggled to keep a straight face. Maria had never served at the table.

I entered the dining room. Despite my efforts, my heart beat in double time, soft for Iacopo and hard for Di Napoli. But, I held my head high, my gaze focused ahead and kept as far away as possible from the table where the daughters, Iacopo and Di Napoli sat, and whose eyes, I felt, bored holes through my back.

———————————— ◆ ————————————

Claudio Trianni lay with the covers pulled up to his chin.
'Come on. Get up. Your presence is required downstairs.'

He grimaced. 'Don't harass me, wench. Serve my dinner here. I'm not going.'

'You must. It's one sure way of getting rid of your daft stepdaughters.'

'Ah. If you put it like that.' Claudio Trianni eased himself out of bed and lifted one arm.

I helped him slip on his padded dressing gown, tied a knot in the belt around his emaciated waist, folded the broad collar and tucked it snug around his neck.

Standing so close, we had no option but to look into each other's eyes. His were opaque.

'Fagiolina.' His voice carried a wistful note.

'No. It is I, your daughter, Hortensia.'

'Don't be ridiculous,' he said. 'I don't have a daughter.'

I sighed with relief. Claudio was closer to death than I had thought. Then the memory of the promise he'd forced me to make in exchange for signing the Paternity document, sent shivers up my back. *If only...* I swiftly killed the rest of that thought.

I wrapped one arm around his waist and placed his other arm around my neck. 'Ready?'

He grimaced. 'Forward march.'

As we made our way down the corridor, I fantasised Claudio Trianni, my father, was walking me proudly down the church aisle on my wedding day, with my mother, Lucia d'Ambrosia, beaming at us. Pietro waited at the altar showing off Arturo's teeth.

Despite this warming fantasy, I had never felt so lonely in my life.

———————————— ◆ ————————————

M aria had already placed a bowl of ginger-spiced broth at Claudio Trianni's place. After a few mouthfuls, he rallied and took control of the dinner conversation.

The meal was a success, but the real reason for the dinner, and the highlight, came when Claudio Trianni called for a bottle of *Prosecco*.

I entered, carrying the bottle and six flutes on a tray.

Di Napoli was faster than Iacopo. He pushed back his chair, stood up and was at my side in a slither of a second. His hot hands covered mine as he took the tray from me. The memory of me lying supine in bright sunshine under the chasteberry tree, my inner calves rubbing Di Napoli's ears, the soles of my ankle boots facing the sky, rose. I wrestled the image down.

'You will always be mine,' he whispered in my ear while his back was turned to the diners at the table.

Dangerous though he was, the dark side of me *wanted* to be his, while the light side of me yearned for Pietro and his relaxed, all-embracing warmth and security.

Di Napoli placed the tray on the table, looked at his host and held up the bottle. 'May I?'

Claudio Trianni gave a feeble wave.

I returned to the kitchen, not caring whether Rubino and Maria would hear my heart's conflicted roars. I stood close to the door, having left it open a crack.

The cork popped, and Di Napoli poured.

'A toast,' Claudio Trianni said, 'to the future marriages of Angelica Barberi's daughters. Camellia to Iacopo Lenzi and Delphina to Gennaro Di Napoli. May God bless you all.'

Glasses clinked.

'Gentlemen, please, I beg you, marry as fast as possible,' Claudio Trianni said. 'I can't afford to keep these beauties anymore.'

The women tittered. The men laughed.

Maria stood behind me. 'That went well.'

Why am I surprised? Whenever Maria is involved, things always work out precisely according to her plan.

'Hortensia.' Claudio Trianni's voice had returned to sounding weak.

I stepped into the dining room.

'Help me to bed. I'm tired.'

———————— ◆ ————————

Claudio Trianni looked at me from the comfort of his soft pillows. 'Hortensia?'

'Yes.'

'Do you know how to tell a lie and get away with it?'

My mind raced backwards. *So, it was you who told me this very phrase after Bea fell out of the window.* 'Yes. Always keep the lie as close to the truth as possible.'

'You remembered. Good girl. Hortensia?'

'Yes?'

'I was joking.'

'About what?'

'Not having a daughter.

Scoundrel. There I thought you were on your last legs.

'Hortensia?'

'Yes?'

'Three things. Above all, I still love your mother and have lived each day regretting my treatment of her.' He ticked off one finger and raised another. 'You are worth one hundredfold more than everyone in the whole of Tuscany, rolled into one.'

'And the third?'

'It's time for you to make good on your promise. Remember, the one you made on your son's life.'

'No. I can't.'

'You must. Or else be warned, you will live to regret it.'

I fell to my knees and clasped both his hands in mine. 'Please, I beg you.'

'Sorry. A promise is a promise. Now. Get a hold of yourself. Think of your son, my grandson.'

Claudio Trianni lay back and shut his eyes.

The air in the bedchamber stilled to what I imagined a century-old, untouched mausoleum would.

'Now do it.'

My arms and hands seemed to belong to someone else. They picked up Angelica's pillow, laid it over my father's face and pressed down.

While counting, I realised that Maria had done exactly this to Giovanni Angeli.

Her voice sounded in my head. *Yes. The final act for the dying: mercy.*

Before I got to one hundred and twenty, my father's body went limp. But, just as he'd said when he whispered the instructions to me, I held the pillow in place and continued to count out another sixty.

I removed the pillow, plumped and smoothed it, removing the imprint of his face and replaced it on Angelica's side of the bed. Once again, I sank to my knees and with my hands clasped, grieved for the father side of him I had never had and at the same time, begged forgiveness.

I heard the front door open and close, and when the bolts were drawn, I stood, dried my face, and slipped out of the room.

———————— ◆ ————————

Angelica's shrieks announced her husband's passing. The daughters acted with decorum perfectly fitting the role of grieving daughters and betrothed young women.

Two days later, Claudio Trianni was buried. After the first clod of earth landed on the coffin, the mourners returned to the church where the double wedding ceremony took place.

Directed by Maria, the village women prepared enough food for a Roman legion. The festivities continued until just before dawn the following day when all manner of carts, a bicycle or two, mopeds and Piaggio Ape vans trundled down the rutted road to the port.

Two boats were to leave with that morning's outgoing tide. One would take Iacopo and Camellia to America, the other, Di Napoli and Delphina to Naples.

The mooring where Pietro anchored his boat was empty. As the boats left, a wind blew up.

Maria sniffed the air. 'It's the *Tramontana*. It's always strongest after sunrise and will help the boats on their way.'

Even before the boats passed the harbour's breakwater, the wind increased, funneling down the valley out to sea. Everyone hastened home. I thought about what Maria had said. If the *Tramontana* was so good at sending boats out to sea, that meant Pietro would find it difficult to steer his fishing vessel back to the harbour.

With the north wind from the Alps whistling and gusting in cool air currents, and despite the rising sun, everyone took to their beds and slept.

I woke several hours later with a start and found myself sitting straight up. Twisting around, I slipped my hand under my pillow and brought out Arturo's teeth. I clutched them close to my heart, seeking comfort through their fixed grin. But in the deep place where that niggly worm had burrowed, and intuition resides, something was amiss.

The moment that knowledge manifested itself, I struggled out of bed, opened the wardrobe and hauled out an old shoebox. I removed the shoes, lifted the tissue paper and stared at the base of the box. The document acknowledging me as Clauido Trianni's daughter and my son, his grandchild, and heir, was not there.

In its place lay a single, black, rigid strand of long hair.

21

With growing disbelief, I scrabbled around the bottom of the shoebox. As the truth dawned, the room swirled around my head, and I blacked out.

Stiff and cold, I woke in the early hours with the shoebox beside me, still empty, except for Delphina's strand of hair. I eased myself off the floor and returned to lie on the bed. With my hands resting upon my domed belly, I stared hard into the dark, trying to fathom how Delphina could have possibly known about the signed Paternity document. More importantly, what she had done with it?

My mother's voice entered my head. *Start at the beginning.*

I summoned the memory of my sparse interaction with Angelica's daughters since my arrival at Villa Trianni, and, not without trepidation, stepped onto the path that opened before me.

I saw Delphina, who stood and stared without blinking out of her bedroom window, and Camellia, who lay and slept in her bed. Both were so still, they might well have been statues only – and not exist at all.

Delphina thrusting the long-playing records into Arturo's hands and blinding the men with her roving lighthouse eye-beams before vanishing.

Camellia, naked, flitting from the stable to the mill. And when Arturo caught sight of me while righting his trousers, his sheepish grin displaying his lovely teeth.

Angelica bolting the sisters in their bedrooms and the different noise they each made; Delphina's terrifying fury and Camellia's heart-wrenching keening.

I relived my surprise at the sisters' spotless bedrooms, and my confusion when I trod upon Delphina's cylindrical hair spike lying in my bedroom.

I had arrived at the end of the path where the impenetrable drawbridge I had erected stood. Stored behind it, were all the memories I wished never to recall. But, now, to discover the reason why Delphina had stolen my Paternity document, I let the bridge down and released this memory.

———————— ◆ ————————

I stood alongside Angelica at the far end of the kitchen courtyard. The invisible force of the two opposing magnets held me back from trying to rescue Camellia from the firepit. I watched her melt away. It had been an act of self-immolation. Why?

As I had experienced before, Time's phosphorescent passage sprang up. It traced backwards along Camellia's life path and came to a stop.

As it had always been in heaven, celestial bodies' written plots and answers to each being's life was there for the reading. One only need know how.

Retfa gnivol dna gnisol orutrA ot htaed, ta reh
s'retsis dnah,
aillimaC lliw esoohc ot evil reh efil sa na
yranidro gnieb.
ehS lliw evig pu reh dnoyeb-erutan srewop,
dna,
ogrednu htrib-er hguorht fles-noitalommi.

With that question answered, I turned my attention back to the firepit. Angelica blew a current of air that caused the coals to re-ignite.

With her gaze locked upon her eldest daughter, she cried out with the force of ten thousand voices, *'Despicable Fury!'*

Delphina darted around the pit to evade the rising flames and her advancing mother. She stood, hands upon hips, her face tilted to the sky and in a sing-song voice, sang out, 'You can't catch me.'

Angelica made as if to run around the firepit, but faster than the blink of an eye, took a shortcut and, barefoot as always, ran through the licking flames. Despite being as light as a floating seed head, she held Delphina's forearms in a vice-like grip and began to pull her daughter into the pit. 'I warned you of the consequences of invoking your powers against mere mortals. With Arturo, you went too far. Now you pay.'

The volume of Delphina's voice changed to an ear-shattering decibel. Fire-fueled rage transformed her lovely face to that of a gargoyle, and her rigid hair strands turned into a coiling mass of serpents.

Anchored by their tails to Delphina's head, the writhing serpents elongated, and with jaws wide open and forked tongues flicking, eased towards Angelica.

'I'm sorry. I promise I won't do it ever again!' Delphina screeched. 'Just don't pull me into the fire, or I'll lose my powers.'

With an effort that would likely match the combined force of ten men or more, Angelica did just that – she held her daughter in the centre of the blazing pit.

Delphina and her head of serpents began to roll and twist. The bodies of mother and daughter became a whirling blur as both women's feet danced in the licking flames.

'Mamma. Please, I beg you.'

'Too late. I condemn you to the existence of an ordinary being.'

Icicles portending doom prickled my skin. Angelica's voice had lost its force. She was tiring fast. Having been in the fire longer, her feet had begun to melt, and the hem of her dress was aflame.

A shriek of demonic joy shattered the air. 'How much stronger I am than you.'

Delphina's feet moved towards the cooler, outer edges of the pit. She now gripped Angelica's forearms and held her mother fast, in the centre of the pit. The serpents engulfed Angelica's head.

With the invisible magnetic force gone, I charged towards the wrestling women and rammed into Delphina who sprawled face down into the pit. At the same time, I pulled Angelica towards me, fell and landed with my back on the cool earth.

Unlike her sister's calm acceptance of the burning flames, Delphina jerked and flipped like a cube of fat sizzling in a hot, dry pan. The serpents disintegrated, except for one or two, whose intact umbilical cords still granted her passage between two worlds.

I lay winded, staring up at the sky. Angelica lay face down upon me. The point where our pregnant bellies met issued forth a heat so hot, I felt my unborn child and I would surely die burning.

Angelica rose, offered me her hand, whispered thank you, and as though a zephyr passed beneath my feet, I tipped upright and stood some distance from the pit. Angelica vanished. I turned my attention to the firepit.

Delphina's fingertips, fingers, then hands emerged. Thereafter, her arms followed and before long, Delphina clawed and hauled the rest of her charred and fragmented body out of the pit.

She lay still while from the earth all manner of insects and reptiles emerged, layering themselves upon each other and filling the burnt holes in Delphina's body until she was whole again.

When reassembled, Delphina looked perfect.

———————— ♦ ————————

'So,' I said aloud, 'as not all her serpents died, she was not rendered to a wholly ordinary being,'

'Correct,' responded a disembodied voice. 'Slowly, over time, those serpents multiplied, restoring her to pure evil.'

I sighed with understanding, then trembled with fear. Having pushed Delphina into the firepit, almost finishing what her mother had started, I had reduced her extraordinary powers. Thus, I had made her my enemy.

Utilising the principle of an eye for an eye, Delphina had stolen my signed Paternity document.

I was relieved, if only for the sake of clarity on events past, and, a little proud of having saved Angelica. Yet, my common sense alerted me: stealing would not be Delphina's only retaliation.

Despite everything that memory revealed I still did not know what Delphina had done with the document.

My mother's voice entered my head. *What if she's destroyed it?*

I knew the answer to that as clearly as if God and the Devil yelled it out in unison. *No. She'd never do that. It's much too valuable a bargaining tool.*

Well, then. What are you waiting for? Write out another and put all the hours you've practised perfecting your father's signature into practice. Sign it yourself.

Knowing what Delphina was capable of, I ignored my mother's advice. I did not want to put my unborn son's life in danger. It took no effort for me to understand that, despite all that I had tried to achieve, my status, and in turn that of my child, remained where it had always been – nowhere. A fist of weary and wary tightness took up residence in my chest.

I would have to look elsewhere to secure my son's future. But to whom? Or where?

———— ◆ ————

After Claudio Trianni's funeral, Angelica was afflicted with lassitude and remained in bed. Without the newly-wed daughters, life in the household slowed.

Maria entered the kitchen, having first checked on Angelica.

Fearful for my child, I asked, 'Is her lassitude catching?'

'No. It only affects and tires women who are too old to be pregnant.'

By my calculation, Angelica was four weeks overdue. 'Shouldn't she have already given birth?'

The bangles might well have been affected with lassitude, too, as they gave a half-hearted rattle.

'A doctor might deem so. But this child is biding her time.'

'What's she waiting for?'

The light in Maria's turned-in eyes flickered. 'Not what, but who.'

The bangles roused themselves and for the first time emitted a sound that hinted at three church bells ringing out after a wedding has taken place.

I changed the subject. 'I feel more exhausted and older than Angelica looks.' My voice hinted misery and not without cause. Angelica carried her pregnancy weight only in her stomach, while my whole body had ballooned.

Easing my workload, Rubino prepared our meals and carried Angelica's tray to the top of the stairs. From there, I'd take the tray into the master bedchamber.

———————— ◆ ————————

Every morning and early evening, I struggled up each step of the ladder to reach the hayloft. Even the walk up the inclined ramp exiting onto the tower's parapet had become more difficult.

Having ascertained Pietro's boat had not docked, I stared hard at the coastline and beyond the islands to the horizon. But, I refused to allow my gaze to wander across the valley to the Angeli Estate. In particular, I ignored the orchard, and the bird's-eye view of the chasteberry tree, under which the violent coupling in broad daylight had occurred between Di Napoli and me.

One lunchtime, while Rubino and I sat quietly digesting our meal, a question I had been meaning to ask but was almost too scared to know the answer to, slipped out of my mouth. 'Rubino, when do you think Pietro will return?'

He glanced at me while cracking walnuts. 'Depends on the wind and the currents.'

My chest grew tighter.

'Rubino?'

'Yes.'

'Is Pietro related to you?'

'He is my nephew. My eldest sister's firstborn.'

'Is it because he is family, you arranged for him to marry me?' To my ears, my voice sounded pathetic.

'No. He'd made his interest in you clear long before.'

Spreading warmth filled my heart, and for a while the tightness in my chest eased. 'He did? When?'

'While you were still living with Maria in her hut.'

'Really?'

Rubino handed me a walnut. 'He was much taken with you. But, having you marry a family member was a safer bet than you marrying an outsider. Just always remember, Hortensia, certain things need to remain only between us – you, me and Maria. *Capisci?*'

'*Sì.*'

'Since we got the labour union to come here and negotiated the sales of the Angeli wine and Trianni oil, workers' conditions have changed for the better. I only pray to God that to ensure the valley workers' Trianni Estate's olive harvest income, Angelica will give birth to a son.'

I pressed my lips, sealing the truth from him. There would be time enough in the future for him and the valley workers to lament the birth of a Trianni daughter.

'Though it wasn't easy,' Rubino continued, 'we each did what needed doing. And, Hortensia,' Rubino stopped cracking walnuts and looked directly at me, 'you played no small part in helping us achieve our goals. Be proud of yourself.'

The warmth filtered through my heart to the rest of my body, not because of Rubino acknowledging my role in securing the valley workers' incomes, but, knowing Pietro indeed loved me from the very beginning. I held on to that warm feeling until tightness reclaimed its grip.

————— ◆ —————

A fortnight passed and still, Pietro did not return. Try as I might, I could not make sense of the ominous dark cloud above my head.

Soon it would be full moon again, and there would be no reason for him to return until the next waning cycle. I could no longer, at will, summon Pietro's face, with or without Arturo's teeth. I put it down to my advancing pregnancy. Would I recognise him when he returned?

'Hortensia,' Angelica said one morning, 'I feel my baby is due soon. Starting tonight, sleep in my bedchamber.'

For the first time, I climbed the stairs in my nightgown, entered the bedchamber, and settled on a cot at the foot of that big bed. Angelica acknowledged me and went back to sleep.

Angelica Barberi's staccato grunts woke me long before the six o'clock church bells.

Before I saw it, I caught a whiff of wet copper, the tangy smell of blood that had no place in that grand, old-fashioned bedroom. I rolled off the cot, grasped a post, and hauled myself upright.

Angelica writhed in a twist of blood-soaked white linen, looking much like the albino serpent discovered in the chicken coop last spring. Halfway along its length, the serpent's body had stretched taut over the egg it had swallowed.

'Hortensia. Send for the doc–' Her face was flushed, and her black-ened tongue peeked between raspberry lips.

I adjusted my dishevelled nightgown as I rushed from the room, as much to get fresh air as to do her bidding.

At the landing, I took in a shallow breath of stale night air and held onto the iron balustrade. Despite the need for speed, my belly refused to let my feet hurry.

With each careful step descended, I pondered why a child had cho-sen to be conceived in the womb of a woman whose childbearing years were fading. And, recalling Maria's mutter, I wondered who she had been waiting for.

Stepping off the last tread, my feet skimmed the icy harlequin-patterned entrance floor. Dawn sneaked between the shutters, highlighting the mark on the wall where a Venetian mirror and the two crystal sconces on either side of it had, until recently, hung.

Supporting my extended belly with both hands, I shouldered open the dining room door.

I passed the hearth that could accommodate half a tree trunk, but since the night of the double-marriage dinner had remained empty and cold.

The kitchen night stove warmed my skin as I headed towards the door and turned the time-worn key. I pushed open the heavy chestnut door, took a deep breath and filled my lungs with fresh, early morning air.

'Rubino,' I called. '*Rubino!*'

The stable door cracked open.

Chicken and rooster heads, adorned with a variety of crimson combs, and studded with lively black-bead eyes, bobbed through the narrow crack. The door swung open, and a flurry of feathers and flashing yellow legs, the flock raced out.

Rubino materialised from behind the stable door. His eyelids blinked against the light.

'Fetch the doctor.'

'You mean Maria. For you?'

'No, the doctor, for Angelica.'

'Something wrong?'

Rubino had delivered countless livestock over decades. But he had not smelled, nor seen what I had: Angelica's blotched bed linen, redder than her raspberry lips. I responded with certainty. 'Yes.'

He held out his treasured, ancient pocket knife. 'Then you may need this.' His forehead furrowed. 'Be careful with it.'

I took the knife. 'Thank you. Be quick.'

But there was nothing quick about Rubino. His gaze lingered upon my protruding belly. 'Are you sure it's not your time?'

'Yes, I'm sure.'

Angelica's muffled scream appeared to convince him; he re-entered the stable. The donkey's hooves beat out a cheerful greeting as Rubino secured the halter.

From habit, and because it calmed me, I counted the flock. Thirty.

Astride the donkey, Rubino exited the courtyard. It was a five-kilometre journey to Dr Baldi's home.

From habit, I shoved a couple of sticks into the smouldering embers inside the night stove and blew carefully until the fire reignited. After adding more wood and heaving the metal kettle onto the surface of the stove, I retraced my steps. Passing the bare wall again in the entrance hall reminded me of the Trianni Estate's precarious financial affairs.

Claudio Trianni had borrowed from the bank using the estate as collateral to fund his predilections. Only when the bank refused to loan him more money, and with no funds and nowhere else to go, Claudio Trianni returned home.

With difficultly I began the climb up the stairs. Yet my thoughts remained on Claudio Trianni's dire financial state that had been hidden for a little while longer with all the brouhaha of bringing home a wife.

From the first oil sale, we managed to pay the first loan repayment, thus keeping the bank from foreclosing on the property. The responsibility of a decade or more of repayments to make felt like an impossible task. Worse, my son's future loomed bleaker, thanks to the theft of the Paternity document. *Damn you, Delphina.*

Halfway up the staircase, my mother's voice intruded again. *Don't be stupid, Hortensia. Compose and sign Claudio Trianni's name to a new document. It's what your father wanted!*

I reached the landing. As I headed down the corridor, Delphina's dark image loomed. Truth be known, I was afraid of her and feared for my son. I did not want jeopardise his life. Not for anything.

About to enter the bedchamber, my belly contracted. Caught by surprise, I sat in one of the chairs outside the door.

Rubino. Why did I doubt you? I fingered the knife. *Please, follow your wisdom and bring Maria back.* When the contraction eased, I pushed the door open.

Angelica lay still. In my vision, the bed had transformed into a layer of meadow-soft leaves dotted with a profusion of tiny lavender and white flowers. Instead of blood, I smelled only the fragrance of delicate mint from the plant, *nepitella*.

'Angelica,' I whispered, holding the door handle for support. 'Angelica?'

I released the handle. The door closed behind me. With each step, the enticing smell of mint grew stronger. Beneath the layer of leaves and flowers there was a movement.

I drew the layer back.

A blue-grey and red lump lay attached to Angelica.

Seemingly of its own volition, the blade easily slid out from the handle. I sliced the infant free.

Using only my fingertips, I massaged her tiny body that fit in the palm of one hand, until she sighed a kitten's mew.

It was useless to attend to Angelica, but I said, 'Angelica, your daughter is born. She shall be called Nepitella.'

I closed Angelica's eyelids and felt her spirit lift as the bells began to summon the faithful to Sunday Mass. My belly contracted again. I placed Nepitella safely next to her mother, fell onto the bed with the force of the contraction, my head landing where my mother's had when she gave birth to me, and where my father's had rested when I brought his life to an end.

I lifted my nightgown. Keeping time with the peals of the church bells, I pushed hard, and before the final peal had faded, I had given birth in a whoosh.

The room filled with the smell of sun-warmed thyme mixing with Angelica's celery and Nepitella's mint. It was useless to try and summon the fragrance of hortensia flower heads; they had none.

Rubino's knife appeared in my hand, its blade still wet with Nepitella's blood.

'You will be called Timo,' I said, cutting my cord and freeing my son. A clear image of Iacopo's face flashed before me, likely driven by that feminine part of his soul, curious to view his child.

Before I could upend Timo, he squalled and waved his clenched fists in the air. I wrapped him in a sheet and nestled him safely beside Nepitella.

Though strong for my seventeen years, I had tired. I inhaled deeply, drawing in the mixed fragrances masking blood's coppery odour, and fell asleep.

———— ◆ ————

By the smell of goat, and chain-rattling bangles, I knew it was Maria before she said a word.

'Hortensia, wake up. There are two babies to nurse.'

Terrified by all that awaited me, I tarried. But the fickle dream-wind, loyal only to itself, changed direction. It delivered me to the crossing I had avoided. I stepped over the Rubicon, letting go of the old me. On the other side, I shyly welcomed the new, motherhood-me.

My eyelids slid open.

Maria, looking ever more like the *Befana*, the mythical witch Italian children either loved or feared, hovered above me. The lights in her turned-in eyes flashed, highlighting her hooked nose.

'You have done well, my child.' Her voice was barely audible through Timo's strident howls demanding nourishment.

With a strength hidden beneath her cloak, she hauled me into a sitting position and settled pillows behind my back. She eased Timo into the crook of my arm. Her gnarled fingers unbuttoned my bodice. 'It's done like this.'

Timo's open mouth latched onto my nipple and he suckled with the adherence of a limpet to a rock.

When I was able to tear my gaze from my son's face, I searched for Angelica, but she was gone. The layer of green had disappeared, and the bloody sheets replaced with fresh linen.

Maria swiftly crossed herself. 'Dr Baldi and Rubino are loading Angelica onto the undertaker's cart. The funeral will be held on Tuesday.'

Timo's mouth slackened, he looked peaceful. My right nipple slipped from his mouth.

Maria replaced Timo with Nepitella. 'Now the left breast.'

The bangles released an encouraging shushing.

Nepitella lay motionless in my arms.

'She must nurse,' Maria said. 'Pinch your nipple between your fingers. Hold her head close. Tease her by rubbing your nipple across her mouth. She needs stimulation. By the looks of it, a lot.'

Nepitella's tiny mouth barely opened wide enough to take in my nipple. She showed no inclination to suckle. Holding her closer, I caressed her exposed cheek with the tip of my little finger. She made a tentative but futile attempt, then went back to sleep.

The lights in Maria's eyes blazed. 'Tease her again, until instinct drives her to latch on.'

While pressing my nipple to her tiny rosebud mouth, I realised in an instant that Nepitella had been waiting for Timo! *Come on, baby girl. I promise, you will be safe with us.*

Maria heard my heart's voice coaxing Nepitella for she gave me a rare, fleeting smile.

Nepitella managed two or three sucks. Timo began to howl and did not let up until Maria swapped Nepitella for him.

'Your son is going to be a fine boy. He is strong, full of life. Just like his grandfather.'

In that moment, the tide stopped, and like a plumb line hung in perfect, vertical balance, I saw how I could change the future.

'Maria.' The tone I used caused her to stop cooing. She gave me her full attention.

Then I did exactly what I vowed I never would. 'Angelica gave birth to a son.' I reached over and caressed the tiny bundle lying beside me. 'I gave birth to a daughter.'

The bangles rippled without making a sound.

Realisation zigzagged across Maria's face.

By presenting Timo as Angelica and Claudio's newborn, I placed him where he belonged: the heir to the Trianni Estates.

The tide reversed and began to flow again. So, too, did Life, along a much different path than what celestial bodies had plotted and written in Heaven.

A t two weeks old, the babies were baptised. Timo's squalls in reaction to the too-cold blessed water poured over the crown of his head, drowned out Nepitella's whimpers.

During the short walk across the road to the town hall, both children fell silent. But when I spelled out Nepitella's surname to the births and deaths recording clerk, she broke out into a fit of ear-piercing wails that had everyone rushing in to see what the matter was.

When I spelled out Timo's surname, his wide-open eyes trained upon me and brimmed, I believed, with disbelief and reproachful accusation.

On the journey home by donkey cart, both babies fell asleep. Rubino, Maria and I were grateful we were no longer subjected to Nepitella's wails. But I more so, as I was relieved of Timo's accusing stare.

Once home, Nepitella and Timo continued to sleep in their cradles, which I had moved into the kitchen. Though the cradles were identical, but for the large pink bow attached to Nepitella's and the large blue one to Timo's, the children could not have been any more different.

Tiny Nepitella weighed hardly anything and was content to sleep. I had to coax her awake and encourage her to feed. On those occasions, I imagined she was looking into my soul.

Timo wanted to feed all the time. He howled lustily if kept waiting and even though tightly swaddled, his feet, knees and elbows poked and jerked about.

The clock showed late afternoon. Exhausted, I stretched my arms above my head, then collapsed into a chair and took advantage of the lull by doing nothing.

A Piaggio Ape's engine clattered in the distance. Since the fortunes of valley workers had improved, several men were now the proud owners of these vehicles. The hills and valley hummed and whined all day, as the three-wheeled vans were used to transport goods of all sorts. As it got closer, the sound of the engine became clearer. *Pietro!* My heart lurched, and I sprang to my feet.

I checked the babies, still sleeping. *Thank goodness.* I righted my apron gingerly; my nipples were tender thanks to Timo. I tucked stray wisps of hair into the bun at the nape of my neck and pinched my cheeks. Ignoring my hammering heart, I stepped into the courtyard and with my hands clasped, waited.

A fisherman who worked on Pietro's boat climbed out of the van. He hastened towards me, carrying a wooden box tucked under one arm.

'Signora d'Ambrosia-il Pescatore, good day.'

'Good day, Lorenzo.' I was surprised to hear my voice; my throat had constricted upon seeing him emerge instead of Pietro.

'I bring news.'

My head and heart synchronised and hammered as one. 'Come in, please. Sit.'

Lorenzo glanced at the two cradles.

'Pietro's daughter, Nepitella,' I said, saving him from asking the question.

'And the boy?'

'Timo. Son of Claudio Trianni and Angelica Barberi. Sadly, both parents passed within a week of each other.'

Lorenzo and I each made the sign of the Holy Cross.

Though it was unnecessary, I added, 'Timo is owner of the Trianni Estate.'

In silence and born out of centuries of servitude, Lorenzo doffed his cap at the blue bowed cradle. Then he placed the safety box on the table.

It smelled of a briny sea and reminded me acutely of my husband. I wanted to reach out and run my fingers lightly over the box as I had done to Pietro's face once he'd fallen asleep alongside me. A profound ache entered my soul.

Rubino hurried into the kitchen. He was breathing hard, his face dripping sweat. He must have run all the way from the olive grove.

How long would Maria take to arrive?

'Signor Rubino Sapienti.' Between his fisherman's hands, Lorenzo turned his cap in circles. 'I bear bad news.'

I staggered. Rubino caught me, pulled out two chairs and side by side we sat at the table.

Mustering the last of my body's strength, I blocked everything out and riveted my attention upon Lorenzo. My ears hurt preparing to listen.

He wasted no time. 'We had an excellent run and were returning from Naples when two fishermen caught fever. In a matter of hours, almost all the crew were down. We threw anchor off the Island of Giglio. I rowed to shore to seek help. By the time I returned with the doctor, three fishermen and Captain Pietro had been taken ill, died and buried at sea.

'The law required us to raise the yellow jack and remain anchored. I'm so sorry.' Lorenzo slapped his cap back on his head, stared ahead with his jaw clenched.

There was no reason to disbelieve Lorenzo's sorrow as genuine. Pietro was well-liked and respected, a true *bello,* particularly in his fishing community.

The fullness in my head cleared. I rose and brought the tray with shot glasses and the last bottle of Anna's *limoncello* to the table. *I must get round to making more of this with this summer's crop. God! Why am I thinking this, when I am hearing of Pietro's death?*

I poured a glass for each of us. 'May my husband,' my voice cracked, 'rest in peace.' I fought hard to hold back my tears. With an unsteady hand, I raised the glass to my lips.

Both men quaffed their *limoncello*. I sipped a tiny amount, worried the unctuous, sticky-sweet liquid might do something to my milk.

The fire in the hearth flared, Maria entered, and after the briefest greeting, joined us at the table. Lorenzo rolled the empty shot glass around in the palm of his hand. 'We waited to ensure the pestilence had run its course. Three weeks later, we dropped the yellow jack, set sail and docked this morning.'

How strange. Because of the joint baptism, I missed going up to the tower this morning.

'Before he died, Captain Pietro wrote orders, putting me in charge.' Lorenzo pushed the box towards me. 'He also said in his letter to deliver this box to you directly, Signora d'Ambrosia.'

In a state of somnambulism, I fetched the black iron key and inserted it into the lock. The lid sprang open. On the top lay a single sheet entitled, *Ultimo Testamento di Capitano Pietro il Pescatore,* The Last Will and Testament of Captain Pietro The Fisherman.

With or without a handwritten will, I already knew my child and I would inherit everything from Pietro in equal parts. It was one of Italy's better laws, ensuring there could be no argument between a surviving spouse and siblings.

I retrieved the will and, not trusting my voice, gave it to Maria to read. When she got to the part about the ownership of the boat, I drew in a sharp breath. I'd never given thought to the possibility I, and in turn my child, would become the owner of a fishing vessel. *Had I acted too soon? Perhaps the boat would have provided Timo with an opportunity for a steady future.* But even faster than those thoughts, in my mind's eye I looked beyond the walls of the Trianni kitchen, to all its land and the 10,000 olive tree grove. No. Timo would still be better served as the proprietor of this estate, to which he now was the undisputed, orphaned owner.

Maria folded the will and returned it to me. Through the tears threatening to spill, I looked in turn at Rubino and Maria. Their wise management of the valley's affairs, ensuring the labour union came to our valley, sales of both wine and oil to the Americans, workers' fixed contracts for a fair share of the profits, had raced through Tuscany like wildfire. Workers from neighbouring valleys hastened to join the union and pressed for the same profit share contracts, covering grape, olive, wheat, fruit or vegetable harvests.

I took a deep breath. 'Lorenzo, are you up to managing the boat and running it no differently than before?'

For a second his mouth slackened then snapped shut. 'Yes.'

'Good. Let me have the names of your crew and ask them to sign a worker's contract. You and I will be partners, and the crew will get a share of the profits once all expenses are paid. Deal?'

Lorenzo looked as surprised as if a whale had swallowed and then spat him out again.

'Oh. And don't forget my standing fish order on Fridays.'

Rubino squeezed my hand. The bangles offered a mellifluous, light applause. The babies woke and began to fuss. I shook hands with Lorenzo. Rubino and Maria saw him to the van and waved him off.

I tended to the babies. An angel must have been looking over my shoulder; for once neither fussed in their own particular way and Timo's accusing stare had disappeared. They slept for another two hours, giving me time to reflect.

Although I had entered marriage with Pietro for the security of my unborn son, I soon realised Pietro loved me deeply.

While I did not return the depth of his feelings, I cherished above all, the knowledge he would defend my child and me. That mattered to me more than anything, and for this, in my way, I cared for him.

Now that he was no more, I could add widow to my growing list of labels. I faced the future alone.

But none of that mattered. Above all, I would defend my son and daughter and ensure their future security.

Taking care of two babies at once was not easy. I began to understand what sleep deprivation meant and fantasised about an unbroken night's sleep.

Maria chuckled. 'It'll be a long time before you can realise that fantasy.'

My arm muscles protested as I stirred the third load of cotton diapers in the laundry pot filled with boiling water.

Rubino continued to prepare meals, and I ate like never before.

'Here, Hortensia, have the last piece,' Rubino said, on one of those rare occasions when the babies were asleep at lunchtime, and together we could eat in peace.

He served me another spoonful of fried onions, along with the last slice of calf liver cooked in equal portions of butter and olive oil, a sage leaf, sprinkled with lemon juice, black pepper, salt and finely chopped parsley. And a large mound of fluffy potato, glossy with melted butter.

I washed down my second helping with a small glass of *Sangiovese*, carried the cradles into the bedroom, fell onto the bed, curled my hand around Pietro's dentures and slept as soundly as Nepitella and Timo.

23

Nepitella and Timo, both four years old, could not be more different, especially at bedtime. Each night, Timo's eyelids went to war and fought off sleep while Nepitella's slid closed as easily as a key turning in a well-oiled lock. Once sleep triumphed over Timo, I returned to the kitchen and joined Rubino and Maria at the table.

That evening we ate *Pollo alla Cacciatora,* hunter's chicken stew, served with golden *polenta* and enriched with grated *Parmigiano-Reggiano.*

It was one of Rubino's favourites, so I could always depend upon him to let me know the moment a hen finished laying. The light in his eyes would gleam with anticipation and he'd say, 'This one's next.'

Four to five hours of low heat cooking in a sauce of pitted olives, sweet red pepper, mushrooms, tomatoes and red wine, ensured the meat turned butter-soft and succulent.

The dish announced its readiness when the meat fell off the bone, and the air was fragrant with pepper, rosemary, sage and onions. We ate slowly and with pleasure, and when there was only sauce left, we mopped it up with pieces of bread.

My belly refused to be disturbed, so I ignored the mess of dishes and remained sitting a while longer.

Rubino pushed back his chair, removed the metal toothpick he kept in a pocket and cleaned his teeth.

Maria slid the silver bangles from her wrist and laid them on the table. With a soft cloth, she lovingly polished each one. I'd forgotten how beautiful they were.

Despite their age, each bangle's decoration remained clear. There was a bangle for the five elements, the earth, the moon, the stars, sun and aether. Once they glowed, she replaced them on her wrist in careful order. When I was little, she'd challenge me. 'Try to remember which one goes next.' It had been my greatest treat to play with them. I sighed with the pleasure of the memory then turned my attention to another matter. 'Do you remember the *scirocco* before I was born and the one after, when Anna and Foxy died? And how the vineyard suffered the worst damage and took longest to recover?'

Rubino and Maria stiffened; I had their attention.

'What will happen, God forbid, if both vineyard and olive grove fail? Then where will we be with no income?'

They remained silent, waiting for me to continue.

'I've been thinking. Last Friday, Lorenzo told me a group of back-packing foreigners asked if accommodation was available in the valley for an overnight stay. They had lost their way to Cinque Terra. As there isn't, he let them spend the night. He fried fish for their dinner and answered their questions about our coastline and islands.'

The bangles, now back on Maria's wrist, cooed, like nesting doves.

'Mmm…' Maria said. 'This is a first. I can't recall a group of tourists coming through our backwater, lost or not.'

I focused on Maria. 'My thoughts precisely. The next morning, they asked Lorenzo to sail them to Monterosso.'

'Did they pay a fair sum?' Rubino asked.

'Yes.'

'So, what you're saying is there's a business opportunity,' Maria said, 'lodging tourists in the valley.'

Rubino pocketed his toothpick. 'With so many workers' children off to other parts of the world, there should be plenty of spare bedrooms.'

'But their homes only have outhouses.' I grimaced, remembering my childhood living with Maria and her pygmy goats in her shepherd's hut. I had to brave all sorts of weather and darkness to get to the outhouse, separated by a flimsy wood wall from the sow's stinking sty.

'The valley is decades overdue in implementing the Sanitation Code,' Rubino said.

'What's that?' I asked.

'A law mandating indoor toilets. It was partially government funded.'

I glanced around the huge kitchen with its ancient gleaming copper pots and pans. My mind travelled through the dining room into the harlequin-patterned entrance hall, passed by the visitor's parlour, which remained closed, furniture shrouded in dustsheets, and up the grand sweeping staircase leading to the first- and second-floor bedrooms.

Soon after Rubino and I moved to the Trianni Estate, I became used to living in the villa and forgot how impressive it was. Villa Angeli, my former place of work on the opposite valley ridge, was similar but smaller. 'Actually, I was thinking of the villas, since we have them at our disposal. Between the two of them, we have twelve bedrooms all with en-suite bathrooms.'

While Maria paused, the tip of her hooked nose crinkled. 'That means,' she said, 'there would be a large price difference between guests paying for a valley worker's bedroom and one of the bedrooms in either villa.'

I nodded.

'It's time to pay our mayor a visit,' Rubino said.

I stifled a giggle. 'Oh dear. Poor Santo Rossi will quake in his boots when he sees you again after the tussle getting the labour union to come to our valley.'

Rubino snorted with derision.

'Be fair,' Maria said. 'Since his wife died, he's mellowed and he is in desperate need of a new one.'

'Hortensia. Keep thinking, and I'll make an appointment with Rossi.' To a series of cracks and creaks, Rubino unfolded his body, excused himself and left.

'Where and how,' Maria asked, 'will you find tourists to come here?'

I shrugged. 'I don't know. Yet.'

———————— ◆ ————————

Three weeks later, Rubino and I presented ourselves at the town hall. Chairs lined either side of the corridor leading to the mayor's office.

'Sit. Relax,' Rubino whispered. 'It's going to be a while before he sees us.'

'Why? Our appointment is for 10 a.m., and we're on time.'

Rubino tsked. 'It's his way of demonstrating who's in charge.'

A number of people, none of whom I recognised, entered the mayor's office with hope on their faces. But most left with disappointed, or worse, despairing looks.

'Rubino?' I whispered. He opened one eye. He'd been taking a nap with the back of his head resting on the corridor wall. 'Why are there more women than men coming to see the mayor?'

Rubino matched my lowered voice. 'Although women can now vote, they still can't do much without a husband. You know, apply for a loan, open a bank account, buy or sell property. The lucky women who have sons, brothers or uncles defer to them for permission. The unlucky ones who have no one are obliged to seek the mayor's help.'

That's not going to happen to me. And then I remembered. I, too, was a widow with a daughter, and the closest either of us had to a family male protector was Rubino.

'Rubino?'

He opened his other eye.

I glanced at the women. They were dressed head to toe in black, and although they appeared to be middle-aged, they all looked worn out. I lowered my voice. 'Surely they could have married again?'

Rubino tilted his head towards my ear and raised his hand to obscure his mouth. 'After the war,' he whispered, 'few men returned. So, these women will likely remain widows until they die.'

The reality of the plight in which these women found themselves seeped into my bones. For my crass insensitivity, guilt chewed at my heart. Then another thought struck. 'But, in our valley,' I whispered, 'families appear to be whole. How come?'

'Most of the villagers, like myself, were too old to be conscripted, so we stayed at home.'

'Yes. But what about their sons? They would have been old enough to go to war.'

From the length of time he paused, I knew he was weighing up and formulating his answer, and that when he spoke I would become party to secret information.

Rubino leaned forward, rested his elbows on his knees and angled his face towards the floor. 'With its difficult access...' Rubino's voice was so low, I had to listen hard to catch his words. 'Our valley has remained largely untouched by the outside world. Our isolation strengthened our independence, so when the war came, we resisted having our lot thrown in with the Germans. We wholly supported the *partigiani*, formed small bands and lived permanently in the forest. Do you remember the hunters and their dogs?'

I nodded.

'Those are the bands of men including fathers and sons, brothers, cousins and uncles who fought against the tyranny. We lost very few men, but I am sad to say, we took the lives of a great many. Our women too, were involved. Take Maria, for instance. Her hut was the storage depot for weapons we took off the enemy.'

My mind raced back to the single room with roof beams, one door and two windows. 'Stored where?'

'Under the earth-hardened floor is a trapdoor leading to the hole we dug.'

I felt my jaw fall open. I knew exactly where the trapdoor was though I had never seen it. As a child, I stood before the nightstand that supported a carafe of water and a basin in which to wash my face and hands before going to bed. Barefoot, I sensed the difference between the hard-packed earth and the hollow wooden trapdoor, believing one day the floor would open and swallow me. I shut off that memory and returned to the present. 'Where did the loyalties of Villas Angeli and Trianni lie?' From the look on Rubino's face, I raised one hand. 'Don't tell me. Giovanni Angeli was a partisan. But Claudio Trianni wasn't.'

Rubino's silence answered my question.

Thus, another reason was revealed as to why my father was still referred to as a *mascalzone* by the valley workers. I felt exhausted. I sat back in the chair and gave my senses time to absorb all this new information.

The wall clock's hands neared midday, when the town hall would close for lunch. The church bell began to toll. On its fifth, the mayor stuck his head out from behind his office door.

Rubino unfolded his body and stood.

'Rubino. You'll have to come back anoth–'

I stepped out from behind Rubino. Close up, Mayor Santo Rossi's bulbous frog-shaped eyes were repugnant.

Though never formally introduced, I knew Rossi prided himself on knowing every valley member by name, which political party they supported, and their voting inclination when it came to mayoral office election time.

The last time I saw the mayor was at Claudio Trianni's funeral. I was very different then; pregnant and as fat as the sow who produced fifteen piglets.

The look of dawning recognition, like watching the sun emerge from behind a drifting cloud, crossed the mayor's face. He wrinkled his nose and sniffed the air. 'Er…' Several black hairs poked from his nostrils.

I inclined my head. 'Signor *Sindaco*.'

His face flushed.

He likes to be addressed by his title.

I picked up the basket containing the delicacies I'd prepared for Santo Rossi. From Anna, I had learned not only how to cook, but the art of persuasion through food.

He sniffed harder. His nose, like a hunting dog, aimed directly at my food basket. He opened the door, revealing the rest of his tubby body. 'Come in. Take a seat.'

Rubino stood aside for me to enter the office first. It was dark, dusty and stank of stale cigarettes. A pole with our nation's flag stood just inside the door. A map of Italy took pride of place on one wall. Behind Mayor Rossi's chair, hung a portrait of Mussolini. In the first ten years since his death in 1945, Italy had no less than seven prime ministers holding office. Changing official portraits to keep up with each new appointment had become problematic. One minister had served only nineteen days in office.

Rubino sat in one of two chairs. I placed the basket at my feet, flicked a corner of the cloth open and sat in the second chair. Soon the mayor's tobacco-stinking office was filled with an aroma of steamed, shelled prawns topped with tangy mayonnaise, chicken liver pâté, vinegar pickled anchovies, creamed pork fat mixed with dry nettles and oregano, and toasted wild asparagus spears wrapped in thin slices of *prosciutto* and sprinkled with wafer-shavings of *Parmigiano-Reggiano*.

The mayor's gaze shifted sideways to Rubino while his head and nose remained turned towards me, from where the aromas originated. 'What can I do for you?'

Rubino was not given to exaggeration, but when he felt the need to press home his point, he'd preface it by clearing his throat before speaking. 'Our valley must be the *very last* in all of Italy with no indoor plumbing.'

Santo Rossi exhaled hard, causing his cheeks to wobble.

'For immediate health reasons, Dr Baldi's report states the need for internal bathrooms.'

'Report? I've not seen it.' The words shot out of Rossi's mouth like fired bullets.

'He's just put the finishing touches to it.' Rubino coughed. 'You'll have your copy on Monday.'

You old fox! Out of the corner of my eye, I saw Rubino cross his swollen fingers.

'So, the valley workers require help from your office to access the financial aid to install bathrooms.'

Santo Rossi drummed his fingers on his desk. 'That law was passed decades ago. I have no idea if the funds are still available.'

'With your connections, Mayor Rossi, I know you'll find out.' Rubino placed a gazette, opened to display the article, on the edge of the desk. 'This will help you. It states funds are marked for the fifty-four households in our valley.'

Where on earth had he found a copy?

As Mayor Rossi reached over, I nudged the basket with my foot. Another waft of aromas rose into the air. *Is that a dribble of saliva at the corner of his mouth?*

'I'll see what I can do. Is that all?'

I kept my voice low. 'No.'

By the look on Rossi's face, he was likely wondering what *this* maid could possibly want.

'While you are sorting the sanitation funding, I'd like you to apply for licences for me to operate Villas Angeli and Trianni, and the valley houses as tourist accommodations.'

Mayor Rossi's eyes distended to bursting point. 'On whose authority?'

'Mine.'

The mayor's face turned white. 'But, you're only a cook, a maid!'

'Not only, mayor, if you check the community hall records, you will see I am the formal guardian to the Angeli and Trianni heirs and their estates until they reach maturity. I have full authority.'

The mayor's face tinged pink. *Is this a precursor to his feeling embarrassed?* I stored his slight for later and stuck to getting my immediate needs met.

'Your help will create jobs since the villas will require maids, cooks – I paused smiling sweetly – and gardeners. And the valley workers can decide whether they want to open their homes to tourists.'

Rubino shifted in his chair. 'I've forgotten, please remind me. When is your term of office up, mayor?'

Mayor Santo Rossi's brows knitted.

'I know, I know.' I held up my hand like a child at school desperate to answer. I put on my brightest smile. 'In two years.'

'The workers will be very grateful for new work opportunities. They will demonstrate their appreciation when you seek re-election,' Rubino said. 'I take it that is your desire?'

While Mayor Santo Rossi grappled for his next words, I lifted and placed the basket on the desk. 'I do hope you will accept this?'

Regret darkened Santo Rossi's face. 'It is forbidden to accept bribes.'

I removed the cloth and tipped the basket towards him. 'This is not a bribe; it's food.'

Longing replaced regret as he peered at the temptations nestled side by side.

'Since your wife passed, you've lost a little weight. You need to keep up your strength to continue all your good work. What a pity.' I made to remove the basket from the table.

Santo Rossi's pudgy hand shot out and grabbed the handle. 'I accept.'

'Best we leave. I hear a storm brewing,' Rubino said. 'Good day, mayor.'

'That was no storm,' I whispered when we were a few paces down the corridor. 'It was Rossi's stomach making all that noise.'

The crevices bracketing Rubino's mouth deepened as he smiled. 'I know.'

'Er...?' Mayor Santo Rossi called.

Rubino and I turned.

Mayor Rossi stared at me. 'What do you want me to do with the basket?'

The smear of mayonnaise on his chin told me Santo Rossi had devoured the steamed prawns. 'When you have news, come to Villa Trianni for lunch. Bring the basket with you.'

He dipped his head and hurried back into his office. I had no doubt he would polish off the rest of the appetisers in a matter of minutes.

'Well, well, well, Hortensia. I think you just made a new friend.'

I gave Rubino a playful pinch on the arm and grimaced. 'Never.'

'Ah, you know what they say – never say never.'

To stress my point, I pinched Rubino again, harder. 'Never.'

As I expected, we stopped at Dr Baldi's home.

Still chewing, and with a large white napkin tied around his neck, he opened the door. He listened intently to Rubino, nodded and said, 'Report by Monday. Okay.'

With a light bounce in his step, belying his age, Rubino returned to the cart. 'Full steam ahead.' He picked up the reins. 'Long Ears, Villa Trianni.'

◆

Sunday afternoon, three weeks later, Mayor Santo Rossi's clattering van's engine announced his arrival.

I removed the headscarf I wore while cooking and stepped into the courtyard. 'Welcome. This is good timing.'

Santo Rossi squeezed himself out of the tight cab. In one hand he held the basket, filled with long-stemmed arum lilies. I knew the marshy glade where he had ripped them from the damp earth. *It's the thought that counts.*

He'd clearly been to the barber. His bald crown gleamed, the hairy nostrils trimmed. Loosely knotted, his tie hid the top button of his shirt. He was wise to keep it undone lest he choke.

Rubino and Maria arrived. With greetings exchanged and wine poured, they sat at the kitchen table and helped themselves to an array of appetisers.

I trimmed the sleek, green stems and placed the lilies in a tall, glass vase. The flared trumpet blooms looked and felt like white velvet. Nestled in each protective spathe, grew a miniature stalk densely clustered with tiny, bright yellow flowers.

I ignored the fact that these white lilies were locally called 'Death Lily' and used to decorate coffins and graves. But the knowledge that some brides carried them to the altar on their wedding day stuck in my head.

Out of the corner of my eye, I watched to see which appetiser was Rossi's favourite.

In no time, the plate of roast peppers and goat cheese canapés served with pieces of rosemary-infused, oven-baked flatbread was bare.

The contrast of the translucent baby onions steeped in piquant vinegar and scattered around the platter of crimson slices of salted beef looked wonderful. The beauty did not last long. That platter, too, was swept clean.

I took my place at the table as we settled in to eat the piping hot spaghetti with oil, garlic and red chilli flakes. Before Rossi was halfway through, his brow broke into a sweat. Unlike Rubino, Maria and I, he could not tolerate spicy heat. The following dish would cool him down.

'Let's take a walk,' Rubino said, 'before Hortensia serves the next course.'

Rossi eased himself away from the table. His belt strained at the last notch. He followed Rubino, his pack of cigarettes clutched in one hand and a box of matches in the other. No sooner had he stepped one pace away from the kitchen, he lit up.

I abhorred smoking.

While Maria carved the lemon-stuffed crisp-roasted chickens, I pan-fried sliced fennel bulbs. An aromatic cloud of anise enveloped my head. 'Do you think he has any news yet?'

Maria wiped her hands. 'We'll know by dessert.'

I plated the chicken and fennel. 'Can you call the men back to the table, please?'

'I'll fetch them. I don't want to wake the children.'

Reinvigorated by his smoke break and walk around the flourishing kitchen garden, Rossi attacked his plate with determined intent. I was pleased but also saddened. Though he ate everything with equal zeal, I was not sure if he really enjoyed eating. He forced the food down. Only starving people did that, and by his size, he was nowhere near starving. *What's driving him to eat?*

'Well, Mayor Rossi,' Rubino said, 'do you have any news for us?'

As I cut into the moist apple cake, Rossi's prominent eyes followed my every hand movement with the acute attention of a cat about to pounce on its prey.

His body is in turmoil. He doesn't know which he likes best – sweet or savoury.

'Sort of.'

Rubino's shaggy eyebrows rose.

'Regarding funding for the valley's sanitation.' Rossi coughed. 'The region says it first has to find the funds – it could take a while.'

'How long?' Maria asked.

Rossi coughed again. 'A year or longer.'

The words shot out of my mouth. 'A year! That's ridiculous.'

Maria gave my shin a sharp kick under the table. Her voice entered my head. *Don't deny him his pleasure playing politics of delay.*

Rossi's face flared puce. 'No. Er...'

You know my name! But still can't or won't address me directly. Why?

'Er...the region's accountants have to find the money earmarked for the valley.' The colour in Rossi's face subsided to red. 'Processing archived documents will take time.'

I held out a bowl. 'A little cream?'

Rubino and Maria declined. I dropped a spoonful on my plate and offered the bowl to Rossi. He emptied its contents and attacked the dessert. For a few minutes, only spoons scraping against the china plates pinged throughout the kitchen. As Rossi swallowed his last mouthful, I asked, 'What about the licences for tourist accommodation?'

'Nothing yet. But when I know, I'll tell you.'

The meal came to an end just as the children woke from their naps.

I stood. 'Thank you for coming and thank you for your help. Goodbye.'

He was likely more taken aback by my dismissal than thanks. He lumbered to his feet. His belt was loose and, the zipper of his trousers had slid down. Not wanting to embarrass him, I never said a word or gave him an indication of his predicament. I held out my hand.

He took my hand. 'Thank you, er...'

'Please, call me Hortensia.'

'Hor…Hortensia. It has been my pleasure.'

The children began to wail. Their noise seeped through the wall that separated my quarters from the kitchen.

'By the way,' my words tumbled out in a rush, 'I'm testing some new recipes. I'd appreciate your opinion. A basket of samples are in the basket in the back of your van. Let me know.'

The children's wails turned to shrieks.

Rossi released my hand, with reluctance I thought. I hurried off to liberate the children from their cot beds and erased the image of the mayor's protuberant eyes.

24

Two weeks after the first luncheon with Mayor Santo Rossi, I received a written request to present myself at his office at an appointed time.

The next morning, I arrived a few minutes after the town hall doors opened, but already the chairs lining the corridor leading to Rossi's office were filled. From the mode of their clothing, the women, all dressed in black, came from distant mountain hamlets more stuck in the ancient past than mine.

I recalled what Rubino said about widows who were obliged to use Mayor Rossi as their protector, advisor and spokesperson. I'd also heard that after the war, many distant hamlets were occupied by women only. Left without male protection and physical help, hamlets, either atop hills or buried in valleys, had been abandoned.

Widows, unbetrothed maidens, and worse, unmarried mothers, as I had already learned, were disadvantaged and marginalised.

As is customary, I greeted them with a respectful good morning.

In anticipation of the foetid air in Rossi's office, a mix of cigarette smoke, sweat and cheap pomade, I mentally pinched my nose closed and knocked on the door.

'Come in.' Mayor Rossi sat behind his desk, and more than ever looked much like a bullfrog. 'Please, take a seat. How are you?'

My gaze was drawn beyond the empty food basket placed on the edge of his desk to the sight of new-grown, wiry hairs that poked out of his nostrils. 'Very well.'

'Your daughter Nepitella and, your ward, Timo Trianni?'

'Good. Thank you for asking.'

'You are well?'

You just asked me that. 'I am. Thank you. How are you?'

'*Cosi-cosi*, so-so.'

'Nothing serious, I hope?'

Mayor Santo Rossi's swollen eyes fixed their gaze to a point behind my left shoulder. He sighed. 'Since my wife died, my life…'

The whispery tail end of his breathy sigh, raw with longing, stirred a memory. One summer evening, a delicate breeze passed over our valley transporting the delicate strains of *Un bel di vadremo*, an aria from the opera *Madama Butterfly*. The poignant melody caused hearts to well up and spill with mourning for loves' lost.

I jerked back to the present. 'You have all my sympathy.' I had used my most sincere voice, but the tone sounded hollow to my ears.

'I knew you would understand.' Rossi's face broke into a crooked, half-grimace, half-smile. 'After all, you and I, well, we're in the same boat, are we not?'

'Yes. And no.'

Santo Rossi flinched.

You're unaccustomed to being told no.

His gaze slow-flicked over me and then reverted to the point beyond my shoulder. 'What do you mean, yes and no?'

'Yes, we are both alone. And, no, because your situation, mayor, is worse than mine. You were married many years. I, less than a year.' A hazy veil of sadness crossed his face. *You loved your wife!* I paused to bat away the creeping vine tendrils of sympathy that reached for my heart. 'You are still in early mourning and have months to go before the traditional grieving period is over. Believe me, after a year, there is a difference. Even if slight.' I bit my lip to keep from spouting any more foolishness.

Rossi's gaze shifted to the empty food basket. 'How is your recipe testing coming along?'

I held back my gasp of surprise at the smooth ease with which he changed the subject. Perhaps he did not love his wife after all, but he certainly wanted the food basket refilled. 'As soon as I've perfected something else, I'd appreciate your opinion.' I could not decide whether it was desire or gluttony that crossed his face. 'So, mayor, why am I here?'

'I have forms for you to sign.' He scratched through a pile of files on his desk. 'They were just here this morning. I know they were.' He began to toss envelopes, files, documents and sheets, some paper-clipped together, some not, from one pile to the next. In a moment his desk looked like the *scirocco* had blown through the office.

Why are you nervous? 'Is this what you are looking for?' I picked up a cardboard file with red cotton loops and the words 'Tourist Accommodation' written on the cover.

'Yes.' His pudgy hands unwound the loops and drew out a thick sheaf of papers while he walked around to where I was sitting.

'Are these the application forms?'

'Yes. One for each villa and one covering the valley houses.' He handed me his pen. 'They need your signature.'

'Oh, Mayor Rossi. I am very sorry. I never sign anything unless I've read it first.'

Rossi's face darkened to puce. 'You don't trust me?'

'I trust you.' I crossed my fingers. 'But I don't trust those *bastardi* in Rome.'

It was clear Rossi was relieved; the colour in his face reduced to a lighter shade of red.

'May I return them next week? I need time. I don't have your excellent training in these legal matters.'

Rossi's mouth opened like a fish out of water.

'And when I return, I'll bring you an apple cake. The one with cream. You liked that, didn't you?'

'Yes, very much.'

'And perhaps a wobbly crème caramel. You know, light set custard with a sweet burnt sauce?'

Rossi's tongue darted between his lips.

'I'll be baking Florentines, too. How about a couple of those? Do you like dark chocolate, cherries and crisp almonds?'

'Yes, yes, yes,' mayor Rossi croaked.

'Very well, then. Thank you. I'll see you next week.' I dropped the file into the empty food basket and closed my hand around the handle. 'Good day, Mayor Rossi.'

'Good day, Hortensia.'

After Rossi's foul-smelling office, the corridor was delightfully fresh, though I detected the waft of fresh croissants. Or was it baked apricot tart?

I greeted the waiting widows once again.

———————— ◆ ————————

Maria walked into the kitchen. 'Aren't you done with those application forms yet? You've been at it for days.'

'I have, but I need to check many of the boxes Mayor Rossi skipped, and add additional information.'

Maria helped herself to a twice-baked almond biscuit. 'Why would he skip boxes?'

'We never discussed what I had in mind. And anyway, now reading through all of this, it turns out to be a lot more complicated.'

Maria poured herself a glass of *vin santo* and dipped the almond biscuit into it. 'For example?' She bit into the biscuit using her side teeth; she could no longer rely on her front teeth.

'Providing meals. Transport service. Personal laundry. Sightseeing information. Speaking another language, preferably English.' I grimaced. 'The tourist board wants to know what entertainment is to be provided in case of inclement weather!'

'Really?' Maria tossed the fiery wine down her throat.

'Really. And then there is a list of questions three pages long wanting an accurate description of each room. Its dimensions, cross-ventilation, and details of an emergency escape route.'

Maria refilled the glass. 'Goodness. Who would have thought?'

'And there is a rating system. One to five stars.'

'No need to tell me – you're aiming for five.'

'Yes. But, what Rossi has filled out barely entitles us to a one-star rating. And the fine print says that applications for one-star locations are unlikely to be granted.'

'Which means?'

'Mayor Rossi has not read through the clauses. Or, if he did, he still did not have a clue as to what he was doing.'

The bangles plinked, sounding like a one-stringed banjo.

Maria paused. 'What do you really think?'

I also paused. 'Stupid, he is not.' I paused again. 'He is deliberately sabotaging my project before it has even had the chance to develop wings.'

'Why would he do that?' After all, it's going to benefit the whole community.'

I waited for the feeling in my belly to develop into a clear thought. 'He feels threatened, and wants to punish me for having risen above my life's station.'

Maria sighed. 'Good girl. Remember, the feeling in your belly is always right.' She tossed down the third glass of sweet, warming wine.

'Maria?'

'Yes?'

'I want to copy the applications so that I have records. Just in case they get lost. I would hate to have to redo this.'

The sound of Rubino stamping off the dirt from his boots announced his arrival. He opened the door, entered the kitchen and glanced at us. 'Something wrong, ladies?'

I repeated what I believed I had discovered.

Rubino paid close attention. 'How many copies do you want, Hortensia?'

'Three of each.'

'That's easy,' he said. 'We'll start right after dinner.'

I hugged the two most important people left in my life, after my son and daughter.

———————— ◆ ————————

B y the second night, I had bowls of warm salt-water at the ready.
'Hortensia,' Rubino submerged his stiff writing hand into the water, 'it's time to buy one of those writing machines.'

Maria flexed her hands and grimaced. 'I second that.'

'Good idea. I'll check the 'For Sale' column in the weekly gazette.'

On the morning after the third night, I left Maria in charge of the children and drove the cart down to Mayor Rossi's office. Samples from a new batch of desserts filled the basket.

'Mayor,' I called as I saw Santo Rossi retreat down the corridor, which for once, was empty.

Rossi turned, his face lit up with undisguised surprise. 'Go in.' He waved his hand. 'I'll return in a few minutes.'

I placed the food basket on the free chair and the application forms on the desk. Then I saw the desktop calendar, its outer edges bordered with colour pictures of Italy's great cities. Turning the calendar towards me, I traced my finger across the top row. Venice, Rome, Milan, Florence. I sighed. *I will visit them, one day.* Halfway down the page a black ink line circled 1 May. Pencilled in tiny writing alongside it the words, Christina's passing.

My finger continued to slide over the bottom row of photos. Verona, Bologna, Sienna, Turin. And then, there it was. In the bottom right-hand corner set in much smaller print the calendar for the following year. A line in red ink circled 30 April. Pencilled alongside it was Christina's name with a line drawn through it. Two words below stared up at me. Marry Hortensia.

I clapped one hand over my mouth to stifle my gasp while with the other I spun the calendar around to its original position. Rubino's voice entered my head and repeated, 'Never say never.'

Never. Never. Never.

I left the office and walked down the corridor as fast as I could without appearing to run.

'Hortensia,' Rossi called.

I half-turned. 'I have to go.'

'But... but...' Santo Rossi hurried towards me.

I held up my hand. Dismay clouded his face. 'Sorry. I just remembered I have to be somewhere. The signed application files are on your desk. Good day, mayor.'

I fled down the steps of the town hall. I could see Long Ears standing with his head lowered, one knee bent, asleep. As I scrambled onto the cart, he jolted awake.

'Ya! Ya!' I called to the donkey. The cart pulled away just as Mayor Rossi appeared on the top step. I caught sight of his face turning from dismay to cold rage. No different to the kitchen cat's face when the mouse evaded capture.

———————— ◆ ————————

A blast of cold air followed Maria as she entered the kitchen. The hearth's flames leaped. Fires always flared upon her arrival whether it was indoors, a pile of burning winter leaves, the pizza oven, or the pit over which whole pigs roasted.

Maria held her gnarled hands over the glowing embers. 'It's been four months. Any news from Rossi?'

I shook my head. 'All this feeding him food samples has produced nothing.'

Maria patted her hands over her black cloak. 'Time for action.'

From one of many pockets sewn into the folds of her cloak, she pulled out a tiny phial and placed it on the table. 'I *knew* it was somewhere.'

'What is that?' I asked.

'Tincture of verbena.'

'What does it do?'

'Reduces anger. Make a fruit jelly and add the tincture. Use that mould.' Maria pointed to a copper tin hooked to the wall. It had a hole in its middle. 'When the jelly is set, fill the hole with custard cream.'

I picked up the phial with a sinking feeling.

'Don't worry.' Maria had read my thoughts. 'It's nothing like chasteberry. Within an hour of eating the jelly, Mayor Rossi will become as amenable as a cuddly bear and answer all questions. Truthfully.'

'Really?'

'Really.'

'Any chance it will restore his eyes to normal?' I pretended to vomit. 'Or for that matter, change the rest of him?'

Maria and the bangles deigned not to respond.

Maria delivered the fruit jelly to Mayor Rossi before lunchtime with a note to say I'd collect the container that afternoon.

A cloud obscured the sun when I stepped down from the donkey cart at four o'clock. A light, cold wind played around my neck. I wrapped my shawl tighter around me.

'Come in, Hortensia.' Mayor Rossi gave me a lopsided smile. Because of the protrusion of his eyes, his lids only met halfway when he blinked.

Shivers snaked up my spine.

'Please, sit.'

I remained standing and pointed to the empty container. 'I'm just here to pick this up.' *Did you eat it all?*

'Don't you want my opinion on your last batch of desserts?'

My heart sank. 'Of course.'

'Then sit and ask me.'

I sat. 'Tell me, Mayor Rossi, what especially did you like about the toasted hazelnut biscuits?'

A look of dreamy contemplation crossed his face. His eyelids closed and his mouth opened, like a baby seeking its mother's nipple. Violently, he bit down and his teeth snapped together, causing me to jump in my seat. In my head, I heard the crunch of the biscuit cracking under his teeth. Still with closed eyes, Rossi began to make chewing sounds. Unable to bear seeing his jaws grinding down the imaginary biscuit, my eyes closed. I heard him swallow.

'Delectable.'

I opened my eyes. He was staring at me and looked hungry all over again.

Surely I don't have to sit through this pretend eating process again with the chocolate and pear slice, orange and rosemary-infused cake, honey fig tart and this afternoon's fruit jelly?

My worst fears were realised. The clock's large hand moved five times before he finished. *Now, it's my turn.*

I smiled sweetly. 'Your opinions are of great help. Thank you.' I stood. 'Oh, by the way, any response from the tourist board regarding the licences?'

Rossi transformed in front of my eyes. The mellow trance the fruit jelly had induced paved the way for Truth to slide past Falsehoods. 'We won't hear from them.'

Truth won.

Rossi heaved himself up. 'No. I mean, not yet.'

Falsehood raced in second.

He showed me to his office door, 'Good day, Hortensia.' He thrust the empty container into my hands. 'Next,' he barked at the dressed-in-black widows.

———— ◆ ————

'What did Rossi say?' Maria asked that evening as she, Rubino and I sat at the kitchen table after dinner.

'I believe he told me both the truth and a lie.'

Rubino's forehead crevasses deepened. 'How so?'

I repeated Rossi's words exactly.

Rubino's shaggy salt and pepper eyebrows rose and fell.

'My intuition tells me he has not sent off the application forms at all.'

The light in Maria's eyes flickered. 'He'll not outfox us.' She paused. 'This is what we'll do. We'll mail a set of the application forms we hand-copied.'

'Good idea.' Rubino dropped another lump of sugar into his coffee. 'Give it to Lorenzo and tell him to mail it from Livorno. That way, our post office staff won't know and can't report it to Rossi. In the meantime, Hortensia, double the samples. That will keep his mind on food.'

'Food is not all he's focused on. He's focused on me. I can't bear it.' My voice ended on a miserable note.

Rubino peeled a sliver of rind from an orange, dropped it into his cup and stirred. Fragrance of zest mixed with coffee rose from the cup. 'Don't be misled, Hortensia. You're not the only one.' He raised the cup to his nose and inhaled.

'What do you mean?'

'Remember all those widows outside his office? Well, whatever he is doing to you, he's doing to them, too.' He swallowed the coffee.

In the form of a knock to the head, realisation dawned. *Good grief. That's why there were croissant and apricot tart smells along the corridor to Rossi's office. How could I be so dense?* I fell into another round of despondency.

'Hortensia.' Maria's practical voice snapped me out of my self-pity and castigation. 'This is all up to you. Decide if this is a battle worth fighting. If no, end of story. If yes, quit whining and get on with it.'

I'd been in this position before when I had to give up something of myself for the benefit of others, and for which I remained deeply ashamed. On cue, my nose filled with the smell of pomade and chocolate. The dark vestment room within the church, Santa Chiara in Naples, Di Napoli and me, naked, flashed through my head. *Banish those thoughts. Think of the future, for you and your children.*

Two weeks later I received a single page letter from the tourism board and read aloud, 'Your applications are under review.'

My heart gave a leap of joy immediately upon which, to my great surprise, I was overwhelmed with the burning desire to punish Mayor Santo Rossi. At the uncharitable thought, Guilt came and flashed by in a second, closely followed by a memory. Di Napoli had taught me well how to administer punishment. Intuition told me Santo Rossi would not only be willing but desired, Chastisement.

I had Lorenzo deliver the mayor a written invitation to lunch on the last Saturday of April. Anna put in an appearance and, together with her, I designed a menu as revenge for all women, past, present and future who had need of Rossi's help.

The late spring days had warmed. By lunchtime, it was the perfect temperature to eat outdoors. I laid the table under the metal pergola supporting the wisteria, whose branches were wrist-thick. From them, pendulous flowering racemes dangled, creating a hazy-lilac canopy under which to sit.

'Hortensia,' Maria said, 'is this wise?'

I glanced at the indigo sky. 'It's warm and unlikely to rain.'

'No. I mean the wisteria pods. What if the children wake and join us? They could put a pod in their mouths. They're poisonous and will give the eater instant diarrhoea.'

'I'll be very careful.' I added this snippet to my store of information I had learned from Maria.

Mayor Santo Rossi arrived. As before, he squeezed out of his van's cab. With the profusion of purple-bearded iris heads sticking out of the food basket, I knew he'd once again plundered nature on his journey to the villa. In his other hand he held a bottle of sparkling wine, the kind used to celebrate an occasion.

'Thank you.' I accepted the flowers and the bottle, trying to avoid touching his hands.

Upon seeing the array of platters, Rossi stumbled and righted himself. His stomach released a low rumble. I would serve each platter as Anna had instructed, in order from the least spicy to the spiciest dish.

I had removed the outer casing from a length of salami and rolled it in chilli powder. Thinly sliced, the tiny circle of red was barely visible. A bowl of green queen olives stuffed with bits of pimento soaked in brine accompanied the salami slices paired with bite-size squares of bread.

By the time the platter and bowl were emptied, Rossi's pasty skin had taken on a healthy, pink glow. I was sure he drank down another glass of *Sangiovese* to wash away any residual piquancy on his tongue.

I served the bowl of chilled *friggitelli,* slender, sweet green peppers, sautéed with tomatoes and garlic. The first mouthful was refreshing, enticing the eater to another cooling forkful. I knew from experience that after a minute or so, taste buds would sting until the entire mouth sizzled.

Trying hard to control himself, Rossi turned away from the table and plunged his tongue deep into the glass of lemon-mint flavoured water.

'The pasta,' I said, 'is almost ready.'

Mayor Santo Rossi could barely get the words out. 'What sauce?'

'A little light *pancetta,* smoked bacon, in tomato.'

A tremor moved from his feet up, passed through his body and ended with a look of relief on his face.

Brace yourself, Rossi. I had omitted to mention *i diavolini,* little devil chili peppers I had added to make the classic, pasta *all'Amartriciana.*

Rossi blew his nose and dabbed his sweating brow umpteen times while eating his way through the pasta and the following dish of grilled spicy sausages served on a bed of deep green, bitter turnip tips.

It was a curious thing to watch. Each mouthful infused his skin with a deeper shade of red. Tears mixed with beads of sweat ran down his face. Despite his obvious discomfort, he was unable to stop eating.

I began to feel sorry for Rossi and decided to wait longer than usual before serving dessert.

Rubino moved his chair away from the table. 'Delicious, Hortensia, thank you.'

'Mmm, the knotty greens contrasted perfectly against the rich, chilli-infused sausage,' Maria said. 'What do you think, Mayor Rossi?'

Rossi's throat and tongue may have swollen as he had difficulty in articulating his words. 'A…as you say, per…perfect.'

I gave him my full attention. 'Good. I'm glad you enjoyed it. After all, this is a celebratory meal.'

He frowned. 'It is?'

'Yes. A celebration of thanks to you.'

'What for?'

I slid the letter from the tourist board across the table towards him. 'For all your hard work regarding the tourist accommodation licences. The application is currently under review.'

Rossi's hand shot out and grabbed the letter. His eyelids slid half-way closed in time with his jaw falling open.

'It's a great step forward.' I used my brightest voice. 'Isn't it?'

Before he could respond, I rose from the table. 'Time for dessert.'

Maria followed me into the kitchen.

'He realised, don't you think?' My voice was low.

Maria's voice was lower. 'For sure. Tread carefully from now on. You called his bluff and exposed him. No man likes that. Especially Rossi.'

Maria was right. I would have to be very careful.

By the time we returned to the table with fresh cutlery, bowls and the container of chocolate and chilli ice cream, Rossi had filled our glasses with the sparkling wine from the bottle he had brought.

'I propose a toast.

Rubino's shaggy eyebrows rose. The bangles clanged once and I felt my chest tighten.

Rossi raised his glass towards me. 'To an excellent cook and tire-less worker.'

Something's wrong. He's taking this news too calmly.

Rubino and Maria remained expressionless but their voices har-monised saying, *'Salute,'* while I could barely open my mouth to say, 'Thank you.' We sipped our wine.

'And another toast,' Rossi raised his glass again, 'to the future suc-cess of *our* tourist accommodation project.'

Our! How dare you. But this time I joined in and said, *'Salute.'*

We sipped again.

'Last but not least,' Rossi coughed and turned his gaze upon me.

Whatever it is, here it comes.

'As of today, my official period of mourning is over.'

My heart dropped to my feet, and my mind flew back to the date pencilled in on his desk calendar.

For the third time Rossi raised his glass. 'I could not have wished to end the past and mark the start of my new future in the company of anyone else.' He stared only at me.

My senses screamed their warning; once caught, he would never let me go. I could hear nothing, only see Rubino's and Maria's mouths move saying *salute*. But I could not; my throat had constricted. The implications of Rossi's words were awful.

God help me.

25

Lorenzo arrived, bearing fresh fish and a black, thundercloud scowl on his face. 'Santo Rossi was here for lunch last Saturday, wasn't he?'

'Yes. Why?'

'The *bastardo* already had this information from the Fishery Department and did not tell you.'

The blood in my veins turned into icy shards. 'Tell me what?'

Lorenzo thrust a fistful of yellow papers at me.

I read. Catch quotas for privately owned boats had been cancelled. Commercial fishing could only be carried out by larger, modern vessels operated by government-appointed agencies. Catches were destined for sale to other markets. Overnight, local, fresh-caught fish had become a thing of the past.

'But that's not all.' Lorenzo handed me the last page. 'See here.' He pointed where Rossi's name was signed.

I read with growing disbelief that it was he who had approached the Fishery Department to ensure that private owned fishing boats no longer catch or sell fish. The shards solidified. 'So, that's it. No more fishing for us.' I scanned through the list of regulatory warnings. 'We'd run the risk of losing the boat. We'll have to let the crew go.'

Lorenzo's face transformed into that of a kicked dog. 'What are we to do? The boat's still got good life in her.'

The freeze in my veins began to thaw. I took a breath. The words to a barely formulated idea tumbled from my mouth. 'What if…what if we turned the fishing boat into a tour boat and you sailed tourists up and down the coast and to the islands?'

No one knew our coast and the islands in our Tuscan Archipelago, dotted like clustered pearls throughout the Ligurian and Tyrrhenian Seas, better than Lorenzo.

'*Idea fantastica!*' An ear-to-ear smile split his face.

'First things first.' I stuck out my thumb. 'Pay off the crew.' I raised an index finger. 'Give them an ex-gratia bonus based on the number of years they have worked on the boat. Then, I raised my middle finger, 'check the boat into the dry dock.'

Lorenzo's face fell. 'Signora, since Mamma died, the boat has been my only home. Can I still live on board?'

The memory of Rubino extracting a promise from me flashed through my head. I placed my hand on Lorenzo's forearm and lowered my voice. 'Of course. But, until I say otherwise, the plan to change the boat to ferrying paying tourists needs to remain between you and me. Understand?'

Lorenzo rotated his cap between his hands. '*Sì*, signora.'

'Above all, this must never reach Rossi's ears. He'll do everything in his power to put a stop to it. Or,' I paused, to give additional weight to what next I was about to say, 'you will lose your home.'

Lorenzo made the sign of the cross. 'On my mother's life, you have my word.'

Did his oath count given his mother died twenty years ago? 'Come inside. Take a seat. Help yourself to *biscotti* and *limoncello*. I have a letter to write.'

I composed a letter to the maritime and tour guide departments in Rome asking for the requirements to turn a fishing vessel into a tour-boat. On instinct, I wrote out copies. *I must buy a typewriter.* I folded the signed originals, inserted them into envelopes and held them out to Lorenzo. 'Here, mail these from the next town along.'

As Lorenzo drove out of the courtyard, I handed over the matter of the boat to God, willing him to favourably influence the outcome of my enquiries. Given how the wheels of bureaucracy turned, it would be a while before I would receive answers. Until then, there was no point in worrying. I turned my focus to the courtyard.

The kitchen garden abounded with energy. Velvety bumblebees hummed around the flowering wisteria in the pergola overhead. Songbirds chirruped and darted between the leafy branches of the lemon trees, fruit suspended like jewels. In the distance, viewed through the courtyard's arch, the cerulean sea sparkled. Not a single cloud wisp broke the expanse of powder-blue sky.

Who was I fooling? Despite my determination, I could not enjoy the beauty around me. Anxiety's invisible, sticky fingers caught me fast like an insect thrashing in a spider's web.

The old familiar tightness settled in my chest. 'Why did you do this to me, Rossi?' I muttered. 'You know the fishing boat is my main livelihood. Are you so determined to keep my daughter and me cooks and maids forever?'

My mother's voice entered my head. *Yes. And, he wants you to go to him for help. That way you will be in his debt. He will extract payment at his leisure.*

———— ◆ ————

Valley housewives lamented the loss of their Friday fish deliveries. Buying fish from the cooperative store in the biggest town more than twenty kilometres away was not an option. They did not trust anything frozen, much less fish that came from foreign waters. Husbands and sons line-fished from the pier or small boats, and some, if lucky, came home with fish for Friday's meal.

Rossi's note, secured with his personal wax seal, thanking me for lunch arrived. He'd added a postscript. 'Please don't hesitate to ask me for help. I am at your service.'

I scoffed.

'What are you going to do?' Maria asked.

I pocketed the note. 'Ignore him.'

'I know that. What I mean is what are you going to do with the boat?'

'For now, it's in the dry dock…' I crossed my fingers. 'Undergoing routine maintenance.'

Long ago, courtesy of my father, I had learned to lie sticking as close to the truth as possible. But by the bangles' profound silence, I knew Maria was not convinced.

———————— ◆ ————————

'Lorenzo, are you sure you mailed the letter?'

'*Si,* signora.'

'It's been three months. I haven't heard anything.'

Lorenzo frowned and scratched his head. 'Maybe, because it did not have the town hall's official stamp or Rossi's signature?'

A rain cloud might as well have burst and dumped its cold water upon my head, shocking me into seeing clearly. *Of course, that's it.* I penned a note to Rossi telling him I needed to see him on Monday morning. 'Here, drop this off at Rossi's office. Hand it to him directly.'

After Lorenzo departed, I wandered over to the pergola and picked up a furry wisteria pod that had fallen to the ground. I cracked it open and removed a single seed. As large as the soft pad of a fingertip, it lay flat and shiny-bright in the centre of my palm.

Maria's earlier caution sounded in my ears, 'They're poisonous and will give the eater instant diarrhoea.' *Dare I?* I could think of no other way.

That evening, after Rubino and Maria had taken their leave and the children were safely in bed, I assembled the ingredients to make "*cannoli siciliani*", a dessert Sicilians claimed as their own even though it had been introduced by the Arabs centuries before when they had ruled the island.

Anna's voice entered my head. *The secret to cannoli success is the texture of its crisped shell. Kneading ensures an even distribution of the fat that creates flawless dough made from flour, sugar and salt.*

While rolling the dough into thin sheets, I thought about the fillings. Like Sicilians, who have long been mad for sweets, sugar was Rossi's first love.

Adding sugar to the ricotta cheese, thoroughly sieved to creamy smoothness was one thing; balancing the mixture with any one of the possible additives was seemingly endless: vanilla or chocolate, crème de cacao, powdered cinnamon or grated nutmeg, rose extract, chopped pistachios, and almond brittle or candied orange peel.

Anna's voice said, *I'd make two fillings, vanilla and chocolate. Afterwards, I'll tell you a little trick to enhance those flavours.*

Using a fine-edged porcelain bowl, I cut the thin sheets of dough into discs. To the deep pot on the stovetop, I added oil to the semi-solid lard and turned up the heat.

Once hot enough, I lowered the dough-wrapped metal *cannoli* tubes into the hot fat. In less than a minute the dough crisped golden brown. I removed and laid them on paper to drain the excess oil. When the metal tubes were cool enough to handle, I slid them out, leaving each delicate shell perfectly rounded on the inside.

Combine the ricotta and granulated sugar, Anna's voice said. *Beat well.*

I did as she instructed. Then I placed the single wisteria seed into the mortar and pestle and began to pound it until pulverised.

Excuse me? What's that you're doing?

I explained my plan to Anna.

That's an extremely dangerous thing to do!

I know. But Maria said it would work almost instantly. And anyhow, I'm going to test it first.

On who?

Myself. Then I'll know for sure how it works and if I need to add more or less powdered wisteria seed.

Hortensia! You are playing with fire. I do not recommend this.

I have no choice.

Why haven't you asked Maria for something she's tried and tested?

What! Like the chasteberry you and she nearly killed Di Napoli
with?

Anna harrumphed.

'I am being careful,' I said aloud to myself and gave the pestle an extra twist. 'Very careful.'

I divided the mixture. To the first two-thirds, I added melted chocolate, filled the piping bag and placed it in the marble cooler. It would serve as my surprise breakfast for the children the following morning.

To the last third, plain vanilla portion, I added the powdered wisteria seed, blended it well, filled a piping bag and piped the mixture into four shells.

I cleared the baking mess, sat down at the table, took note of the time on the wall clock and bit into the first *cannolo*. Two more bites and it was finished.

I waited fifteen minutes before I started on the second. Within minutes, a wave of searing pain wracked my abdomen and caused me to double over. I grabbed the dish containing the last two shells and ran to my bedroom. I dumped the dish on my bedside table and made it to the bathroom just in time.

Hours later, when I was sure I had no more need to remain in the bathroom, I crawled into bed. I was cold, dehydrated and weak. Too scared to drink any water lest I retch again, I closed my eyes, held onto the edge of the mattress and drifted off. Not to sleep, but a hallucinatory walk down the path of my life past, flanked on either side by an alignment of luminant celestial bodies. Then I fell into oblivion.

I woke the following morning at dawn's call. A film of what I'd done the night before played out. I became aware of a terrible thirst, and I was experiencing slight sensitivity in my belly. I wiggled my fingers and toes, pointed my feet, bent my knees and once I'd ascertained I was in good enough shape, I flung back the covers, dressed and went to the kitchen.

In preparation for the children's breakfast, I piped the empty shells with the chocolate mixture I'd left in the marble cooler. In no time, a platter, piled pyramid-high with chocolate *cannoli*, stood in the centre of the table. I set a pan to warm for the children's milk and my coffee.

'Nepitella. Timo. *Cannoli* for breakfast.'

Within seconds, Timo, wide-eyed, entered the kitchen. 'Yum.'

'Eat one at a time,' I cautioned him, as he took his place at the table and reached for the pile.

Nepitella, dainty and airy-light, emerged. She reached for her first *cannolo* as Timo reached for his second. As delicate as a cat lapping a saucer of milk, Nepitella licked the chocolate oozing from the shell's open ends first. 'The chocolate is delicious, but I preferred the vanilla.'

I spun around from the counter where I was preparing coffee. My heart plummeted. 'You what?'

'I smelled vanilla, woke and saw two in a bowl on the table next to your side of the bed. I couldn't resist.'

'What time was that?'

'I don't know. But you were fast asleep.'

'And you feel all right?'

'Yes. Why shouldn't I?'

'Umm…eating such richness in the early hours of the morning might have had a bad effect on your tummy?'

'No. I'm fine.'

Even a large, adult man with a cast-iron stomach would suffer. But then again, Nepitella was beyond ordinary. Thus, it stood to reason: beyond ordinary would be met with beyond ordinary reactions. I offered grateful thanks.

———————— ◆ ————————

On Sunday evening after the children had gone to bed, I prepared the shells and ricotta mixture with vanilla again. I filled two piping bags, one without wisteria powder and one with and locked both in the marble cooler. I placed the key on a chain around my neck and went to sleep. The following morning before the children woke, I filled the shells.

Anna's voice entered my head. *I'm glad to see you survived your experiment.*

Me too. Are you going to teach me the trick to enhance the vanilla flavour?

Yes. Push a maraschino cherry into each end, just so they peek out.

Ooh…that'll look wonderful.

Don't forget to sift icing sugar over them.

I won't. Thank you, Anna.

I layered the *cannoli*, knowing the exact position of the two wisteria-treated ones.

I hitched Long Ears to the cart, and with the container secure at my feet, waited until Maria arrived.

'Good morning,' I called as she entered the courtyard. 'I'm going to drop off some samples with Rossi. Please give the children breakfast.'

Maria waved and disappeared into the kitchen as I flicked the reins over the donkey's back.

◆

I was the first to enter the town hall. I headed down the empty corridor and tapped at Mayor Rossi's door, which was ajar. Cigarette smoke curled out from the narrow opening.

'Yes,' Rossi growled.

'Good morning, Mayor.' I purposefully made my voice sound light.

'Ah, Hortensia. Come in.' His tone of his voice changed. 'Please take a seat. What can I do for you?'

'Nothing. I have brought you some more samples… Oh, dear, I…'

Rossi's eyes swivelled. 'What is it?' He jumped to his feet and came around to where I stood clutching the back of the chair with one hand.

I held the container in the other hand and swayed. 'I feel faint…'

'Here, let me help you.'

'The *cannoli*…' I thrust the container at Rossi and sank into the chair.

'*Can…cannoli?*'

I lowered my voice to a whisper. 'Yes.'

'Sweet or savoury?'

'Sweet. Vanilla. Just for you.' I watched Rossi through a forest of eyelashes.

His tongue darted between his lips as he, with exaggerated care, placed the container on his desk.

'A little water, please.'

'Yes. Yes. Water.' Rossi poured a glass and offered it to me.

My hand shook as I took the glass, spilling a little. Alarm clouded Rossi's face.

I kept my voice low and weak. 'I need sugar.'

Desperation replaced alarm. He looked around his office. 'I'm afraid, I don't...'

With the back of one hand against my forehead, I feebly waved my other hand in the direction of the container. 'A *cannolo* will do the trick.'

Relief replaced alarm. Rossi eased open the lid, and a fragrant cloud of sugar and cream filled the air. This time, the look on his face changed to pure joy. He picked up the top shell and handed it to me.

'Ah, thank you.'

His gaze followed the *cannolo* as I brought the shell up to my mouth. The tip of my tongue plunged into the exposed ricotta and then teased the liqueur-soaked maraschino cherry from the cream. For a moment, I held the cherry between my teeth then bit it in two. With the inside of my mouth filled with the syrupy, warming liquor, I swallowed the cherry. Then my mouth closed over the edge of the shell. At the sound of the crackly crunch, I could feel the heat radiating from Rossi's body. I believe he came close to the point of exploding.

I took my time chewing and swallowing after which I sipped some water. Only then did I open my eyes and give him a tender, soft smile. 'You saved me. Thank you.'

Rossi's dilemma of whether to keep looking at me or the *cannoli* pyramid was laughable and pathetic. 'Please. Have one.'

'I'm not sure...It's a little early.'

'I need another. Join me.'

Rossi returned to his side of the desk and sat.

'Here.' I handed him the first wisteria-treated shell which he devoured in two bites. I held out the second.

Rossi needed little encouraging. He stuffed it into his mouth and watched me as I slowly ate my way through mine.

'Don't wait for me. Please have another. *Cannoli* must be eaten within an hour of being filled. Otherwise the shells go limp. Neither of us wants that to happen, now do we?'

Rossi gulped, and his face turned red.

Did he just grab his crotch under his desk?

Twenty minutes had passed, and Rossi had eaten three more when the expression on his face changed to one I recognised, having experienced it two nights before.

'I...I just have to give instructions to the staff.' Rossi jumped to his feet and rushed out.

I pushed the office door closed, walked around the desk, sat in his chair and pulled open the top drawer. All in a row lay several stamps in varying sizes, each with the town hall's insignia and an inkpad. I pulled out the new letter I'd written to the Fishery Department in Rome, inked the medium stamp and pressed it down hard at the bottom of the page. I picked up Rossi's pen. Having practised his signature from the thank you note he'd sent me, I had no problem replicating his name over the official insignia.

My mother's voice entered my head. *Take one of the stamps. You may need it in the future.*

Dead calm descended upon me. *That's stealing.*

That's surviving.

I pocketed one of the stamps, closed the drawer and returned to the visitor's seat. A hesitant knock sounded on the door. 'Yes.'

The town hall's secretary, tall and skeletal-thin, entered. 'Mayor Rossi offers his regrets. He has been called to a meeting.'

'Of course. Oh dear. These *cannoli* won't be any good in a little while. Would you like one?' I tipped the container towards him. 'Offer the rest to the staff. But make sure they are eaten within the hour. Promise me?

I don't want anyone saying the kitchen at Villa Trianni turned out soggy *cannoli.*'

'I promise. Thank you, signora. Good day.'

'Good day.'

A week later I received Rossi's personal wax sealed note. 'Thank you,' I said to the minion who shifted from one foot to another. 'You may go.'

The minion wrung his hands, 'Please, signora, the mayor says I am not to return without your written response.'

'Wait here.' I entered the kitchen, cut through the seal, unfolded the page and read.

Rossi thanked me for the *cannoli*; he and his staff claimed it to be the best they had ever eaten. He begged my forgiveness for abandoning me to attend an unexpected and urgent meeting. I giggled and then choked it back when I read the postscript.

The phrase he used asking permission to call upon me was a request to court me. If I agreed, he would make his claim over me public. Worse, it would be one step away from a formal marriage proposal, which, unless I died, I would, by custom, be obliged to accept.

Picking up a pen and a clean sheet of paper I wrote, 'Thank you for your note. Please accept my humble apologies, but I need time to consider your request. I will respond six months from now.'

I reread my note ensuring I gave no inkling of a formal rejection or acceptance. After all, I did not want to annoy him. I sealed a fresh envelope, wrote Rossi's name on it and handed it to the minion for delivery.

———— ◆ ————

The valley church bell sounded out a few preliminary chimes and then gonged twelve times.

Nepitella slept spread out like a starfish alongside me.

Timo stood next to my side of the bed. He tugged my hand. 'Zee-ya. Let me in.'

I raised the covers. My child crept in and shivered against me. Attempts at getting him to sleep in the master bedchamber upstairs had so far failed. 'What happened this time?'

'Shadows pulled my eyelids open.'

I tightened my arms around him. 'Oh dear. You must be very tired now.'

He nodded in earnest.

'We'll try again tomorrow night. Okay?'

No nod this time.

'But now, go to sleep.' I kissed the top of his head.

He wriggled about, then like a flipped-off switch, his body sagged against mine.

Wedged between the two children, and the memories triggered by the light of the full moon, I lay awake. The air filled with the children's combined scent of mint and thyme. That made good company while I pondered the details of the bed and breakfast project, and then my mind turned to the boat.

So far, it had spent months in a dry dock being overhauled and re-fitted to the stringent demands of the Italian Sea Vessel Regulating office. Every *lire*, down to the last cent I had saved, spent on the licences demanded by that department and the Ministry of Cultural Heritage and Activities and Tourism, was gone.

Since receiving Mayor Santo Rossi's note requesting permission to call upon me, I counted down the months I had left before I gave him a formal rejection. The thought hovered like the sword of Damocles above my head.

———— ◆ ————

Nepitella and Timo tumbled about on the bed. Their voices, Nepitella's sweet and melodious, Timo's loud and demanding, urged me to wake. Playing the game, I feigned sleep. Judging when they least expected it, I made a terrible face, roared, jumped out of bed and gave chase.

Screaming with delight, they ran from the bedroom through my small living room and into the kitchen. Their voices fell silent, like a water spigot turned off.

Thinking they were hiding, I shrugged on my dressing gown and called out in a sing-song voice, 'I'm coming to get you.' I entered the kitchen and came to an abrupt stop as though I'd slammed into an invisible wall.

The open door framed Di Napoli and his six-year-old son, my godson, Massimiliano. Both wore matching fedoras atop their heads and cashmere coats casually slung over their shoulders. Their images pulled me back to the first time I spied Di Napoli while leaning over Mistress Letizia's bedchamber windowsill. I clutched the neckline of my dressing gown closed. Not for modesty's sake, but to stop my heart from crashing through my chest. *He's looking old. Tired.*

Di Napoli doffed his hat. 'I knocked and didn't mean to startle you.'

The three children, more or less the same height, gazed curiously at each other. Nepitella and Timo had never seen a child dressed like Max. Perhaps Max had never seen children dressed like them: barefoot, mismatched pyjamas and with tousled hair.

My throat turned gritty, but I managed to rasp out a good morning. Di Napoli stepped past his son who, like my children, remained as though nailed to the floor. Buried memories and the fragrance of pomade and chocolate, surfaced. *Was that a box of gianduiotti under his arm?*

My chocolate demon uncoiled. I'd not eaten a *gianduiotto* since Iacopo's gift of two foil-covered chocolates on the night of our mutual seduction, seven years ago.

'Hortensia. You look wonderful.'

If ever there was a blatant lie. 'What brings you here?' My clipped voice camouflaged my racing heart.

Head cocked, the lights in his black eyes flashing amusement, Di Napoli's full lips curled up in an insouciant smile.

Did my heart just soften?

'Come on, Hortensia. This is me, Di Napoli. We know each other.'

The resonance of his rich voice set my core to thrum. *No need to remind me.* He slid the box of chocolates onto the table and raised his hands palm-side up, inviting me to step into his arms for a welcome hug, which I ignored. There was nothing but the scent of chocolate and pomade to breathe.

Timo's feet unglued from the floor. He stepped forward, placing himself between Di Napoli and me.

Undeterred, Di Napoli changed tactics. He looked over his shoulder. 'Come, Max, greet your godmother, Hortensia d'Ambrosia-il Pescatore.'

Though Max's body moved towards me, he kept Nepitella in his line of sight. His face glowed with rapture. Delicate and elfin-like, she inspired visions of wizardry and enchanted forest meadows teeming with mythical beings.

Timo glared alternately between Max and Di Napoli.

Following his father's order, Max came forward.

'Call me Zeeya,' I said.

Timo had learned to speak first, but could not pronounce my name. He shortened it to the last three letters that sounded like *zia*, meaning aunt. As in everything she could, Nepitella copied Timo. Thus, neither child called me Mamma.

Max held out his hand and graced me with a quick glance from under his lashes, dark and long, like his father's. 'Zeeya, I'm pleased to meet you.'

I was not surprised by Max's rehearsed phrase. But underneath its smooth delivery, there trailed a forlorn and lonely breeze, in search of one of its kind.

With her eyes glowing with aeons-old wisdom, Nepitella watched the scenario play out. Timo had turned into an immovable, stone-carved sentinel forcing me to step around him.

I sank to the floor and drew the child into my arms. His little body, not delicate like Nepitella's, nor robust as Timo's, stiffened. I held him close and would not let go until I heard his heart beat in response to mine. His guard forced to stand down, Max angled his head and whispered in my ear, 'You knew my mamma?'

Reminded of my never-ceasing thoughts about my mother, his words tore my heart in two. I gave him an extra squeeze and whispered, 'Yes.'

'Will you tell me about her?'

'Of course.' I glanced up. If he'd been a rooster, Di Napoli would have crowed with triumph. He'd skilfully and knowingly played the pulling-of-my-heartstrings card. *Bastardo!*

Nepitella's and Timo's mouths hung open. They had never seen me hug another child.

Fear overpowered the former glow of wisdom emanating from Nepitella's eyes. Her tiny body appeared to shrink and crawl into a spiral shell. Just in time, I drew her close to where I remained on my knees with Max standing alongside me. 'Nepitella, meet Max. Max, my daughter, Nepitella.'

Both looked sombrely at each other. I grasped Timo by the wrist before he could withdraw into an underground den, jealousy gnawing a hole through his soul. 'Timo, this is Max, heir to Villa Angeli. Max, this is Timo, heir to Villa Trianni.'

'Go on.' The kitchen walls reverberated with Di Napoli's voice. 'You can shake hands like I taught you. Timo is your equal.'

With the order of rank addressed, I stood. Timo glanced at me, for permission or guidance, perhaps? I stared hard, willing him to shake hands without my prompting.

An almost imperceptible shudder, but a shudder nonetheless rippled through Timo's body. Warning bells jangled in my head. That Di Napoli did not suggest Max shake hands with Nepitella caused my heart to smoulder.

A burst of flames from the night stove and a flurry of tinny chimes announced Maria's arrival, breaking the tension that gripped us.

My children rushed to her and clamoured. 'What have you brought?' Their faces glowed shiny-bright with anticipation.

'Mmm. Let me see.' Maria searched through the many pockets sewn into her voluminous cloak.

Max backed away.

Di Napoli gripped his son by the shoulder. 'Nothing to be afraid of, my boy, that's just Maria.'

I always forgot how alarming Maria looked at first sight, with her long black cloak, hooked nose, flickering, squinty eyes, and tinkling bangles.

'Where did I put them? Ah. Here they are.' From her pockets, Maria retrieved yellow chicks, one each for Nepitella and Timo. 'And, one for you.' Maria turned and held out a cheeping chick to Max.

His body stiffened but he stepped forward and received the ball of fluff. Raised in the chaotic city of Naples, this was likely his first time seeing, let alone holding, an adorable, vulnerable chick.

Each chick had a tiny ribbon around its neck. Pink for Nepitella's, blue for Timo's and red for Max's.

'Nepitella, Timo, take Max with you,' I said. 'Put the chicks in their nursery.'

The ice broken, the children left the kitchen each holding a chick in their cupped hands.

As Max passed Maria, she whipped the hat off his head and coat from his shoulders. 'Those don't belong in a chicken coop.'

'It was a long journey from Naples,' Di Napoli said. 'Any chance of breakfast?'

Maria stood with her arms akimbo. The lights in her eyes flashed. 'Di Napoli, is this a social call?'

Di Napoli bristled. 'You forget your place, woman.'

If he suspected Maria had almost killed him with incorrect dosage extracts from the chasteberry tree, I'd understand the reason for his domineering and condescending rudity; it had taken years for his health to recover. Moreover, if rumours were correct, to the great disappointment of vast numbers of women, he never attained his former legendary talent for all manner of sexual escapades.

Before Maria could retort, Rubino entered.

'Ha, *il Capo* has arrived.' Di Napoli slapped Rubino on the back.

I bridled at Di Napoli's patronising attitude towards the very people who'd helped him get to where he was. For remuneration, he had married Mistress Letizia Angeli. But, before his marriage, he had been no better off than any of us. Now, as the father of the heir to the Angeli Estate, he assumed superiority, wore showy clothes and carried himself as if he were the boss of us all.

Through the kitchen window, I saw the children leave the stable housing the chicken coop. Max trailed behind, gingerly sidestepping foraging chickens. The children headed towards the kitchen garden bursting with spring vegetables. There were enough plants, earthworms, frogs and lizards to keep them occupied for a while.

I filled the large espresso pot's chamber with water, tamped down finely ground coffee beans in the funnel, screwed the two halves of the pot together and set it on a low heat.

It was not long before Di Napoli spoke. 'I'm leaving on an extended business trip, introducing *gianduiotti* to new markets. Delphina is joining me but Max can't. Nor can I leave him in Naples; he's to start school. So, I thought, what better than for him to come and attend school here and put down his roots in the place he owns?'

Maria snorted. 'Who is to care for him?'

Di Napoli gave Maria a look as if she had lost her mind. With a nonchalant tip of his head in my direction, he said, 'She's already caring for one heir, isn't she?'

I beat the heating milk to froth with anger rather than vigour.

'But,' Rubino said, 'Hortensia lives here. Having Max live alone in Villa Angeli is not practical.'

I reached for the croissants I'd prepared the night before, removed the cloth and slipped the tray into the heated oven.

Di Napoli fell silent. I refused to say a word until he addressed me directly. Maria read my thoughts and held her tongue. Rubino wisely followed suit.

I handed Rubino an unopened jar of last season's wild, black fig jam. With his large hands, he unscrewed and set it down on the table.

I placed a tub of fresh *Fior di Latte* on the table, a pale yellow cheese with a tangy bite preferred by adults. And a hunk of *fontina*, a buttery, nutty-flavoured cheese children prefer. Reaching into the back of the cooler, I drew out a ceramic bowl, fashioned to look like a cherry cut in half. It brimmed with red cherries. Their slippery, taut skins were bright with a light, oily sheen.

My taste buds sprang to alert, anticipating the first bite when crisp, clean and very sweet juice would spurt in my mouth.

Di Napoli eyed the cherries and then caught my eye. His face hinted desire to devour them. Or, devour me?

I remained unaware, but at that moment a hairline crack appeared in the years-old wall of defence I had built against Di Napoli.

A memory fragmented and lighter than a will-o'-the-wisp seeped through the crack. As fast as the memory of us sharing just such a bowl of cherries, naked upon sarcophagi in the dark bowels of the gothic Church of Santa Chiara in Naples, began to re-assemble, I caught and smothered it. I returned to the present.

'What say you, Hortensia?'

Ah. Getting closer.

The fragrance of baking croissants escaped the oven and wafted through the air. That, along with the aroma of percolated coffee, strong and bitter, and sweet, warm and airy-light frothed milk, caused my breakfast belly to groan. 'How long will you be gone?'

'A year.'

The bangles trilled. Di Napoli was lying.

I placed dishes and cutlery upon the table.

'Will you take care of Max?' Di Napoli asked.

Finally.

Like soldiers massed in preparation to heave and break down a portcullis, long-buried memories threw their weight against the cracked wall. The hairline crack increased, and my head and heart took up arms. My head was saying, *Di Napoli, you took your pleasure with me, and for that, you owe me.*

I switched off the oven and refocused, keeping Max in my line of sight through the window standing in the kitchen garden. My heart was saying, *Max, despite me being your godmother you are a soul in need. I will take and raise you as my own, but only after washing your head free of pomade.*

Di Napoli's deep voice reverberated against the kitchen walls. 'I'll pay for his keep.'

Now that's what I was waiting to hear! I placed the coffee pot and frothed milk on the table.

Di Napoli sighed. 'Spit it out, Hortensia. How much?'

I retrieved the crisp, golden croissants from the oven and placed them in a basket. 'Your share of the next wine sale to America.'

'Christ!' Di Napoli sprang to his feet. 'That's daylight robbery. How in hell am I to live?'

Like the chestnut tree, Rubino remained immovable. So, too, did Maria and the bangles.

'That's your problem.' I picked up Max's hat and coat in one hand and held them out to Di Napoli. With the other, I gestured, 'Take it or leave it.'

Di Napoli faced Rubino. 'My friend…'

Maria and I inhaled sharply. *The man was beyond rude.*

'Help me out here. What's the long-term forecast for the grape harvests?'

Rubino held Di Napoli's gaze. 'Bar natural disasters, each harvest in quantity and quality will improve.'

Di Napoli sat down. He wiped his face with his handkerchief. 'Okay. Okay. I agree. I guess I will have to survive on my chocolate sales. Now, let's eat. I'm starving.'

I did it! I suppressed an exuberant yell.

Midway bringing the cup of coffee to his mouth, Di Napoli stopped. He focused on Maria. 'You haven't put anything in my coffee, have you?'

Maria raised her cup and, taking a slow sip, avoided replying or lying. I knew not which.

'Children. Breakfast.' I watched them racing towards the villa, three glorious rainbows, side by side. So caught up in the sight, it escaped me that the hairline crack in my years-old wall of built-up defences against Di Napoli, had turned into a fracture.

Rubino and Maria took their leave.

'Son,' Di Napoli said, as the Max entered the kitchen. 'Come here. I have news.'

Max stood beside his father.

The closest person to a father Nepitella and Timo had was Rubino. Wide-eyed, they looked on.

Di Napoli placed his arm around his son's shoulder. 'Remember I told you about coming here to live?'

Max fidgeted and looked downward.

'Your godmother has agreed. I'll write. Learn how and write back. Okay?'

Timo looked as though he was about to explode. 'Where's Max to sleep?'

Ah. I should have known. Timo's sleeping arrangement was his current nemesis. 'Where would you like Max to sleep?'

For once Timo was speechless.

'Tell you what. Why don't you all go upstairs? Timo you choose–'

'But what about breakfast?' Timo eyed the table.

'You can have breakfast after.'

'Okay. But only if you and Nepitella come and sleep upstairs in the bedrooms I choose, too.'

'A big bedroom for me?' Nepitella's eyes grew as round as two pizzas.

It struck me that now was the right time for all of us to move upstairs. We had long outgrown my small bedroom and living room. 'Okay.'

'Come on,' Timo yelled. 'Last one is a *buffo*.'

Laughing like circus clowns, the children raced out of the kitchen, through the dining room, over the harlequin-patterned hall floor and up the staircase. Their voices faded as they reached the landing; doors systematically banged open and closed.

Di Napoli stood behind me. I stiffened, the fracture widened. His body heat seeped through my dressing gown and scorched my skin.

'Hortensia.' His breath danced along my neck.

Oh, God. It's been so long.

His lips brushed my ear. He placed his arms around my waist. One hand found its way to my breast, the other cupped my mons pubis. He nuzzled my neck and squeezed both hands at the same time. I swooned with the pleasure of it.

The children's voices grew louder; they were returning.

'Come to me tonight.' His voice was low and deep, turning my bones to jelly.

Give me strength.

I pushed his hands and stepped away.

27

I threw together one of my children's favourite meals: *fettina panata*, paper-thin slices of breaded veal, fried crispy, served with potatoes sautéed in brown butter, and a bowl of shelled peas sprinkled with sprigs of mint.

Di Napoli squeezed lemon over the golden escalope on his plate. 'Isn't this good, Max?'

Max's cheeks bulged like a squirrel's full of acorns. He nodded his head with vigour. Timo skewered three pieces of potato and tried to jam them all into his mouth.

To get his attention, I touched his hand. 'Slowly. One piece at a time. And chew properly before you swallow.'

As fast as Timo gobbled his food, Nepitella picked at hers. Using her fork, she pushed a pea in circles around her plate. After the third circle, she'd spear it and pop it into her mouth. What little she ate was consumed in this manner. If anyone commented, she'd not eat at all.

Di Napoli and Max noticed, but fortunately, they said nothing. I would explain Nepitella's eating habits to Max as soon as possible. *If I could just find a way to encourage her eating.* Even Maria was at a loss.

'Wine, Hortensia?' Without waiting for my response, Di Napoli filled my glass. *'Salute.'* His gaze sought mine. I brushed a hand across my brow, trying to keep from being lured into those dark pools.

What if things were different, if this was a normal everyday family gathering? My thoughts took to the air and soared. *How would it be if Di Napoli and I were married, and these were our children? Would we be happy? Would life be ordered, tranquil?*

My head and heart went to war.

'*Whaaat!*' screamed the voice in my head voice. '*Get ahold of yourself.*'

My heart responded. '*You're right. You're right.*'

How can I be so stupid? He's married to my archenemy. He is a manipulator, an opportunist, arrogant, a womaniser, and most of the time a rude bully.

I berated my former foolish girl's heart, which still clung to the remnants of the notion we were as connected as I had felt the first moment I saw him. In truth, the only things that tied me to him were those events, best left buried. The warm swelling in my heart cooled and deflated, leaving me feeling so heavy I could hardly move.

The fracture gaped. Fragments of memories escaped so fast I swatted them like one does pesky midges, flying in a cloud above one's head.

Following dinner and the bedtime rituals, the children piled into Timo's large bed. Di Napoli leaned against a wall and melded with the shadows. My head throbbed, yet I picked up the storybook and began to read. Before long, the children fell asleep.

I carried Nepitella into the bedroom Timo had assigned to her and pulled the covers up to her chin. Then I watched Di Napoli carry his son to his new bedroom. He leaned over and gave his sleeping boy a kiss.

My heart fluttered at the sight, then fell, as my head beat hope into a hasty retreat, leaving the bitter taste of reality. Nepitella and Timo would never know paternal love.

The villa had gone quiet. I put on the coffee pot and waited until the last of the smoky-sweet liquid bubbled through the spout. At the very moment Di Napoli entered the kitchen, the male barn owl outside shrieked, announcing his presence.

Di Napoli pulled up a chair and sat.

The box of *gianduiotti* remained unopened. Its voice, which only my chocolate demon and I could hear, whispered, 'Open me. Eat me.'

I poured the coffee and placed two cups on the table. 'How is Delphina?'

'She's a mystery.'

'How so?' I held my breath.

The light in Di Napoli's dark eyes dimmed. He paused. 'I can speak freely?'

'Of course.'

'You won't judge me?'

What! When did you care what I thought? I lowered my voice to an encouraging tone. 'I won't.'

My mother's voice entered my head. *Don't be foolish, Hortensia. He's using flattery to soften you.*

'More than a mystery.' Di Napoli paused, then drew in a sharp breath. 'She's downright strange. I married Delphina for several reasons, not least because she enchanted me. Soon on, I…' He stabbed his chest several times with his index finger. 'I, of all men, struggled. Despite my earnest efforts, to the point of endangering my health, I could no longer satisfy her voracious appetite. Then, she lost interest in *me!*'

Di Napoli's voice conveyed mild shock and surprise, though, at that time, his feelings must have been extreme. A look of incredulity and disbelief crossed his face with the memory of it.

I restrained an escaping giggle. *How could any woman lose interest in him? He was an exceptional lover; devoted to the art of pleasuring.* And, through less natural means, which he preferred, Di Napoli could take two bodies to places unknown and heights unscaled.

The gaping fracture turned into a yawning maw. Memories of acts undertaken in the dark bowels of the church in Naples streaked out, like bats leaving a cave at dusk.

First, Di Napoli pleasured me until I thought I had died and entered paradise. Then, no different to dangling the carrot in front of the donkey's nose, he coaxed me to perform boundless, unspeakable acts for his pleasure.

Though I had no taste for administering the unnatural, when I realised I had developed a talent for it, shame swallowed me whole, like a snake ingesting itself. The only way I could withstand that shameful feeling was when I took control and made Di Napoli scream for more, and then beg for merciful release. So continued our endless round of intimacies each afternoon for six weeks.

I stood before the broken wall and peered into the empty space behind. *Memories. Damn you all.* I wrenched my grim thoughts back to the present.

'Also, half the time I don't think she belongs to this world.' Di Napoli's brow creased. 'Do you have any idea what I mean?'

I was not going to enlighten him. 'No.'

Di Napoli sighed. 'I receive more warmth and affection from my dog than I do from her.'

It took all my energy to curb my heart edging towards feeling sorrow for him.

'When I discovered her blithely entertaining any man she chose, regardless of station, and sometimes, two at a time,' Di Napoli slumped back into the chair, 'I gave up.'

The owl's mate responded.

'Then, there was the mysterious death of the only man I know who tried to resist her – on the night before his wedding.'

My head and heart rallied, and my thoughts flew to Arturo. Of course! *He* had resisted Delphina. He had been in love with Camellia. The scar with Arturo's name written upon it reopened. For a second, I relived the same, spine-tingling horror when I found him in the tower, surrounded by Rubino and Maria.

'Rumours of the way he met his end rippled through Naples. What was used to impale and kill him,' Di Napoli simulated turning a key to lock his mouth, 'I won't repeat. But it convinced me Delphina was responsible.'

Visions of those hair strands, which turned into spikes, flashed in my head.

'So, my dear, sweet, Hortensia, Delphina has released me from my conjugal obligations. But, should I deny her other desires and demands, which by far, exceed her beauty, I fear for my life. She's an oddity at best, a freak at worst.'

I invoked my calm, rational head to respond. 'For this reason, you have brought Max here.'

'Thanks be to God! I knew you would understand.' Di Napoli buried his head in his hands, while the barn owls alternately shrieked.

My heart betrayed me again by feeling sorry for him. Then the question burning to be answered slipped out of my mouth. 'What do you plan to do?'

'Do? Sweet Hortensia. I have grown too tired and too old for new dalliances. I seek only companionship.' He reached for my hand. 'Unless of course…'

Vibrant memories of the sweet relief we experienced in the torture of each other danced like whirling dervishes upon my weakened heart. I removed my hand from the table and set it, away from temptation, in my lap.

My head had triumphed.

The edges of Di Napoli's mouth turned down in a sad, wry smile. 'You know the Church's rule. My bed is made, I must lie in it 'til death do us part. Until then, I will continue to do her bidding, and play the role of "cuckold".'

My, how the wheels have turned. I could not imagine the number of men who suffered the ignominy of having to play that role, thanks to Di Napoli.

The owls found each other. Their hoots shrieked in unison.

I recalled the bangles warning me of his lie. 'So, you're leaving Max here permanently.'

Di Napoli threw me a surprised look from under his long lashes. His internal thoughts were indiscreet, for I heard them clearly; as if he'd uttered aloud – *you're not so slow after all.*

I bristled in an instant, and it took all my strength not to shout out loud. *Vaffanculo!* Fuck you!

'Yes. But, I will come back as often as I can to see him.' Di Napoli extended one arm and left it resting upon the table, his hand, palm-side up. 'And, have the pleasure of your food and companionship, too, I hope?'

The owls fell silent.

I bit my bottom lip hard. *My God. How persistent you are.*

My mother's voice entered my head. *That's what it's all about: chase, conquer, and discard.*

I needed no more reminders of how atrociously he had spoiled me, a mere maid, on the brink of womanhood. What he'd done to me and taught me to do to him for his depraved pleasure was knowledge only for the unfit.

A mellifluous voice, perhaps, of an angel, sounded in my ears. *You are not unfit.* Caring, guiding hands eased me into a calm sea. Weighed by my shame, I sank like a stone to the seabed where I rested in the pitch dark until faced with the choice of either dying or living.

I chose the latter.

Striking my feet upon the sand, I shot arrow-straight upward and emerged into the light, cleansed and shame-free.

I pushed the *gianduiotti* aside and slid a cup towards his outstretched hand. 'Your coffee's getting cold.'

The gleam of hope that had sparked in Di Napoli's dark eyes died. 'Hortensia, is there anything about me and you…us that needs talking about? Clearing up?'

Watch out, my mother's voice urged. *He's still trying to hook you.*

The owls started up again, and old questions, sounding like the discordant notes from the Puccini lakeside theatre's orchestra, warming up, clamoured in my head. My former maid's heart cried out. *Yes. Tell me. Was I really only ever a plaything, a dalliance, to you? Did you ever love me? Did you mean it when you said, if you could have, you would have married me? If so, why didn't you ask me?*

Di Napoli's intense gaze could have melted the entire box of *gianduiotti*. 'Well?'

'No.' And then before I could stop the words, they slipped out. 'And you?'

'Yes.'

My head froze. My heart froze. I was sure the kitchen froze. And because the owls fell silent once more, they might have frozen, too.

'Why didn't you reply to my letters?'

'I never received them.' *Pietro, what did you do with them?*

'And the last time we were together?'

The last memory of him striking me, his heartfelt cries seeking comfort, my comforting him and then seeking comfort from him, lit the inside of my head like the flash of the shooting star's luminescent path.

'Forgive me.'

Did I hear right?

Yes, my mother's voice said. *But stay strong. He is at his most lethal now that he is caught up in the chase. He will bring you down like a predator does its prey.*

My mother's words were as effective as dumping a bucket of ice-cold water over me.

I blinked hard as tears threatened to spill, and waved one hand with nonchalance. 'It's been a long day. I'm retiring. Goodnight.'

Di Napoli inclined his head. 'I'll be leaving in the morning. Good night.'

Despite the raw ugliness of our past, the resonance of his deep, rich voice still turned my bones to jelly. It was easy to imagine that every chocolate in the box had unwrapped their foils and popped into my mouth.

I left the kitchen, feeling his eyes bore holes in my back. Exercising prudence, my hips did not sway. For his loving was not what I ever wanted again. My thoughts turned to Pietro, whose kind of lovemaking was what I yearned for.

———————— ◆ ————————

E ntering my bedroom, I picked up a pen and, now having a legitimate excuse, wrote, 'Signor Rossi, regretfully, an unexpected additional responsibility, being the guardianship of the heir to Villa Angeli, Massimil-iano Di Napoli, has been tossed into my life, preventing me from considering your request…'

I rested my elbows on the table, covered my face with my hands and imagined a bridal bouquet made up of long, green-stalked death lilies. For the whole of its life, each white spathe would protect – or hold captive – the miniature yellow stalk.

My heart leaped with joy at having evaded a fate worse than death.

I sealed the envelope and wrote Rossi's name on it. On Friday, I'd have Lorenzo deliver my rejection of Rossi's courtship leading to a marriage proposal.

————— ♦ —————

Early the next morning, I opened Nepitella's door and saw she was not in her bed. Nor was Max in his, but I did see the imprint of Di Napoli's head on the pillow alongside his son's. He'd left earlier than I expected.

The master bedchamber's door was open. The three children slept in a tangle of limbs like kittens in a basket.

In the kitchen, the single sheet I had asked Di Napoli to sign lay on the table. A quick glance confirmed his signature. But he'd added something. I picked it up and in dawn's filtering light, read. He had agreed to give me his share of not only next season's wine sale, but every season's, until Max turned eighteen.

I clutched the edge of the table for support and stared hard, doubt-ing my sight, my heart and my head. Restitution, more than I imagined, had been paid.

My mother's voice entered my head with a resounding squawk. *See what results when women keep their heads and hearts and hold men at bay?*

I folded the sheet and slipped it into my apron pocket. *This one will not go missing.*

I turned my attention to breakfast. The rich fragrance of warm milk mixed with powdered cacao wafted up the stairs. I heard the boys' feet hit the floor, then their footfalls before they flung open their doors and raced to the landing. Though I never heard the sound of Nepitella's feet, she materialised first at the top of the stairs. Both boys scowled their annoyance.

Although Timo was fast, he always allowed Nepitella to reach me first. Or, was it because he did not want it known she was faster than him?

'Cos she's a girl,' he'd say. But this morning, he held back, allowing Max to be second in line. Timo cocked his head and gave me a beady look. 'Cos she's your daughter, he's your godson, and cos I'm nothing to you.'

My heart snapped. 'All the same,' my voice squeaked, 'I love you.'

'No.' Timo's voice had risen. His bottom lip quivered. I reached for him. He dodged my groping hands. 'You're nothing to me.'

'But, Timo, even though not everyone is related, we are all one big family. Look at Rubino and Maria for example. They are our family and family doesn't always mean blood relatives.'

Timo turned his head and refused to look at me.

The bangles tinkled, and the fire turned blue.

Maria walked into the kitchen and caught me in the act of using the edge of my apron to wipe the tears streaming down my face.

'I wonder,' she said, patting her cloak pockets. 'I wonder. Now, where did I put that….put that…?'

'Put what?' the children yelled.

I staggered up the stairs. *I am dying. Dying in agony like a wretched beast.* I shut my bedroom door and lay on the bed.

My son's words hurt me, one hundredfold more than any wrong done to me in my life. But nothing could compare to the sight of the pain spilling from his eyes. And it was that, *his torment*, I could not bear.

Several hours later, I woke to the sound of whispers and shuffling coming from behind the door. Then, a series of tentative knocks.

'Zeeya, are you better? Max asked.

'Can we come in?' Nepitella and Timo asked.

'Yes.'

The door flew open. Max carried a small tray holding biscuits and fruit. Nepitella proffered a bunch of mixed herbs and flowers from the kitchen garden. Timo held something between his close-cupped hands.

With rising anxiety, I searched for signs of the pain that had flooded him earlier. There was none. His eyes were clear, bright and brimming with mischief. An enormous sigh of relief escaped me.

The bangles rang, sounding like Mistress Letizia's bell that she used to summon me when I had been her maid.

Maria stood in the doorway. 'A mid-morning snack is served.'

'What's wrong?' Nepitella asked.

'A simple headache. But it's gone now.'

'You need to eat. To keep up your strength.' Nepitella used my exact words and tone of voice when I encouraged her to eat.

I held back a smile and made my voice sound serious. 'Yes, nurse. You are right.' I refocused to include the two boys. 'Share this with me. You all need strength for the surprise I have in store for you today.'

'What surprise?' Nepitella and Max asked.

'Don't you want to see mine first?' Timo held out his arms towards me. His voice crackled with reproach.

'Of course, I do.'

'Zeeya, close your eyes,' Timo commanded. 'Don't peek.'

'I won't.'

'Hold out your hand.'

I did.

'Look now.'

I looked. It was so light I did not feel it, but on my hand rested a butterfly. Its mauve and orange wings fanned open and closed as if in preparation for flight.

Is this the sign my son is returned to me?

My mother's voice entered my head. *Yes.*

The remnants of my headache and heartache vanished. I had never felt better.

Three heads crowded together close enough for me to kiss one after another and say, 'Thank you, thank you, thank you.'

'Shall I release it outside where it belongs?' Without waiting for an answer, Maria retrieved the butterfly and disappeared.

'Snack time,' I said. 'Let's play a game. In turn, each person gets to choose what to eat, and everyone follows.'

'And then will you tell us the surprise?' Max asked.

'Yes.'

The children tumbled about on my bed like scattered *bocce* balls, then righted themselves.

'Timo, share out the biscuits. Max, divide the mandarin segments into four parts. Nepitella, pour the milk.'

We took turns to choose, and we ate. I sighed with relief – Nepitella ate without fuss.

'The surprise!' Timo yelled. 'Tell us the surprise.'

'We are going to learn how to swim.'

Timo straightened. His face was inscrutable.

'I don't like water,' Nepitella said.

I turned to my new child. 'Max, can you swim?'

'Swimming is no good.'

'Why?'

Max's face became solemn. 'Cos, water gets in the ear and swells up the head like a watermelon. When your brain bursts, your head explodes.'

Good grief! What have those Neapolitans been teaching him?

Nepitella scrunched her face. 'Ew.'

Timo shoved his elbow into Max. 'Liar.'

'Am not.'

'Are.'

'But Zeeya,' Nepitella said, 'why do we have to learn how to swim?'

'So we can go sailing.'

'In a boat?' Max asked.

'Yes.'

Timo frowned. 'A big boat on the sea?'

'Yes.'

Timo's eyebrows rose just as mine did when my curiosity piqued. 'Where will we go?'

'Anywhere you want.'

Timo bounced around on the bed. 'Yay!'

'Why do we have to know how to swim if we're on a boat?' Nepitella asked.

I hugged her. 'No one can go on a boat unless they can swim.'

'But why?'

'Because, when the boat stops we can jump in and swim in the sea. Won't that be fun?'

Nepitella's face crumpled in dismay. I noticed her fingers had crept along the cover and found Max's hand.

Timo noticed, too.

I changed tactics. 'But before we swim in the sea, we have to start with lesson one.'

'What's lesson one?' Max said.

'Learning to paddle our feet in the river.'

'In the *Frigido*?' Nepitella and Timo asked.

I ignored their exaggerated shivers. 'Yes. Boys, go and find Rubino. Timo, you ask him to hitch the donkey. And Max, you tell him we're starting our swimming lessons today.'

Nepitella remained sceptical. 'Does Rubino know how to swim?'

'Yes, of course.'

'Is Rubino going to teach us?' Timo asked.

'Yes. Now off you go and don't yell for Rubino. Find him and speak in polite, normal voices. Nepitella and I will meet you downstairs.'

The two boys sprang up like hares and raced down the stairs, elbowing and jostling one another.

28

The summer drew to an end, but the labour necessary to maintain our self-sustaining valley did not.

Workers prepared for the grape harvest at the end of September immediately followed by the olive harvest in November. For centuries, the financial results from their intense physical labour only benefitted the often-absent landowner. Now with the workers signed up as members of the labour union, and individual estate contracts signed, they were assured of their wages and a bonus, whether the landlord was there or not. Households also received a portion of wine and olive oil to see them through the year.

In preparation for storing, housewives poured a handful of gravel through the narrow necks of hundreds of bulbous, dark green demijohns. They added water and shook the glass containers. The swirling gravel loosened the hardened dregs. Once rinsed, the containers were ready for storing a year's worth of wine and oil. On average, a family of four consumed two litres of oil a month and a litre of wine per day.

Anticipated yields for both harvests were high. I wrote to Iacopo in America, giving him Rubino's opinion on the quality and volume of wine and oil we expected.

In recent years, Rubino's eyesight had weakened, and he handed over the profit distribution process to me. Workers' names filled the dense cream pages of the leather-bound ledger. Each person's share was penned alongside his name and upon receipt, signed for. Few workers could write. The signature column reflected the soul of our valley with a mix of hieroglyphic squiggles, thumbprints and crosses.

After the harvests, each worker tended to his patch of land. One part was left fallow and the other, planted in late summer, ensured a supply of vegetables through the winter.

Farmers slaughtered pigs, turned the butchered meat into sausages, with lengths of salami suspended from lines in barns to air-dry.

Housewives organised their jars of homemade jam, basil-infused tomato sauce, pickled onions, cucumbers, and cauliflower florets. They packed jars of blanched artichokes and green beans, roasted peppers and grilled zucchini filled to the brim in oil. Groaning pantry shelves attested to their bottling proficiency.

The trickier it was to negotiate around standing baskets overflowing with chestnuts, hazelnuts and walnuts, potatoes and apples, interspersed with orange pumpkins of all shapes, the more people regarded it as a blessing, for it meant there was an abundance of food laid in for winter.

Until tripped by a basket, or sporting a lump on one's head from the ropes of garlic, onions and corn strung from every conceivable hook, one remained a novice in the art of food storage.

'Time to measure how tall you've grown,' I said. Stand straight, Nepitella.' After squashing down her springy hair, I marked off her height on the wall and wrote her name, month and year alongside.

I could see Timo struggling to keep himself in check. He likely had wanted to go first.

'Flip a coin,' I said. 'The winner goes next.'

Both boys gave me their undivided attention.

'Flip a coin?' Max's voice ended in a gulp.

'How?' Timo's voice ended on a too-high note.

I pulled a coin out of my pocket. 'You balance the coin like this on your thumbnail and call out heads or tails.'

'Heads,' Timo yelled.

'Tails,' Max yelled.

'Then flick it like so.' The coin spun into the air. I caught it on the way down in one hand, flipped it over the palm of my other hand and revealed the coin.

'Tail side is up. You win, Max. You're next.'

In a matter of minutes, the children's heights had been recorded. Their summer growth spurt was significant.

'I'm taller than you.' Timo's face showed smug satisfaction.

'But you are younger, and nothing will ever change that,' Max said, reclaiming an advantage over Timo.

'Here are another two coins,' I said, breaking the tension. 'Go outside and practise.'

The children raced through the kitchen door and out into the courtyard. Through the window I watched them flicking their coins into the air.

Though her height had changed, Nepitella's alabaster skin had not. It refused to burn under the hot caress of the Tuscan sun. By contrast, the boys' skin turned nut-brown.

Max's hair, finally rid of his father's pomade, remained jet black and curly. Similar to his father Iacopo's fair hair, Timo's fell to his shoulders in heavy locks that sported sun-bleached ends. Nepitella had inherited her mother's shade of copper, which when seen caught in the sun's rays, appeared to explode into flaming, licking tongues of fire.

That afternoon we trundled down to the bend in the river where, despite the long, hot summer, a substantial pool of water remained. I collared Max, drew him close to me and lowered my voice. 'Max, you will never be able to swim properly unless your face goes in the water.'

Max gave me a beseeching look. 'I really can't, Zeeya. My head will explode.'

'We've been swimming the whole summer and none of our heads have exploded, have they?'

'No. But mine will.'

I sighed. Knowing how ingrained quirky superstitions were, I let the subject go. 'Come on, everyone. Jump in. Ten alternating lengths of breaststroke and freestyle.'

Timo swam as though he was on the attack, determined to domi-
nate the water. Nepitella mastered the strokes and became one with the
water. Although Max swam with his head above water and one eye fixed
on the riverbank, I felt they were ready to swim in the sea.

The next morning, around the kitchen table, the children practised
writing their names. Even at this early stage, they had already developed
their peculiar writing style. In September, school would start, and they
could already count to one hundred and knew the alphabet.

Determined they would not continue speaking like most valley
workers who would use only the present perfect to talk of past events, I
introduced them to the imperfect, perfect and remote past tenses. This
caused them to squirm in their seats, frown and chew their pencils. Timo
rebelled by finding all sorts of excuses to leave the table. Max laboured
diligently, and Nepitella, who alternated between daydreaming and razor-
sharp clarity, surprised me by repeating the verb conjugations as though
they had always been firmly planted in her head.

The clatter of Pietro's old van engine sounded through the kitch-
en's open doorway.

'Uncle Lorenzo,' the children yelled. Chair legs scraped the floor as
the boys dashed from the table. Nepitella, as light as a dandelion puffball
floating in the air, joined them in the courtyard.

On this day we received fresh fish which had been line-caught,
mail and, I hoped, news of the changeover of the licence from fishing to
tourist boat, about which only Lorenzo knew.

Lorenzo bounced out of the cab. 'Greetings, children.' He was af-
fable, practical and, above all, honest. Right from the start, I understood
why Pietro had put him in charge of the fishing boat.

'Good morning, signora.' Though I had told him many times not
to, he doffed his cap.

'Morning, Lorenzo. Any mail?'

He handed me a cloth bag, heavier than usual.

Max focused on the bag. He was still waiting for his first letter
from his father.

'What fish do you have?' Timo's voice was buoyant, filled with eager curiosity.

Lorenzo opened the van's back door. 'Take a look.'

The children crowded to see the array of fish in containers.

Nepitella scrunched up her face. 'Ew! 'What is it?'

'An octopus,' Timo said.

'And its Latin name?' Lorenzo asked.

Timo frowned. 'Cephalopod mol–'

'Mollusc. Of the order Octopoda,' Max chimed in.

'Show-off,' Timo said.

'And its species?' Lorenzo asked.

'O. vulgaris,' the boys shouted trying to outdo each other.

Lorenzo's face broke into a broad smile. 'Good job.'

'Look! It's watching us,' Timo said. 'It's still alive.'

I was grateful to Lorenzo for his method of instructing the children. Though Timo and Max showed a keen interest in all the fish he brought on Fridays, Nepitella couldn't care less.

'Pay attention,' Lorenzo said. 'This is a big one. It's got a beak and has a nasty bite.' One tentacle whipped around Lorenzo's forearm, its circular cups sucking his skin. 'Fancy *Polpo alla Luciana* for dinner?'

Anna's voice entered my head. *It'll need thorough cleaning.*

I swallowed. I'd never cleaned or cooked octopus. But then knowing Anna was close at hand, I said with confidence, 'Good idea. But only if the children help.'

'Not me.' Nepitella's response was like a gunshot. For all her airiness, she could be fast and determined. She scooted back into the kitchen.

'How do we kill it?' Timo asked.

'Ah. Unlike other fish,' Lorenzo said, 'we must beat this one to death.'

The boys' mouths gaped, and they stared goggle-eyed.

'Show me,' Timo said.

'First, you need two rocks.'

I joined my daughter in the kitchen and opened the bag of mail. Within minutes, the sound of the smaller rock beating against a larger one filtered into the kitchen. Then, repetitive slapping as someone bashed the octopus's body to tenderise the flesh.

After a knock at the door, Lorenzo stood on the step with his fishing cap in his ink-blackened hands. *What must the boys look like?* I waved my hand indicating a chair. 'Come in.' He sat. 'Well?'

Lorenzo could not hold onto the dour mask he'd plastered to his weather-beaten face. It cracked, and his face broke out into a wide grin. 'The tour boat licence,' he stage-whispered, 'has been granted.'

A surge of delight shot through my body. I clapped my hands. 'Finally! Well done, Lorenzo.'

'No. No. This is all your doing.'

My belly fluttered. What would Mayor Santo Rossi do when he discovered I had bypassed him and applied for the boat licence? I did not even want to think what he'd do if he knew I'd forged his signature and stolen one of the ink stamps from his office. 'Now all we need to do is outfit the galley, and we're good for our first sailing,' I said.

Lorenzo's face dropped. 'But there is no more money until the next wine and oil sales.'

'True. But I do have one last resource. How long will it take for the shipbuilders to outfit the galley?'

'Five days.'

'What's the weather forecast for next Saturday?'

'Fine and mild.'

'Safe for the children's first swim in the sea?'

'Certainly.'

'Good. On your way down, let the valley women know they are invited on board for our first sailing in exchange for a prepared dish.'

Nepitella, who rarely bothered with adult conversation, had listened with quiet intensity. 'We're going sailing?'

'Yes,' I said. 'And you are going to get a very big surprise.'

'A surprise? For me?'

'Just for you.'

Lights flared in her eyes. 'What's the surprise?'

'I'll ruin it if I tell you.'

She crinkled her pert nose.

'Er…' Lorenzo said. 'What colour should I paint the boat's new name?'

'Ask Nepitella what her favourite colour is.'

Before he could, Nepitella answered. 'Pink.' The flares in her eyes blazed.

Has she put two and two together?

In mock horror, Lorenzo threw his hands in the air and then winked. 'Pink it will be, princess. See you on Saturday. Goodbye.'

The boys entered with a pail from which several limp, marble-grey tentacles dragged.

Anna's voice entered my head. *The octopus needs to be cleaned before…'*

'Are you ready to clean and cook this octopus for dinner tonight?' I asked.

'Yes,' they said.

I repeated Anna's instructions and watched as the two boys cleaned out the spongy mass that was the insides of its head, popped out the beak and cut away its eyes. Stripped of its skin, the empty, cleaned head pouch soon lay to one side.

'Now for the tentacles,' I said. 'See how the suckers are filled with sand?'

Heads together, the boys peered hard.

'Submerge the tentacles in the hot water. Count slowly to thirty, then remove it. You'll see the sand loosen and float out.'

Timo lowered and then lifted the octopus's tentacles out of the water.

'Wow!' Max said. 'Look how they have shrunk.'

'And the colour,' Timo said. 'It's changed from grey to red.'

Drawn by the awed excitement in the boy's voices, Nepitella peered over their shoulders.

Dip it in once more. Check the suckers are completely clear. I repeated Anna's instructions.

'Yes. Make sure it's clean,' Nepitella said. 'I don't want to eat sand.'

I spluttered, held my hand over my mouth, and pretended to cough. Her words even broke the boys' attention. They cast her swift glances over their shoulders and then returned to the task at hand. I wasn't going to hold my breath. There was little chance Nepitella would eat the octopus. *On the other hand...*

'Because this octopus is so big, cut the tentacles into bite-sized pieces, like this. See?' I demonstrated. 'And for goodness' sake, be careful with the knives. No horsing around.'

While the boys diligently cut the tentacles, I placed ingredients I was going to use on the table and then went in search and returned with a large, deep pot and its lid. 'Pat the pieces dry.'

'Why?' Timo asked.

'Hot oil coming into contact with water, will cause it to spit, jump out of the pot and burn the cook's hands.' I peeled the garlic and sautéed it with a pinch of chilli pepper in the olive oil. 'Timo, carefully spoon the pieces into the bottom of the pot, don't drop them in. The oil will splash. Okay?' Timo added the patted-dry tentacle pieces. 'Now, stir until each piece is well coated.'

I poured in a glass of white wine and turned up the heat to evaporate the alcohol. 'Max, put in the tomatoes, parsley, capers and pitted olives.'

In the past, fishermen used to simmer the stew in a crockpot wrapped in a wet cloth. I had no need to use a wet cloth. But to make sure the least amount of liquid evaporated, I cut a disc of parchment paper, wet it and rested it just above the level of the liquid. I placed the lid on the pot and set the heat to low.

'Zeeya,' Max said, 'how long does it have to cook?'

'Three, maybe four hours. Boys, go and find Rubino. Remind him to join us for dinner tonight at seven o'clock, *pronto.*'

During the harvesting season, and now even with it over and everything stored, a myriad of tasks remained. Rubino fell into bed exhausted and often in too much pain to eat. Consequently, he'd lost weight, though his thick hands and sausage-like fingers remained.

'And Maria?' Timo asked.

'Yes. Maria too.'

Max's hand shot into the air. 'Can I raise the flag?'

'Yes.' I had the village seamstress sew flags in different colours. The orange flag indicated the children were to bring their game to an end and make their way home. The green flag was for Rubino and the white for Maria. The message was the same. Come to the villa when you can. The red one indicated an emergency and everyone was to come to the villa immediately. Thankfully, I hadn't had reason to raise it. Not yet.

'I'll hoist the flag,' Timo said.

'I asked first,' Max said.

'I don't care. I'm doing it.'

'You're not.'

'Watch me.'

The boys tried to hold each other back as they rushed out of the kitchen and into the mill where they would nimbly scale the ladder into the loft, and race up the inclined ramp that opened out onto the tower's parapet. Their constant headbutting, challenging and contradicting each other left me feeling drained. 'Nepitella, 'I'd like you to set the table tonight. Okay?'

'Can we use the silver?'

The best cutlery was hardly ever used. I felt this evening's meal would be my personal celebration of having the boat licence approved. 'Sure. And pick some fresh flowers for the table, too.'

Nepitella flashed me a rare smile, so beautiful I blinked several times. Not at Nepitella's transformed face, but in worry of the day when she and Timo would learn what had taken place after their births.

The boys rushed into the kitchen and came to an abrupt halt. They eyed the table, gleaming family Trianni silverware, fragile crockery, candles and a vase of flowers. They went upstairs to wash their hands and faces, changed into clean shirts without being told, returned and took their places at the table.

That's a first. They are retaining some of my nagging after all. My heart warmed. That they had forgotten to brush their hair did not matter. I'd learned the prudence of picking my battles.

'Zeeya,' Max said, 'may I open the wine?'

'No.' Timo said. 'I will.'

'This is my wine from my estate. I will open it.'

Timo glared at Max and paused.

I could almost hear the wheels in Timo's brain turn.

Timo's chin jutted out at a sharp angle. 'That may be so, but I am the boss of this estate. You are my guest. So, do as I say.'

The warmth in my heart cooled.

Rubino arrived and overheard the exchange as he stepped into the kitchen. 'No. Hand me the bottle and corkscrew. I will open the wine. The day you can bring in your harvest, you will earn the right to use your titles. Until then, you are both nothing but pups and will listen to your elders. That means me, Hortensia and Maria. No exceptions.'

No doubt startled by Rubino's quiet, serious voice, the boys fell silent. But likely more so, because it was the most they had heard him speak. They stepped forward and handed over the bottle and corkscrew.

I threw Rubino a grateful look.

The kitchen fire flared. A second later Maria entered and addressed the boys. 'Before you ask, I've brought nothing this evening.'

'We don't *always* need you to bring us something, do we?' Timo shot Max a direct look.

'Right,' Max said. 'Not that it means we don't appreciate it when you *do*, though.'

My head spun with this quick turnaround and unaccustomed show of solidarity.

'Where's Nepitella?' Max asked. I'm starving.'

'Coming.'

We all turned to see Nepitella glide down the staircase. She'd draped a gossamer shawl around her shoulders; one Angelica Barberi had once worn.

Miniature flashes of lightning lit up Maria's turned-in eyes. Rubino, in the act of pouring wine, stopped. The boys' jaws slackened.

Though she had grown over the summer, she remained delicate and petite. Another change had taken place. What I had glimpsed earlier, when she had flashed me a rare smile, suffused her face. She would become more beautiful than her mother and two half-sisters. *How long before people realise Nepitella is not my child? Will the valley workers, bound by the unspoken rule of keeping valley secrets, remain silent?*

I thrust these thoughts, which haunted me day and night, to the back of my mind. *Time to serve dinner.*

To my surprise, Nepitella ate two pieces of tentacles without protest and like everyone else, used a piece of bread to wipe her plate clean.

'Children,' I said, 'there is a surprise outing tomorrow.'

Three pairs of eyes locked onto mine.

'Do we have to get up early?' Timo asked.

'I am afraid so.'

'How early?'

'Very early.'

Timo screwed up his face.

'What's the surprise?' Max asked.

Before I could reply, Nepitella answered. 'Sailing. But you can't go on board unless you are properly dressed.'

Timo frowned. 'Do you mean sailor clothes?'

'No. Pirate clothes.'

Max whistled. 'You mean fancy dress costume?'

Nepitella fingered her mother's gossamer shawl around her shoulders. 'Yes.'

'Whose boat?' Timo asked.

'Ah,' Nepitella said. 'That's the real surprise.'

'But,' Max said, 'where are the pirate outfits?'

'You'll have to make them yourselves,' I said. 'And, use only your old clothes.'

Though it was early autumn, Saturday dawned with the promise of being the perfect day for sailing, and swimming at noon.

I stood at the bottom of the staircase, one hand resting on the wrought-iron balustrade. 'Children, are you ready?'

'Coming.' Their voices harmonised, yet were distinct.

The night before, after the children politely requested permission to leave the table, they exploded into a flurry of activity. They raced upstairs and disappeared into Nepitella's room where they most likely held a council of war. Soon after, Timo returned to the kitchen. 'Where's the large pair of scissors?' He began to rummage through the drawers.

'Here,' Maria said. 'In the top drawer.'

He flashed her a smile and taking the stairs two at a time raced back up with the scissors held aloft in one hand.

'Zeeya,' Nepitella called down from the landing, 'where is your sewing basket?'

'Where it always is,' I replied. 'In my bedroom.'

A few minutes later, Max appeared. 'Rubino, do you have a spare ball of twine?'

Rubino searched in his trouser pockets. 'Will this do?'

'Yes. Thank you.'

After the dinner dishes had been put away and Rubino and Maria had left, I went upstairs and was met with squeals and yells and banging shut bedroom doors. 'Don't come in. You can't see until tomorrow.'

Although I grinned to myself, I put on my serious voice 'Don't forget to brush your teeth.'

'We won't.'

'Goodnight.'

One after another the children wished me goodnight from behind their closed bedroom doors. I entered my bedroom with a stabbing pain in my heart. It was the first time I had not kissed them goodnight or tucked them in.

But now I was eager to see what they had achieved and looked like.

As always, Nepitella appeared first. Unbeknownst to her, she wore her birthmother's aquamarine shawl draped over her dress like the robes of the Greek sea goddess, Amphitrite. With her back held straight and eyes looking ahead, she floated down the stairs.

I saw she'd threaded a ribbon, adorned with luminous white clam-shells, through her red hair. She had also tied a string of linked shells around her waist. *Ah. So, that was why she needed the sewing basket.* As she stepped closer, I realised the shells were mine. Each Friday, when I was Nepitella's age, and Pietro delivered Anna's fish order, he'd present me with a gift of shells. 'You look lovely, sea princess.'

Her little face flushed with pleasure as she exited into the court-yard.

The boys appeared. I swallowed my giggles. Side by side, they swaggered down the steps. Max wore a black tri-corn hat. He'd chalked a skull and crossbones dead centre. Timo wore my favourite blue and yellow scarf wound around his head and clasped at the base of his skull, falling into a long ponytail. Black patches covered an eye each, and an earring adorned one ear each. *Those are mine!* I should have spoken to them about raiding my things without permission. But they looked so precious in their borrowed finery, I hadn't the heart. 'My goodness, gracious me! What fearsome and handsome pirates you both are.'

Chuffed with my response, they tightened the twine holding up their cut-off trousers, increased their swagger as they clumped down the stairs, entered the courtyard and climbed aboard the cart.

Rubino and Nepitella sat up front. The deep furrows bracketing Rubino's mouth twitched. But like me, he held down his amusement and said in a serious voice, '*Andiamo.*'

'Wait,' Nepitella said. 'Where's Maria?'

'She'll meet us at the harbour.' I climbed aboard and settled myself in the back of the cart. 'She attended to a mother and newborn there last night.'

Rubino released the cart's brake and urged the donkey forward.

The journey through the olive grove and chestnut forest was faster than normal. We had an appointment to keep.

The boys took turns standing up with an imaginary telescope pressed to their unpatched eyes. Likely imagining how pirate lookouts would sound, Timo changed his voice to a scratchy high-pitch that set my teeth on edge. But it was nothing compared to Max. He dropped his voice, coming close to his father's rich resonance that sent shivers up my spine.

But for chickens scratching in the dirt, hunting dogs chained to posts and the goats chomping down anything green, the valley, and all the houses in it, appeared deserted. *Where is everyone?*

Maria's voice entered my head. *They are all at the harbour.*

Surely not!

Wait and see.

As the cart crested the rise, the limpid, opalescent sea spread before us. Three islands dimpled the horizon's arrow-straight line: Capraia, home to four hundred souls and the centre of anchovy fishing; Gorgona, an agricultural prison where inmates worked outdoors, and whose large cells and soccer field were much envied by inmates in other prisons around Italy; and Corsica, the birthplace of Napoleon.

The boys jumped up onto their seats, causing the cart to bounce. They held on to each other for balance and yelled, 'The sea! the sea!'

Without looking back at them, Rubino said, 'Get down and sit, before you both land on your heads.'

They sat, craned their necks, but continued to squirm and wiggle.

And then, there she was, rocking ever so gently, gleaming re-splendent in her multi-layered coats of indigo. New white canvas sails wrapped snug against her boom, and her mast reached pencil-straight into the sky.

Clusters of valley workers crowded the quay. The women were apronless and instead of their everyday slippers they wore their Sunday shoes. Baskets lay at their feet, which I knew held their culinary specialties.

Don Antonio, his hands clasped around his black prayer book and rosary, and to my dismay, Mayor Santo Rossi, who wore his official bronze chain, stood waiting, too. Topping all this was the valley's band. The conductor waved his baton. The band struck up a march; a discordant tune heralding our arrival. Rubino tugged the reins and brought the cart to a halt. He twisted around in his seat and gave me a wink.

I silently mouthed, *thank you.*

The boys sprang off the cart. Rubino stepped down, clasped them firmly by their shoulders and whispered in their ears. Looks of understanding passed across their faces. Timo turned and, with courtesy befitting a chivalrous knight, held out his hand to help me. Max assumed the air of a prince, and with one arm tucked behind his back, took Nepitella's hand to assist her.

Lorenzo appeared on deck and waved. He could not, I was sure, smile any wider.

At the last dreadful cymbal clashing, the out-of-tune march came to an end. The crowd hooted and hollered, and Rossi called for silence. He gave a speech ending with, '...a new prosperous horizon for our valley, with thanks to Signora Hortensia d'Ambrosia-il Pescatore, without whose foresight...' *and my money* '...this venture would not be possible.'

I could not bring myself to look directly at Rossi. He had acknowledged my refusal of his proposal in ways that would make a love-struck poet blush. He ended by promising he would wait for me only, no matter how long. Now, his imploring gaze never left my face. It was more than I could bear.

A photographer thrust his camera into my face. Light bulbs popped. Flashes of heat – red-hot embarrassment at being made such a spectacle, flushed my skin. I drew my children close. Clutching Rubino's sleeve, I walked towards the boat.

Maria, whose black cloak billowed even in the calm air, stood statue-still, dwarfed by the boat's prow. A bottle of *Sangiovese* from Max's estate stood on a makeshift table next to her.

Don Antonio led us in prayer and ended by blessing the boat.

Lorenzo tossed a rope over its edge, which Rubino caught. 'Come here, boys.' They shuffled over to stand next to him. 'Timo, hold the bottle. Max, tie the end of the rope around the neck. Knot it well.'

The boy-pirates did as told.

Maria pressed Nepitella forward. 'Take the bottle. Say aloud, "To the crew and passengers, to *la Nepitella*, may you always return safely to harbour". Then, on the count of three, hurl the bottle against the hull.'

'Help me,' Nepitella said in a small voice.

Maria lowered hers. 'No. This is your boat. You need to christen it. How well you throw and break the bottle will decide this boat's future. You can do it. Concentrate.'

'Give her space,' Rubino said.

We all stepped back and focused on the sea princess. She drew the bottle backwards, repeated Maria's words, then flung it hard against the hull. The bottle smashed and red wine splashed. More yells and clapping broke out.

Timo stilled. 'Why is Nepitella's name on the boat?'

Max leaned into Timo. 'Because she is the owner.'

Timo looked at me. I nodded.

'Now,' Max said, 'Nepitella is equal to us.'

I could almost hear the wheels turning in Timo's head as he digested this new information.

Lorenzo lowered the gangplank. 'Family d'Ambrosia-il Pescatore first,' he yelled.

Maria gave Nepitella a little shove. Alone, she stepped onto the polished deck of her very own boat.

My heart lurched. *I did it. I did it!* Right then I couldn't have cared less that I had not one *lire* left to my name. My mother's voice entered my head. *I knew you would.*

I felt for the pouch that held Arturo's loose teeth, all thirty-four of them. To cover the last cost of outfitting the galley, I had sold the dentures to the jeweller for the value of the gold that had originally come from the necklace and horn pendant Pietro had given me in place of a wedding ring. The boat needed the gold. I had my memories, and the boat to remember him by. *Thank you, Pietro.*

Dentures had advanced from human to cheaper fake teeth, and Arturo's, now yellowed were worthless. Thus, I planned to throw his teeth into the sea after we set sail. *I will never forget you. Thank you, Arturo.*

Soon the deck heaved with curious valley workers. They lined up to shake my hand and offer compliments. Their rough hands were a pleasure compared to Mayor Rossi's hot sweaty palm. He raised my hand to his mouth and left a slither of spittle upon it. I stemmed the shudder that rose from my feet.

The boys reverted to their madcap behaviour; nothing escaped their investigation. When they went below deck, their excitement frothed like an overfilled glass of *Prosecco*. The sound of their voices rose through the open hatches.

'There are three bedrooms,' Timo yelled. 'Two with bunk beds and one with a double bed.'

'And a kitchen,' Max yelled, 'with gas burners.'

'Look at this.' Nepitella's voice conveyed awe. 'A real bathroom.'

'It's time to get going,' Lorenzo said. 'All men, please leave.'

The men's faces clouded and the air rang with disappointed retorts. This first outing was for our valley women and children only.

Guided by Lorenzo, and powered by twin diesel engines, *la Nepitella* left the harbour and turned north. The boat glided past the fancy seaside beach resorts that sported a colourful array of umbrellas and beach chairs.

'We leave Tuscany at this point,' Lorenzo shouted, pointing landward. All passengers turned starboard and faced the coastline.

Nepitella sat between Maria and me. Visible only to us, we saw a rod of shimmering light pass through Nepitella as the boat crossed from Tuscany into Liguria. It was from here her mother Angelica Barberi came, and likely conceived Nepitella. I did not doubt that deep within her, Nepitella would remember the present moment. One day, when she added up other moments like these, she'd arrive near to, if not directly, at the truth. *God help me.*

Maria must have read my thoughts. She placed a cold, bony hand on my forearm and squeezed. Even the bangles rumbled their sympathy.

I pushed away those terrifying, piercing feelings of fear of the reactions and consequences when my conspiracies were revealed.

As we passed the narrow mouth of the river, appropriately called, *Bocca di Magra*, The Thin Mouth, Lorenzo lifted his voice again. This time, for Timo's and Max's benefit.

'Over there is the fishing village of Tellaro, the smuggling haunt of many notorious pirates. It can only be reached by foot or by sea.'

That was enough for the boys to fling themselves against the rail. The excited look on their faces changed to wistfulness as they stared at the tiny fishing village clinging precariously to the cliff.

Some adults visibly froze. An anti-ship battery of reinforced concrete sat atop the steep and rocky promontory, *Punta Bianca*. Its name was taken from the white limestone rocks, which blazed in the sunlight. A relic from World War II no one wished to see, let alone remember all that it represented.

The boat turned to port and we sailed across the crystal-clear water of The Gulf of Poets in the Ligurian Sea.

Lorenzo dropped anchor in front of the seaside village, Portovenere. Its houses' facades were painted in creamy peach, mint and orange pastels, reminding me of an antique patchwork cover. Directly behind us lay the island of Palmaria, behind it the island of Tino, open to the public once a year, and behind that, Tinetto, the perfect rock for diving daredevils.

'Zeeya?' There was a sharp note of enquiry in Timo's voice. I had a pretty good idea of what he was after. 'Can we swim?'

'From here?' Max's voice hinted half in disbelief and half in hope my answer would be no.

'Yes.'

Nepitella threw her hands in the air. 'But we don't have our swim-suits.'

I pointed to the basket at my feet. 'I do. In here.'

'Hooray!' Timo yelled and flashed me such a warm smile, my heart melted. My arms reached out to hug him. But he dodged my grasping hands and all I clutched was air. He grabbed his suit and disappeared below deck.

I followed Max's gaze from boat to shore and lowered my voice. 'If you like, you can swim around the boat.'

Timo, whose ears worked best when they should not, overheard and yelled, 'I'm swimming to shore and back.'

The gauntlet had been thrown. Max's jaw clenched. He took his suit and disappeared.

Nepitella turned to me. 'Are you swimming, too?'

'Of course I am.'

Nepitella turned to Maria. 'What about you?'

'I'm going to try out the new dinghy.'

The bangles tinkled with a youthful zest that belied their age.

'Zeeya?'

'Yes.'

'See all the valley ladies sitting over there.'

I wanted to laugh. No different to how I once had, on the occasion of my first boat trip to Naples, the women sat clumped centre to the deck, terrified of the sea.

'Yes.'

Nepitella leaned towards me. 'They say,' she whispered, 'none of them can swim.'

'I know,' I whispered back. 'That's why you needed to learn in case you ever had to help someone who can't.'

Nepitella's mouth formed the shape of an O.

I held out my hand. 'Come on, let's go below and change.'

Nepitella slipped her hand into mine. My heart sprouted wings and soared skyward.

The boys rushed past us going back up on deck. 'Wait for us,' I said.

'Hurry!' they yelled.

By the time Nepitella and I appeared, Lorenzo had let down the ladder and Maria sat hugging her knees in the bobbing dingy.

A flash bulb went off. *What! How did he manage to stay on board?*

Lorenzo whispered in my ear, 'He's the photojournalist. I've made him promise to take a tonne of photos. We are going to need a lot of tourists from HA MER E KA.'

The exception Lorenzo had made was good. But I felt so self-conscious in my new, all-in-one, white bathing suit, I might as well have been naked.

Regaining my composure, I turned to the boys. Barely able to contain their excitement, they bounced on the balls of their feet and swung their arms in windmill circles, like sprinters warming up before a race.

Oh, what the hell. This is what I want, isn't it? I grabbed Nepitella by the hand and yelled, 'Last one in is a *buffo*.'

I caught the boys and everyone else by surprise. Nepitella held my hand as we streaked past the boys and beat them to it, landing in the glorious celadon sea first.

We came up spluttering and laughing and then got water-bombed by Timo. Max slipped into the water via the ladder.

A group of *Portoveneresi* gathered on the shore, clapping and calling out their compliments as we emerged from the sea and stepped on to the beach.

I wasn't sure if it was us they were complimenting, or *la Nepitella*. From the beach, she looked lovely and fresh, like the new feelings surging through my body.

A spokesperson for the group called out, 'With that paint job, it's not a fishing boat. What is it?'

'A tour boat.' Another rush of excitement surged through me as I explained *la Nepitella's* conversion to members of the public for the first time.

'Who's the owner?'

The boys who had been following this exchange pointed at Nepitella. 'She is.'

'That's crazy. A child can't be the owner of a boat.'

'She is.' The boys' voices rang with aggression.

'Enough,' I hissed. 'Swim back.'

They ran and dove into the sea. *Yay! Max finally dunked his head.* I turned back to the group. 'Crazy? Maybe.' I grinned. 'But you'll be seeing a lot of us next year from early summer. Bye. Come on Nepitella, I'll race you.'

To admiring whistles – a new sound in my ears – we dove into the sea. I struggled to keep up; Nepitella streaked through the water.

As we neared the dinghy, I slowed. 'You go ahead.' I grabbed hold of the dinghy's side, and half-pulled myself up when another flash bulb popped. *What's he doing in the dingy with Maria?*

'Grab my hand. I'll help you,' the photographer shouted. He put his camera down and reached his hands out to me.

Maria's sense of humour, unleashed, rose to the occasion. She gave him a quick kick on the backside, sending him flying over my head.

Side-splitting, roaring laughter came from the valley women who had inched closer to the boat's rail.

He came up spluttering, with surprise all over his face. 'Help me.' His head went under and bobbed back up. 'Ca…can't swim.'

The riotous laughter from those who could not swim, turned to moaning angst.

'I'm coming!' I yelled, glaring at Maria.

But Nepitella had already reached the floundering man.

Maria unhooked a lifebuoy ring and threw it in our direction. Her aim was so accurate the photographer's head popped up through its centre just as his head broke the surface of the water.

'Steady.' Nepitella sounded just like me. 'Focus, mister. Here. Look at me. You are going to be all right.'

I could hardly believe what I was hearing and seeing. He focused on her and calmed. As Nepitella swam him safely to the dinghy, I glanced up. The boys pressed against the rail, their jaws slack. Likely they'd never given thought that a grown man could not swim.

Hushing, the sound mothers make to comfort a distressed child, rolled down from *la Nepitella's* rails, where the valley women now leaned, their hands clasped in prayer, their faces pale, aghast at the near accident.

'I'm okay now. Thank you, sea princess.' The photographer clutched the dinghy's looped rope.

Like the Striped dolphin, native to the Ligurian Sea, Nepitella flip-turned and headed back to the ladder dangling from the boat. Her sleek little body looped and sliced through the water, barely creating a ripple.

I searched the photographer's face. For what I was not sure – an injury perhaps? *His eyes are the colour of la Nepitella's paint job.* 'It wasn't me. I promise.' I used my children's favourite excuse.

'I know,' he said. 'More like a mule.'

'Where are your manners?' Maria's retort sounded like a whip crack, but was an attempt at disguising her humour. 'How can you blame a poor old woman when it was your foot that slipped?'

He grinned and leaned his head to whisper in my ear. 'You're marvellous. Do you know that?'

To my ears, his voice sounded warm and sure. I liked that. But, I especially liked what he had to say about me.

'Andreas Crespo. I already know you are Hortensia d'Ambrosia. I'm very pleased to meet you.'

I noted that his surname, Crespo, aptly described the tight curls adorning his head. 'Pleased to meet you, too.'

We each released one hand from holding onto the dinghy and shook hands above the sea's surface. Being in the water meant that despite the difference in our heights, our heads were at the same level. It felt strangely intimate, helped by my sudden desire to wrap my legs around his waist.

'Get me back to the boat.' Maria smacked her palm against the side of the dinghy. 'It's way past lunchtime.'

Despite the ring under his armpits Andreas hoisted himself out of the water in a single fluid motion. His wet clothes sucked and slicked flat against his body.

The valley women's silence deepened. A sure sign they too were fully engaged, appreciating the clear outline of his slim musculature, and broad shoulders.

'I'll swim.' I said this to give my heart time to start beating again. He eased the buoy ring off, picked up the oars and rowed towards the boat.

By the time I got back up on deck, the valley women had unpacked their picnic baskets. The children sat at the table Lorenzo had placed under a makeshift awning.

I was certain the table legs were about to buckle under the weight of platters, dishes and bowls from which a riot of colour sprang and mouth-watering smells rose. But I was not interested in food. My gaze slid over the feast, drawn to Andreas. To make sure he was okay? *Who are you kidding?* It was to take advantage of looking again at the impossible colour of his glorious eyes. And the rest of him.

He wore a spare pair of Lorenzo's too-short trousers, showing off his calves and bare feet. The boys had followed suit and rolled up their cut-off trouser legs a little more and were barefoot, too.

His white shirt was air-drying. The buttons were open down to his navel, showing off a broad smooth chest bronzed from the summer sun. My heartbeat had stopped again. Wrestling my focus away from his chest, I said, 'Let's eat.'

To ensure everyone understood Nepitella was half owner of the boat, I let her serve herself first. She carefully chose from the array of food and settled on *polpette*, fried meatballs mixed with onions, parsley and grated *Parmigiano-Reggiano*. She pushed each ball around her plate only once, ate, albeit slowly, one by one.

I exchanged a swift glance with Maria. She had clearly briefed the valley women, as none of them encouraged Nepitella to eat any more. On the other hand, they encouraged the boys, who ate like they had been starved and went back for seconds and then thirds.

Once everyone had eaten and the table cleared, I repeated the reasons for the boat's change from fishing to tourist island-hopper. Then I explained my next plan: to open the bedrooms in both villas to paying guests. That the tourist board had recently awarded me the first licence to operate both villas, as tourist accommodation with meals on working farms, called *Agritourismi*. Some women's stoic faces changed slowly as they grappled with the concept.

'So, I'll need new staff for both Villa Trianni and Villa Angeli,' I said. More faces changed.

'Not only maids. Cooks, too,' Maria said.

Cleaning and cooking was something all valley women understood. All faces broke into smiles.

'What about payment?' asked one.

'Fixed seasonal contracts,' Maria said.

The sound of a murmuring wave of approval washed over all of us.

My mother's voice entered my head. *Now, make them that offer they won't be able to refuse.*

'There's more,' I said, 'Recently many of you got your first indoor bathroom installed, right?' I looked around at the nodding heads. 'If you've got a spare bedroom with a new bathroom to offer paying guests, you, not your husband, will receive payment.'

Like I knew it would be, my statement was a shocker. The women took in a collective breath. Earning money of their own? That was unheard of.

'What will my husband say?' one said.

'Mine will never stand for it,' another said, releasing a regretful sigh.

'Don't be fools,' Maria said. 'Since when have any of you told your husbands all of the truth?'

Giggles and guffaws escaped the valley women's mouths.

'You only need tell them half of what you earn,' Maria said.

'But,' I held up one hand, 'there is still a lot to plan and do. Paying guests can't stay in anything less than comfortable accommodation. Consider giving the walls a fresh coat of paint. Sew up a new bedcover perhaps, with matching cushions. Here, these may help.' I handed out glossy home decorating magazines, the likes of which they had never seen. 'It will be all up to you.' Straightaway, I could see imaginations had been fired. 'Think about it and let me know what you decide.'

Clanking sounded as the anchor was hauled up and the deck vibrated underfoot. 'We return,' Lorenzo announced, 'under sail.'

A light breeze had picked up. I watched as Andreas raised the sails under Lorenzo's precise instuctions. The children got in the way, but their enthusiasm was so infectious no one had the heart to reprimand them.

In a matter of minutes, the sails cracked and went taut, and *la Nepitella* headed back to our harbour, where Rubino and valley husbands waited. Exhausted by the day's events, Maria and the bangles fell asleep. Nepitella folded into my arms and fell asleep, too. Under Lorenzo's guidance, the boys took turns holding the wheel. I had never seen them so serious.

Andreas glanced my way every so often, then looked back down at his writing pad and scribbled some more. The sun began its descent, sending red rays along the horizon. *La Nepitella* glided through the pale green sea and my heart slipped into her smooth rhythm and matched it.

This has been the best day of my life.

30

Rubino drove the children down to school and I collected them in the afternoons.

Before heading out, I checked on the valley women who had reorganised their homes to free up a room or two to accommodate paying guests. That day, my first stop was the home of Luisa Prosperi.

'Luisa,' I said. 'You can't sleep in the stable and give up your matrimonial bedroom.'

'Nonsense. I kicked my husband into the stable years ago. Now that I will be joining him there, he's delighted. With the money I'll earn, I'll visit my son in America, meet his American wife and my three grandchildren. For that I'll put up with my husband!' She wiggled her ample hips. 'Who knows? I might just have a little bit of fun.'

My face felt hot. 'Well, if you put it like that…'

The truth was, I did not want to hear about her intimacies with her husband, nor did I want to be reminded of my own, non-existent intimacies. That was something I had long ago relegated to the back of my mind, and found Luisa's natural and casual talk disconcerting. Not least of which was the splendid outline of Andreas's body that crept into my consciousness at inopportune times.

Luisa opened the door to her marriage bedroom. 'Ta-da.'

I'd been dreading this moment, thinking perhaps she'd not followed the ideas in the home decorating magazines I had handed out. Or, perhaps not understood the significance of the before and after pictures on de-cluttering. I stepped into the room. My fears were unfounded. 'Goodness.'

She'd taken the magazines' suggestions and removed all the gew-gaws that had adorned the walls and surfaces – mainly, a myriad of vases filled with faded and dusty plastic flowers and a boggling array of pictures and statues of the Holy Family.

Luisa ran the palm of her hand against the wall. 'I did all the paint-ing.' Her face glowed. 'It's a lime- and water-based paint that breathes, preventing that horrible, creeping black mould.'

I touched the polished-to-gleam ornamental brass curlicues on the iron headboard. 'Where did this bed come from?'

'It's the same one as before.'

'No!' I turned my attention to the bedside lamps with pink, tulip-shaped, glass shades. 'And these?'

'Wedding gifts. I decided it's time to put them to use.'

I pointed to a rocking chair in one corner.

'That,' Luisa said, 'has been in our family for over one hundred years. Generations of women nursed their children sitting in it, including me.'

'It looks new.'

'Now it does. I reupholstered it with a tapestry my mother stitched.'

The tapestry bursting with red poppies evoked our Tuscan coun-tryside in May.

From the centre of the room, I took in the new linen curtains that diffused the strong sunlight and the well-scrubbed terracotta tiled floors. The chestnut beams overhead had been dusted and oiled. The transfor-mation was amazing, and I hoped the photographs Andreas planned to take would show off the room's simplicity in the very best way. 'And the bathroom?'

'Come.' Luisa led me to a door that had not been there before.

I had heard about her husband knocking a doorway through to the lean-to shed on the other side that had housed their chickens. From other en-suite bathroom additions, I knew that opening doorways in metre-thick walls constructed with boulders a hundred years ago or more were feats of engineering and brute force.

As if Luisa had read my mind, she said, 'It required the strength of three strong men and chains attached to the ox to remove each boulder. And six men to install the iron lintel to support the weight above.' She opened the door and stood aside.

I stepped into a box of white marked here and there with chrome. 'Oh my! It's beautiful.' *It's exactly how a bathroom should be. No more, no less.* A window overlooked a patch of land where a new coop had been built for the chickens, dispossessed of their previous home.

After confirming the day and time Andreas would arrive for the photo shoot, I departed for the valley school.

Groups of waiting grandmothers and mothers clustered around the gate. Hearing the cart, they turned towards me. The looks on their faces ranged from surprise to curiosity but most showed confusion. Owning a boat was one thing; being in charge of dispensing earnings from the harvests was another. But now, opening the villas to tourists and helping the women turn rooms in their homes into accommodation was altogether too much. I had risen way above my former station. They had no idea how to address me.

'Good afternoon, ladies.'

Don't move. Stay sitting. My mother's voice in my head said. *Or you will lose the advantage.*

I clenched the reins, forced myself not to squirm and to remain seated. The image of my father, Claudio Trianni, rose before me. Like a true feudal lord, he had been a master at keeping everyone in their place. He nodded, clearly in agreement with my mother's advice. I took a breath, and spoke in a voice far different from the one he would have used. 'Gina, Silvia, be ready to come to Villa Trianni tomorrow morning. Rubino will give you both a ride up. I want to open the rooms on the second floor.'

'*Si*, Signora d'Ambrosia.'

And just like that, from that moment forward, there was no more confusion regarding my title, and only my closest and dearest continued to call me by my first name.

The school bell clanged, doors flew open and children raced out. The air filled with a cacophony of young, energetic voices. As I did each day, I checked my children as they headed towards the cart, wondering what scrapes they might have gotten into, or caused.

Nepitella clambered up, sat beside me and smoothed her skirt over her knees. Other than scuffed shoes and shirttails hanging out, the boys appeared to be fine. They scrambled onto the cart and threw down their satchels.

I ya-d at the donkey and to the women I called out, 'Good afternoon.'

'Good afternoon, Signora d'Ambroisia,' the valley women responded in unison.

For a few moments the children were startled into silence. I sensed they were trying to fathom what my title meant.

Nepitella fingered the light wool cardigan I wore over my sleeveless A-line dress. 'It's new.'

'Yes.' When I had selected bathing suits from a Florentine apparel catalogue, I treated myself to several new store-bought dresses. The catalogue claimed the First Lady of America inspired the style. I determined never to wear an apron again unless I was cooking. I'd also bought several pairs of shoes with matching bags. In no time I figured what women carried in their bags: pale pink lipstick, a comb, a lacy handkerchief, a nail file and a small bottle of perfume with the number five on it. And, I could not resist a pair of overly large, black-framed sunglasses and a pair of cotton gloves.

Nepitella let go of the fabric. 'It's lovely.'

I was thrilled. It had only taken her a minute or so to speak. 'Thank you.'

From her first day at school, Nepitella refused to open her mouth, and it took her until around dinnertime before she'd utter a word. It was, I assumed, her way to protect herself against the valley children, who regarded her with distrust given her unusual looks. My thoughts flew back to the children's first day of school.

———————— ◆ ————————

Timo climbed onto the cart sporting a black eye. Before I could ask, Max enlightened me.

'Timo punched Dario because he called Nepitella, *Piccola Strega*, Little Witch. And he returned the punch.'

'Yes. But you punched him, too,' Timo said.

Max sat up a little straighter. 'Yes, I did.'

'Max,' I said, 'why did you punch Dario?'

'To teach him a lesson. He had no right to punch Timo back.'

'What do you mean?'

Max threw me a pitiful look and explained speaking slowly. 'Because, Dario deserved it. He shouldn't have said what he did about Nepitella. All actions have consequences which one has to take like a man.'

Who taught you this? I scanned Max for signs of injury. 'Did Dario punch you back?'

Beside me, Nepitella giggled. 'He couldn't.'

I caught sight of the valley women collaring and questioning their children over Dario's black eye. I looked closely. *Good grief. He's got two black eyes.*

After an animated discussion, his mother clipped Dario on the back of the head, fixed her fingers to one of his ears and dragged her blinded son home. His caterwauls followed us as the cart pulled away.

On this day, the boys broke out into their usual sparring banter. I breathed a sigh of relief. *All's well.*

My children, through fair means and foul, had inherited an elevated status, of which others could only dream. Timo and Max would one day be their school friends' bosses. And Nepitella, already so unusual looking, was the part-owner of a tour boat, that come next summer, would further benefit our valley.

The *Portoveneresi* had been right. It was strange. And strange did not fare well in our valley. Throw into the mix change, and all heels dug deep. Now I had begun the process of turning our medieval valley's world upside down, how would we all cope?

————— ◆ —————

The children were already asleep, and I was preparing for bed, when Andreas arrived on Thursday evening. He looked better than my memory served me.

'I'm sorry for my late arrival.' He removed his coat and hung it on the rack. 'The train from Rome was delayed.'

I felt vulnerable even though my dressing gown covered more of me than the white bathing suit he'd seen me in a month before. 'No matter. I left you something to eat if you're hungry. It's on a tray in the kitchen.' I pulled the cord to my gown tighter. 'Let me show you to your room.'

As the villa's upstairs bedrooms were still not yet ready, I had prepared my old room on the ground floor with its bathroom and little sitting room just off the kitchen.

I entered the room with Andreas close behind me. A small pool of light gleamed on the bedside table. But it had nothing on the full moon's light flooding the room. I wrenched my thoughts away from those nights when Pietro had pulled the bed directly under the window and made love to me, whispering the words of the song, *Marechiaro. How long ago it seems.* 'Be prepared to leave with Rubino tomorrow morning when he takes the children to school,' I said. 'He'll drop you off at Luisa Prosperi's home.'

Andreas dug around in his satchel and pulled out a brown envelope. 'Here, please, take a look and let me know what you think. Anything you don't like can be changed.'

'Thank you. See you in the morning.' I clutched the weighty envelope to my chest and left. *Why are my feet not touching the stairs?*

Sitting up in bed, I opened the envelope and pulled out the article he had written, which was more than several pages long. I put it aside, took a deep breath, and braced myself to view the plain me caught in glossy print. I picked up the first photograph from the top of the pile. *Who's that?* I stared hard at the woman in a white bathing suit, a flash of long slim legs,

326

small waist, and cupped breasts ensconced in the padded bodice. Her face was tilted to the sun. She was laughing, bursting with unrestrained joy and had abandoned herself to the tingling anticipation of jumping into the celadon sea. My hand trembled. *Is this really me? Dare it be said, dare I believe it? Lovely. I am lovely.*

The next photograph was of Nepitella wearing her matching, mother and daughter, bathing suit. Her hair blazed redder than a glowing sunset accented with the ribbon of white clamshells. She stared straight ahead, her mouth curved in a dolphin smile.

Thereafter was a photograph of Timo, with knees bent, hitting the water, causing the surface of the pale green sea to explode around him in a perfect circle of sparkling water diamonds.

And Max, as he descended the ladder, glancing warily over his shoulder at Nepitella, Timo and me, urging him to join us.

The rest of the photographs included moments of everyone on the boat, laughing, eating, talking, dozing, and upon our return, *la Nepitella's* white sails against a crimson, setting sun, her indigo bow slicing through the glass-green sea.

I picked up the first photograph again, fascinated at my physical image. Scrambling out of bed, I pulled off my gown and stood naked in front of the mirror. I assessed myself with a critical eye and compared it to the photo I held in one hand. I turned around and looked over my shoulder at the curve of my spine running down to my pert, apple-shaped buttocks. *Yes, definitely me.*

Turning to face the mirror again I appraised my breasts and flat belly. Using the tip of my index finger I traced the faintest shadow-line of golden hair running from my navel to my mons pubis. Andreas's words repeated in my head, 'You're marvellous. Do you know that?'

No, Andreas, I had no idea, until now. Thank you.

The memory of Andreas's outlined body replaced my image in the mirror. My hand cupped the nest of gold in the V between my legs. The photo fell to the floor while my other hand found its way to my breasts.

For the first time in years, I pleasured myself. I had no need to conjure up the smell of pomade or chocolate.

The next morning Maria, Rubino, Andreas and the children assembled in the kitchen for breakfast. When Maria caught sight of me, more importantly, caught sight of what I was wearing: a green, three-quarter sleeve, tight midriff and pencil skirt dress, the bangles clinked their approval. That was good enough for me. Rubino's deep facial crevices lifted and settled as he, too, gave me a quick smile.

I avoided making eye contact with Andreas and focused on getting the children their breakfast.

In a final mad scramble, everyone, except Maria and me, climbed onto the donkey cart and set off.

The silence in the kitchen was bliss.

'He likes you,' Maria said.

'I like him, too.' I paused. 'I'm afraid.'

'That's understandable. But remember, Hortensia, decisions taken in the past were done in the best interests of everyone. You don't have to justify your part to anyone. If ever asked, admit nothing.'

I remembered all too well her and Rubino's advice, when I was still in the early stages of pregnancy and had no clue who the father of my child was. 'I know. I know. But what about the children?'

'Cross that bridge when you come to it. By the way, your hair needs touching up.'

'What!' I raced to the mirror on the wall and peered. Soon after Nepitella's birth, when her hair showed its propensity for red, I began to colour my nondescript hair.

Each month, I boiled three beetroots, reduced the liquid until only a concentrated amount was left. After rinsing my hair in apple vinegar, I combed the beetroot liquid, mixed with a tiny amount of olive oil, through my hair. It was all I could do to demonstrate Nepitella and I had something in common. Now, eight years later, most people took it for granted that I had naturally reddish hair, while my daughter had a mop of fire-red ringlets. I peered closely at my hair in the mirror and grimaced. 'I look forward to the day my hair turns grey and I don't have to bother with this messy subterfuge.'

'That's unlikely to happen for a long while yet,' Maria said. 'How old are you now?'

'Twenty-six next birthday.'

'Twenty-six! Ah. That's right. It will be an auspicious year for you.'

'Please, please tell me that means an abundance of luck is coming my way. The month of June will be the start of the Bed and Breakfast, and island boat-hopping summer. Oh God, Maria, what happens if all this planning amounts to nothing?'

The lights in Maria's eyes flickered. Her cold, bony hand gripped my forearm. 'Hortensia, there are ten more years to go before the boys take up their rightful ownership of their estates. In these last four years, you have been nothing short of a miracle getting everything sorted, from the boat conversion, to the *agriturismi* for the villas and the valley farmhouses. Neither Rubino, nor I, would have achieved what you have. Look at you, badgering Mayor Rossi, taking your ideas to the region, petitioning the Tourism board and those *bastardi* sitting on their fat arses in Rome. No one has achieved what you have.'

For the first time in years, Maria hugged me. I was so desperate for comfort, my body sagged against hers. For fleeting, blissful seconds I was once again a child in her arms. 'All thanks to you and Rubino getting the labour union here and estate contracts in place,' I mumbled into her shoulder.

'Ah. But the secret is, you learned and took what you learned to a whole new place.' Maria held me at arm's length. Her turned-in gaze travelled down her nose, over the bump and launched itself from the hook of her nose to land on my face, and held me captive. 'Just ensure that each person involved in your enterprises has a vested interest. Then it will be a guaranteed success. Meantime, where are the beets?'

An hour later, Rubino returned with the sisters, Gina and Silvia, dressed in their cleaning clothes and armed with their mops, pails and cloths.

I lifted a wrought-iron key from the rack that would unlock the door leading to the five bedrooms on the top floor that had been left undisturbed for years.

'I'd smear a little olive oil on that key,' Rubino said. 'That will help ease the lock.'

I did as he suggested. 'Come, Gina, Silvia. Let's go and see what awaits.'

After a few jiggles, the key turned the lock and the door swung open. The air in the corridor was dank. The cleaning ladies lit a candle each, pushed open the first bedroom door, unlatched the windows and swung back the shutters whose grated hinges squeaked in protest.

'Oooh,' they exclaimed.

Being the top floor, the view was astounding. The ultramarine sea glistened in the distance and the chain of islands, making up the Tuscan Archipelago between the Ligurian and Tyrrhenian Sea, were clear. My heart gave a skip of joy. *Those islands are going to be a big draw card for our Tuscan-coast-exploring American guests.*

Morning light flooded the room. Odd-shaped lumps of furniture were covered in thick cotton sheets. A quick look at all the bedrooms with en-suite bathrooms revealed them to be similar.

'Gina, which suite do you think should be cleaned first?'

She stepped into the corridor. 'This one,' she said, indicating the fifth room. 'Then when it's complete we can work our way down the corridor without tracking dirt back up.'

'Good thinking. Silvia, how long will it take to get each one ship-shape?'

Silvia's face broke into a smile. She was clearly pleased to be asked her opinion, rather than be told. 'Five days, at least.'

'Ladies, it's all over to you. When the first bedroom is complete, let me know, and we'll celebrate. Good luck with those cobwebs.'

We looked up. Dust-laden webbing stretched between the angles of all four corners of the room. The cleaning ladies thrust their brooms in the air and wielded them like swords. We laughed.

Thank goodness I'm not going to be tackling those monster-webs.

———— ◆ ————

Autumn had crept up on us. Niggling winds menaced leaves until they fell and then chased them in the air and on the ground. On that September morning, I pulled on a coat and threw an extra jersey into a carrier bag for each child. I glanced at my refreshed red hair, and just in time, remembered to colour my lips with my new pink lipstick. I was ready to collect the children from school and Andreas from Luisa's house on our way back home.

'Here, Long Ears, eat this.' I offered the grey donkey the boiled beets. It was a treat for him as much as it was a way of getting rid of my hair colour evidence. 'This is the last journey for today. You'll have the weekend to laze.' *I must buy a car before winter sets in.*

I smiled. How excited the boys would be. They had complained of the cold in the mornings on the way to school. Nepitella on the other hand rarely suffered the effects of heat or cold. Aside from the *Apes*, it would be the first car in the valley. That would upset Mayor Santo Rossi. Regional funds for a mayoral vehicle had still not been made available to him.

Maria's voice entered my head. *Remember what I said about vested interest?*

Yes. I'll figure a way to give him a helping hand. I shuddered at the thought.

I climbed aboard, picked up the reins and started the journey down to the valley.

Lorenzo waited for me at the school gates. He doffed his cap, smiled and walked over. 'The mail.' He held out the cloth bag.

I noted it was heavier than usual as I tucked it between the cushions on the bench.

He placed a bucket with its lid fixed closed behind me. 'Here are a couple of line-caught sea bass for your dinner tonight.'

'Thank you, Lorenzo. How was the exam?'

'Ah, well, you know.' He looked up at me, but could not hold the serious mask in place any longer. 'First-class pass!' He tossed his fisherman's cap into the air and caught it with a deft hand.

'Congratulations! This Christmas, stop by the villa for a meal and we'll celebrate.' Inwardly I sighed with relief. I had worried Lorenzo would not pass. *Then who would be the licensed marine guide to run island-hopping and coastal tours?* 'Lorenzo, bring me the books. I'd like to start studying as soon as Christmas is over.'

He frowned.

'It's so that if you can't be the tour guide, I can.'

A smile replaced his frown. 'Good idea.' He doffed his cap at me once more. 'Goodbye, signora. See you next week.'

'Goodbye and congratulations, again!'

The school bell rang. Classroom doors opened, releasing racing children. A quick scan and the sound of their bubbly conversation told me all I needed to know. 'Here, put these on.' I handed out the jerseys.

'But, I'm not cold.'

'Please, Nepitella. Just put it on to make me happy.'

Nepitella scrunched up her pert nose as she shrugged her arms into the jersey's sleeves.

'Don't forget to button up.'

She inhaled, puffed, and her bottom lip trembled with the force of exhaled air.

I ignored her, and turned to look over my shoulder. 'Ready?' I called out to the boys.

'Ready,' they yelled.

The cart pulled away to the sound of gusting leaves and various valley women's voices calling out, 'Good weekend, Signora d'Ambrosia.'

I barely heard them, or the boys cavorting behind me. My thoughts were full of Andreas who I would see again in a few minutes. I took the road to Luisa's house and forgot all about the heavier than usual mailbag I had tucked between the cushions.

31

A single glance confirmed that Luisa Prosperi was infatuated with Andreas Crespo. Though she was old enough to be his mother, undisguised passion flushed her skin. Her feelings were understandable. He was the most handsome man, *un bel ragazzo*, our valley had seen in years.

It was rumoured that my father, Claudio Trianni, had once been equally handsome. But his reprehensible treatment of the valley workers, let alone of my mother, was cause enough for him to be nicknamed *mascalzone.*

Better than his good looks was when Andreas gave you his attention. It felt as though nothing else in the world mattered. A natural tonic for all ages, he charmed my children, who never took to strangers.

Luisa's flock of white chickens pecked their way around her kitchen garden. Standing knee-deep in a profusion of verdant spinach plants, she blew him air kisses. 'Andreas, my heart's treasure, take care of yourself. Come back soon.'

He snapped one more photograph, capturing her farewell, before settling on the cart's bench with Nepitella between us. 'I will. Thank you for everything.' He returned the blown kisses.

'Sit down, boys,' I said to Timo and Max, who attempted to keep their balance as the cart pulled away.

I tried to ignore the twinge of jealousy that stabbed me. *I wanted to be the recipient of those blown kisses.* 'Successful day?'

Andreas deftly unscrewed the lens from his camera. 'Very. And I got to visit Gilda Fabbri, too.'

No doubt Gilda's equally smitten.

'So, your work photographing the valley *Agriturismi*, working farm guest houses, is done?'

'Yes.'

'You'll be leaving tomorrow?'

'I'll leave on Sunday, if that's okay with you?'

Good. He'll be here another night.

Andreas placed the lens in its soft black pouch. 'I'd like to photograph Villa Angeli's exotic trees, before they all lose their leaves to winter.'

I kept my focus ahead and nodded, wondering what it would be like to bury my fingers in his mop of curls.

'Can I go, too?' Max piped up.

'And me,' Timo yelled.

'You have to ask me first,' Max said. 'It's my villa and my garden.'

Will they ever outgrow this relentless one-upmanship?

'No, boys, you've both got it wrong.' Andreas ran his hand through his hair. 'You have to ask Hortensia. Only she can give you permission.'

I threw Andreas a grateful look. He clearly knew something about managing spoiled, privileged children.

'Zeeya,' they chorused, 'can we?'

Bad memories of my early years serving as Mistress Letizia's personal maid hurtled into my head. Most of the people I had known at Villa Angeli died – Bea, Anna, Foxy the dog and Max's mother, Mistress Letizia. The only good to come from there was Max, whom I pulled from his dead mother by slitting her stomach open.

I would soon not only have to face those memories, but also the rooms in which those events took place. Given the miracle of his birth, I determined to ensure Max's first visit home would be a positive experience. I turned my head so that my words flew over my shoulder. 'Mmm. We could take a picnic lunch, and after, open the villa.'

'Yay!' the boys cried.

I turned my head again. 'On one condition.' For a few moments, only the steady clop of Long Ears' feet could be heard. 'Don't get in Andreas's way. Deal?'

'Deal!' they shouted.

'Zeeya?'

'Yes, Max.'

'Will I see the room where I was born?' His voice was unusually quiet and shy.

'Yes.'

'I'm starving. What's to eat?' Timo asked, swiftly changing the subject. He always did this when he thought Max was getting too much of my attention.

Knowing the route to Villa Trianni, Long Ears needed no guidance getting home. He trotted along at a brisk pace.

'Look!' Nepitella pointed upward. 'The red flag.'

We all looked up, searching out the tower. My heart began to beat in time with the fluttering flag. Only Rubino and Maria were at Villa Trianni. We entered the courtyard to see Maria standing in the kitchen doorway. I scrambled down from the cart. 'What's the matter?'

She held out a light brown rectangular envelope, our very first telegram.

'It came this afternoon.'

'Did you read it?'

She nodded.

The bangles sounded the notes to a ponderous death march.

'Boys, take Long Ears to the stable. Feed and water him. Muck out the stable. I'm coming back in thirty minutes to check if you've done it right. If not, there will be no visit to Villa Angeli tomorrow. Understand?'

Heads nodded with vigour.

Taking his cue from me, Andreas said, 'Nepitella, can you please carry this pouch? Take care. It's the lens to my camera and very delicate.'

Her little face lit up. She took the black pouch and followed him.

I retrieved the single sheet of paper and read the clipped words. *'With immediate effect, wine and oil sale contracts are cancelled'*. My spirits plunged into the abyss of despair. 'Iacopo can't be serious.' My throat released a dying croak.

'It stands to reason the contracts have been cancelled,' Maria said. 'The American's vineyards and olive trees have been bearing fruit these last two seasons. Given his vast acreage, he no longer needs our harvests.'

'But, what am I to do with our harvests? I can't sell our produce to the Italian government's cooperative for a pittance, can I? But if I don't sell, there'll be no money. How will I make the Trianni bank loans? The whole valley depends on this income.' *As do I!*

'We'll think of something.'

'Have you told Rubino?' I asked.

'Ah,' Maria said. 'There lies another, very real and immediate problem.'

The hair stood up on the back of my neck. 'The real reason for the red flag?'

'Yes. Come.'

I followed Maria towards the stable, and glimpsed the boys sweeping out the stall while Long Ears munched his way through a mound of barley straw. A bucket of fresh water stood beside him.

We climbed the external stone staircase that led to Rubino's quarters above the stables. Maria pushed open the door, stood aside and let me pass. Fully clothed in his Sunday best including his finest pair of old but well-shined boots, Rubino lay on his bed.

'Rubino?' My voice rose.

'*La mia carissima ragazza.* You have come.' His voice was barely audible.

It was the first time he'd ever called me his dearest girl. A knife blade, sharper than a shard of glass, sliced through my heart. My breath left my body. Trembling, I fell to my knees beside his bed and enfolded one huge hand in both of mine.

'*Cara*, don't be sad,' he said. 'It's long past my time. I'm happy to go.'

'Nooooo.' The sound that issued from my chest did not belong to me. Rather, it sounded like a primeval voice that belonged to all humankind, hinging on the anticipated loss of a loved one. 'Not yet. Not yet. I need you still.'

'I must, *cara*. Carry on the good work. With your care, the valley workers are in good hands. They depend on you.'

Rubino's eyelids slid closed as he released his last breath.

The room started to turn. I lay my head on his chest. No different than when I was three years old and my mother, in her butterfly form, left, my grieving heart whispered over, and over again, 'Come back, don't leave me. Please, don't go.' My words faded and disappeared into the void along with him.

Why, oh why, didn't I find more time to prepare him hot salt-baths?
Guilt made a feast of me.

It was dusk by the time I lifted my head from Rubino's cold chest, soaked with my tears. In the meagre light, I saw his still wrinkled face, but smoother and more relaxed than I could recall.

Just how old were you?

A hesitant knock sounded, and the door scraped open. The children, followed by Andreas and Maria, entered. Each carried a lighted candle and their rosaries laced between their fingers. The boys' faces were masks of sombre scowls. Nepitella's looked peaceful.

'Time,' Maria said, 'to say your goodbyes.'

We all made the sign of the Holy Cross.

Timo stepped up first, kissed Rubino on the forehead and said, 'Thank you for looking after me like a papa would.' He moved aside, pretended to wipe his nose but brushed away a tear.

Pain for my son gripped my heart and squeezed until I could barely breathe.

Max stepped forward. 'Thank you for welcoming me, when I had nowhere else to go.'

Oh my God. All the time Max knew his father was leaving him here permanently.

Max sniffed. 'And thank you especially for teaching me how to swim.' He stepped aside for Nepitella.

Being shorter than the boys, she stood on tiptoe but still could not reach his forehead. Instead, she whispered something in his ear. A tiny frown drew her eyebrows together. She stretched harder, angled her head pressing her ear towards his mouth and listened.

The boys' jaws dropped. 'What did he say?'

The corners of her mouth curled into the beginnings of her dolphin smile. 'He says to tell you, Zeeya, that he was one hundred and four years old. Oh, and look in the drawer, there is something there for you.'

Andreas clapped his hands over his mouth.

'Tell Rubino,' I said, 'I say, thank you.'

Nepitella conveyed my message by whispering again in Rubino's ear.

Maria materialised from the shadows. 'Everyone back to the kitchen.'

Subdued, Andreas and Neptiella led the way. As the boys clumped down the steps, their awed but excited voices rose.

Pinpricks of starlight and a sickle moon glowed against the black, velvet sky. Owls from their treetop perches readied their vocal chords for the night's screeching serenade. In his stall below, Long Ears stamped his feet. Fingers of unusually cold night air reached out, joined, and settled over everything.

'Check the bedside drawer.' Maria's voice jolted me back to the present.

It's a day for single sheets of paper. I drew it out and read aloud. Rubino's handwritten will left everything he had to me. At the bottom of the sheet there was a postscript. *Money's under the mattress. Buy a red car. Call it Rubino. Xxxx.*

Maria and I eyed the mattress and Rubino's body. Though he was frail, he was still a big man.

'Let's roll him over,' Maria said.

'Good idea,' I said. 'On the count of three, heave.'

Together, we eased him onto his side close to the edge of the mattress.

'Have you got him?'

Maria grunted.

I stuck my hands under the edge of the mattress and heaved. It never moved. 'Dear God, this mattress weighs a tonne.'

'Breathe, put your back into it.' Maria's voice was barely audible.

I did as she said and managed to lift a corner. 'I can't see.'

Maria pointed a bony finger to the candle.

Supporting the mattress's weight with my back bowed, leaving my other hand free, I lifted the candle. 'Oh my goodness.'

'What is it?' Maria's voice cracked with effort.

'You've got to see this…'

'Aiiieee…' Maria lost her grip and fell. Rubino rolled off the bed and landed on top of her. By the sudden release of Rubino's weight, the mattress flipped over, pinning him and Maria to the floor.

'Help!' Maria's voice was muffled.

'Are you hurt?'

'No.'

'No problem, then. Stay there until I've cleared this lot.'

'Hurry.'

The base of the bed frame was packed with stacks of *lire* interspersed with loose silver coins 'I will.' *I'll need a wheelbarrow to transport this much cash.*

By the time I rescued Maria and we got the mattress back on its frame, Rubino back onto the mattress and covered him with sheet, we were both sweating. Under the glow of the candle, we stuffed two pillowcases with the pile of notes and coins.

'Maria, I hope you haven't left your money under your mattress?'

'Sadly yes. My goats recently ate their way through it. So, when I die, you'll find what little money I now have hanging from the beams in hessian bags.'

'Please, tell me you're not planning to die just yet?'

'Er…no.'

The bangles trilled the loudest I ever heard. I knew better than to ask another question.

'On my way home, I'll let Don Antonio know,' Maria said. 'My guess is that Rubino's funeral will be held tomorrow afternoon.' She wrapped her bony arms around me and gave me a hug. 'Hortensia, Rubino would tell us not to grieve. Life is for the living.' Maria vanished into the black night.

I swung the pillowcases over my right shoulder and entered the oil mill. Finding an empty barrel, I stuffed the pillowcases into it and secured the lid. So I could tell this barrel apart, I placed a dark green glass demijohn on top of the barrel. The demijohn was less than half full of wine.

Stepping away, the memory of Iacopo emerging from behind the row of stored barrels flashed through my head. I rubbed my eyes and stared harder. It was my imagination. No one was there.

After splashing water from the well onto my face, running my fingers through my hair, and straightening my dress, I entered the kitchen.

Following Andreas's instructions, the children busied themselves chopping and dicing, boiling and frying.

'You okay?' Andreas mouthed.

I nodded.

'I hope you don't mind, I opened a bottle of wine.'

'Not at all. I'm ready for a glass.' *Or the whole bottle.*

Andreas handed me a glass half-filled with *Sangiovese.* In the flickering firelight, it glowed like spilled blood.

'Zeeya,' Timo said. 'Sit. Dinner is ready.'

The children and I sat while Andreas placed the serving dishes on the table.

'I cleaned and cut the potatoes and fried them,' Max said. 'Look.'

I ignored the burnt, blackened bits that under normal circumstances the children refused to eat. 'Oh my, they look wonderful.'

'I shelled the peas and boiled them in butter and mint, just like you do,' Nepitella said.

'They smell delicious.' By the look of the over-cooked-to-a-mush peas, Nepitella would be scooping rather than chasing her peas around her plate.

'And I grilled the seabass,' Timo said.

At least it looked edible. 'Children, thank you. What a surprise!'

'And, I have an announcement to make,' Max said. 'We're going to each cook a meal once a week.'

Anna matched my strangled gasp of dismay.

I cast a glance at Andreas, whose mouth widened with mirth. 'What a wonderful idea!' *Wouldn't it be nice, if every evening was like this?*

As soon as my heart formed the thought, my head chased it out. My relationships with men had brought complications. Except for Pietro. And he was no more.

Andreas washed the dishes while I put the children to bed. As usual, we piled into Timo's grand bed, and I read them a story. One after another they fell asleep. I could still carry Nepitella to her bedroom as she weighed hardly anything, but I could not carry Max.

I descended the stairs and went into the kitchen. Andreas's camera equipment lay in pieces spread over the cleaned table.

He looked up. My heart, still tender at Rubino's passing, nevertheless quickened. His broad shoulders and hard chest were clearly defined under his shirt.

'Can you carry Max to his room, please?'

He stood graceful as a sleek cat, or a dancer. 'Of course. Lead the way.'

After closing Max's bedroom door, we walked down the corridor. I was aware of Andreas and his radiating warmth. I stopped at my bedroom door. *Does he feel the way I do?* I turned to him. 'Andreas, I want to thank you. You've been so very good with the children…' I could not help it. Tears pricked my lids and began their escape down my cheeks.

He wrapped his arms around me. 'It's okay.'

His comforting warmth was what I needed. What I wanted. I raised my face to meet his. He turned his head away, so I kissed his cheek instead of his mouth.

'Hortensia,' he said, 'with Rubino's passing, you're in shock. To-morrow you'll feel different. Sleep well.'

He kissed my forehead, gave me a tight squeeze and let me go.

I watched him disappearing down the staircase. A whirlwind of emotions threatened to overwhelm me, biggest of all – embarrassment. *You fool. You fool. You fool.*

In the middle of the night, I awoke and sat straight up. *The mail-bag!*

Then I remembered my embarrassment. I wanted to die. I pulled the covers over my head and forgot about the mailbag again.

I woke to Timo and Max bouncing on my bed.

'Zeeya,' Max said, 'what time are we going to my villa?'

'As soon as you are dressed and have eaten breakfast.'

The boys tore out of my bedroom.

'Come back.' My voice rose.

Two tousled heads stuck around the door frame.

'Wear Sunday clothes and your coats and don't forget to brush your hair. We're attending Rubino's funeral this afternoon.'

Their faces flushed. Likely they only now remembered Rubino's passing yesterday. *Goodness, children can be so absorbed in their own little worlds.*

'Yes, Zeeya.' Instead of running, they walked to their bedrooms.

At least that slowed them down. My head felt ready to split; I had not slept well. Aside from my stupid attempt to kiss Andreas, my mind was swimming with questions: who will take charge of the harvests and oversee the mammoth task of pruning? I could think of no answers. *Why, oh why, didn't I learn as much from Rubino as I should have? Stupid. Stupid. Stupid. But, none of this matters, unless I find new buyers. But from where? And how?* Yet for all that, my heart ached far worse than my head. *Rubino, I miss you.*

An hour later, we walked in single file. I led, the children in the middle, Andreas last. The knife-edge ridge path, cresting the steep incline appeared more treacherous than I'd remembered. *Should I have taken the easier, much longer route?*

I knew the boys were struggling; their banter had slowly dwindled. I glanced over my shoulder. They, including Andreas, were concentrating on where to place their feet. Nimble as Maria's pygmy goats, and seemingly without having to look, Nepitella negotiated the tricky path with ease.

Halfway, I called a halt. Everyone except Nepitella crouched. As they raised their heads and looked seaward, their jaws slackened at the stupendous view.

I had never travelled anywhere, other than once to Naples. But I knew, as the sun set the limpid purple-blue sea ablaze, that nowhere could be more sublime than our Tuscan coastline. Andreas's camera clicked in a continuous stream as he snapped one photo after another. When I deemed we'd all had our fill of the visual splendour before us, I said, 'Forward march?'

'Forward march,' everyone replied in unison.

The row of cherry trees came into sight. I took the left fork and entered the Villa Angeli's orchard filled with exotic trees.

'Let's stop here,' I said. 'Boys, take off your coats. Go. Explore. Come back when the sun is directly above your head. After our picnic, we'll go up to the villa.'

Timo and Max dropped their coats, and, like colts off their halters, disappeared into the hortensia thicket, whose delicate flower heads, already faded and dried to brown, crackled and quivered.

'See you in a while.' Andreas adjusted the camera strap around his neck and walked off.

I eased from my back the rucksack that contained the picnic and spread the blanket on the meadow grass.

'Ready to explore, Nepitella?'

'First, I want to visit with Foxy.'

My mouth gaped. I had never mentioned Foxy to the children, so how did she know?

No different to Long Ears' homeward surefootedness, Nepitella led me directly to Foxy's grave. She knelt beside the patch upon which a single rose bush grew. I did not have to think what colour roses it put out. *But, who planted it?*

I did.

Oh, Rubino. You're here!

Yes. To help with the harvests. Grape picking needs to start on Monday. Put the word out after my funeral. You are going to need every single hand.

The ache in my heart eased. *Rubino... I've a lot of questions. Rubino?*

He did not reply.

The sun had reached its zenith. Only a hint of short shadows smudged the bases of Villa Angeli's orchard and exotic trees.

'Come, Nepitella,' I said. 'Oh! Where did you find that?'

Nepitella held up a familiar-looking ball. 'In the grass. I've been throwing it for Foxy.'

'Good. It's his favourite game.'

Her face had transformed. The corners of her mouth curved into a dolphin smile, the lights in her eyes danced, and the end of her nose wiggled with delight. 'I know.' She slipped her hand into mine.

My heart gave a joyful skip.

We walked hand in hand towards the chasteberry tree. The memory of when I'd lain under it with Di Napoli raced into my head. I glanced up. From precisely that spot, the view across the valley to Villa Trianni's tower was clear. Anyone with good sight could have seen us. I thrust the memory away.

Andreas lay stretched out on the picnic blanket snapping photos through foliage reaching into the sky. My throat constricted. He was breathtakingly handsome.

As the boys got closer, their whooping and hollering grew louder. They raced out of the hortensia thicket, elbowing each other. The colour in their cheeks mirrored the small red fruits suspended from the branches in the crab apple tree.

I raised my arm. 'Stop. Calm down. Catch your breath.' They jolted against each other to a halt, drawing in deep breaths. Then, in a flurry of gangly arms and legs, they collapsed onto the blanket.

I unwrapped and handed out sandwiches slathered with soft goat cheese, layered with slices of *mortadella* with pistachios, or slices of *peperoli* stuck with black olives and red peppers. For a while, I heard only the sound of contented munching.

Andreas cocked his thumb and smiled at me over the children's heads. I could not help myself. The sting of last night's rebuff still smarted but I returned his smile.

Max bolted down his sandwich and watched each of us as we finished ours. I knew he was bursting to get to the villa he owned and see the room in which he'd been born.

'It's time,' I said.

We scrambled to our feet and headed uphill.

Even though Villa Angeli did not have a tower and was smaller, it was more impressive in its simplicity than the sprawling and imposing Villa Trianni. Perhaps Timo noticed. If he did, he did not say a word.

But Nepitella did. Her mouth formed an O, and whispered, 'It's beautiful.'

Wait until the pink roses clinging to the walls are in full bloom.

Andreas's camera clicked in quick staccato as we walked along the gravel path leading to the imposing front door. On either side, in perfect symmetry, were four sets of closed shutters. Above, on the second floor the symmetry was replicated, but with matching wrought-iron Romeo and Juliet balconies jutting from the façade. The third floor, being the attic, sported round windows, rather like giant portholes. The villa's green shutters, although faded, contrasted with the apricot walls and terracotta tiled roof.

'The key?' Max asked.

I pointed. 'Under that vase.'

Andreas stepped forward. 'Here, I'll help you.' He tilted the heavy terracotta container.

As always, Timo tried to unnerve Max. 'Watch out for scorpions and spiders.'

Max shuddered, but despite Timo's warning, he thrust his hand under the vase without hesitation. 'Got it.' He held the key aloft and his mouth split into a grin. He inserted the key, turned it and pushed. The door did not budge.

'Everyone, shoulder to the door,' Andreas said. 'On the count of three, push. One, two three…'

The door swung open, and the children tumbled in, landing on the entrance hall floor. Andreas and I clutched each other as we, too, landed in a tangled mess on top of the children. My fingers delighted in the feel of his hard body.

'Ouch!' Max cried.

'My hand!' Timo yelled.

Nepitella's muffled giggles rose from beneath the pile.

Andreas extricated his limbs and got to his feet first. He helped me up and then the boys. Nepitella, who had borne the heaviest weight, emerged last, unscathed and still smiling.

'We have two hours at most,' I said, 'before we head to Rubino's funeral. If you open the shutters, make sure you close them. Okay?'

'Okay.' The children's voices rang out happily.

By his face, Max's anticipation had reached epic proportions. He had no interest in the ordinary, everyday rooms on the ground floor. He eyed the staircase. 'Can I go up?'

I inclined my head. 'Lead the way.'

He released a pent-up sigh, one that sounded aeons old.

The first set of double doors at the top of the staircase opened into the library. The leather-bound books with their gold leaf titles winked at me like old friends. The four-seater sofa, table and chaperone chair remained in situ. As did the waist-high, free-standing *capodimonte* porcelain vase in which Max had been baptised. And in front of which Pietro and I had stood upon the occasion of our marriage.

Max walked towards the three hanging portraits. He ignored the ones of his grandparents and stood for the longest time in front of the portrait of his mother. Her soft round face and celestial blue eyes appeared to focus only on him. Without saying a word, Max left the library and turned right into the corridor.

A billowing draught of air ruffled my hair. *Letizia, are you following me?* No sooner had I asked the question, I realised it was her son she was following.

Max pushed against the master bedchamber door. It swung open. Even after all this time, the faint smell of Letizia's favourite chocolates wrapped in silver and gold foil hung in the air.

As the master bedchamber was not nearly as big as his, Timo immediately lost interest, and with a smug look, left the room.

Andreas read my lips as I mouthed, 'Follow him, please.'

Max advanced into the room with Nepitella close behind. From the corner of my eye, I saw one of Foxy's balls roll out from under the bed. It came to rest against Nepitella's foot.

She picked it up. 'I'm going outside to play with Foxy.'

I nodded and turned all my attention to Max.

He stood at his mother's dressing table. One after the other, he picked up Letizia's hairbrush, comb and hand mirror. He looked at himself closely. 'I don't look like her.'

'No. You don't.' I crossed my fingers for the lie I was about to tell. 'But you have her lovely, warm spirit.'

He turned towards the bed, seemingly oblivious of the draught that had followed us into the room. At first, it was caressing. Then it gathered force. The crystal bottles on the dressing table shook and knocked against each other. The canopy drapes fluttered, and windowpanes rattled in their frames.

Max began to tremble and, like a leaf freed from its point of connection, was airily adrift.

The draught turned into a swirling wind, achieving maelstrom proportions. Feather pillows, bedside lamps, the hairbrush, comb, hand mirror and bottles, their stoppers freed, collided mid-air.

Maria's urgent voice entered my head. *Help him!*

Her words jolted me out of the grip of the wind's hypnotising pitched howls and just in time, I reached Max before the last of his spirit exited his body. His hands were ice-cold, skin the colour of white marble. Like a somnambulist, he walked in a trance. I turned him to face me, pressed his shoulders until he sat, swung his legs up and laid him upon the bed. I lowered myself beside him, pulled the dustsheet over the two of us, folded my body around his and held him tight.

Ignoring the wind and its howling fury, I breathed steadily, each breath a whisper in Max's ear. I concentrated, willing my heart to thump against his back; encouraging pleas to persuade him to stay with the living, rather than follow the desperate, urgent drumming of his dead mother's heartbeats.

An eternity might have passed before the wind relented, and I felt warmth return to Max's limbs. I lifted my head and looked at his face. His colour was normal. His dark lashes, longer than his father's, fluttered. His lids opened.

'You're back,' I said.

He smiled like an angel. 'Yes. I've been on a long journey with my mother.'

'Did you have a lovely time?'

'Oh yes. Very much.'

I threw back the dustsheet. We stood and hugged. The room had returned to normal. Realising I'd come within a hair's breadth of losing him caused every fibre in my body to tingle with bone-chilling fear before turning into ecstatic joy for his reprieve.

'Zeeya. My mother says you are doing a good job of taking care of me.'

Timo's voice sounded before his arrival. 'It's time to leave.' He entered the chamber just as Max and I released each other. Timo's face flushed red, burning with undisguised jealousy.

'Maria's waiting downstairs.' His voice was dagger-sharp.

———————— ◆ ————————

V illagers packed the valley church. Those who could not squeeze in were obliged to stand outside. The dipped sun had lost its warmth and despite the now icy wind Don Antonio had all the church doors open so the Requiem Mass could be heard by everyone.

Upon seeing Andreas, Luisa Prosperi and Gilda Fabbri waved frantically. Ignoring their husbands' grunts of disapproval, and a wave of mutterings from the rest of the congregation, the two women insisted he sit between them, trapped and squashed by their ample buttocks.

Maria, Nepitella and I sat in the front pew with a clear view of Rubino's simple wood coffin placed in front of the altar.

I forbid you to waste money on a fancy box, he had written in his will.

Timo and Max sat alone in their separate family pews, facing each other. Throughout the ceremony, Timo fixed his glare upon Max. Max ignored him. Or, perhaps he was unaware? I did not know, but I felt cross with Timo and uncomfortable for Max.

Mayor Santo Rossi gave the eulogy. He praised Rubino saying that throughout his life he had been a pillar of support to those in need and that he had needed only a little help in getting the labour union to come to the valley. Help that he, Mayor Santo Rossi, had been only too happy to provide.

Maria and I exchanged glances.

More like hampered.

While the valley workers were simple, they were not stupid. The sound of shuffling hobnailed boots and leather soles against the mosaic floor increased; a clear message to Rossi to stop. He'd aggrandised himself enough.

Rossi took heed. 'But even with his passing, not all is lost.' His bulbous eyes focused on me. 'We have in our midst one of our own who continues Rubino's work of improving the lot of our community…' He paused.

'Wait for it,' I whispered to Maria. Bang on cue, Rossi drew in a short breath and finished by saying, 'guided and assisted by me.'

Though separated by Nepitella sitting between us on the hard pew bench, Maria's voice entered my head. *Don't let him upset you.*

I'm not. He can say whatever he wants. We all know the truth. And, anyhow I don't need him.

My mother's voice entered my head. *Be careful of being too sure. You never know what life might throw your way.*

I ignored her.

———————— ◆ ————————

Rubino's coffin was interred in the area reserved for the poor and laid to rest next to Anna.

If the Church had an inkling of how much money he had accumulated... I decided I would make a donation to the church for its upkeep.

Before the mourners turned to go home, I stood balanced upon an empty barrel and clapped. The large group of weather-beaten faces stared in surprise. 'Everyone. Attention, please. The grape harvest will start on Monday. Those wishing to work and share in the profits, sign up early on Monday morning.' *What am I thinking? What profits? I don't have a buyer yet.* I crossed my fingers.

A murmur, like a wave lapping the shore, sounded from the crowd.

'Same terms as before?' A voice rose from the centre of the crowd.

'Yes. But there will be an increase in your share of the profit. This year's harvest is our best yet, thanks to God and your work.' *I must be mad. Why am I saying this?*

A shout of approval rose from the crowd.

'Who's in charge now that Rubino is gone?' the same voice asked.

I listened hard and matched the voice to Dino, who went by the nickname of, *il Mangiatore di Carne di Maiale*.

'Step forward Dino, so I can see you.'

The crowd parted to reveal Dino, who looked exactly like his namesake, a wild boar; short, compact and very tough.

'Upon his deathbed, Rubino said you should replace him.' Again, I crossed my fingers for the lie I had just told. I paused. 'Does anyone have a problem taking orders from Dino?'

There was silence.

'Dino, are you up to the task?'

'Do I get a title?'

'What title would you like?'

'How about, *capo*?'

'On one condition.'

'What's that?'

'You take these two boys.' I leaned down and placed a hand on each of Timo's and Max's shoulders. 'Embrace them like they are your own sons. Teach them everything you know. Let them work as hard as the rest of you.'

The crowd murmured its approval.

Both boys squirmed under my grip and cast me aggrieved looks.

Rubino's voice entered my head. *Brava.*

In the background, I could hear the bangles clink their approval.

'And, *piccola rossi-capelli strega*. Is she to be put to work, too?' A voice I did not know piped up from the edge of the crowd.

Silence fell.

My heart hammered. Irrespective of their size and hair colour, witches of any kind were not welcome in our closed community. 'Show yourself, and I will answer.'

The crowd parted.

Thank you, God. He is an outsider. I recognised the brown jacket. *But from where?* I gazed over the crowd and lowered my voice. 'Anyone who feels this question deserves an answer, say so now.'

The crowd froze.

Dino held out his hand to help me step down from the pail. Our faces were centimetres apart. I whispered, 'Deal with him.'

Dino nodded.

I removed my hand from his. 'Thank you, *capo.'*

Dino grinned.

He and the valley workers would not lay a hand on the outsider. There were far more effective ways than physical violence for an ousting. They would ignore, not serve, nor permit him to buy anything from the local store. The family who'd given him accommodation would suddenly have need of the space. Starving, thirsty and friendless, he would, for his survival, leave our valley of his own volition.

———— ◆ ————

For the journey back to Villa Trianni, Maria and Andreas sat upfront. I sat in the back of the cart. Nepitella fell asleep in my arms, and the boys huddled under some blankets.

'We'll miss school,' Max said.

'No, you won't,' I said. 'You'll go to school as normal and work with *capo* Dino and the valley workers in the afternoons until the work for the day is over. And that can be long after sunset. So, prepare yourselves.'

'But,' Timo had a whiny note to his voice. 'I don't want to learn how grapes are harvested and turned into wine. I'm only interested in the oil harvest.'

'Don't worry. As soon as the grape harvest is over, the olive harvest begins. Then you'll both be working and learning all about making olive oil, too.'

'Are we to be paid?' Max asked.

I hadn't thought about that. 'When you sign up on Monday afternoon, ask *capo* Dino what your payment terms will be.'

'Sign up?' Max's voice expressed shock. 'I don't have to sign up. I am the owner.'

'Not until you turn eighteen. And that applies to you too, Timo.'

'Who says?' Timo's voice was edgy with defiance.

'The law… If you want to argue that, you'll have to hire a lawyer and present your case to the seat of Government in Rome.' *Why am I having this nonsensical discussion?*

'Nah. I'll become a lawyer and represent myself.' Timo straightened, filled with bravado.

'Good. That means you'll have to study hard at school and then go to university.'

'University?' Both boys spat out the word as if it was dirty. It was one hardly ever used in our valley.

'Sure.'

'Did my father go to university?' Max asked.

'No. He became a chocolate salesman and was successful because he could sell anything to anyone.' *Ouch. That was harsh. But it's fact. Better he knows the truth.* I softened my tone. 'But your grandfather was a learned man. Remember all those books in the library?'

Max nodded.

'And my father? Did he go to university?' Timo asked.

I could not believe my ears. It was the first time Timo had ever asked a question about his father. My heart contracted in agony. *What am I to say? Describe his real father, my first lover, Iacopo. My husband, Pietro. Or, describe Claudio Trianni, the man I have presented as his father, but who is my father, and Timo's grandfather?*

Maria brought the cart to a halt.

So engrossed, I did not realise the passing of time. The boys jumped off before I could answer Timo's question.

Thank you, God, for saving me. 'Boys, straight to bed,' I called after them. 'It's been a long day.'

Andreas came around and took Nepitella from my arms, so I could climb down from the cart. 'Can you carry her upstairs for me, please?'

'Sure thing.'

I uncoupled Long Ears and led him into his stall. Maria entered and helped me feed and water the donkey. Her energy never ceased to amaze me.

'That was some conversation you were having with the boys,' Maria said. 'Try to keep the subterfuge going for as long as possible. The older Timo is when you finally tell him, the more likely he will understand.'

'I hope he'll forgive me.'

Maria never responded and vanished into the darkness. Then I re-alised she'd not said anything about Nepitella's likely response to learning the truth about her parents.

Maria's voice entered my head. *Nepitella's response will be the least of your worries.*

I sighed with relief and tiredness, entered the kitchen and locked the door. Had I not been so tired, I might have thought to ask what my next, greatest worry would be.

Andreas and I met on the staircase halfway.

He smiled. 'Their heads hardly hit their pillows before they were out like a light.'

'It's been a long day,' I said. 'I'm exhausted, too.'

'Hortensia?'

'Yes.'

'You are really, quite simply, bloody marvellous. The way you handled that crowd. If I didn't know any better, you might as well have been "to the manor born".'

'Is that what stopped you from kissing me last night? You too be-lieve I am only a cook. A maid, the boys' guardian?' *Dear God. What's gotten into me?* I smacked my free hand over my mouth and began to tremble. *Were those knocking sounds coming from my knees?* When I looked up, Andreas's face had turned ash-white.

'No,' he barely managed to stammer. 'God, no. Not at all.'

My knees could no longer hold me up. I collapsed inelegantly on the step, frightened I'd fall if I didn't.

He sat beside me and took one of my hands in his. 'Hortensia. Please believe me. That's not it.'

'You keep saying how marvellous I am. So, what's the problem? Are you married?'

'No.'

'Are you engaged?'

'Yes. No. Well, sort of.'

'You mean she doesn't know?'

Andreas took a deep breath. 'I am afraid to tell you.'

'You don't think I'll understand?'

'Yes. I am afraid you won't.'

'Try me.'

'You'll likely never speak to me again.'

'Try me.'

He lowered his voice to a whisper. 'I'm…' He paused, 'I'm homosexual.'

'I'm sorry. You're what?'

'Homosexual.'

'You mean…you mean… What does that mean, exactly?'

'I prefer men to women.'

Oh my God. The undercurrent wave of whispers I'd heard when we entered the church for Rubino's funeral became clear. Whispers of a degrading word, a term that uneducated valley workers, men in particular, used whenever they deemed a man 'not man enough'.

'You're disgusted?'

'No. Surprised. A little embarrassed.' I felt my face blush. *And embarrassed for all the other valley women fawning over you.* 'I'm sorry. My actions last night must have been very awkward.'

'To tell the truth, I'm an old hand at it. Women do find me attractive. Especially middle-aged women.'

I swatted him on his arm. 'I'm not middle-aged!'

'No. Not you! I meant what I said before. Hortensia, you are marvellous.'

Silence.

A chasm opened to the deepest recesses of my heart. A question I'd hidden surfaced. In a barely audible voice, I asked, 'But then why am I partnerless?'

'Are you crazy? Where are you going to find a partner worthy of you here in this valley?'

'Well, there is Mayor Santo Rossi.'

'What! That bald, pot-bellied, greaseball? Never. Not over my dead body. You'll come to Rome with me. You'll be toasted, hosted and feted.

My God, Hortensia, men will fall over themselves to have a moment in your company.'

He really is a tonic.

'You think?'

'I know.'

We sat for a while, close and warm. It was a closeness I once dreamed I might have if I had a sister or brother.

'Andreas?'

'Yes.'

'Will you be my brother?'

'I already am.'

'Andreas?'

'Yes.'

'Can you drive?'

'Yes.'

'Will you teach me how?'

'Yes. What kind of car?'

'A red one?'

Andreas chortled. 'By when?'

'Before Christmas. I want to take the children to Mass on Christmas morning by car. To surprise them. Oh, and you are invited. Bring your friend, too.'

'Are you sure?'

'Of course. What's his name?'

'Gino. He's a journalist. Did you read the article I included with the photos?'

I grimaced. 'No. I'm sorry. I was too tired, and then too busy.'

'He wrote the article. He writes for American home, fashion and travel magazines. He wants your permission to print the article and others.'

'He writes in English for Americans?'

'Yes. Publishing articles will help you get your tourism enterprise on the road.'

'It will?'

'For sure.'

'Okay. I'll read it tonight.' I stretched out my legs. 'Time for bed.' I grinned. 'Don't worry. I mean alone.'

Andreas stood. He flashed me an ice-melting smile. We hugged in the middle of the staircase and parted.

Is Gino as gorgeous as Andreas? 'Goodnight,' I called softly from the top of the stairs.

I checked on the children asleep in their beds and returned to my bedroom.

Once in bed, I found the envelope and pulled out the typed article, but I fell asleep before I got past the first page.

Sometime in the night, I woke and bolted upright.

Drat. I had forgotten the mailbag again.

33

I woke to a warbling dawn chorus of golden orioles, recently arrived from North Africa. I unlocked the door and stepped into the kitchen courtyard. A salt-laden fog rendered the sea invisible. To ward off the cool air, I rubbed my palms against the tops of my arms and scooted into the oil mill to retrieve the pillowcases.

The demijohn was not on the barrel where I had placed it to remind me in in which barrel I had stored the pillowcases filled with Rubino's money.

My heart doubled its beat. Easing off the barrel's lid, an odour of cloying richness enveloped my head as I extended one arm down as far as I could. My fingers touched the oil-smooth bottom. *What!* My belly plummeted to my feet. I scrabbled my hand around its sides. Nothing. *It's not possible.* Both pillowcases were gone. I stood and looked at the adjacent barrel. I eased off its lid, and once again scrabbled around within. Nothing. I did the same with the other ten.

So, it was a person I'd seen, not a figment of my imagination, when I'd stored the pillowcases after Rubino's death. Only, the person had not been emerging from behind the row of barrels, but disappearing behind them.

I forced my legs to move and stepped behind the barrels. My sight adjusted to the deep gloom. The space was empty but for the demijohn, lying on its side. Turning, I stubbed my toe on it, which sent the heavy glass container spinning aimlessly in circles.

A ball of rage ignited in my belly. The shape of the brown jacket materialised in my head. *The outsider!* He had stolen my inheritance. My fists clenched. The ball erupted and melted the ice around my heart until my entire body burned. *Why was he here? How dare he trespass? Spy. Steal from me. My children! Steal our future!*

All my plans, hopes and dreams crushed, I crumpled to my knees. I sat back on my haunches and with my arms crossing my chest rocked with the monotonous rhythm of a metronome. By the time my rage and disbelief were spent, I was shivering from the cold, or the shock, or maybe both.

The outsider would not have suffered the ignominy of being ousted by the valley workers for having insulted my daughter when he called her a little red-headed witch, thereby also insulting me. He'd be long gone, a marauder sprinting away, bearing spoils. Now where was I going to get the money for the car? The boat? The Trianni Estate's outstanding loan? The villas' staff salaries? Payment to the valley workers for the harvests, let alone a share of the profits? I should have heeded my mother's advice. *Stupid. Stupid. Stupid.*

I returned to the villa. As I passed through the dining room, I saw the last pair of silver candelabras on the table. I'd sell them. Or, I could ask Santo Rossi to stand surety for a bank loan. No sooner had the thought entered my head than I chased it away. I'd send the candelabras to the antique market in the walled city of Lucca, where I had sold the Venetian mirror and the two crystal sconces, the proceeds of which had covered the cost of my father's funeral, handsome wedding gifts for Angelica Barberi's daughters, and Angelica's funeral costs following the birth of Nepitella.

Compared to the looming expenses, the proceeds of the candelabra would not be nearly enough. My mind raced through both Villa Trianni and Villa Angeli, sorting, discarding and selecting items that could be easily transported and sold. Like a wounded animal seeking refuge in its den, I slid into bed, and just like I'd done as a frightened child, I pulled the covers over my head.

That did not stop my mother's voice entering my head. *Money or not, life carries on.*

At least it was not 'I told you so', in response to my former and very recent pooh-poohing the notion of needing Santo Rossi. I was now paying the penalty of being cocksure. She'd been right. One could never be sure what obstacle life would toss in one's way.

Cocooned in darkness, my brain calmed. I tossed fragments of ideas into the air. First one, then another, like a juggler slowly adding more apples to tumble. I mixed and matched. But there was a piece missing, and I needed it to reveal itself before I could formulate a plan of action. By then my body had warmed. I sat, switched on the lamp, removed Gino's article from the envelope, and in the spirit of 'life carrying on', began to read.

His description of our coastline and islands was accurate and detailed, but the section of things to do and places to see in the valley needed work.

I picked up one of the children's pencils and made additions to the text, including a list of classic Tuscan dishes for hands-on cooking classes, and cheese and *limoncello* making. Olive oil and wine tastings. My mind flew back to the night of my first wine tasting instruction, and how Rubino and Maria had laughed when they tricked me into tasting turned-to-vinegar wine. I paused, immersing myself in the warmth of that memory. Then I put pencil to paper and began to write again: donkey cart rides to and from the harbour through the chestnut forests surrounding us. *Sorry, Long Ears, your retirement may not happen just yet.* And I scribbled a note about the opportunity to join the valley workers for an authentic experience of bringing in the harvests.

Where is the gramophone and all those records? Find it and order some new LPs. Argh... How am I to pay for all this? My thoughts returned to my stolen inheritance, possible items for sale and then back to the tourist activity list.

There was wild asparagus and nut gathering, mushroom hunting, and boar hunting. Boars were prolific breeders and would give the hunters a chance to earn something extra.

Satisfied with my notations, I returned the article to the envelope and picked up a fresh sheet of paper. Under two headings, Villa Trianni and Villa Angeli, I listed the articles I would sell at the antique market, folded the paper and slipped it into my bedside drawer. I dressed and headed down to the kitchen. Despite the triple loss of my inheritance and the wine and oil contracts – all of which lodged like a boulder in my heart – hunger pangs shot through my belly.

I set a pan of milk on the still warm stove. There was some bread left over from yesterday. While the coffee percolated, I tossed slices on the open fire grill to toast, twisted the lid off a new bottle of last season's cherry jam. Once the hot liquid had bubbled and gurgled its way through the funnel, I poured myself a coffee, smeared a dollop of glistening, sticky jam onto singed toast and sat down to eat.

The fragrance of toasted bread wafted upstairs and likely teased the children's breakfast bellies awake.

Overhead, Max shuffled his slipper-shod feet across the floor. I began to count. His door opened, and in another forty-seven steps he would enter the kitchen.

Andreas stuck his head around the door frame. 'Any coffee for me?'

Through the opening, I glimpsed his naked body. 'Of course. Once you're dressed.' Strange. Less than ten hours ago I had lusted after him. Now, I felt no trace of desire.

I tilted my chin to the ceiling as Timo's feet thudded to the floor. I braced myself for the sound of his bedchamber door being wrenched open and then slammed closed.

'Race you!' he yelled, streaking past Max coming down the stairs.

I was always struck by how fast Timo could move. And, like always, he beat Max. It wasn't competition; it was total domination.

And then, the biggest surprise of all, Nepitella materialised and took her place at the table before Timo entered.

'But you were still in bed when I passed your bedroom.' His bottom lip pushed forward into a sulky pout. 'How did you do it?'

As Nepitella shrugged, fragments of forest undergrowth fell from her damp corkscrew-curly hair. Memories of her half-sister, Camellia Barberi, who had roamed the countryside naked at night, jammed my thoughts. I looked harder. Bits of leaves and earth were stuck to her dressing gown. *Oh God no. Please. Not her, too.* My energy drained, flowing out of my feet, leaving me hollow and spent.

Andreas entered dressed in a tailored, stone-coloured linen jacket and matching trousers. Under the jacket, he wore a blue crew-neck sweater that fit snug to the contours of his impressive body. He placed his travel bags on the floor. 'You okay?'

I offered him a cup of coffee and put on a brave face. In my other hand, I held the envelope. 'For Gino. I've added a lot of extra information.'

'Okay.' Andreas winked at me, turned his head and caught the children's attention by deliberately slurping his coffee, causing the boys to guffaw and Nepitella to grimace.

The fire's flames leaped and turned blue, announcing Maria's imminent arrival. The kitchen door opened.

'Hurry,' Maria said, 'or you'll miss the train.'

Andreas held up his coffee cup. 'I'll come as soon as I've finished this.'

Maria turned on her heel, her black cloak billowing out behind her. The flames burned red once again.

Timo and Max mimicked Andreas, raised their cups to their mouths and together slurped their warm milk. The boys howled at my very serious that's-not-the-way-we-drink face.

Andreas gave me a crushing hug and whispered in my ear, 'Just horsing around.'

I whispered back. 'Andreas, I don't have the money for the car...'

'Don't worry. You'll pay me once I deliver it.'

'But–'

'Deliver what?' Timo always heard what he shouldn't. 'Bring what? Tell me.'

'It's a surprise,' Andreas said.

The boys scrambled to help with his bags and headed out to Long
Ears and the cart where Maria waited.

'Goodbye. See you soon.' Andreas blew air kisses.

We stood in the courtyard until Long Ears passed under the arch.
Dear God. What's wrong with me? I'd forgotten the mailbag again.

◆

That afternoon, after collecting the children from school, I took the left
fork and travelled on the dry riverbed where the *Frigido* had once
flowed. I stopped the cart at the first row of vines that snaked their way up
towards Villa Angeli. *Vendemmia* was already well underway. Valley
workers stretched out along the rows, snipping and dropping bunches of
grapes into baskets.

I brought the cart to a halt and twisted to face the boys. 'Report to
capo Dino. He'll bring you back to Villa Trianni when work for the night
has stopped.'

I returned the valley workers' greetings while the boys, who usually
sprang from the cart like goats, took their time getting down.

'Is Nepitella going to work, too?' Timo asked.

'Yes, but she is going to clean demijohns.'

Timo's frown disappeared. Cleaning glass containers was laborious
and his least favourite task.

'Zeeya?'

'Yes, Max.'

'How much will we be paid?'

'Depends on the weight you pick. See those baskets over there?' I
pointed to two new baskets the women had woven attached to leather
straps.

'Yes.'

'There is one each for you and Timo. You slide your arms through
the straps, so the basket rests on your chest. When they are full, *capo* Dino
will weigh them and enter the weight into the logbook.'

'But, how much will I be paid?'

'The same amount as every other worker.'

'Okay.'

Max, why are you so focused on money?

'I'm going to pick more and earn more money than you,' Timo said.

'No, you won't.'

'Watch and see.'

I lowered my voice and hissed. 'Boys. Best behaviour. Don't disappoint me.'

I left them in *capo* Dino's hands, ya-ed at Long Ears and turned the cart around. With Nepitella sitting beside me, quieter than usual, I headed to the barn at Villa Angeli. Several times I glanced sideways. Her mop of red curls was clear of twigs and underbrush. *Perhaps it had been my imagination?*

Along with several other women renowned for their cleaning abilities, we attacked the vats. Entering each vat was a tricky affair. Women paired off in twos. A stepladder leaned against the exterior, which one woman climbed. Her partner raised a second ladder, which the woman at the top then lowered into the vat's belly. That way, the pair descended and standing back to back, scrubbed every inch of the insides of the wood walls. I hated being on the inside of the vat. Despite its yawning mouth and four-metre depth, I felt entrapped and worse, the residual fumes gave me a headache.

After a good scrubbing and thorough rinsing, the plughole was stoppered and the vat filled to the brim with water. As the wood absorbed the water and expanded, the water level dropped. When it stopped dropping, the plug was removed, the water washed away, and the vat was ready to receive the harvest.

Donkeys pulled the laden carts into the barn and the women, standing barefoot on the pile, shovelled the grapes into the vats. When they were almost full, they turned the giant screw, forcing the metal plate downward, crushing the fruit.

The warmth of the autumn day started the natural fermentation process. Several times a day for the next three days or until bubbles appeared on the surface, the mass of crushed fruit got a good stir with a long-handled wood paddle.

———————— ◆ ————————

Nepitella was already in bed asleep by the time Dino delivered the boys home. Exhausted, they staggered into the villa, stinking of sweat, dust and *pomace:* being grape juice containing skins, seeds and fruit stems. Their faces, hands and clothes were uniformly stained the colour of dried blood.

'Shower,' I called to them. 'I'll be up in a minute.'

I turned towards Dino. 'Did they eat?'

Dino's teeth flashed white from behind his grape-stained skin. 'Like young lions.'

'What happened to the outsider?' I asked.

Dino scratched his head and looked blank.

'You know. Rubino's funeral. The man in the brown jacket who insulted my daughter.'

'Long gone. Did not even bother to collect his belongings. Left. Just like that. Poof.' Dino snapped his fingers in the air. 'But you can ask Rossi. Mattia Rossi is his favourite nephew.'

A bolt of lightning might as well have struck me, as the last piece of the puzzle slotted into place.

'By the way, the boys worked well. Will they return tomorrow?'

'Yes.' My voice cracked. 'I'll drop them off after school. Goodnight.'

Dino doffed his cap, sprang up onto the cart, flicked the reins and left.

I returned to the kitchen, locked the door and headed upstairs. I wanted to review and tweak my plan of action, now that the puzzle was complete.

I passed Nepitella's bedroom and entered Max's. Through the bathroom door, I heard him turn off the shower. I folded down his bedcovers and plumped up the pillows. Dressed in his pyjamas, he stepped into the bedroom, followed by a cloud of steam.

'Into bed.'

He slipped in, and I pulled the cover up under his chin. 'Did you have a good day?'

'Yes. Very. I picked a lot of grapes.'

'So I hear. What are you planning to do with all the money you'll earn?'

Max's eyelids fluttered. 'Save it.'

'Oh.'

'I want to make Villa Angeli's winery the best in Tuscany.'

'Good thinking.'

'And...'

'And what?'

Max's upper and lower dark lashes merged. 'Take care of you for-ever.'

I leaned over and planted a goodnight kiss on his forehead. He sighed and fell asleep.

Watching his face relax my thoughts turned to his mother, Letizia. Max had inherited the sweet side of her disposition and so far, thank goodness, I recognised nothing of Di Napoli's dark underbelly in him. *But you're going to have to toughen up.* I turned off the lamp and headed to the master bedchamber.

Asleep, Timo sprawled fully dressed face up on the bed. I removed his boots and drew the bedcover over him. The mixed smell of pomace and sweat was so strong I could not bring myself to kiss my own son. *Was it the smell, or him?* I did not venture any further along that thought.

Walking back down the corridor, I paused, eased Nepitella's door open and entered. Revealed by the corridor's light spilling into the room, her slight form showed under the covers. I walked closer and reached out to draw back the covers from her face. I tugged the sheet. A pillow, placed lengthwise, lay where her body should have been.

My hidden fears, like the coils of giant snakes waking, stirred. *Ne-pitella! Where are you?*

I pulled on my coat, descended the stairs, exited the kitchen, locked the door and pocketed the key. No need for a lamp. The full moon shone brightly. I slipped under the archway and headed down the rutted track.

My footsteps cracked and crunched through the thin crust of night-cold earth. Instinctively I tried to reduce the weight of my footfalls. In the distance, an owl's hoots, like an undulating ribbon, floated in the air. The track entered the olive grove. Moonlight beams shone through the branches with olives dripping like black polished pearls. My breath, in the cool night air, formed opaque puffs. The peace and grace of the ancient grove at night was lost on me. My heart hammered, and I struggled to breathe.

A rustle in the undergrowth brought me to a sudden halt, every fibre in my body alert, poised to flee. I looked down. Nothing but an *istrice toscano,* on its nightly roam in search of roots and tubers, and also known for its notorious appetite for grapes, crossed the track. *Silly porcupine. The grapes are on the other side of the valley.* I walked on.

The distant howl of a leader-wolf resonated through the cold night air. *Nepitella?*

Maria's voice entered my head. *She's fine. Go home.* I needed no urging. Facing the grove dappled in moonlight was one thing, but I had no wish to confront a wolf pack. To the rising sound of answering howls, I turned on my heel and hurried home.

When I passed down the corridor, I opened Nepitella's door. The corridor's pool of light showed Nepitella asleep in her bed – her red corkscrew-curly hair fanned across the pillow. She was peaceful, dainty as always, her hair clear of twigs and leaves.

As I drifted off, a hazy thought wafted through my exhausted mind. *How did Nepitella get back in with the kitchen door locked?* Then the thought dissolved as I fell into sleep.

———— ◆ ————

Timo stood in the middle of the kitchen with his hands on his hips, his chin jutting out. 'But why do I have to shower if I am only going to get dirty again?'

I released a controlled sigh. 'Because you stink and have to be clean to go to school. So, go back upstairs, shower, dress in clean clothes and come down for breakfast.'

'But the other kids don't shower every day.'

'Do I have to remind you: *you are* not other kids.'

By the change in his posture, I could see my words had struck home. Timo turned and raced back upstairs.

Nepitella and Max sat mute, drinking their warm milk and eating their biscuits.

'Did you sleep well, Max? Are you rested?'

'Yes. I am looking forward to picking grapes again this afternoon.'

'Good. I'm pleased to hear that. And what about you, Nepitella?' Not trusting myself, I turned my back to her and busied myself at the counter.

'I slept very well.' Her voice was scratchy.

I spun around. 'Are you ill?' I felt her brow.

She touched her throat gingerly. 'It tickles.'

The sound of howling entered my head. All sympathy vanished. *That's what happens when you socialise with wolves.* 'Here, put some honey in your milk.' I placed the jar and a teaspoon on the table. 'That should help.'

'Thank you.' Nepitella added a teaspoon of honey to her bowl of milk.

Good Lord! What on earth? Nepitella had several bald patches on her skull, which she'd tried to cover by arranging her hair in a new style. I bit my lip, trusting that one day the reason would be revealed.

'And what about you, Zeeya?'

'What about me?'

'Did you sleep well?'

I turned back to face the counter. 'Yes.' I didn't bother to cross my fingers. It was an insignificant, tiny drop of a lie, in an ocean of mistruths.

The routine of the previous day followed: school, joining the grape harvest at Villa Angeli, and Nepitella and I returning home before the boys. But that night I patrolled the corridor and entered Nepitella's room hourly. Before daybreak, the thought struck me. *Stupid. Stupid. Stupid. Of course, she did not go roaming. Full moon had passed.*

I fell into bed to sleep for an hour, grateful in the knowledge that I wouldn't need to worry about her for another month.

34

The fermenting grape juice stopped bubbling after three days. The seeds and other heavy sediments layered the bottom of the vat, the juice formed the middle layer, and the stems and skins formed the cap. Sandwiched, the liquid would turn into wine with potency and body before being strained and poured into smaller oak barrels.

On the tenth day, each barrel was filled to the neck and sealed, ensuring no air was present thus preventing the liquid from turning to vinegar. Once stoppered, the men rolled the barrels to the darkest, coolest part of the barn.

The last barrel in place, the valley workers stopped off at church before heading home. They lit candles, clasped their hands and prayed with fervour, the way God intended, for the wine to mature the way it ought. They then returned to their homes for a much-needed rest. The valley workers knew the process well. While the wine was ageing, the olive harvest would begin. After the oil was pressed and stored in barrels, wine and oil were shipped to America. After that, they would expect payment for all their work and a share of the profits. But I still had no idea of how or to whom I would sell the wine or oil. *Damn you, Iacopo! Damn you, HA MER E KA NEE!* It was time to speak to Maria. And Rubino and Anna.

Dinner was over, and Maria had begun to clear the table.

'Children, brush your teeth, put on your pyjamas and get into bed. I'll be up in a minute.'

Timo was about to protest, but I silenced him with a direct hand gesture. Contorting his face, he followed Nepitella and Max.

'Maria, leave the clearing. I'll do it. But don't go. We need to talk.'

She squinted, and likely through the crosshairs of her turned-in eyes, tracked Nepitella disappearing up the stairs. I shook my head, indicating it had nothing to do with Nepitella.

Once the children were settled in bed, I returned to the kitchen. Maria was dozing, her head nodding. In profile, her hooked nose looked more pronounced than ever. The bangles hummed. She jolted awake and stared at me like an eagle on the hunt.

I sensed Rubino's calming, then Anna's ebullient, ethereal presence. For the first time in years, the four of us sat around the table. Taking a deep breath, I started with Iacopo's telegram cancelling wine and oil orders. This Maria already knew, but Rubino and Anna did not. 'So now we are midway between the two harvests with no buyers. In another two weeks, valley workers will be wondering why we aren't shipping. Christmas will soon be upon us with no payouts.'

Anna spoke first. *Write to Di Napoli. He's an experienced salesman and will know how to sell both wine and oil.*

As fast as a snap of the fingers, I wanted to shout, No! but in deference to her and the fact that Di Napoli was her nephew, I said, 'Good idea.'

Maria inclined her head and turned her attention to me. 'Anything else you want to discuss?'

The boulder lodged in my heart got heavier. I proceeded to tell them of the theft of Rubino's money, my inheritance. After their collective shocked intakes of breath, the silence in the kitchen was deafening. Anna tapped her temples and Rubino's eyebrows hid under his cap.

Again Anna spoke first. *Go to Mayor Santo Rossi. You'll have to exert pressure on him to crack and tell you what's happened to the money.*

Rubino shifted in his chair. *More like offer him something he really wants in return for his help.*

I'd known all along I would have to go to Rossi, but reluctance and disgust held me back. It was clear: if I wanted my money back, I'd have to face my fears.

———————— ◆ ————————

The church bell chimed the twelfth toll, indicating midday. In a few minutes, the town hall would empty and reopen three hours later. I knocked and entered Santo Rossi's smoke-choked office. His eyes grew larger.

'Hortensia! What a pleasant surprise.'

I wore a pair of heeled slingbacks, an on-the-knee, emerald green, crossover skirt, and matching three-quarter-sleeved jacket that ended where my slim hips started. The green contrasted well with my dyed red hair and glossed pink lips. Though what Rossi could see of it, I did not know. The light in his office was dark but for the single lamp that pooled a circle of light on the desk. I turned to shut the door behind me, and, under the cover of pretending my clutch bag had slipped, I turned the key and locked the door.

Rossi left his seat and pulled up a chair for me. 'Please, sit.' Still standing close to me he stepped back, rested his buttocks against the edge of the desk and folded his arms.

I placed my bag and the basket on the vacant chair and sat perched on the edge of the chair with my knees and ankles touching. I made no attempt to close the flap of my skirt, which fell open, revealing a stocking-clad thigh. Removing my black gloves, I eased out one finger at a time and placed the pair on his desk. My varnished nails matched my lip gloss.

Rossi tore his gaze from my exposed thigh to the basket. 'Is there something in there for me?'

'For us, actually.' *Did Rossi's ears wiggle?*

'Are you here because of my second…' He consulted the desk calendar. 'Four-months-and-thirteen-days-old, proposal?'

For the first time I understood the phrase *La speranza eterna*, as a profound look of hope flushed Rossi's face.

'It depends,' I said. 'But–'

Under his jacket, Rossi's chest expanded. 'Oh, my dear, I am hon-our–'

I interrupted him. 'But first, a delicate matter needs to be dis-cussed.'

Rossi's chest deflated, yet he kept one frog eye on the basket and the other on my face. 'Go on.'

'Mayor–'

'Please, call me Santo. Or, *caro* Santo, if you like.'

'Is that what you would like?'

He flashed me an attempt at a cute toddler's smile when presented with a much-wanted piece of candy.

You look ridiculous. 'Dear Santo, a terrible thing has happened.'

Not a muscle twitched in his face. 'Terrible enough to have already gone to the police?'

It was an unwritten code of honour and pride in our valley to take matters into our own hands and resolve disputes without seeking the assistance of the police. I shook my head. 'I'm sure we can resolve this.'

'We?'

Surely his eyes can't get any bigger.

Both the basket and my exposed thigh forgotten, he asked, 'What has this got to do with me?'

'It involves one of your close family members.'

'It does?'

'Yes.'

'Who?'

'Your nephew, Mattia Rossi.'

Santo Rossi's eyelids lowered halfway. A red line encircled his white collar and then crept up his neck. 'How do you know it's Mattia?'

'I caught him.' The thought of crossing my fingers for the use of the word 'caught' rather than the correct phrase, 'I imagined I saw him', flashed through my mind. But adding this tiny deception to my ocean of untruths would hardly make a difference.

A muscle in Rossi's lower jaw twitched. 'You caught him?'

What the hell. 'Yes.'

'What was he doing?'

'Trespassing. Spying on me and my family. Hiding in the mill.'

'Oh, my dear. I am so sorry.'

'So am I. Because I have been considering your marriage proposal. But when this happened, it upset me enough to change my mind.'

Rossi's eyes bulged. He clasped his hands begging forgiveness. 'I shall speak to him.'

It was my turn to receive a visit from 'eternal hope'. I reined in my voice to prevent the words from tumbling out, and asked as lightly as possible, 'Mattia's still here?'

'Yes. No. Actually, I don't know. I've not seen him.'

I adjusted my position on the edge of the seat. My skirt flapped open wider, revealing the floral pattern on the tops of my stockings, held up by garters.

Rossi fell to his knees, and his gaze shifted downward.

I cooed sweetly, '*Caro* Santo, don't lie. Tell me the truth.'

'It…it is the truth. I…I've not seen him these last two weeks.'

As Rossi's stuttered, the only hope of finding my money died. *Plan B.* I shifted about some more. 'You must find him. He needs to be punished.'

Rossi's voice cracked. 'Punished?'

'Yes. Just like you. You've been a naughty boy, too, haven't you?' Whether his head hung in shame or he was fascinated with my thighs, I did not care. His head fell forward, inching closer. I wriggled and thought how grateful I was for the dim light. 'You did send him to spy on me, didn't you?' Rossi groaned. I could only see the top of his bald head. I sneaked my hand under the cloth covering the basket and removed the long birch whip coiled on the inside. Released, it sprang erect with a snap. 'Why?'

'Be…because I was jealous. I wanted to know who the photographer was. What he was doing with you.'

My palm closed over the handle. I was alarmed at how comfortable and snug it fit and then felt a surge of grateful relief; for as long as I held the whip I was in control. Buried memories flashed through my head,

instantly releasing the smell of pomade, chocolate and Di Napoli's sweat.
'What did you think we were doing?'

'Things.'

I lowered my voice. 'What things?'

'Naughty things.'

'Naughty things you want to do with me?'

'Yes.' He groaned. 'Forgive me.'

You'll be screaming for mercy by the time I'm through with you. My
grip on the handle tightened. I brought the birch whip down hard over
Rossi's trousered buttocks.

He cried out in genuine surprise.

I brought the whip down again. This time he cried out in pain. But
it was not painful enough. '*Caro* Santo, drop your trousers.'

While Rossi eagerly, hastily fumbled with his belt, I slipped off my
shoes, placed the my soles of my feet against the waistband of his trousers
and pushed down. The moment his trousers and underpants pooled
around his knees, I lifted my arm high and brought the whip down upon
his fleshy buttocks. He bit down onto one fist muffling his screech of pain.

My mother's voice entered my head. *Are you sure you locked the
door?*

Yes. Go away.

Okay. Okay. I'm going. Just asking.

'Dear Santo. Tell me the truth now. Are you sure you sent Mattia
only to spy on me?' From my position, I could see Rossi's buttocks had
flamed red. The saggy folds of lumpy flesh quivered.

'Yes, I'm sure.'

I brought the whip down again. 'How sure?'

Whether he grunted with pleasure or pain, I did not know.

'Very, very sure?' The whip whistled through the air again.

'Yes.' Rossi screeched. 'I'm very, very, very sure.'

This time, his buttocks quaked. And from under his jacket, I could
see his back and arms vibrate, too. *Good.* 'Tell you what I think, *caro* Santo.
I think you sent Mattia to steal from me.'

'Steal? Steal what?'

'You sent him to steal my money.' I raised my arm again.

'Aieeee… Money? What money?' From his kneeling position, Rossi eased his bleeding buttocks to rest on his calves. His face coloured puce, bulging eyes streamed wet, and mouth dribbled saliva.

'I'm going to ask you once more. Did you send Mattia to steal my money?'

'On my life, I did not.'

The whip whistled through the air. Once. Twice. Thrice.

'*Christ!* I'll hunt him down and get your money back.'

That's what I've been waiting to hear. 'You've got one week. If it's not returned, I'm going to the police. And just in case you don't find him in time, let me tell you how much you are to refund me.'

I gave him my estimation of the amount. Though he blanched, he agreed. I could not bear to look at his face any longer and needed to change his focus from my face back to my crotch. I reclined, raised and hooked each thigh over an armrest.

With a subdued howl of joy, he pitched face forward into my pantyless crotch. I angled the whip, and for good measure, and with all my muster, I brought it down for each word I sang out, 'You…very…very…naughty…boy.'

Even in the gloomy light, I could see Rossi's buttocks were as latticed as the lead in the church windows.

———————— ◆ ————————

Before the week was up, true to his word, and likely when his buttocks could stand the jolting of his rattling van, Mayor Santo Rossi paid me a visit. The children were at school, and Maria was down in the village.

Out in the open, we greeted each other formally. There was no telling who would be watching. But once inside the kitchen, Mayor Santo Rossi became meek and began to paw me. I knew what he wanted, but I would have to see his money first. There would have to be a vast amount of it.

He heaved a large leather bag up onto the kitchen table. 'As promised.'

I peered into the bag. There were wads and wads of *lire* rolled into bundles, held in place with rubber bands. Why was I surprised and disappointed when I saw no coins? I was still not sure whether Rossi had told me the truth, but it stood to reason that the paper money he had brought was not Rubino's, so there was no reason for any coins to be present. My head kicked in. 'This is not all of it.'

'You'll get the balance once we are married.'

'Who said anything about *marriage?*'

'You did.'

'I most certainly did not.'

'You most certainly did. You said you had reconsidered your decision.'

'Yes, but then the theft happened, courtesy of you sending your nephew to spy on me.'

'Ah. But here, your money is restored and thus reverts your decision to now accepting my marriage proposal.' Rossi reached for the bag and made as if to leave. 'But then again…'

My mother's voice entered my head. *Don't fall for it. He's playing with you. He wants you more than you'll ever need him.*

This time I heeded my mother's advice. I surprised Rossi by fixing one of his ears between my thumb and forefinger. 'Bring the bag. Follow me.'

Rossi did as he was told, whimpering in pain and yowling with delight. As we passed the stove, I reached for the long wooden spoon. I beat him for each step we climbed. Panting, Rossi paused on the landing, likely hopeful that any one of the bedroom doors would magically spring open. I let go of his ear and grabbed the other, dragged him up the next flight and pulled him into the furthermost bedroom that Gina and Silvia had recently spring-cleaned. I locked the door, removed my housedress and stood clad only in cheap, bright red underwear, fishnet stockings and a pair of black heels.

Rossi paled to the point where I thought he might faint. I tossed a Venetian carnival mask at him. 'Put it on. Undress. *Pronto!'* From the moment I affixed my mask, my heart slipped into its calcareous shell, and my head changed from ordinary to dominant; a necessity if I was to make Mayor Santo Rossi's dreams come true. I swapped the wooden spoon for the leather whip, and the sound of clinking metal chains, collar and cuffs filled the room.

In the back of my mind, I heard Di Napoli's rich chuckle.

◆

On Friday night, when I began to prepare dinner, a strange sound vibrated through the thick walls.

I watched the boys' faces as they tried to make out what it was.

'I know, I know, it's a *car*.' Timo flung open the kitchen door and streaked into the courtyard, Max and Nepitella following behind.

Andreas pulled up in a red car. My hands clapped over my mouth. The way the boys were running around whooping and hollering, they too were thrilled. For once, even Nepitella looked impressed.

Andreas slipped out of the vehicle, elegant and gorgeous. '*Buona sera a tutti.*'

The boys neither returned the greeting nor glanced at him; their gazes were glued to the vehicle.

'Is it ours?' Timo's voice rang with excitement.

'It is,' Andreas said.

'What is it? Wait. I know. I know,' Timo said. He covered the red, blue and white emblem on the bonnet with his hand. 'Don't tell me. It's a Rivo... Rivo–'

'A Rivolta GT300!' Max shouted.

Timo spun around and punched Max. 'I said, don't tell.'

Max returned the punch. In a matter of moments they were rolling about, flattening the vegetables in the kitchen garden.

'Whoa.' Andreas bent down to separate the boys. A flying fist punched him in the face. 'Ouch. *Basta!*' He held a hand to his nose. A trickle of red ran over his lips.

I picked up a pail of water standing beside the well and dashed its contents into the boys' faces. They coughed and spluttered, but it brought them to a halt.

Stored frustration caused me to yell so, my throat and ears hurt. 'Have you both gone mad?' Perhaps it was due to my recent interaction with Santo Rossi – I latched onto an ear each. Holding my arms straight out at my sides, I kept them apart until they calmed, or more likely when their burning ears brought them to their senses.

'That's it. I've had enough.' I probably yanked too hard on their ears as I had no trouble getting them to follow me into the kitchen. 'Timo, go to that far corner. Sit and don't move. Max, you to the other corner.'

Both boys had begun to shiver, their wet clothes sticking to them.

Timo opened his mouth, about to remonstrate.

I stuck my face in his and growled, 'Not a word. Do you hear me? Not a word. Stay in your corner and don't move.'

Nepitella and Andreas stood like statues. Andreas likely even forgot about his bleeding nose.

My mother's voice entered my head. *It's about time.*

The flames leaped and Maria entered. 'I thought you could do with some help.' She began to pat her black cloak.

'Andreas, let's see to you first.' I led him through my former living room and bedroom to the small bathroom.

He submitted to my cleaning and anointing his swollen nose and ready-formed bruises with squeaks and squawks. 'What's up, Hortensia? Ouch. Be careful. You're on edge.'

'Believe me, you don't want to know.'

'Of course I do. I'm your brother, remember?'

'I'll tell you later.' *Sorry, Andreas, you'll never know. Not even the half of it.* 'But right now I think we could both do with a glass of wine.'

'Hortensia?'

'Yes?' I lightly smeared ointment over the broken skin on his face.

Andreas jerked his head away. '*Yikes!* That stings.'

I blew softly knowing it would cool the burn.

'Ah. That's better. Hortensia, the car is second-hand but in really good condition. The owner was desperate for cash immediately. So, I got it for a fabulous price.'

'That's wonderful. Thank you.' Good price or not, I still had no means to pay for it. But now was not the time to discuss that.

I left Andreas to re-inspect his injuries in the bathroom mirror and entered the kitchen.

Maria had just finished attending to Timo and Max, assisted by Nepitella. 'Good job,' I said.

The corners of Nepitella's mouth turned up.

Although I kept my voice low, it rang with determination. 'Come here, the two of you.' I stood in the centre of the kitchen. 'Timo, don't drag your feet. Hop to it. Both of you.'

Andreas entered.

'Apologise to Andreas.'

'Sorry, Uncle Andreas,' they mumbled.

'Now apologise to each other and shake hands like gentlemen.'

Max said sorry and stuck out his hand first. It took Timo a second longer than I would have liked, but I let it go. 'Off to your bedrooms. Shower, to bed and lights out.'

Timo's mouth opened. 'What about dinner? I'm starving.'

I dug deep to maintain my new-found determination. 'No dinner for either of you. Let this be a lesson on how to behave.'

Everyone's jaws, including Maria's, dropped. My mother's voice entered my head again. *You can't send them to bed with no dinner!*

Watch me.

A dawning light appeared on the boys' faces, especially Timo's. Without a word they exited the kitchen, walked side by side through the dining room, and I watched their progress up the stairs. After they both closed their bedrooms, I turned to find Andreas offering me a glass of wine. Maria already had one in her hand, and Nepitella had a watered-down version.

'*Salute*,' we chimed and clinked glasses.

'To new beginnings.' I crossed my fingers and took a long swallow. 'Come on. I'm dying to inspect our car. Andreas, lead the way.'

After we had taken turns sitting in the plush seats, deeply inhaled the enticing smell of the leather several times over, oohed and aahed at the controls, the steering wheel, flicked the lights on and off, wound the windows up and down, and blew the hooter several times, which I knew would make the boys burn with envy – I was convinced I would never master driving. Empty glasses in hand, we watched Andreas pull the vehicle into the mill and park alongside the cart.

The mailbag! I found it caught under the cart bench cushions, tucked it under my arm and followed the others back into the kitchen. It was way past our usual dinnertime and I was starving. Guilt pierced me. *How did the boys feel?*

Rubino's voice entered my head. *Stay strong.*

I laid the mailbag to one side, and after years of practice set about preparing dinner as quickly as possible.

35

Immersed in deep sleep, I heard a voice calling me, and sensed being touched. Having had far too much wine the night before, my brain was befuddled, and I had no desire to face the headache that had already begun to throb. The voice and touch became more insistent. With reluctance, I dragged myself towards the surface of consciousness.

'Zeeya.' Nepitella shook my shoulder.

I lifted the covers in the hope she'd slip in beside me and allow me to sink back into oblivion.

'Come.' Her voice rang with urgency. 'You must come.'

'What is it?'

But she had already left my room. Groaning, I sat up, slipped my feet into slippers, fumbled my way into a dressing gown and stood swaying. *I'm never going to drink again.* I stumbled into the corridor. Nepitella stood poised at Max's bedroom door, her little face creased with worry. Upon seeing me, she disappeared into his room.

I tied the belt of my gown and, despite the roaring in my head, hurried after her.

I felt the heat from Max's fevered body before I got to the bed. His long dark eyelashes fanned out against his chalk-white skin that bore a smattering of bright-red spots. His breath was rapid, and his pulse throbbed visibly to one side of his throat.

I recognised the chickenpox immediately. *But, dear God, why is he burning up with this fever?* Then the thought struck me. *It's my fault. I should never have left him in the kitchen soaking wet. This is my doing. Timo!* Forgetting the thump in my head, I dashed to the master bedchamber. An effervescent wave of spine-tingling relief flooded through me. My son lay curled, sleeping peacefully and showing no signs of illness or fever. I returned to Max. Nepitella hovered over him like a dragonfly.

'Nepitella, take a torch. Go into the kitchen garden–'

'I don't need a torch. I can see in the dark.'

I did not let her answer distract me. 'Heat a pot of water. Pick a handful of nepitella.'

'Shall I make tisane?'

'Do you know how?'

'Maria taught me.'

'Okay. Good girl.'

'Shall I bring the apple vinegar, too?'

The mention of vinegar jolted my memory. Mixed with water, apple vinegar was an old remedy used to bring down a fever. 'Yes.'

Nepitella disappeared, and I went in search of rags. She returned with a bowl and the bottle of vinegar.

'Tisane steeping?' I asked.

She nodded.

I filled the bowl with cold water, added vinegar, and dunked the cloths into the mixture. Then I wrapped a cloth around each wrist and placed one over Max's forehead. I used another to dab his neck and chest. In less than a minute, the cloths had dried, and I refreshed them. The fever had de-hydrated Max. His skin felt crisp to the touch, and his lips were cracked. I wanted to believe it was my imagination, but with each cooling cloth I applied more spots appeared.

Timo stood in the doorway. 'What's going on?' As his eyes lost the last vestiges of sleepiness his face registered shock at the sight of Max.

'Timo, get dressed. Go and wake Andreas. Show him the way to Dr Baldi and bring him back with you. Don't delay.'

'*I* can go in the car with Andreas?'

'Yes.'

Without another word, Timo went off to do my bidding. A few minutes later, I heard the sound of the car's engine roar into life and the courtyard gravel crunch beneath its wheels.

'Maria will be here any minute.' Nepitella's voice was airy-light.

I did not bother to ask how she knew. She and Maria shared perceptive abilities. No sooner had I thought this that the bangles tinkled, and Maria appeared. She approached Max and began to pat her billowing cloak's pockets. Nepitella stood with her hands cupped, waiting for whatever Maria would place in them. They were the epitome of the wise woman and her apprentice.

Max began to shake and then convulse. Maria slipped a metal spoon, bowl side down, into his mouth to prevent him from swallowing his tongue. He moaned and cried and, had it not been for Nepitella pressing down his body, I'm sure he would have flipped off the bed. How Nepitella found the strength was something I also did not want to consider.

'Hortensia,' Maria said, 'this is bad.'

The scream that had been building in my belly hurtled towards my throat. But the stare from Maria's turned-in eyes held me fast until I calmed, and the scream died.

'Check the address on the last letter Di Napoli sent Max.' she said. 'He must come.'

I turned to the writing desk and pulled open the drawer in which Max kept his father's letters. The top letter, the most recent, reflected the hotel's name and address in Rome where Di Napoli was staying.

'Hortensia.' Maria lowered her voice. 'Go to Mayor Santo Rossi and use his new phone to call Di Napoli. While there, get Rossi to apply for the telephone line to this villa.'

Convulsions over, Max lay like a rag doll. Not a flicker of life crossed his face.

Dawn peaked through the shutters. The car's engine sounded again and came to a sharp stop. The front door, rarely used because it was so heavy, opened and banged closed, and footsteps thudded up the staircase.

385

Dr Baldi wore his dressing gown over his pyjamas, and his hair stood up in a crest much like the migratory African hoopoes who graced our valley from spring to late summer.

Timo placed Dr Baldi's black leather medicine bag on the table and flicked the catch. It was something Dr Baldi promised all children they could do if they took their medication and got better. The bag snapped open and transformed into a miniature apothecary with pop-out compartments holding all manner of labelled crystal bottles and small leather boxes. I motioned to Andreas not to come beyond the doorway.

'Is it catching?' His voice quavered in fear.

Dr Baldi glanced up at Andreas. 'It usually isn't a concern, but sometimes…'

Andreas paled, heightening the colour of his nose that had been struck by the boys during the crossfire of last night's traded blows.

'Andreas, we need to do another car trip, please, as soon as I change.'

His relief at leaving the sickroom was palpable. He headed downstairs with the leaping spring of a hare on the run.

I picked up Di Napoli's last letter, and though I walked away from Max, I left most of my heart with him. In minutes, I was dressed and sitting in the car alongside Andreas. If he noticed what I was wearing, and I am sure he did, he did not comment.

'Where to?'

'Mayor Santo Rossi's house.'

Andreas's mouth hardened. I was grateful he did not press me with questions. Other than my directions, we remained silent throughout the journey.

'Pull up here, please.' I exited the car when it stopped.

From the corner of my eye, I saw the neighbours' curtains twitch. Wary of my heeled, slingbacked shoes, I walked with care to Rossi's front door and pressed the buzzer.

A window on the first floor cranked open, sounding much like the clank of a boat's anchor chain. '*Chi è?*' Rossi called.

'Hortensia d'Ambrosia.' From above, I heard him gasp. Rossi cranked the window shut and a minute later, pulled back the front door's night bolts.

Rossi peered over my shoulder, seemingly mesmerised. *Was it because of the red car or Andreas in the driving seat?*

'Come in.'

I stepped in.

He shut the door. 'What can I do for you?'

My words came tumbling out in a rush during which Rossi's gaze upon me never waived. 'I must ask that we go directly to your office to call Max's father. Please.'

The direction of his gaze began to slide up, and then down, the length of my body. 'Of course. But first, tell me, Hortensia, do you have something for me?'

My skin crawled, and my feet instinctively turned towards the door ready to flee. I held out my empty hands. 'As you can see I was in a rush.'

'I meant your acceptance of my marriage proposal.'

I had not bothered replying to his last letter wherein he'd begged me to re-consider. There are added benefits of being the wife of a mayor and we share a common interest in the delights of...' his postscript read. I had no need to fill in what he'd left out. I shook my head.

'I am desolate. But I see you are wearing heels. Are they my consolation prize? Or, do you have a surprise for me? Under that skirt, for instance?'

My throat filled with grit. From the croaking sound it made, *I* had turned into a frog.

'Was that a yes? Come, let me see.' Rossi placed one arm around my waist and pulled me up against him. He fumbled his other hand between the crossover fabric of my skirt. Like a homing pigeon, his fingers wormed their way beneath the elastic thread in one of my panty leg holes.

'Stand with your feet apart,' he whispered and poked his slimy tongue into my ear. He slid his index finger between the folds of my flesh. 'Ah, good. You're ready for me.' He removed his finger, sniffed it delicately like a dog sniffing a bitch in heat. Then he stuck his finger in his mouth and sucked. He removed his finger from his mouth to the sound of a pop. 'Delectable.'

Di Napoli's voice instructing me years ago entered my head. *Take control. Be in charge.*

My heart and head emerged from their hiding places. There was too much at stake for me to become squeamish now. I snapped my heels together and gave Rossi a hefty push. I spied the container of walking sticks near the door and selected one best used in the mountains. It had an iron point at the end. I grabbed it by the handle and poked Rossi with it. His bulging eyes lit up like the car's headlights.

'Dress.' I gave him another sharp jab, causing him to yelp half in pain and half in delight.

Halfway up the stairs, Rossi turned to face me. 'Refusing my offer will cost you.'

My mother's voice entered my head. *Trade hard.*

'In exchange for withdrawing your proposal of marriage, now and forever, I'll donate the car to the town hall to be used by the incumbent mayor.'

Rossi stood still. It took him a moment to figure that if I was at liberty to donate the car, it must be mine. He gave his finger another sniff and quick suck. And, just as I knew he would, he said, 'You're right. I can have you any time. I don't have to marry you for it. So the car it'll be.'

Hiding my relief, I threw down the walking stick, opened his front door and walked out.

By now Rossi's neighbours had recognised Andreas behind the wheel. Curiosity forced them to set aside their disapproval of him. The men, still wearing their pyjamas – never would they allow their wives or daughters to be seen in their nightwear – gathered around the car. Upon seeing me, their grunts, signifying their approval of the car, stopped and changed to sympathetic tongue clicks and speedy recovery wishes for Max.

Andreas had clearly informed them, and rightfully so, of the reason for this unprecedented early morning visit, rousing Mayor Santo Rossi from his bed.

But all I could think of was what had happened in the short space of time I had spent in Rossi's house. I had finally negotiated an escape from a fate worse than death, and the image of those haunting, white, lily bridal bouquets, vanished.

Ten minutes later, Rossi, with a smug look on his jowled face, walked towards the car. He nodded left and right, greeting each neighbour by name and enquired after their health. He even asked one if the bunion on his left foot had increased its size overnight. This caused guffawing all round. It was impressive. He oozed his way around his neighbours with intimate familiarity.

Rossi waved goodbye and without hesitation, slipped into the front seat. After a rudimentary salutation, he bombarded Andreas with questions about the vehicle on the short journey to the town hall.

In the rear-view mirror, Andreas caught the look on my face and understood immediately that the ownership of the car, for whatever reason, had changed.

I was worried about speaking to Di Napoli on the telephone. Though it would be a first, getting back home as fast as possible was more important. I imagined myself covering Max's sweet, dear face, red spots and all, with kisses. He would pretend to hate them, screw up his face and make argh sounds. But I knew Max secretly loved being cuddled and made a fuss of, and after a perfunctory protest, he would yield.

And, at last, I'd be able to take a long, cleansing shower.

———— ◆ ————

Rossi and I stood in front of the small door cut into one of the town hall's massive, ancient-arched doors.

With a key attached to a large ring, chock-full of other keys, he unlocked the door. Perhaps, the rumour was true after all. Rossi may indeed have a key to everyone's house, especially the houses of widows.

The building was deserted and deathly still. In another hour, it would open to the public. He re-locked the door behind him. We were entirely alone.

'Walk ahead of me,' Rossi said. 'I want to see your hips sway in those heels.'

My jaw tightened.

'Not enough,' he growled and gave my behind a wallop.

I swung around, spat and raked his face with my fingernails. Stark streaks sprang up, dotted with blood.

'You bitch!' he cried. 'Never the face. Never the face.' He pressed his handkerchief to his cheek. When he removed it and saw it marked with red, his face changed again. This time, to pure ecstasy. Rossi liked to see blood.

We entered his cigarette-stinking office. I scanned the room and my gaze fell on the telephone taking pride of place on his desk. I unfolded Di Napoli's letter to Max.

'Read the number,' Rossi barked, no different from the way he spoke to the waiting widows. Now that it was all business, his demeanour changed, the face-scratching instantly forgotten.

It was very much the same way Di Napoli had behaved after he'd gotten what he wanted from me. The only difference was Di Napoli always made sure to pleasure me first. Rossi had no clue as to how to administer honey first before the bitter medicine.

'*Pronto*, hello,' Rossi put on his best mayoral voice. 'Signor Di Napoli, Suite 21.' He paused and responded, 'Mayor Santo Rossi, *Comune di Valle*.' He listened. 'Yes, I'll hold.'

After a while, Santo Rossi said, 'Di Napoli? Signora d'Ambrosia-il Pescatore wants to speak to you.' He thrust the phone at me.

'Hel…hello?' How I managed to utter a single word was a wonder. I felt trapped between the two men. The one next to me, I loathed with all my heart. The other at the end of a telephone line, I had once loved with the infatuation of a silly maid's heart.

'Hortensia?'

'Si.'

'Max. Something wrong?'

'Si.' I could barely whisper the word, my throat had clogged so.

'I'm leaving within the hour.'

I could not reply. Nor was it necessary. The telephone made a re-sounding click in my ear. I fumbled putting the mouthpiece back into its cradle. I wanted to cry.

My mother' voice entered my head. *This is not the time for tears. Recover yourself. You have work to do.*

Having learned my lesson, I listened to her, took a deep breath and turned to Rossi. 'You are getting too much with that car.'

'What! You can't reclaim a donation.'

I'm not. But, not even the mayor of Rome gets to drive a car like this.'

'I know.' A mixed look of glee and smugness crossed Rossi's face, then disappeared as likely another thought entered his head. Rossi's eyes half narrowed. 'Don't play games with me. What else are you after?'

'Apply to the telephone company and have our entire valley pro-vided with telephone lines. *Subito.*'

'Don't be ridiculous, Hortensia. I've only gotten mine after a four-year wait.'

'Now that the main overhead cable is installed, it's no problem to extend lines to each house.' I paused. 'Or, do you want me to tell the valley you are hell-bent on keeping them in the dark ages while the rest of world advances?'

His response was as fast as a striking serpent. 'You mean, no dif-ferent to what your father used to do?'

I was not surprised Rossi knew who my father was. But if he thought I would be embarrassed by my father's legendary gross behaviour, he was wrong. I stared Rossi down and called his bluff. 'Precisely.' My memory flew back to the first time I sat in this office with Rubino, who wisely asked the question I was about to repeat. 'I've forgotten, please remind me. When is your term of office up, Mayor?'

Rossi sat dead still in his chair. I could hear the town hall staff walking down the corridor, greeting each other. I could also hear Rossi's brain churn, but unfortunately, I could not read what was going on in there.

'Get the hell out of here, before I announce our marriage instead.'

I left his office and walked down the corridor, raising eyebrows and surprised looks. I did not care. Soon, everyone would know about Max and the call to his father. I only hoped and prayed to God Max would recover – nothing else mattered.

I hurried back to the car, once again surrounded by a crowd. This time by men and women, dressed in daywear and all of whom spoke at once. It seemed for the moment, they had forgotten Andreas was *un bucco*, a hole, the derogatory term homophobic Tuscans call homosexuals.

I exchanged greetings with the crowd. The women passed on heartfelt wishes for Max's recovery, followed by the sign of the cross. The men, in contrast, asked when Di Napoli would put in an appearance. They would take no chances. If they did not lock up their wives and daughters, they would accompany them everywhere until Di Napoli was safely out of the valley.

Andreas pulled away from the kerb and headed home.

In between changing gears and steering, and pressing the foot pedals – I again convinced myself I would never master any of it – Andreas squeezed my hand. 'I cannot tell a lie. I do want to know what's going on between you and that odious sleazeball. But I'm not asking. Only, please make sure you take care of yourself. One never gets the better of degenerates like him.'

'Thank you for not lying and not asking. And yes, I am taking care of myself.'

And everyone else. Again.

◆

Before Andreas had brought the car to a complete stop, I opened the door, kicked off the heels, raced up the stairs and entered Max's bedroom. 'How is he?'

Maria sat in a chair beside his bed. 'He's sleeping. Deeply.'

My eyebrows rose like Rubino's used to when displaying alarmed concern or alarmed surprise.

Maria gave an exaggerated sigh of resignation. 'No. Not one of my potions. Dr Baldi gave him a sleeping draught.'

Thank goodness. 'Why are his fingertips bandaged?'

'To stop him from scratching. Those sores itch something awful. He even scratches in his sleep.'

'His fever?'

'Still spiking.'

'So, he's not out of the woods yet?'

'No.'

My belly contracted but my heart and head remained steady.

Maria glanced up at me. 'Di Napoli?'

'Said he would leave within the hour. Should be here mid-afternoon.'

'Telephone?'

'Sorted. Including lines for every valley household.'

The bangles gave a low trilling applause.

Maria inclined her head. 'Good girl.'

'Where are the children?'

'Gone out to play. They'll return in time for afternoon tea.'

Okay. 'I'm off to shower.'

Maria wiggled the tip of her hooked nose. 'Good idea. You stink of Rossi.'

———— ◆ ————

Upon his arrival at the villa, Di Napoli went straight upstairs to his son. Andreas opened the back passenger door. I gulped down my surprise as Delphina emerged looking like one of those models gracing the pages of the glossy fashion magazines I subscribed to. As she eased herself out of the car, her dead-straight hair fell forward like a curtain on either side of her face and made its distinctive rattling sound. She stared about her, perhaps recalling her short time living in this villa. But when her head tilted up towards the turreted tower, my belly boiled with rage.

Get a grip, Hortensia. I walked through the kitchen and dining room and stood waiting for her in the grand, harlequin-patterned entrance hall.

As Delphina entered, I could not help but acknowledge how lovely she was. So lovely it was enough to take one's breath away unless one knew better.

Seeing me, she paused, removed her sunglasses and stared me up and down. 'You're missing your apron, Hortensia.'

'You're missing your heart.' My voice rang clear and strong.

The lights in her eyes glittered and her face cracked into a smile. 'Touché. Any chance of a cup of tea?'

'As much chance as you telling me where my signed Paternity document is.'

'Aha.' She removed her gloves, held one hand in the air and snapped her fingers. 'How did I know you would ask that question straight away?'

'Well, where is it?'

With a nonchalant air, she waved one hand in a circle. 'Closer than you think. But believe me, Hortensia, what you really should be asking is what knowledge your husband, Pietro, went away with on his last fishing voyage.'

I turned statue-still. Every nerve in my body jangled, yet I made not a sound.

'Aw. You're lost for words. How your poor little brain must be spinning. Think, Hortensia, think.'

Silence.

'Oh, dear. Brain not working? I see I'm going to have to tell you after all.'

Silence.

'Ever notice what a perfectly lovely view there is from the turret?'

Then I knew. Delphina had clearly seen Di Napoli and me under the chasteberry tree. 'You told Pietro.'

'Stopped him when he was halfway across the river. Poor man. You should have seen his face. It was a picture. Your betrayal hurt him terribly.'

A stake pierced my heart. How I managed not to crumple to the floor was a miracle.

'Oh my. You look just like he did. Mmm… I think you could do with a cup of tea, too. So, how about it?' Delphina flicked her fingers in a shooing motion. 'Off you go, into the kitchen, where you belong.'

I found my voice and almost spat, 'Get it yourself', but thought better of it. I did not want her anywhere near the kitchen. 'Five minutes in the dining room.'

I turned and, dragging my heart behind me like a dead weight, I entered the kitchen.

My mother's voice entered my head. *Now is not the time to grieve. Set it aside for later. Focus on the here and now.*

I listened to my mother.

Through the window, I saw Andreas struggling with more suitcases than I could ever have imagined. They were all the same brown colour with a gold fleur-de-lis design and ranged in size from small to overlarge.

Andreas entered the kitchen and set the middle-sized suitcase down. He wiped his brow and lowered his voice to a conspiratorial whisper. 'You didn't tell me she was a man-eating spider.'

I matched his voice. 'If I knew she was coming, I would have. Be very careful.' Right then I gave thanks Andreas was homosexual. In the next moment that premature relief shattered.

'She's already propositioned me twice, in front of her husband!' He sounded outraged. 'What a cuckold! How does he stand for it? She doesn't take no for an answer. Nor does she seem to understand that I don't fuck women.'

I dug my nails into his arm. 'Listen to me. You are leaving. Go back to Rome. Don't come back until I say. Never, ever have anything to do with her. Ever. Promise me.'

'Whoa.' Andreas's handsome face broke into a huge smile. 'I'm a big boy. I can take care of myself.'

'No. Not with her you can't. No one she sets her sights on gets away.'

Andrea grimaced. 'Okay. Okay. Message received. How do I get to the station?'

I made a snap decision. 'Nepitella and Timo will harness Long Ears. They can take you in the cart. They're old enough and know the way. Go and pack. And Andreas,' I put my hand on his arm, 'if you never take me seriously again, that's all right. But this time, you must. Promise me again.'

'I promise.'

'I'll get the children. You can catch the five o'clock train.'

I rushed to the turret and hesitated. Which colour flag? The vision of Arutro's body lying on the parapet was replaced by that of Andreas. I raised the red flag.

I had decided to put Di Napoli and Delphina in the fifth bedroom on the top floor. All the bedrooms had great views of the sea, but this room had a spectacular view up and down the coast.

But, the monster's suitcases lying at the bottom of the stairs was a sobering eye-opener. *I'm going to have to install an elevator. Tourists won't want to struggle with their luggage to the top floor. Damn. Di Napoli and that monster will have to stay in the small suite of rooms Andreas is about to vacate.*

I smiled to myself. *This is good practice. I'm thinking how a bed and breakfast hostess should!*

The children appeared, both wide-eyed and teary. Realisation knocked me on the head. *Oh, dear God, how stupid I am!* 'No. No. No. Max is not dead. He's fine. Well, not fine. But recovering.'

Palpable relief flashed across their faces.

'Here's what I need you to do.' I explained their responsibility to harness Long Ears to the cart and drive Andreas to the train station.

Their tears and funereal masks disappeared and were replaced with bright-eyed eagerness.

'I know it's further than you've ever gone, but I trust you both to be reliable. Come home directly. No stopping. Not for any reason. And don't push Long Ears. He is getting old. Easy, steady trot. Do you understand?'

Both children squealed a resounding 'Yes!' and raced off to the stable as though they had wings for feet.

Ten minutes later, I entered the stable. 'Here are some apples and water for your journey.' I checked the straps and reins. Long Ears stamped his feet.

'I'm ready.' Andreas threw his clothes bag into the back of the cart. The soft, black pouch holding his camera hung around his neck.

'Where are the car keys?'

'In the kitchen on the table.' Andreas gave me a hug and climbed aboard.

Nepitella clambered into the back of the cart and covered herself with the travel blankets. Timo picked up the reins.

'Timo, when you pass the house of the sisters, Gina and Silvia, call out and tell them I want them to come up here now.'

Timo nodded. He sat very straight, full of pride with the tasks he had been assigned.

'See you soon, Andreas. Children, remember everything that I said. Goodbye.' I crossed my hands and held them against my chest as I watched the cart leave the courtyard.

Though it was a perfect autumn Tuscan day, I did not see it. I had to relieve Maria and face Di Napoli. The monster was nowhere and the pot of tea on the tray in dining room was cooling. And then, the thought struck me: it would be wise if the valley women locked up their husbands and sons.

I stepped into the bedroom. Di Napoli and Maria were focused on Max. From his flushed face I could see his fever was spiking again.

Maria looked up. 'His temperature is not so high and there are no more convulsions.'

Thank you, God.

Di Napoli knelt at his son's bedside with his fingers interlaced and whispered. 'My son. Oh, my son.'

When Di Napoli dropped his forehead to rest upon his hands, I looked closer. There was something wrong with him. I caught Maria's eye. Her voice entered my head. *Di Napoli is dying, only he doesn't know it.*

How long does he have?

A few days, at most.

A blow from nowhere punched me in the belly. The intensity of pain and sorrow was shocking, and swiftly replaced by pure panic. *Is it catching? Will Max get it?*

Calm down, Hortensia. Max can't get any worse.

The kitchen doorbell tringed.

'That must be Gina and Silvia,' I said. 'Maria instruct them to prepare my old suite of rooms for Di Napoli and his wife.'

'No. Not for me.' Di Napoli's voice was hoarse. 'I'm staying with my son, right here. Delphina can have the room to herself.'

The bangles' tinny beat ordered me to join Maria, out of Di Napoli's earshot. Without another word, I followed and stood in the corridor.

Maria lowered her voice. 'Why your old suite?'

I matched Maria's voice. 'Because, that monster has a tonne of luggage. There is no one to haul it up two flights of stairs, and I'm certainly not. I'm thinking we are going to have to install an elevator before next summer.'

Understanding dawned on Maria's face. Her cloak billowed around her as she disappeared down the stairs.

I re-entered the bedroom and stood next to Di Napoli. 'Gennaro, get up and go to the other side of Max's bed. You need to lie down.'

He needed no persuasion. Even with my help, he rose unsteadily. *He's shrunk!* I recalled how once we matched in height, and how, at this close proximity, arousal flared through my body like a struck match. I pushed those old, silly maid's thoughts away, helped him shuffle his way around the bed and pulled back the covers, careful not to disturb Max. I helped Di Napoli out of his jacket and tie, undid his shirt collar button, knelt to ease off his shoes and stopped short. *My goodness! These are the same pointy shoes he wore all those years ago when he first arrived at Villa Angeli. And the pair Foxy pissed on to demonstrate his canine opinion of him.*

As I knelt, I saw that his shirt cuffs were frayed, and his trousers were shiny at the knees. *Why is he wearing old clothes?*

Di Napoli sensed my thoughts because he said in a voice with no hint of its former deep resonance, 'I told you. I cannot deny Delphina anything for fear of my life. I give her everything I earn from the chocolate sales, and you, everything I earn from the wine sales for taking care of my son.' He gave a low rasping cry. 'And, yet, despite my giving up all my income, and pursuit of former delights, I am dying.'

Maria, you are losing your powers. He knows.

She was quick to retort. *I told you once before, I am not always correct!*

'And to boot,' Di Napoli continued, 'it appears, my son is dying, too.'

I straightened and looked him in the eye. 'Hush. No one is dying.' In an attempt to lighten his mood, I lowered my voice. 'Off with those trousers and get into bed.'

The Di Napoli of old appeared, if only for a moment. The light in his dark-pool eyes flickered as his lips drew back in a sardonic smile. 'Had you said that to me only once, with the same passion I have always felt for you, my heart would have been yours.'

He was right. I'd never said anything remotely like that to him. But I had, I realised with shy surprise, said those very words in a playful manner to Pietro. But that was in another life, a long time ago.

Di Napoli fumbled with his belt and let his trousers fall to the floor, revealing a pair of threadbare leggings. I averted my gaze but could not help noticing that the natural state of his manhood was no larger than the size of a pea pod.

Chasteberry! Maria! This is the result of your overdosing.

Maria's voice entered my head again. *No. He's paying the price for excessive sexual activity with uncountable partners.*

I eased Di Napoli down, guided his thin legs onto the bed and pulled the cover to his chin. 'Better?'

He closed his eyes. 'Sweet Hortensia. Yes. Thank you.'

I could not help notice how father and son's fanned, lush eyelashes matched.

Maria?

Yes.

Tell Gina to prepare a large pot of bean soup. She's the better cook. And when the sisters are finished, they can go home.

Okay.

And you go home and rest.

———— ◆ ————

In no time, Di Napoli developed a fever. All afternoon I alternated placing cool cloths upon the brows of father and son and dripping nepitella tisane upon their lips. Their fevers spiked and reduced in synchronisation – perhaps, in sympathy and support of each other.

At dusk, when Nepitella and Timo ought to have been home, Max's eyelids slid open. He gave me a wan smile, turned his head and stared at his father's face in profile on the pillow alongside him.

'Is he sick, too?' Max whispered.

Torn between telling the truth or a lie, I said, 'He's very tired.'

'But then why have you been treating him the same way you have me?'

'Because he caught a fever–'

'My fever?' Panic flashed across Max's face.

'No. A fever from travelling.'

'Travelling here to visit me?'

'No. A fever from all the travelling he's done before he got here.'

'Is he going to be okay?'

'I hope so.'

'Does that mean he might not?'

'Yes.'

'Does that mean he might die?'

'We all have to die one day.'

Max remained quiet for a moment. 'Then it's best he dies here with me rather than somewhere else.'

Pain and sorrow for what Max would soon experience caused my heart to contract in sympathy. 'Yes. It would be best.'

Night replaced dusk. My ears strained to hear the sound of Long Ears' clip-clop coming into the courtyard. The smell of the slow-cooking soup wafted up the staircase and tormented my belly. Not having eaten all day I was hungry, but I did not want to leave Di Napoli. His breathing had become labored, and Max had fallen into an exhausted but tranquil sleep.

For the umpteenth time, I reached out to Maria. *Where are you?*

When I caught the first acrid whiff of the bean soup scorching the bottom of the pot, I sprang from the bedside and raced down the stairs. Delphina's suitcases, still piled at the bottom of the staircase, caused me to trip. I righted, raced into the kitchen and yanked the pot from the stove. I poured the contents into a clean pot, to prevent the soup from spoiling.

I couldn't help serving myself a bowlful, and ate while standing, doing exactly what I always told my children not to do. I shovelled one spoonful after another into my mouth, did not chew but swallowed, with no pause in between. I eyed the wall clock. Something had happened. *Nepitella and Timo. Maria. Where are you all?* I could not begin to imagine the monster's whereabouts. I walked through my former sitting room and peeked into the bedroom, which I had assigned to Delphina. Gina and Silvia had done a good job. It was spotless. The monster was not there.

At the very moment I heard Long Ears pulling the cart into the courtyard, Max's bloodcurdling scream filtered down the staircase.

I was trapped again. The first time, in the morning, between Mayor Santo Rossi and Di Napoli while on the phone, and now, the second time, in the evening, between my children. The decision was the hardest I had ever made in my life. I stepped towards the kitchen door, but when Max screamed again, I changed direction.

I'd forgotten to turn on a lamp, so when I entered, the room was in darkness which somehow intensified a light scent lingering in the air. I scrabbled around to switch on the bedside lamp. Max cradled his father's head against his chest. The bedcovers were awry, and from his ashen skin, I knew Di Napoli was dead.

I grasped Max's hands with their bandaged fingertips and pulled him into my arms. He clung to me like a limpet and pressed his face into my neck. His body shook.

'What happened?'

'Delphina killed my papa. Then she tried to kill me, too.'

I glanced around the room. Besides the distinct fragrance of delphiniums, and disorganised bedcovers, nothing seemed out of place. Then I saw the spare pillow lying on the floor upon which the outline of Di Napoli's face was imprinted. Fury burned deep in my belly. At the same time, I was overcome by a terrible, overwhelming desire to gather my children and keep them safe with me. I could not leave Max alone.

I clapped my hands over Max's ears and yelled at the top of my voice like never before. 'Nepitella. Timo. Get up here immediately!'

I listened hard to the ensuing silence. Nothing. Finally, there was a noise. One set of footsteps. My heart sank. I recognised the steps. My heart somersaulted with joy.

Timo materialised in the doorway, his face whiter than a bleached sheet.

I mouthed, 'Nepitella?'

His lips barely moved, and he spoke in such a low voice I almost did not hear. 'The wolves came and surrounded the cart. Long Ears panicked. I yelled at Nepitella to come up front with me. I looked back. She…she wasn't there. I…I am afraid the wolves took her.'

I held out my free arm and Timo stumbled towards me like a poor wretch dying of thirst arriving at a pool of water. Max and I embraced him. The boys shivered. My rage turned to ice. I glanced up. The monster stood in the doorway melding with the shadows. She was laughing silently at me with her head tossed back, full of writhing serpents. In the next second she was gone.

Maria's voice entered my head. *There is only one thing to be done, Hortensia.*

I know.

You do?

Yes. Where are you?

Never mind that now. To protect yourself and the boys, do exactly as I say.

And Nepitella?

We'll deal with her later.

I assumed this meant she was safe and sighed with relief. *What am I to do?*

See the phial on Di Napoli's side of the bed?

I looked.

Empty it into the tisane and make the boys drink it all, half each. Sleep will come quickly to them. When they wake, Max will only remember up to seeing his father sleeping peacefully alongside him. Timo will only remember driving home with Nepitella sleeping peacefully in the back of the cart. Go. Do it now.

I eased myself from the boys who clung to one another, and did all Maria had instructed.

'Here. Drink this.' My voice was gentle but firm.

Without retort the boys swallowed the tisane. I had barely enough time to remove the glasses from their hands before they both slumped into deep sleep. I rolled them over to lie one on either side of Di Napoli and covered them.

Hortensia, it's time. Go to the far end of the courtyard and prepare yourself.

There was no need for Maria to warn me of what I was about to witness.

The glowing firepit was visible from the open kitchen door. The cold, early winter's night was dark. Neither moon nor starlight could pierce the unseasonal sea fog rolling in.

Hortensia, fetch the rake from the stable.

The light in the stable glowed feebly. Timo, bless his soul, had followed my rule: animals, after serving us, needed to be cared for before we attended to our needs. He had stalled Long Ears, fed and watered him and made sure the chickens were safely housed in their coop, before entering the villa. I picked up the rake and after switching off the stable light, headed towards the pit.

Rake over the coals carefully. You must find all eight bangles.

Why are your bangles in the pit? My skin prickled, but I was too focused on carrying out Maria's precise instructions to think any more of it.

Put the bangles onto your right wrist in the order I taught you. Don't make a mistake. You only get one chance to get it right or they will never be able to serve you.

No pressure then!

Maria chuckled.

I was barefoot and wore clothes too light for the evening's cool temperature. I stepped closer to the fire and, reaching out with the rake, turned over the glowing coals. The fire reluctantly gave up each bangle. I placed them aside to cool. Once I retrieved all eight, I assembled them in a line, as I had done as a child, and slipped them in the right order onto my right wrist.

What now?

Step into the fire. And just like Camellia did, fall face forward and remain there until you wholly disintegrate.

Whaaat! Me?

Yes.

I can't. You should be doing this!

I cannot.

Why not?

I am no longer.

Silence.

Delphina's doing?

I am afraid so. And now, Hortensia, only you, and only in this way will you receive the powers to overcome her.

Silence.

If not, Delphina will kill every one of you and, being the last one left, she will inherit both Villa Angeli, through her husband, Gennaro di Napoli, and stepson, Massimiliano di Napoli, and Villa Trianni through your son whom you have presented as heir and therefore is her stepbrother Timo.

Silence.

It's your choice.

Silence.

Hortensia! Time is of the essence!

———— ◆ ————

It took me a while to grasp that Maria was now speaking to me from the other side and that I would never see her again. When considering what needed to done, I grappled with my fear. But as the meaning of her words trickled like water through a shale bed, becoming clearer with each layer passed, I knew not only did it need doing, I wanted to do it. Delphina was not going to take any more lives if I could help it. Nor would she take all that Rubino, Maria, Anna and I strived to achieve. That would mean the death of the valley.

In order to halt the forces bringing darkness to my world, I had to be reborn into theirs. And I would only be released again through a second, wholly complete burning.

There was no point in delaying the inevitable. It was going to be terrible. I stepped forward and stood with both feet in the glowing coals. I lifted my arms sideways to shoulder height. 'Dear God,' I prayed, 'help me,' and pitched forward face first into the burning coals.

———— ◆ ————

The bangles, rattling like sabres, woke me. I lay to the side of the firepit, still underdressed for the too-cool night air but awoke with a burning in my belly and purpose in my heart. I rose. 'Delphina, where are you?'

'Here I am.'

I spun around and there was Delphina, her bare feet skimming a few centimetres from the ground. Her head of serpents whipped about in a frenzy.

'Are you going to play in the fire?'

I shook my head.

'Hortensia's afraid of the fire,' Delphina sang out in her sing-song voice. She darted and streaked around me, like a minnow in the shallows. I felt awkward comparing and lumping a minnow with Delphina, let alone comparing its movements to hers. I erased that thought.

'Who is the scaredy-cat? Who is the scaredy-cat? She is, she is.'

Delphina sang the refrain, again and again, until I was sure that alone would drive me mad.

Her serpents had grown longer. They entwined sinuously down to her buttocks and fell about her shoulders in great swathes. Instinct told me they would overpower me before I could lay a hand on her.

'Think, Hortensia. Think,' I muttered. *What is the single thing Delphina is most afraid of?* Before the answer could wholly manifest itself, I suppressed it. I had always known and did not want her to realise it.

'Are you really the boss of those serpents?' I laced my voice with awed fear.

The lights in Delphina's eyes sparked with manic joy. 'Are you afraid of them?'

'Yes, I am. Oh, Delphina, please do be careful, don't go so close to the fire!'

She spun around and faced me. 'Ah! So you are afraid of my serpents and the fire.'

I cowered and trembled.

'Of which are you more afraid?'

I lowered my voice so she could not hear.

'What? What did you say?'

I raised my voice slightly. 'The fire.'

Pure evil replaced the glints of manic joy in her eyes. 'I'll teach you how not to be such a scaredy-cat. Come on, stand in the fire.'

If she suspects I have Maria's bangles and their power... 'I can't.'

'Oh yes you can.'

I followed my boys' example of contradicting one another. 'Oh no I can't.'

Delphina's evil glints blazed. 'It'll only be for a few seconds.'

I whimpered a small, 'Okay,' and stepped to the edge of the firepit. I screwed up my face, pointed my foot and dipped my big toe into the hot coals. 'Ow! I can't, I can't!' I jumped back.

'Who would have believed you're such a sissy. Come on, try again.'

'Help me.'

Delphina's glints danced. 'I'll stand in the fire with you for as long as you can, okay?'

'Okay.' My squeaks and squeals rivalled Andreas's as I matched Delphina step for step until we both stood facing each other. 'Aiii!' I screeched, jumping from one foot to the other. 'I can't anymore.'

The serpents were wary of the game. With forked tongues flicking, they hissed.

'See,' Delphina said, 'it's not so bad, is it?'

'It's terrible. I don't want to play this game anymore.' I jumped out of the fire and stamped my feet on the cool earth. 'I'm in agony.'

'Oh, come on, Hortensia. Just one more time.'

'I tell you. I cannot.'

Delphina made to move out of the fire, but knowing I had to keep her in there for as long as possible, I changed tactic. 'But, look at you! Delphina, you are so good at this game!'

Delphina remained, despite her burning feet. The serpents fought each other, trying to escape the increasing heat. When she could no longer remain, she glided out of the pit, at which point the serpents crashed around her shoulders. Then, they turned on her.

'Stop biting me, you imbeciles. I am in charge here.'

'Delphina, don't berate your serpents so. They deserve better. After all, they have served you well on your many adventures.'

To my horror, which I quickly deflected lest they see, the serpents turned their heads in my direction. Their oval-shaped pupils gleamed, likely calculating if I would be a more sympathetic host.

'Get back in the fire,' Delphina growled.

'Okay. But please,' I said in a meek voice, 'can we do cartwheels instead? It'll be faster. My feet will only get half-burnt, your serpents will get half as angry, and you will be bitten only half as many times.'

Clearly not thinking right, she agreed.

'I'll go first.' I cartwheeled through the firepit as though my life depended upon it. 'See,' I clapped my hands and stomped my feet. 'Much better.'

'Step aside,' Delphina yelled. 'I'm the Cartwheel Queen.'

'Oh, no you're not.'

Delphina's mouth opened so wide I could see the pink fleshy nub at the back of her throat vibrate. 'I am. I am.'

'Show me.' I changed the tone of my voice, so it could be concluded I was as mad as her.

The serpents did not like the cartwheel game at all. Several, weakened, dropped into the fire.

Bouyed with relief from fewer bites, Delphina yelled, 'Again!'

Off I went cartwheeling through the firepit pretending I was a starfish flipping over from one point to the next on cool, wet sea sand.

Each time Delphina cartwheeled, more serpents fell from her head. Like me, she had become patchy with holes burned through her body.

'Tell you what, Delphina, why don't you show me what you really can do? Handstands, for instance. You know, like we all did as children?'

The remaining serpents hissed and aimed their flicking forked tongues in my direction.

What was left of Delphina's blackened face spread into a patchy grin. She placed her hands on her hips. 'Walking handstands! Let *me* show you how.'

I stood aside. My bangles had protested vigorously at each of my madcap suggestions. Now they fell silent but remained alert.

Delphina went head down, balanced on her hands and with her legs bent behind her, walked. When she reached the middle of the pit, the last serpent dropped, sizzled and vaporized.

Seizing my chance, I took a flying leap and landed on her. She collapsed and, twisting an arm behind her, I held her down with my bangles banging out the counts towards a knock-out. In her case, total annihilation.

Caught by surprise, Delphina had no time to catch her breath before the rest of her began to melt, and I began to burn. But I held on, as my bangles counted, and each piece of her that tried to escape, I grabbed and plunged back into the fire. This time, all of Delphina would be consumed. My life, my children's lives, and the valley's continued existence depended upon it.

———— ◆ ————

Although the cacophony was enough to cause the sea tides to halt in abeyance, I did not heed my bangles, but Maria's voice. *Hortensia. Get out of that fire.*

I pulled myself to the edge of the pit and rolled onto the cool earth. 'It's over.' My voice cracked with relief.

No, it isn't. There's one more baptism.

I had no need to ask whose. Despite my attempt at denial, I had known all along.

By the time I reached the kitchen door, my patchy body had filled out and my flimsy clothes for this overly cool night looked as new as if I'd bought them yesterday.

I entered Nepitella's bedroom. Her beautiful, curly, fire-red hair spread across her pillow. Still as light as a seed head, I easily picked her up and carried her to the firepit. As I got to its edge, she woke, stiffened and suddenly weighed heavier than the two boys together.

'This has to be done for both your sake and everyone else's.' With strength and courage that came from who knows where I again stepped into the firepit. Nepitella screamed with such piercing cries my eardrums nearly burst, but I held her then almost lost my grip when I heard a low growl at my side. I looked up to see the pit surrounded by wolves; their eyeballs glowed brighter than the coals. If anything, this increased my determination. My love for her made me all-powerful and I held the child down until every bit of her had melted, and the wolves vanished. I crawled out of the pit and lay on the earth. Soft rain mingled with my tears.

What I had accomplished was, by any stretch of the imagination, inconceivable, but right from the start, Maria had taught me to do the impossible.

37

The next morning, I woke to a silent household. Visible through the window a steady, fine drizzle fell from a dove-grey sky; the first of our winter rain.

Max appeared at my bedside. I raised my covers. 'Are you better?'

He slipped in and snuggled against me. 'Yes.'

Thank you, God. 'That makes me happy.'

'Zeeya, I have bad news.'

'Tell me.'

'Papa has died. I held him in my arms until he got too cold.'

'Oh, Max, I'm so very, very sorry.'

Max sniffed. 'Me too. He was sicker than we thought. He's better off with the angels.'

'I believe you are right. We'll send for Don Antonio and Dr Baldi a little later.

'Zeeya?

'Yes.'

Max wriggled around to face me. 'I have a secret message for you from Papa.'

'Really?'

'Really.' Max lowered his voice. 'Papa says to tell you he loved you very much, next best after my mamma, and that you are the very best godmother I could ever have.'

I squeezed him tight. 'I have a secret, too. Just for you.'

'Really?'

'Really.' I lowered my voice, 'I loved both your mother and father, but I love you very, very much and you are the very, very, best godson I could ever have.'

The effect of my words caused Max's body to soften, with, I hoped, the irrefutable knowledge that he was much loved and wanted.

Timo entered my bedroom followed by Nepitella. They piled in and snuggled tight.

In a low, solemn voice Max shared the news of his father's passing to which both Nepitella and Timo responded by conveying their heartfelt sympathy.

Gosh. They are learning and maturing. 'Someone else passed away last night.'

'Who did?' Max asked.

'Maria.'

'Oh no!' Nepitella cried. 'Who's going to teach me how to make more tisanes?'

I squeezed her hand. 'I will.'

'How did she die?' Timo asked.

The augury I had been avoiding flashed, revealing Delphina ambushing Maria as she walked home along the treacherous path with her cloak billowing, and calling out to her pygmy goats, 'Mamma's coming home.'

Pierced and weakened by Delphina's hair spikes, Maria barely resisted being dragged and dumped into the firepit. What Delphina did not see was Maria removing her bangles and burying them below the burning coals before she melted.

I extinguished the vision and lied. 'Maria died of old age.'

'Wasn't she even older than Rubino?' Timo asked.

'Never,' Max said. 'No one could be older than Rubino.'

'Can,' Timo said.

'Can't,' Max retorted.

The normality of their quick, cut and thrust dialogue was music to my ears.

'I know,' Nepitella said. 'I'll ask her.'

I held my breath.

Nepitella closed her eyes, and the boys waited. Her brow crinkled, then smoothed and crinkled again. She opened her eyes. 'Maria's not answering.'

I breathed, and my heart did another joyous somersault. Nepitella no longer had the ability to commune with the dead.

'Zeeya, why isn't Maria talking to me?'

'My guess is she's really tired. Perhaps she wants to be left alone so she can rest.'

Nepitella's lovely dolphin-shaped mouth formed an O.

'Zeeya?'

'Yes, Timo.'

'I have a story to tell about our trip home from the station last night.'

I lay still, gripped with a deep sense of foreboding.

'Nepitella,' Max said, 'is it a good story?'

She shrugged. 'How would I know? I was sleeping in the back of the cart.'

'You'll know if you both stop talking and listen.' Timo's voice sounded peeved, a warning he could soon resort to silent sulking.

He would never know how much I desired to hear what he had to say. 'Tell us.'

He sat up and pulled the edge of the covers around his shoulders. 'But you have to promise you will believe me.'

'Timo, I will certainly believe you. So now, please, the story.'

'It was dusk, but halfway through the forest it was already dark.' Timo threw me an apologetic glance. 'I had forgotten to attach the lamps, so I had nothing to guide me except my memory and Long Ears' ability to find his way home. He was trotting along nicely when, all of a sudden, lights like small burning coals lit up either side of the forest track.'

Maria! You said Timo would not remember anything except return-
ing home with Nepitella sleeping peacefully in the back of the cart!

I know, I know. I'm sorry. I didn't do this part exactly right.

Max's feet sought the warmth of my calves. I waited for the touch
of Nepitella's and almost swooned with delight when her feet turned out to
be warm rather than ice-cold. It was another indication her baptism by fire
and return to the ordinary world had been successful.

'Long Ears stumbled or tripped, then jumped straight up in the air
with four stiff legs and crash-landed back to the ground.'

Max was about to giggle when I gave his calf a warning pinch with
my toes.

'Long Ears began to run. No, race. No, fly as fast as the wind and
the cart flew right along behind him. I had to hold onto the footboard with
both hands to keep from falling off.'

'And me?' Nepitella said. 'What about me?'

'You did not answer my shouts, and when I could look, saw you
still slept. How, I don't know. You were tumbling in the air like Zeeya flips
pancakes.'

'You're not going to believe this, Zeeya, but...' My son gave me an
imploring look.

'Those eyes were the eyes of a pack of...of...wolves.'

'That's not possible. There haven't been wolves in this forest for a
century or more,' Max said. 'We learned that in school.'

My mouth was dry. 'What happened then?'

Timo cast me another grateful glance.

Nepitella's sweet mouth compressed into a thin line. 'Don't wolves
communicate by howling?'

'Yes,' my son said with certainty.

Max's mouth compressed, too.

'The funny thing is,' Timo said, 'when Long Ears exited the forest,
the wolves disappeared and when I picked up the reins, a soft, peaceful
feeling covered me.'

Okay, I forgive you, Maria.

Nepitella and Max stared in silence at Timo.

A tiny crease appeared between Nepitella's eyebrows. 'That's the story?

'Nice,' Max said.

'And, I believe every bit of it.' I pinched Nepitella and Max's calves with my toes.

Nepitella's crease faded. 'Me too.'

'And me,' Max said.

I eased into a sitting position and gave my son a warm embrace. For once, he did not try to evade me.

'Any chance of breakfast?' Not only did Max use his father's exact phrase and inflection, but his voice carried unmistakable hints of his father's deep resonance, too.

'Of course.'

'Yay.' The children sprang out of bed as fast as rabbits escaping down a hole.

'Race you,' Timo shouted.

'You're on,' Max yelled.

'Wait for me,' Nepitella called.

All three children sprinted out of the room. I heard their footsteps pound down the staircase and come to an abrupt halt. I slipped out of bed and stepped into the corridor. They turned and looked back up at me.

'Whose suitcases are those?' Nepitella asked.

'Mine.'

The children turned again and looked down the staircase. Delphina emerged from the dining room. She was graceful, regal and more beautiful than ever.

'Good morning, Max. You look well recovered.'

'Good morning, Delphina,' Max said. 'I am, thank you.' He whispered to Nepitella and Timo. 'That's my papa's wife, Delphina.'

'Come. Introduce me to your friends.'

Max led the way. At the bottom of the stairs, he presented Timo first and then Nepitella. I watched keenly, but Delphina made no sign of recognising Nepitella as her half-sister, even though, from where I stood at the top of the stairs, it was glaringly obvious.

Maria's voice entered my head. *Only to you. Not to others.*

I allowed myself a small sigh of relief.

'A little bird tells me you are all budding cooks,' Delphina continued. 'Does that include American breakfast?'

Nepitella and Timo stared at Max, who turned red. He had written to his father about their weekly cooking attempts. Clearly, Di Napoli had shared this snippet of information with Delphina.

'Yes. We can,' Nepitella said. 'I make the toast.'

'I fry the eggs,' Timo said.

'And I,' Max puffed his chest out more than Timo's, 'fry the bacon crispy.'

'Really? I can't believe it.'

'Shall we show you?' Nepitella said.

'Oh, yes, please.'

The children took off, rushing through the dining room into the kitchen.

'We'll call you when it's ready,' Nepitella shouted over her shoulder.

I motioned to Delphina to come on up and watched carefully; she trod solidly on the stairs. Her hair was no longer ramrod straight, but twisted, ending in a beehive atop her head. I stood aside for her to enter Max's bedroom that had once, for a short while, been hers. 'Bad news.'

She gasped, 'Gennaro?' She rushed to the bedside, bent over her husband and kissed him tenderly on the forehead. She straightened. Her face filled with grief. 'The funeral arrangements?'

I watched Delphina even more closely. 'It'll be a double.'

'Oh no! Who else?'

'Maria.'

'Goodness. I had forgotten her. I am so sorry. Maria was not my husband's favourite person. I could never understand why. Her scary looks, perhaps?'

Treading in unchartered waters, I began to feel confused. Exactly what did Delphina, in her new existence as an ordinary being, remember? My bangles hummed.

Maria's voice entered my head. *She has no recollection of anything bad she ever did.*

Not a single memory?

No.

This time, are you sure?

Yes.

So, she doesn't know Nepitella is her half-sister, that she killed Arturo, you, and God who knows who else, stole my Paternity document, and told Pietro about Di Napoli and me?

Correct. She has no memory of any of that, or the rest, which would fill several books.

Does that mean my children and I are now safe around her?

Yes. And now she is a widow in need. Remember, no Di Napoli, no income. Even as Max's stepmother, she will remain penniless until Max turns eighteen. Unless of course, you step in?

I could send her to Mayor Santo Rossi for help. I paused. *Just joking.*

Maria chuckled.

But Maria, if she recalls nothing, how do I find the Paternity document? She said it was closer than I thought.

Why do you need it?

I'm being careful. You never know what life might throw your way.

Silence.

Maria had gone.

I turned to Delphina. 'I'll send for Don Antonio and Dr Baldi after breakfast. It is still too early to wake them. My thought is that the funerals will be held this afternoon or tomorrow morning latest.' I looked Delphina straight in the eye. 'What are you going to do?'

She covered her lovely face with her hands. 'I truly don't know. I never expected to be a widow so soon.'

The cogs in the part of my brain devoted to the bed and breakfast project began to turn.

I left the children with Delphina washing the breakfast dishes, entered the stable, harnessed Long Ears and set off for Dr Baldi and Don Antonio. I slipped Rubino's old rain cape over my head and immediately felt enveloped by his warm, comforting presence. The cape had its practical uses too; it kept me dry from the drizzle. Light though it was, it soaked everything. It was always the best kind of rain after the long, dry summer spell.

———— ◆ ————

'But,' Don Antonio said, 'how do you know Maria's dead, without seeing the body?'

Dr Baldi shrugged. From past experience, he knew well enough anything that had to do with Maria was simply, best accepted, no questions asked. 'Just have the carpenter provide two coffins. One lavish and one simple.'

Don Antonio did not question which coffin was for whom, and confirmed the funerals for four o'clock that afternoon.

I headed off to Maria's hut. Her pygmy goats scampered out to greet me, bleating as if they were competing for an award. They would have to come to Villa Trianni, there being no one to take care of them. I pushed the old wood door further open and entered.

As I expected, after melting in the fire, Maria's ether reassembled in her shepherd's hut. She lay on her narrow bed, wearing one of her black cloaks. I winced, seeing the minute holes where Delphina's spikes had pierced Maria's bony hands, nailing her down in the firepit. I shut off the thought wondering what the rest of her body looked like. I found a pair of gloves and eased her hands, finger by finger, into them. Thus, when Don Antonio arrived along with helpers, and placed her body in the coffin, they would not see the marks. All the while, my bangles respected their former mistress by remaining silent.

As I also expected, two long, thin sacks hung from the rafters. I felt around in Rubino's cape pockets for his knife. With care I flicked it open and cut through the rope and let the two sacks drop to the floor. I flicked the knife closed and opened the neck of one sack. In it were wads of rolled up *lire* held in place with twine. And, as she had warned, it was nowhere near the cache Rubino had left.

I suddenly felt exhausted. During the supernatural events of the last twenty-four hours I had no time to think about the precarious situation I found myself in. No income, monies to be paid out, Rossi threatening me, a season's worth of oil and wine that needed selling and no buyers.

The lamenting refrain Max's mother, Letizia, had once crooned came to mind. My voice, like a seesaw tipping back and forth, rose – 'What am I to do?' – and then fell, 'Dear God, what am I to do?' I barely paused before repeating it again.

Maria's voice entered my head. *Get a grip, Hortensia. Or it will drive you mad.*

I took in a long, slow breath and released it, just as long and just as slow.

I kissed Maria's forehead. 'I love you. Thank you for everything.' Out of childhood habit, I skirted the spot where a hidden trapdoor led to hole in the hard-packed earth. I pocketed the knife, picked up the two sacks, whipped off the rest of Maria's cloaks hanging from the nail hooks and threw them all into the back of the cart. The fine drizzle turned to steady raindrops and I headed home.

If I'd delayed a moment longer, I would have seen, instead of glinting arrows of sunlight, angels' tears fall through the cracked terracotta tiles and splash against the hard-packed earth.

———— ◆ ————

When I crossed the *Frigido,* I pulled Long Ears to a halt in the middle of it. From the gathering rivulets rushing down the mountains behind me, the river had widened and deepened. If the rain continued, in a few days we might be cut off. But I did not stop the cart to assess the river, but rather to enter that moment when Delphina, in her former mad state, had divulged my disloyalty to Pietro. *My darling, I am so very sorry. I wish you were here. I need you. I love you.* My heart spoke the words so loud, they might as well have issued from my mouth.

The sweetest voice, made up of the collective voices of God's angels I'd heard only once before in the ceramic garden in Naples, responded, 'Now you know what it is to truly love a man.'

Long Ears made to move. He could not be happy standing in the ice-cold current swirling around his feet.

'Ya,' I called, and Long Ears pulled forward.

Halfway through the forest, Long Ears stumbled, or tripped, I do not know. Then he broke into a quick trot building up for an all-out run. With minnow-speed, Timo's story darted into my head.

'Easy,' I called to Long Ears. 'Easy.' The donkey slowed and I bought him to a stop. I jumped off the cart and hooked the feedbag over his ears. Notwithstanding a prickle of anxiety, I retraced the cart's path to the place where I thought Long Ears had taken fright.

Something glistened in the stony path. It was hard to tell what it was, there being a high content of flint in all the stones, but none as shiny as this. I scraped the tip of my boot on the ground, revealing a silver coin. I picked it up and held it against the gloomy light. At that moment with my head tilted, and from the corner of my eye, I caught the flash of something spin down. My head reflexed sideways and whatever it was landed on the ground with a tinny plink. It was another silver coin. I crouched, picked it up and saw another and then another more or less embedded in the ground. One more plink landed close to me. Still crouched, I looked up into the boughs of the tree spreading over the track.

'It can't be.' Suspended above my head were the two pillowcases I'd stuffed with Rubino's money. There was a tear in the bottom of one, and each time a gust of wind blew, another silver coin dropped out of the bag.

I glanced around, wondering how I could reach the pillowcases and cut them down. *The cart.* I'd back Long Ears down the track until the cart was under the pillowcases. *If I stand on the bench, I might just reach.*

'Sorry, Long Ears, you can snack again later.' I removed the feedbag, and called out to him, 'Back up, back up, back up,' in the way I remembered Rubino doing during the harvests. To my relief, Long Ears took a step back, and then another. I placed my hands under the running board, and still calling 'back up, back up,' steered the cart in a straight line until it stood where I wanted. I engaged the brake. 'Good job, Long Ears.' I rehooked the feedbag over the donkey's head. *Rubino, you always said donkeys are superior to horses in all ways. This proves it!*

I balanced on the cart's bench with my arms raised above my head. Drat! I was way short of reaching the top of the bulging pillowcases. In frustration, I glanced down and saw Maria's sacks. I realised then that if I slit a hole in the bottom of the pillowcase hanging above my head and held open the neck of Maria's sack, I would likely catch the money as it drained out of the pillowcase.

I retrieved Rubino's knife and widened the tear in the pillowcase.

It took several minutes to drain the first pillowcase and less for the second. I tied a knot in the bulging sacks and stowed them under the bench. *I can't leave the two split pillowcases flapping in the wind for anyone to see.* Tightening my muscles and bending my knees, I poised to spring skyward. I grabbed at the bottom of the first pillowcase. With my weight, the branch supporting the pillowcases snapped. I sprawled on the bed of the cart cushioned by the travel rugs. 'Easy,' I called out to Long Ears, who, despite the feedbag over his head, skittered.

The breeze changed direction, and as I caught that most odious of smells so, too, did Long Ears. He reared forward. Only the cart's brake prevented him from taking off.

'Easy! Easy!' I cried to the ruffled donkey. 'We know that smell, Long Ears. Whatever it is, it's long dead.'

The wind changed direction again, taking the smell away with it. I jumped down from the cart and went in search of the origin of the smell.

I didn't need to get close to recognise the fragments of the brown jacket belonging to Rossi's favourite nephew and thief. From the teeth marks on the remnants of the jacket, and one well-chewed boot, I assumed the wolves had ambushed him. Not wishing to see any more, I returned to the cart.

I disentangled the necks of the pillowcases from the broken branch and froze. Clumps of long, fire-red hair curls had been used to secure the pillowcases to the branch.

My belly cramped, and threatened to throw up its contents. Had Nepitella come upon him already dead or, had she been a part of his death?

Maria's voice entered my head. *Don't concern yourself about that. Whatever happened, she hooked the pillowcases into the trees for safekeeping. And from this day forward, Nepitella is no different than any other ordinary nine-year-old girl.*

Taking enormous comfort from Maria's words, I removed the donkey's feedbag, climbed on board, released the brake and ya-d until Long Ears pulled away.

After stabling the donkey, I picked up both sacks and headed up to my bedroom. Reluctant to leave anything to chance, I locked the sacks along with the reimbursement monies made by Santo Rossi in my wardrobe and buttoned the key into one of the hidden pockets in Rubino's rain cape, which I hung on a hook behind my door.

I calculated there was enough money to cover immediate expenses, including paying Andreas for the car. But I still needed to find a new buyer for the wine and oil harvests.

My mother's voice entered my head. *Why only one buyer? Perhaps you can sell the produce to several buyers?*

I climbed the ladder to the hayloft, walked up the inclined ramp and exited onto the turret. In deference to Arturo, I skirted the spot where he had been impaled and headed for the flagpole. I raised the orange flag, signaling to the children to return home. I clutched Rubino's green flag, and Maria's white one between my fingers while my mother's words sank in.

What if...what if the bottles of wine and oil were gift-wrapped and shipped via mail-order to buyers in America? I can take out an advertisement in the magazine Andreas and Gino work for. The magazine sells a lot of copies; they must have a lot of customers.

In unison, the voices of Rubino, Maria, Anna and my mother, clamoured, *Idea fantastica!*

38

The news of Maria's passing spread fast. Within hours, people arrived by foot, old bicycles, rickety carts, three-wheeler vans and scooters in a myriad of colours to pay their respects.

They parked their vehicles higgledy-piggledy and gathered in our valley churchyard, which soon heaved with winter-dressed bodies. Fourteen members from one family spreading over five generations claimed to have all been delivered by Maria, and each recounted the very moment they first caught sight of her.

'That can't be,' Max whispered. 'That would make her…one hundred and twenty years old, sixteen years older than Rubino.'

Timo drew himself up. 'I told you she was older than Rubino, but you didn't listen.'

I held them by a shoulder each. 'Boys, with so many people here today, you need to share your pews.'

Timo frowned. 'I want to choose who can enter my pew.'

'No. Keep the door open, and let in anyone until the pew is full.'

Timo's frown deepened. 'But I don't want just anyone sitting with me.'

The bangles sounded their disapproval.

'I order you to go to the oldest people, invite and help them in.'

Timo's face darkened.

My answer was not what he expected. 'Do it now. You too, Max.'

Max was quick to respond. 'Okay. But I'm saving three places. One for Zeeya, Nepitella and Delphina.'

Timo glared. 'Zeeya can't sit in your pew. She's my guardian, too.'

'True. But she isn't your godmother.'

My heart contracted simultaneously with the sparks of pain that flashed in Timo eyes. 'Enough,' I hissed. 'Delphina will sit with Max. Nepitella and I will stand at the back of the church. Off you go, and if you can't do yourselves proud, do it for me.'

Timo and Max glared at each other for a second longer. Then, as if angels entered their bodies, they displayed kind consideration as they invited and guided the elderly through the two private side doors leading into their family pews.

On the outskirts of the churchyard, the valley housewives arrived laden with food baskets, and their menfolk laden with tables and chairs. Before the church bell struck four, several tables and chairs stood under the chasteberry tree. The rest of the tables that did not fit under the tree were placed between the tombstones.

Covered platters of sliced meat, pickled vegetables, rounds of cheese, bowls of olives, glasses, six one-litre demijohns of oil and ten four-litre demijohns of wine, and rough-shaped oven-baked bread-rounds sat upon the tables.

Don Antonio opened the church doors. The congregation surged down the aisle and came to a stumbling halt, seeing not one but two coffins, side by side at the altar. He waved the dumbstruck mass forward. 'Be seated.'

Footwear scraped and shuffled against the mosaic floor, and buttocks of all shapes and sizes settled on the creaking wood benches. Everyone focused on Don Antonio as he raised his arms calling for silence.

'We are gathered here today to honour the passing of our venerable sister, Maria Fortunato.' He waved his hand to the simple coffin. The congregation sighed softly. 'And,' Don Antonio paused and pointed his finger at the expensive coffin, 'our brother, Gennaro Di Napoli.'

The votive candle flames bent, and the white altar cloth undulated with the force of the expelled breaths of air the women generated. Then they broke out into coughing fits, attempts to disguise their shock. The men went on the alert, counted the heads of their womenfolk and puffed up, like the cock in his hen-coop into which a fox has brazenly entered.

Don Antonio continued. 'Gennaro Di Napoli's second wife, Delphina Barberi, is present, as is his son, Massimiliano Di Napoli, who has been living among us these last five years.' Don Antonio inclined his head towards Delphina and Max. 'On behalf of this congregation, please accept our deepest sympathies.'

Just then, I caught sight of Mayor Santo Rossi and pressed my lips harder for an altogether different reason. His bulbous eyes stared unblinking at the new widow. Despite Delphina's red-rims, partially obscured by the black lacy veil she wore upon her head, she had never looked lovelier.

I would protect her from the mayor. Indeed, I determined to protect all women as best I can from him. I clamped a hand over my bangles to silence their tinkling applause.

Don Antonio proceeded with the service, but what more he said, I did not hear. Like a bird, my mind took flight. After going full circle, it returned to the nest still filled with seemingly insurmountable problems I had to resolve.

At the end, Don Antonio called for pallbearers to carry Di Napoli's coffin to the graveyard. Lorenzo was the first to raise his hand, thereafter *la Nepitella's* old fishing crew followed. My heart warmed towards Lorenzo for his kindness. He had saved Max the embarrassment that would have come with realising no man wanted to carry his father's coffin. Perhaps the same could not have been said about the women. I spied more than several waterfalls of tears that I knew had nothing to do with Maria's passing, but everything to do with the loss of never having been bedded by Di Napoli, and the knowledge that the opportunity was now lost forever.

Don Antonio raised his hand for attention. 'In keeping with Maria Fortunato's request, only women shall bear her coffin to the graveyard.'

I stepped forward with Nepitella beside me, as did the villas' cleaning sisters, Gina and Silvia.

Luisa Prosperi stood and shook off her husband's clutching hands. 'What are you afraid of, you fool?' she hissed. 'The *brutto ragazzo* is dead and nailed closed in his coffin.'

Gaining confidence, Gilda Fabbri was next. She too fought with her husband before stepping forward.

Another pallbearer was needed. I looked around. Delphina gave me a tiny wave. I nodded, and she took her place beside me.

Because Max was still too short to be a pallbearer, he walked ahead of his father's coffin and led the way to the graveyard. Maria's coffin followed, led by Nepitella.

Timo, where are you? As far as I could turn my head while bearing the front left corner of Maria's coffin on my right shoulder, I searched for my son.

Maria's voice entered my head. *Don't worry. He's currying favour by helping the ancients to the tables beneath the chasteberry tree. He's even pouring them wine!*

Once the coffins were interred, Maria's coffin alongside those of Rubino and Anna in the paupers' graveyard, and Di Napoli's alongside that of Letizia Angeli in the Angeli family's mausoleum, the mourners returned to the churchyard.

It was dusk. In the distance, the sea lay flat and grey. Cold winter air funnelling down the mountain slopes behind us sliced through our coats and jackets.

Don Antonio handed out boxes of candles. Stood upright in jars, and then lit, the light from the candles offered a bedazzling view of the food platters. Voices rose, and the funeral event seemed more like a festival.

But due to the cold, the festive air lasted only as long as the food and wine did. Soon the churchyard emptied, the church doors closed and the children, Delphina and I started the journey home to Villa Trianni.

———— ♦ ————

L ong Ears kept up a steady clip despite nearing the spot where I had discovered the pillowcases storing Rubino's money, and to the left where I knew the scraps of Mayor Rossi's favourite nephew, Mattia Rossi, still lay. My senses went on the alert. Though there was a light breeze, I did not even catch a hint of the former ghastly smell. I turned my head at a slight angle and kept a close watch on Nepitella, and by default, Delphina, but neither showed any sign of recognition as the cart drew closer.

My sigh of relief was premature.

Timo jumped to his feet. 'Here!' he shouted. His pointed finger changed direction as the cart clattered past the spot. 'It was right there.'

'What was where?' Max asked.

'Where Long Ears jumped and the cart was surrounded by wolves.'

'Aw,' Max said, 'tell us another tale. An even taller one this time.'

'It's the truth. Zeeya, you tell him.'

'Nah. It isn't,' Max said.

'It is.' Timo's voice tinged with a desperate edge.

'Isn't.'

In the next second, the boys tumbled down onto the cart's bed.

'Whoa,' I called out to Long Ears, whose trot had been broken by the lurching.

'Timo. Max. Stop.' Grunts and groans, thuds and thumps drowned Nepitella's anguished voice.

Delphina twisted around on the cart's front bench, her face creased in dismay. I engaged the brake and stepped over the backrest into a flurry of kicking legs and punching fists.

I braced myself against their blows, but managed to find one ear and pulled for all I was worth. Max's caterwauling split the air. I found another ear. Next came Timo's cries. They separated instantly.

'Let go.' Timo hopped from one foot to the other.

'And me–' Max said.

The front rows of the ancient olive trees guarded both sides of the track, forming a channel down which the sustained howl of a lone wolf raced, bearing down upon us like the first surge of floodwaters. The boys halted, struck still by fright. Delphina and Nepitella wrapped their arms around each other, their faces screwed up as the full force of the sound passed over our heads, lengthened and finally diminished in the far distance.

I let go of the boys' ears. They scrambled to sit upright, visibly shaking.

'It's all right,' I said. 'Relax. The wolf has gone.'

'Wow, did you hear that?' Max asked.

I interrupted with a cold, hard voice. 'Hold on. I have something to say. Do I have your attention?'

'Yes, Zeeya.' But the boys still peered into the darkness, terror and fascination plastered across their faces.

'If you continue behaving in this outrageous way, I will start behaving like a madwoman.'

That caught their attention. They turned from the darkness encapsulating the cart and focused on me. I calculated my arms' reach to the distance of each boy's head. In a flash, I smacked their heads together. With perhaps too much force, I latched on to their outer ears and drew their heads apart. 'This is what I mean!' I screeched. 'If you insist on crazy behaviour, you will be met with crazy behaviour.' Before they could react, I knocked their heads together again.

'Owwww!' Timo yelled. Tears began to run down his face.

'Ouch, ouch, ouch. I'm sorry,' Max snivelled.

Nepitella and Delphina shut their eyes again; this time against the spectacle of me beating the boys.

'Now, once and for all, let's get this straight. I am the boss of you both. Animals don't behave the way you two do. For God's sake, don't be jumped-up, ignorant, arrogant idiots as your fathers were. Grow up and be men. Good men. Proper men. Not delinquents. Am I making myself clear?'

With their hands cupped over their ears they nodded. Delphina and Nepitella stared.

'We are a family. A family needs solid, responsible young men, not morons. Now, as you are both always so eager to prove yourselves as fighting warriors, get off the cart.'

'Wha–'

'You heard me. Get off.' I made a move to grab their ears again. Both boys scuttled off the back of the cart. 'It's five kilometres to the villa from here. Walk together. Protect one another.'

I climbed back into the front of the cart, sat down and twisted around on the bench. 'Oh, and one last thing.'

The boys stood side by side, shivering, their eyes about to pop out of their sockets.

'When you get home, don't make a noise. Go to bed. See you in the morning.' I turned, released the brake, ya-d at Long Ears, and the cart took off.

The bangles never made a sound, for which I was grateful, but I had to break the silence between Nepitella and Delphina.

I reverted to my normal persona. 'God help us. If that doesn't teach them a lesson, I don't know what will.'

Nepitella and Delphina relaxed, and by the time we reached home, they were giggling out of control at the idea of Timo and Max walking home together in the dark, in a forest filled with vicious wolves.

In the kitchen, Delphina surprised me by giving me a warm hug.

'Good job with the boys, and thank you for everything,' she said. 'Goodnight.'

I hid my surprise and hugged her back. 'Sleep well. Tomorrow is another day. We'll discuss a few ideas about your future I have floating around in my head.'

'Pyjamas, brush your teeth and to bed,' I said to Nepitella as we walked up the stairs.

'Zeeya?'

'Yes.'

'Are you sure the boys will be safe walking home?'

'Absolutely.'

'Zeeya?'

'Yes.'

'From now I am going to call you Mamma.'

A kick from nowhere connected with my belly.

'Mamma?'

'Yes.'

'You don't have to dye your hair anymore.'

My belly cramped. 'Okay.'

'Mama?'

'Yes.'

'I love you.'

I knelt and enveloped my daughter in a huge hug. 'I love you, too.'

I walked down the corridor to my bedroom. Never had I felt so elated and exhausted. Or so lonely.

I entered and shut my bedroom door. The bangles tinkled in fond greeting.

Maria's voice entered my head. *I'm glad you didn't overdo it. One howl-imitation was enough to bring the boys back into line. And good thinking ensuring Long Ears did not hear it.*

Thanks. I only hope it does teach them a lasting lesson.

I climbed into bed and lay awake until I heard the boys' treads along the corridor, stopping outside their respective rooms.

'Goodnight,' Timo whispered.

'Timo, is Zeeya going to believe us when we tell her we saw the wolf?'

I smiled to myself. The boys' imaginations knew no bounds.

'Don't know.'

'So, we shouldn't tell her?'

'Right, let's just keep it a secret.'

'Okay.'

'Night,' Timo said.

'Night. And Timo, I'm glad I've got you as my brother.'

'Me too.'

I sighed, snuggled down in my bed and soon fell into a dream of wolves and bags raining money, clouds of butterflies and a frog waiting to turn into a prince who looked suspiciously similar to Pietro.

———————— ◆ ————————

I jolted awake. Mayor Santo Rossi's bulbous, unblinking eyes intruded on my dream, turning it into a nightmare.

Staring into the dark I visualised the two sacks containing my inheritance, and the heavy leather case holding Rossi's reimbursement monies. I'd stowed all of it at the bottom of my wardrobe. Now, the sound of monotonous dripping, like water from a loose tap was, I realised, my conscience pricking me. Since I'd found my inheritance from Rubino, I would return Rossi's money. But how?

My mother's voice entered my head. *Set up a charity in his name to benefit all the widows, unbetrothed maidens and unmarried mothers.*

Brilliant idea! But the thought of Rossi driving my car peeved me. It would be handed over in a few days after the paperwork was signed confirming it as a donation to our town hall for the incumbent mayor's use. A niggling thought finally emerged with such clarity it took my breath away. I *would* get the vehicle back. I would run for mayor! Was that possible?

Maria's voice entered my head. *Anything is possible. You already know that.*

Imagining Rossi's face when he learned of my intention to run against him caused giggles to escape from between my lips. Adding up all the women in our valley – they outnumbered the men – I knew with as much certainty as the sun rose and set each day, they would vote for me.

Another niggling thought revealed itself in the form of the old bag of mail I'd retrieved from under the cart's bench, and that now lay on the kitchen counter.

Peeking through the shutters, I saw dawn was still far off. The outside air was visible; opaque and thick from the cold. I pulled on my dressing gown, shoved my feet into slippers and descended the stairs. The bangles rattled in protest at the early hour but I ignored them.

I entered the kitchen, stoked the fire in the night stove, and a few minutes later with a cup of fresh coffee in my hand, pulled the mailbag towards me.

My mind raced back three months to September, during the children's first week of school when Lorenzo gave me this mailbag. So much had happened since then. The best of which: I'd found a friend in Andreas; my status in the eyes of the valley was unquestionable; Rossi had reimbursed my stolen inheritance, now doubled since I had discovered it. In exchange for the mayoral use of the red Rivolta GT300, I had Rossi renounce all past, current and future marriage designs upon me. The worst of which: losing the wine and olive oil sale contracts; Rubino, Maria and Di Napoli passing on; the sexual trades with Rossi; the terrifying self-immolation in order to overpower Delphina's dark persona and, by plunging Nepitella into the fire, expunged the darkness in her.

Nothing could top all of that.

I sighed and opened the mailbag, heavy with the weight of the magazines to which I had subscribed. I set them aside to read in bed when I was least likely to be disturbed and could indulge in wondering and delighting over the clothes and innovative home decorating ideas.

A notification from Torino informing me my new typewriter was on its way, was lodged between two official brown envelopes inked with the Tourism and Maritime department stamps in Rome. *More bureaucratic paperwork!* To make sure there was nothing else in the bag, I tipped it upside down. A white envelope with a foreign postmark and addressed to me fell onto the table. I slid the butter knife under the flap, retrieved a folded sheaf of flimsy blue writing paper and carefully pressed the several pages flat on the table.

The world reduced to the letter, the distance between it and my eyes.

September 1968

My very dear wife, try not to be shocked, but it is I, your husband, Pietro. Asking you this is silly I know, given you believe me dead. Of course you will be... Are you still reading? Please, don't throw this away, at least not until you have read to the end.

First, I must tell you what has demented me these last years. I live in abject dread of each month's full moon, when the lyrics of Marechiaro, and the feel of you lying in my arms turns my heart inside out – a torment I would not wish upon a living soul. In the hope of freeing myself before I go completely mad and am unable to write to you as I do now, I must confess my actions and beg your forgiveness.

I return to the day I left. You were preparing the marriage dinner for Di Napoli, Iacopo Lenzi and the Barberi sisters. I felt uncomfortable all morning while you were in search of ginger over at the Angeli Estate. When you arrived home, disheveled and claiming you had taken a tumble, my alarm bells would not be silenced. My instinct told me it had to do with Di Napoli. But my hope that I was wrong was stronger. Yet, I left, with a dark shadow in place of my heart, and my blood boiling.

Halfway over the Frigido, Delphina Barberi flagged me down. Without preamble, she disclosed the coupling she'd seen taking place between you and Di Napoli from the turret. Worse, she handed me the document she admitted stealing, which confirmed your parentage and that your (our) child is heir to the Trianni Estate.

My dearest, why was I so stupid? Suffice to say, it is a question I have never been able to answer. Anyone in his right mind would have seen by the scratches and bruises blooming on your face, that the consensual coupling Delphina claimed that took place was wholly untrue.

And why was I angry you'd not confided in me about the Paternity document? Truth be told, was it any of my business? Who was I to assume total ownership of you by sheer dint of marriage?

The answers to these questions fall firmly at the door of my insecurity, jealousy and lack of trust.

Please, don't stop reading now. There is more. My writing hand is freezing up, yet this too, I must disclose. After Delphina poisoned my mind, and I was heartless and out of my head, I lay with her, thinking it sweet revenge against you. Never has anyone been so wrong. Revenge is a bitter pill that remains, like a cancer, growing in my throat each day.

After the briefest coupling since Time began, I thrust the document back into Delphina's hands. I recall my words with acute clarity. 'Hide it in the parlour, a vase perhaps, where one day she may find it'. I confess, at that moment the idea of your angst searching for the document while it lay so very close to you, gave me macabre comfort. Delphina instantly understood my diabolic intention, agreed, and together we laughed at your expense.

Are you still reading? Can you bear to? I know if it were me, I would have already dropped this in the fire to be forgotten forever. Sadly, there is more, for you are not the only person I have hurt with my duplicity.

To ensure my "death" was wholly believable, I pretended to become ill, along with several of my other crew. I summoned Lorenzo, gave him instructions to ensure my safety box reached your hands, should I die. What an admirable, first-class man and friend! He immediately asked if all the papers were in order, that should I die, my wife and child would have no trouble inheriting my fishing boat. We fought. I wanted to leave the boat to him, but he would not hear of it. Under his scrutiny, I signed the boat to you and our child.

Once Lorenzo left for shore to find a doctor, I searched for the box in order to change my will, making him the owner of the boat. But I could not find it. Dawn was creeping in and I had run out of time. I weighted down my body bag awaiting sea burial, slipped overboard and swam to shore in nothing but rags.

Fury gave me the energy to flee to Genoa, where under another name I boarded a fishing trawler headed for the Atlantic Ocean.

All through these years, my anger raged until the onset of full moon. Then my heart returned to its rightful place in my chest, and my love for you resurfaced, no different to fish swimming to the surface of the sea under the full moon to dance and make love with the one they love.

Now the truth is out, Hortensia, I beg only your forgiveness. I cannot hope for more.

Your forever-loving husband,
Pietro il Pescatore

P.S. I have new dentures.

Calm like I had never experienced settled upon me. I walked through the dining room, crossed the black-and-white marble floor tiles in the entrance hall and came to a stop in front of the double doors leading into the parlour. I turned the key, pulled down the handle and pushed the door open.

Dawn filtered through the shutters outlining the furniture shrouded in dustsheets. It was not furniture I was looking for, but another *capodimonte* floor-standing vase. I walked to the oblong pedestal, removed the dustsheet and peered inside. Right at the very bottom lay my Paternity document. I tilted the vase, lowered it to the ground and tipped its base up until the document slipped out like a child on a playground slide.

With it in hand, I returned to the kitchen. I pulled out a fresh sheet of paper, and suddenly realised the years-old fist of wary and weary tightness in my chest had gone.

Relieved, I sighed with ease, lowered the poised pen in my hand to the sheet and began to write.

THE END

If you'd like to share your thoughts with me, I'd really like that! Please visit my website at www.jacquelinefalcomer.com to contact me.

About The Author

Jacqueline Falcomer was born in Natal, South Africa, and grew up between Johannesburg and Durban. She has travelled extensively, living in the UK as well as the USA, twice, and dreams of returning.

Perhaps one day… For the last decade she has lived in a small hilltop house in Italy, with a splendid view of the Mediterranean.

She still travels, including to new places likely to be used as a backdrop in future books.

Love Me Not only features the Tuscan hamlet where she currently resides. The third book in her trilogy, *Tell Me Not*, is set primarily in the Italian Alps and Salzburg, Austria.

More information about Jacqueline, her inspirations, audio versions, and first chapters of upcoming books may be viewed at www.jacquelinefalcomer.com.

The Journey to *Love Me Not*

Hard on the heels of *Forget Me Not*, new characters popped up in my head, all demanding their story be told. Once again, I hung on and went for the ride… never knowing where I would land.

I do hope you enjoyed *Love Me Not's* characters and their stories as much as I did writing them.

The third novel in this trilogy, *Tell Me Not*, is a work in progress. Publication updates can be found on www.jacquelinefalcomer.com